The Enchantment

By
Juliet Peterson

Dedication
To Andrew and Stephyn Maria

Prologue

The night was starless and utterly still. A grey blanket of cloud had been draped over the area for some days now, and a pall mist hung heavily in the air. An armor-hung guard stood stiffly near the castle's back entrance grumpily breathing the muggy mist. This night of the week had customarily been free for him. At another time he would have been home in his four room cottage, his stomach full of cod and potatoes, smoking his pipe and talking with his wife and sons, or playing tug with his dog.

But the past two months had brought an abrupt end to such happiness in his life with hardly an explanation. The king had put out orders to increase the security of the castle. To stand; to do nothing but blink and breathe in and out air thick with fog, with no explanation.

The guard thought it all an utmost absurdity. He was only one of five men standing around the back entrance gazing dumbly into the darkness. He wanted to go home. He wanted to eat cod and potatoes and he wanted to sleep – for he had had little sleep in days. Perhaps he would rest a little now; just a little. Just close his eyes for a few minutes. It would be all right; there were four other men here, and they had not seen or heard anything in weeks.

He leaned casually against the cold stone wall and closed his eyes heavily. He hardly noticed that on his left and right, the four other guards were doing the same. In a wink of time, he was dreaming deeply of cod and of potatoes. A hooded black figure glided slowly past the five guards, now as useful as tin cans.

The large wooden door cracked silently open, and the figure crept inside.

***

Chapter One

Arnaud did not notice the heat. He didn't notice the humid air smothering like a woolen blanket. At another time it would have been unbearable, and the perspiration that trickled over his forehead and into his eyes would've been an impediment and an irritation. But as with all who have been recently struck with sudden grief, Arnaud had ceased to care about things like the boiling sun. His hands were wrapped securely in large and heavy nets and had been so for the last quarter of an hour. The cords dug painfully into his skin, but Arnaud was grateful for it. He didn't exactly notice the pinching sting but it somehow kept his mind carefully away from deeper and greater pains.

"A fine time to be tangled," M. Liam said in his rough tone, glancing to the east. Black clouds were rolling and grumbling toward the shore. His calloused hands darted skillfully over the netting.

"Pull it in a bit more."

Arnaud was lost in nothingness and did not hear.

"A bit more I say!"

Arnaud pulled himself back to the present and heaved. Meters of thick cord scraped over the side of the small boat, dripping salt water onto the deck. The captain tipped his hat back and readjusted it before he leaned forward and began scouring the fresh netting. Arnaud blinked fiercely over dry eyes.

"Pull the rest," Captain Liam said, waving a hand with bleak resign.

Arnaud heaved until the remaining netting had squelched down onto the cracking wood. He untangled his arms and wiped the sweat from his burning face. But still he did not feel the heat.

"Third time this month." The captain tossed an evil glance at the net. Arnaud could see it now. The rough cords had been cleanly sawed; a round hole the size and shape of a small barrel gaped up at them.

"It's the oddest thing," the captain said, "feels like I do more patching than fishing these days." He pursed his lips and shook his head at the net. "All right, "he sighed dejectedly, "let's put in for shore."

The sky had half blackened by the time they'd fully docked. Arnaud noticed the captain watching him closely with an expression of worry but was gratefully the man said nothing.

"I hope the rain doesn't hit you, Arnaud, before you make it home." The captain removed his cap. He ran a weathered hand through his thinning hair and glared up at thunder gaiting over the horizon.

"And pray mercy from God." He slipped a small paper package into Arnaud's hand. "One net is not enough to make it. Not by a long shot."

"No, Sir, I—" Arnaud had not spoken a word that day and his voice was dry and difficult to find. But Captain Liam decidedly did not notice. He held his palms up in refusal as Arnaud offered the package back.

"You support others, Arnaud, it's no charity. You have to be thinking of them."

"But you—"

"Don't you worry about me. I'll get along; always have." He pulled his hat tight over his snowy hair and laid a hand on Arnaud's shoulder. "Hurry before the collectors come along, or we'll neither of us have anything to show for the day."

He began to walk away, but turned back as if struck with a sudden thought. "Arnaud, try not to get into any more trouble with the collectors. Now, I say this as a friend," he added quickly, "you're like your father: high-spirited, but it only did him harm with Lord

Gualhart and his collectors. You know it came to a bad end."

Arnaud knew the man was harmless, that, though his ill-timing and words cut deeply, he meant well. He was only referring to Arnaud's recent brawl with one of the collectors. But Arnaud was indeed as his father was, not one to stand by as men robbed his home in the name of false law. If others would set aside their cowardice and join me, there would be no need to sneak the day's catch ashore.

But none of that mattered now. The old man was right. He couldn't afford the trouble, not now. Arnaud gripped the pack tightly under his arm, touched his hat to the captain, and started down the water-side street.

Not far ahead he could see two men easily spotted by their bright and meticulous wardrobe. Arnaud gritted his teeth and hid the package in his pocket with an easy movement; he bowed his head as they went by. One of the men, a wide portly fellow with a ruddy complexion, stared at him suspiciously with squinty eyes. He seemed ready to stop Arnaud, but his burly companion engaged him in questioning another poor sailor before he could act. Arnaud lengthened his stride.

The budding storm had driven in all manner of vessels. As Arnaud tramped over cobblestones, directional calls of docking barked all around him. This street also hosted the open market, and as he walked further along, Arnaud was confronted by stands arrayed with all objects imaginable squatting in blocks.

Calais was a trade city with dock and market open to the free world. At one time it was booming with enterprise. Arnaud could remember making his way through the crowded streets...

Here, a man with three gold hoops through his ear calling figs five pounds a franc. There, a man with skin as dark as midnight bartering beads in all the colors and sizes of sky and earth. Further on, bolts of fabrics from the balmy deserts and dew-hung jungles hanging out on racks, their hues as vibrant and exotic as their homelands. A little round faced monkey chattering as he passed displays of melons and nuts, its tail curled around its blue-turbaned owner as they disappeared into the crowd while catching the lush scents of figs and rosemary.

But the scene had long been chased away. Foreign ships had dubbed the port of Calais an unlucky haunt. Even the fish would not come.

Arnaud walked through sheets of invisible rain without seeing the ghost of a vibrant market. Long shadows followed him along the sides of stone buildings as he turned onto a side street. Arnaud walked faster. The sun was out ahead of him but was being quickly swallowed by black clouds spilling over the sky like ink.

Yet even in light Arnaud's familiar path was blurred as his thoughts were. Each step and each thought came without recognition of the last, like the repetition of a song sung since childhood. His mind raced and his feet moved, but his thoughts were not coherent enough to take shape.

By the time he finally saw through his opened eyes, Arnaud had left the city streets and was within view of the thatched roof that had sheltered his childhood. It had been a strong place, a strong home for generations, but had begun to crumble under frequent tax collections; under his father's death; under Arnaud's watch. An unworthy shame managed to creep its way into Arnaud's feverish mind.

And this small bitterness and fear that had lain dormant within him for years pulled on the corners of his thoughts and scratched and bit at them until it ripped

6

them open and all that Arnaud had been avoiding spilled out suddenly like blood from a deep wound.

He was dead.

Only six years and he was dead.

"He was too young. Much too young," Arnaud spoke the words aloud as if saying it, convincing God of it, would bring his brother back to life.

Too young. Much too young to die of brain fever, a death that perhaps could have been prevented if there had been money enough to send for a physician. But there had not been, and no hope of ever having even such little excess lay in the future. If sickness struck a second time, he could do nothing for his family but watch them drop out of this life. Such bitter thoughts screamed through a mind that had henceforth been brimming with whispers.

When after indiscernible time the screams finally dulled, Arnaud looked around him and realized that he had walked up to the barn and that he had been weeping hot tears. He pressed his face up against the outer wall to cool his burning skin and wiped his eyes with the back of his dusty hand, but tears sprang up again each time like morning dew on the underside of a leaf.

Time sped on until the sky was quite black with clouds and the air was thick and darker than night. And still the tears came. Arnaud tried to quell them and tried to block his grievous thoughts but to no avail. His lamentations seemed to increase rather than decrease. He would not enter his home weeping, would not let his mother and sisters see him like this. They had too much to worry over as it was. So he stood long up against the wall as the clouds grew heavier and heavier until Arnaud could almost feel their weight pushing down on him.

Here, in this barn, only a month ago, he had been teaching Anhault how to milk the cow and how to change straw. And there outside the barn, Anhault had for years looked on in admiration as Arnaud split wood for the fire. In a few years he would have been old enough to help. And by that time he might have become apprentice to a blacksmith or a carpenter as Arnaud had been for a short while. But Arnaud's education had been prevented in a similar way, by a cloak of fiercest black.

Arnaud drew himself quickly away from these thoughts. He'd hit a wall, one that had gone up very quickly a long while ago and had been greatly fortified through time. The tears stopped as suddenly as they had come.

It was raining now, and had been for a while though Arnaud could not say when it had started. He was cold and wet through by the time he crossed the short distance to the threshold, but he was grateful for it. Thick raindrops covered any trace of tears.

Despite the utter cold and darkness outside, Arnaud walked into the gold of fire spilling out onto board walls and floors and a rough table surrounded by rough chairs. A short week ago his young brother had been sitting at that table memorizing Latin and working out sums as his mother had insisted despite their destitution. As Arnaud had at that age.

Don't think.

"Arnaud."

Arnaud felt the jolt of being pulled from deep thoughts, though he'd carefully been thinking of nothing. His sister, Clarice, stood in the doorway from the kitchen. She was paler than ice and stood staring at him for a long while as if she'd forgotten who he was.

"She hasn't come back," she said very quietly.

"Who hasn't come back?"

"Mother. She – she said she would be back shortly but that was hours ago. I wanted to go after her, but—."

"Where did she go?" Arnaud asked sternly. He could hear the frigid rain pounding every moment harder and harder upon the roof.

"I think— to the—to the—" Clarice pointed vaguely, choking on her words. But Arnaud already knew where, and he bounded out the door before Clarice could manage to finish her thought.

It fell in glass sheets, hard and fast, almost impenetrable with the eyes. For a moment, Arnaud had to see with his hands along the outer walls of the house. He moved slowly until it seemed either his vision had improved or the tempest had slightly lessened. But still he could not see far.

And even as it was difficult to see, it was difficult to walk. The ground was slippery, and where it was not, thick mud gripped and pulled on his boots with squelching fingers.

But she hadn't gone far, not too far. The cemetery had long expanded to the outskirts of the city. It was not far from their home to the last grave where he was buried. Yet navigation through blind rain took Arnaud many long wetting minutes. And he could almost touch the cross that marked it before he saw her.

She was still standing but barely, hunched over in grief. The hood of her cloak had been thrown back and rain water ran down her face and off her chin in a thin stream. Arnaud, whose resolve was generally clear suddenly felt desperate. He did not know what to do. Since his father's death she'd been continually ill. Subjection to weather on top of the death of a second child might prove too much for her delicate constitution, though Arnaud daren't think it.

"Mother," he said gently, "Mother, the storm. It isn't safe to be here."

He placed his arm around her shrugged shoulders and guided her carefully away from Anhault's grave.

She let him lift her hood back over her head and moved slowly, but without resistance.

The rain's impossible intensity only increased as they made their careful way down the slope. And it seemed they could not even see the house before Arnaud was shutting the crooked door on the black. A heavy clatter resounded through the room like thunder. Arnaud looked around; it wasn't thunder, the old sword of some ancestor that had displayed symbolically above the door had slipped from its frame and pounded to the ground.

"Help her," Arnaud told Clarice, who stood as they entered.

Her eyes were red, but thankfully dry. He bent down and retrieved the old weapon. A large stone set in its hilt glowed in the firelight as he placed it gently back above the door.

"Where is Anais?"

"Cooking," Clarice managed to whisper as she led her mother by the hand out of the room.

Cooking what? There had been less and less to eat each week. Lord Gualhart's tax collectors made sure of it. Each day was a new struggle to procure food and Arnaud hadn't had the energy or resources today. It struck him hard now that there would be nothing for his mother and sisters to eat tonight.

Yet as he took a rag and began to dry his dripping hair, he could smell the thick aroma of frying fish.

"Anais, where did you get fish?" he asked, entering the small kitchen.

"It was in the package you left on the table, Arnaud. Did you not want me to cook it? We have little else."

Oh yes. The package Captain Liam had handed him before he left the ship. How could he have forgotten?

She moved quickly from the table where she'd been slicing a shriveled potato into the sizzling pan over the fire. She smiled at him very widely which confused him. He couldn't think of smiling yet or for a very long while.

"I heard some talk in town today of ruined nets. Henri Bonnet had to sell his milk cow to pay the tax because he wasn't bringing in enough fish to sell at market. Like us a few months ago."

She spoke very quickly. It reminded Arnaud of an angry bird. And the whole time she never stopped smiling, but her eyes were nervous as she waited for him to speak.

Arnaud had already heard about the cow, but he couldn't think what to tell her. He had no reassurances to give or to keep for himself.

"Well, don't speak of it to mother. She's –"

She hoisted the smile back up and stirred the potato vigorously with the fish.

They sat in silence for several minutes. Arnaud picked at drying mud on his hands and tried to think, but he found it difficult. Thunder boomed outside thin walls.

"I . . . didn't want to say anything now, Arnaud," the smile dropped off, "but our stores are . . . they'll be gone in a week. And— and in town today, they won't let me borrow anymore. The butcher says he knows that hooks are disappearing and there are holes in the nets and he's worried you won't be able to pay him." Her eyes were downcast in either fear or shame.

Arnaud remained silent for a long while; attempting to collect his thoughts. But they were too scattered and he couldn't seem to form a solution. He knew Captain Liam could not afford to keep him on as things were; that there would be many without work like him, and no future employ. But Arnaud needed work if they were to eat. They were fortunate to be among the few living on the outskirts of the city where they could grow their food, but where they'd once had chickens and a cow they now had none, and too early this year they'd begun relying upon their stores. Gardens wouldn't even be planted again for several months.

"Arnaud, I—" Anais' voice was as nervous now as her eyes. "Alphonse de Gaulle has . . . made indications that he wishes to ask for my hand."

"The baker?"

She nodded, but lowered her eyes to the fish and kept them there. "He's very wealthy, and –and food would no longer be as scarce." Her hands shook a little, but she kept her countenance hidden.

Arnaud watched her intently. She was two years younger than himself and very pretty. Alphonse de Gaulle must be thirty-five years and Arnaud knew him to be sly and crafty. Anais would be secured from destitution, but mother and Clarice; it would be shaky dependence on another man's wealth. Arnaud shook himself. What am I thinking? His sisters were not bartering tools! It was no solution.

"Couldn't you—do you think you might get work on a shipping vessel again?" Anais asked timidly. "Gileta overheard her father saying you would likely have risen very high in ranks if you could've stayed on. If mother hadn't gotten so ill." Her voice trailed off as if afraid of what he might say.

"I have an understanding with Captain Liam," Arnaud replied not unkindly.

"But you make hardly a centime under him."

"And you think that sufficient cause to break my word?" Arnaud said harshly. But when he saw her flinch he softened his tone. "Where would I find a shipping vessel besides? They will no longer port in

Calais." He sighed. "I wish you would just leave it to me, Anais. There's no need for you to be worrying. I'll figure something out."

Anais seemed to detect the sincerity in his gruff words. She nodded and busied herself with their meager dinner.

But Arnaud was cut by this lack of faith in him. The weight upon his shoulders was heavy enough without doubt. He felt acutely the pressure to find a fast solution to their problems.

His eyes strayed to the dusty sword propped above the door. It had always been there; longer than Arnaud could remember anyway. It must be worth something. When cleaned up it would likely shine. Perhaps it would fetch a high price as decorative for an extravagant nobleman.

Arnaud shook himself again. No, he couldn't do that to his mother. He couldn't sell an heirloom that had belonged to her father, one of the few possessions left to kindle dying memories. No, there must be something else. There must be an answer.

Through the night, Arnaud's thoughts raged on like the tempest, now and again broken by the mournful voices of his sisters and by the awful silence of his mother, unstoppably determined.

***

Chapter Two

Days passed; and then a week, and each night offered less to slacken their hunger. When Captain Liam looked at Arnaud now it was with a pitying sadness that increased every moment, until finally even the mended nets gave out under few fish, and the captain had nothing to keep or to pay. Though the sun was out and the birds were singing, it was a very grey morning.

Arnaud strode quickly past squat buildings and bustling people. He walked and walked, but had no destination. Everything was blurred and hazy like the world was spinning wildly around him while he stood very still.

"Arnaud! It's been a long while since I've seen you. I thought you'd be captain aboard the Nitona by now the way things were going. Tire of the life at sea, did you?"

Arnaud looked up, finding himself walking through a bustling street. He stood before a black smith's shop and a man robed in a leather apron strode toward him removing heavy black gloves.

"Charles!" Arnaud said, immediately covering his thoughtful distress as he recognized the blacksmith. A boatswain aboard the same ship years ago, before Arnaud's mother had fallen ill and he'd taken lesser work closer to home. "The smithy bring you ashore, then?" he asked, avoiding the man's like question.

"Ah, I never was much good on a ship," Charles laughed. "Eh! Frances! This here is the man I've been telling about." Always a great chatty fellow, the blacksmith pulled an associate under his arm and gestured to Arnaud. "This man here rose from the lowest sailor to second mate in under three years."

Arnaud stood still, feeling more and more uncomfortable by the second.

"And I am positive if he ever had a mind for mutiny, which I'm sure none of us ever did," he added in a mock whisper, "the entire crew would've followed him. Myself included."

"You're a good man, Charles," Arnaud said, desirous of changing the subject, unwilling to let the man know how low he'd fallen in two years. "How is business?"

"It's as to be expected," the smith accepted the shift without a wink, "fairly steady, but no extravagancies. Nothing fun lately, just shoeing and carts and the most necessary repairs. This lull in catches has affected everyone, even the wealthiest." He shook his head. "Hey, if ever you have mind or means to lead a crew, I'd be keen to join. And I know a pretty few who'd be as well. Surprisingly, I rather long to be out on the water again."

"If ever that happens, I'll call on you first," Arnaud humored.

"You're free to come at any time whether looking for hands or not."

Arnaud shook the man's hand and left, grateful the smith had not pressed to know his current situation. He dropped easily back into his thoughts. Again he walked with no direction searching for any solution that wouldn't compromise honor or decency. But no matter where his feet or his mind took him, he couldn't seem to find anything. There was no work. Not in Calais.

"What are you doing here so early?"

Anais' voice made Arnaud jump. She was standing quite close to him with a yellow bonnet drawn over her brown hair. "Shouldn't you be out—" She stopped suddenly and looked very grave. "It's happened, then?"

15

Arnaud looked around. They were standing at the edge of a crowded street.

"I don't want you to worry about this, Anais," Arnaud said taking her arm and leading her aimlessly down a side street. "I'll find something. I will." He said it to convince himself as much as his sister.

But Captain Liam had held on to Arnaud as long as he could and now even the lowest positions were filled. There was nothing; nothing left for him to do. Nothing short of begging. As he focused on this grim thought, his eyes caught on a metal cross peering gloriously out over the tops of residential roofs. An idea flashed through his mind. Begging of God, of the church; it was better than begging of his fellow man, wasn't it?

Arnaud began to steer his steps toward the steeple. He'd almost forgotten Anais, but her hand grabbed his arm tightly.

"What is it, Anais?" What looked like terror had sprung into her eyes. "Anais—?"

"Arnaud!" Arnaud spun around and found himself face to face with the baker. "Well this is convenient." Alphonse's eyes feasted on Anais, who fixed her gaze intently upon the ground. "I thought you'd be out on the water. Not anymore, I guess." Arnaud pursed his lips. "I wonder if I might speak with you on something." He ran an eye over Anais again. Arnaud could feel her stiffen beside him. "Here, come into my shop."

"I won't be long, Anais. Wait for me." Arnaud removed her grip on his arm.

"Arnaud . . . Please—" Tears clung to her eyelashes.

Arnaud squeezed her hand. "I'll only be a minute."

Arnaud had been inside Alphonse's bakery many times in his life, but not recently. He worked from dawn to dusk daily and left necessary purchases from here to his sisters. He glanced around. Nothing seemed to have changed in the past few years. Loaves and rolls sat on display and a heavy aroma of yeast and flour hung pleasantly in the warm air. Arnaud's stomach growled involuntarily at the scent.

"These are hard times, Arnaud." Alphonse said conversationally as he strolled behind his little counter. "Particularly for a fisherman such as yourself. Such hard times that for some it has even become difficult to procure food. Naturally," he gave a little chuckle. It sounded hollow to Arnaud's ears. "Naturally, I am not one of those people." He gestured vaguely around him with a long-fingered hand.

As the baker caught sight of Arnaud's stony stare he seemed to lose a bit of his swagger. He swallowed and shifted his gaze to the open shutter. Anais was across the street looking into the opened door of a shop. The man took a steady breath and avoided looking at Arnaud. "I was sorry to hear of your young brother. Armand, was it?"

"Anhault."

"Yes, of course, Anhault. Most unfortunate." He laid his spidery hands on his counter, and as if feeling again the power of his position. The determinable pomp returned. He plowed on. "I am a man of business, Arnaud, and I have a . . . proposition. I assume you have some idea of what I speak." He smiled a yellow smile. Arnaud had a sudden urge to break it.

"I believe I do."

"Good. Let's get down to business then. I know, Arnaud, that as of today you are out of work. I also know that you have been borrowing off the butcher and are unable to pay your debts there. I can help where you are lacking.

"For one year, I will provide bread for your family. Of course, there will be a limit, say five loaves per week. In everything there must be a limit. And it cannot be the choicest loaves. Obviously I will need those to sell. I would like to give you my best breads, Arnaud, but if I worked on charity I would go out of business." He chuckled his hollow chuckle.

"All of this, a hand up from starvation, for Anais. And even there I will be of help. By taking Anais off your hands, you will have one less to worry about feeding. Recently, I think, you have experienced those benefits," he nodded his head solemnly, alluding to Anhault. "I know you are not a business man, Arnaud, but surely you can see how my proposition would benefit you."

It took all of Arnaud's strength to keep his head cool and his feet upon the ground.

Alphonse smiled at him, though he still seemed wary of Arnaud's strong stance and look. He turned to stare again out the shutters at Anais. "It's unlikely your sister will receive a better offer. Even a biased man can see she is no—"

Arnaud, whose every muscle had been twitching to injure this man whose insults dripped freely like poison from his tongue, let himself go. Alphonse's mouth was suddenly choked with blood. He looked up in utter shock and pain. Arnaud swung again before he could stop himself. A small pop filled his ears as his fist cracked the baker's nose.

"Stay away from her," he said. He turned and walked out of the shop, leaving Alphonse with intense shock in his eyes, his hands shaking while covering his nose and mouth.

Anais was still staring blankly into the shop across the street when Arnaud left the store. He could see her trembling, even from a distance.

"You tell me if he bothers you again, Anais," Arnaud said as he came up to her, suddenly feeling the bruising pain in hand. "You'll have to buy bread across town. I'm sorry it will be such a long walk." She was so pale and frightened Arnaud almost laughed. "In fact, it's probably best if you don't walk down this street at all," he said jokingly. "Go around the long way."

Anais' face lit up, just a little, a real smile this time. "Come," Arnaud said, "I'll walk you part of the way home. I have some business to attend to."

Anais did not speak as they went, but Arnaud could tell she had questions. She continually glanced at him as they walked, and several times began to speak but stopped short. He didn't offer any information. He didn't want to raise any false hopes, including his own.

They had reached the edge of town and their house was in view. "Goodbye, Anais. Don't worry on it," Arnaud said, "and don't tell mother or Clarice. There's no need for them to know anything until I've got it settled."

Anais nodded and set off toward the little cottage.

Arnaud turned the other direction, found the cross over the sea of roof tops, and began walking.

***

As he stood on the step of the large building with the wooden cross staring down upon him, he wished he had crossed those steps more often in his life. Since his father's death he had scarcely attended services at all. He'd been mending sails or nets for foreign sailors on the Sabbath; anything to bring in a little more.

Now, standing here at the door, he felt foolish to ask anything of the church when he had given it nothing. And though God was his last resort, his only resort, Arnaud almost turned around. But he didn't. He stood staring at those heavy oak doors for a long time, struggling to swallow his pride on behalf of his family. People passed on the street behind him and birds chattered high in the still air.

Finally, but without quite coming to a decision, he stepped confidently forward and reached for the door. But before he could grasp the handle, it swung open.

"Arnaud!" Pere Michel stood before him, his expression revealing as much astonishment as his voice. "Well, this is a pleasant surprise. Please, come in."

The chapel was much as Arnaud remembered it: dim yet somehow still full of light, with hard oak pews and a few detailed statues. Pere Michel said what Arnaud hoped he would not notice.

"It's been a while, hasn't it, since you were last here? You may notice that we've had some paintings shipped in from Italy. They came only, oh . . . two weeks ago? Very beautiful. Here, let me show you."

For several minutes they gazed upon a vibrant Last Supper and Christ Triumphant. While the priest spoke of art, Arnaud remained silent. He knew little of such subjects and his predicament weighed heavily upon him, making concentration difficult.

"But I think, Arnaud, you did not come here today to hear my long-winded appraisal of olive frames. Was there something I can do for you?" Pere Michel asked at length.

Waves of foolishness and guilt nearly crushed Arnaud's determination. But he had no choice. He must do something, or watch his family starve.

"Father, today I . . . my captain, M. Liam, has come to the point where he is unable to pay me."

Pere Michel nodded his head. The motion made his brown robe shake over his round belly.

"I understand. Here, let's go into my private office to discuss."

The priest opened a little door along a wall of the long cathedral. Arnaud stepped through and Pere Michel followed, pulling the door closed. It snapped shut behind him.

"You are out of work," the priest said without preamble. "I understand many are right now with few fish to bring in. It is as good a time as any to turn to God. But am I correct in thinking concern for your soul is not why you are here, Arnaud?"

Arnaud almost hung his head in shame. He looked down at his hands and saw that his knuckles had indeed bruised a deep purple. He attempted to hide this from the priest, sure that the man shunned violence, no matter how necessary.

"I believe in God, Father," he said with a determined stare. "In truth that is why I am here. I believed that those who turn to Him in their greatest need will find his aid and mercy."

The priest looked evenly into Arnaud's eyes. He felt hope drain from him. Were his mother and sisters to be deprived the help of the church because of his unattendence?

"I ask nothing for myself. I would not be here if I had not others to think of. And you may be sure I will pay back every centime, every crumb, no matter how long it takes me."

Pere Michel smiled warmly at him.

"You are a very determined man, Arnaud," he said conversationally, "have been since you were a boy, even while your father lived. Always had a plan in your head. I remember about a year after your father's death your mother musing to some women in the congregation that life would be much easier if she had a milk cow. Later I learned from Jean de Collier and Symon Dubois that you worked many hours for each of them, helping to dig a well and shoe horses in addition to fishing, to get the cow for her."

Arnaud smiled. The priest must know he had sold that cow months ago to pay debt to that slimy baker, Alphonse de Gaulle.

"I'm only curious, Arnaud, what is your plan now?" Pere Michel looked very intently at him.

"I know I must find work," Arnaud said, avoiding the priest's gaze, "where, I don't know. I fear it will be very difficult. There are so many now facing my predicament. But I am willing to take any work for any pay I might get."

Pere Michel nodded thoughtfully, "Oh, of course, Arnaud, we will be glad to help." Pere Michel stood to his feet. "And I will make a suggestion, if I may? Travel to another city and temporarily seek work there. Boulogne is composed of as many farmers as fishermen, and right now the ground is more fruitful than the water."

"But I don't know anything about farming."

"Oh, I don't think it matters much as long as you're strong . . . and determined. Do you have enough to eat tonight?"

They didn't. No more than perhaps a few beets.

The priest walked through a small door and returned a moment later with a hard loaf of bread. "I'm afraid at this moment it is all I have," he said, handing it to Arnaud, "and I'm sorry, Arnaud. But, as I said, you caught me on my way to an appointment, and I really shouldn't keep them waiting any longer."

"Of course. I am sorry to have detained."

They strode back through the cathedral and out the heavy doors into the sun.

Pere Michel placed a hand on Arnaud's shoulder, "If you do take my advice and have difficulties while in Boulogne, pay a visit to Pere Estienne of the Boulogne parish. He is an old friend of mine and may be able to help you."

"Thank you, Pere Michel."

"I am very sorry I must leave you so soon. May God guide you, Arnaud."

As Arnaud made his way back through muddy streets he thought he would feel uneasy about his decisions to beg help of the church and to follow Pere Michel's advice; that he would be overpowered by the guilt that had nearly kept him from entering the church at all and by fear and uncertainty of the unknown. Instead, he felt light with relief. A burden of worry had been lifted from him. And beneath it he was surprised to find excitement and life.

Boulogne might be different from this oppressively taxing city. Perhaps Arnaud would make enough money to easily repay the church. Perhaps even a surplus to buy another cow, or supplies for needed repairs on the house; maybe even enough to adopt the smith's idea and buy his own skiff. Then he would be dependent only upon himself.

He was filled with a small sense of adventure. Simply laying eyes on a tree different from those thick in the forests around the city would be somehow adventurous. Arnaud attempted to rid his mind of likely false hopes, and he very nearly succeeded. But he could not control his heart. There, hope grew wild like ivy over stone walls of grief and disappointment.

***

Chapter Three

It was several days before Arnaud departed. He had
to be sure of the church's aid before he would leave.
But the very next day a man came with two long loaves,
three eggs and a thin cut of ham. They ate more heartily
than they had in months.

And then there was the difficulty of telling his
family of his decision to leave. Arnaud was concerned
how his mother would react to this news. She had
calmed greatly in the past weeks, but she still seemed
very fragile, and terrible grief shone yet in her eyes.
Arnaud could hardly bring himself to tell her he would
be leaving them, even if only for a short while. But
when one morning in the kitchen he did find the right
moment, it turned out his concerns had no ground. She
heard him and accepted his decision, only asking when
he would be leaving.

Arnaud was relieved that the seriousness of their
destitution was not such a terrible blow upon her. But
he was almost disappointed. He had prepared sound
arguments to back his decision, and now he had nothing
to do with them.

He set out at dawn the next day. His mother and
sisters gathered at the door to see him off. Clarice
fought tears and Anais stood very still and very pale.

"I've asked Antoine to watch over you and the
house while I'm away," he said awkwardly, "I'll try to
send word when I arrive."

His mother nodded once, distractedly wringing her
hands.

He smiled reassuringly at them all before hoisting
his pack onto his shoulders and turning towards town.

"Wait! Arnaud, wait," his mother called after him.
She disappeared into the shadowed doorway of their
home and returned two minutes later with a long parcel

wrapped in a thick grey cloth. She walked up to him, leaving Anais and Clarice to watch from the door, and pressed the parcel into Arnaud's hands looking very near to tears. It was heavier than he had anticipated.

"If you're unable to find work," she said, "per--perhaps you can sell this."

Arnaud slowly unraveled part of the cloth to reveal the golden hilt of the sword that had lived above their doorway. It glowed like the sun through a grey morning newly cleaned. She ran shaking fingertips over it longingly, but without greed.

"I can't take this, mother. I can't sell it," Arnaud refused, offering it back.

She pulled her hand away. "There are more important things now than silly heirlooms," she said, "it is yours now. Do what you feel is right. But—but, please . . . please don't quarrel with any collectors, Arnaud. Your father—" A sudden sob choked her words.

He placed his hand on his mother's wasted cheek and smiled reassuringly.

"Don't worry."

She smiled weakly.

Arnaud rewrapped the sword carefully, slung it onto his back beside his satchel, and turned. Rocks crunched beneath his feet and a salty breezed played upon his face as he walked away from home and family.

***

The city had not yet begun to stir in earnest, but local fishermen were already making final preparations to set sail while shop owners and market keepers began laying out their few items for the once busy market, along the docks.

Arnaud felt awkward as he walked past them, gazing ahead. He had recently bought hens from the man he now silently strode past, who was now arranging dates into appealing piles. Normally, Arnaud would have been pulling rigging and hoisting sales, perhaps untangling nets and preparing to cast them out.

He felt strangely as if he would never return to these docks and it was unsettling. He rebuked the feeling; it was unfounded and nonsensical, simply the result of uncertainty in the unknown. He quickened his pace but was unable to shake the feeling as he passed neat rows of small wooden houses. The flicker of candlelight could be seen glowing from several otherwise cold shutters. The sun was beginning to rise in earnest now, and the young heat prickled on his arms and neck.

He looked out and realized that without giving a thought to direction, his feet had led him to the unmarked line drawn between Calais and wilderness. But here they stopped. A thickness of leaves and branches now stared innocently at him. A faint path had long been marked through the wood between Calais and Boulogne, but it was not often tread, and sprigs of grass and newborn thatches had sprung up, littering the brown with clouds of green. But Arnaud could only see a few feet into the leafy darkness. The sun's rays were not yet strong enough to stab the black shade. Perhaps they were never strong enough.

As Arnaud gazed into the thick, he was seized with a sudden urge to return to his family's farm; to turn back; to look back. He stood as still as the towering trees before him, the toes of his worn boots just inches from the untended trail. A salty breeze whipped around him from the West. He stepped into the darkness refusing to look behind him at the wakening town and his entire life.

* * *

The wood was absent of heat as it was of sun. But even though there was little warmth, there still hung a

26

dewy wetness. It made the still air smell thickly of moss and the heavy fragrance of rich flowers; a sting of salt hid beneath them reminding Arnaud that the sea laid just beyond the black. He could see nothing and blindly trusted his feet to stay to the path as he drew his cloak tighter against the icy mist. But the sun was not so easily put down and often leaked through twisted branches above painting the path with black and white stripes. To Arnaud, the rays of sun that managed to penetrate looked like glittering walls or a bit of the magic that littered children's tales. He half expected to run flat into them or turn into a great warty toad as he stepped through.

He continued on through the day without pause; unable to determine time or distance as he walked. The sun's orb was blocked from his view, and he could judge little from the scattered rays struggling through the leafy canopy. He trod on and on for what felt like many days, until the yellow slits upon the ground began to dim and were painted blood red.

Arnaud halted directly beneath a large porthole to the sky, and shrugged his pack from his shoulders. The thickly bound heirloom thudded down upon the path as well. Arnaud had forgotten about it, and wondered vaguely how that was possible— it must be very heavy. He reached out for it and weighed it in his palms. It was heavy; much heavier than his pack, and yet he had scarcely noticed it. He laid it gently in his lap and stared bemused at it for a moment, actually wishing it were a loaf of bread and some meat instead of an old relic, no matter what its potential worth. He'd been watching his mother and sisters waste away too long to take any food they might have for himself. He would just have to get something in Boulogne, somehow.

He sat still, attempting to not feel his aching insides, to not hear his protesting stomach. The moon

27

was a fraction short of full, and it glittered through every leaf in a way that the sun could not. The air around Arnaud seemed to him heavy with twinkling emeralds and diamonds. He looked back down at the swathed relic in his lap and began to unravel it. A sheathed sword flopped heavily onto his knees. The single green stone embedded into its hilt glinted against the moonlight sending green prisms to hang in the air above.

It couldn't be an emerald or it would have been sold long ago. He turned it in his hand admiring the sheath. My father was no knight. I wonder where he got it.

He took the great thing into his calloused hands and slowly slid the blade from its sheath. He had never held a sword before and was rather clumsy with it. But the thing slipped out more easily than he had expected, having been collecting dust for more years than Arnaud could guess. With a feeling of expectancy, he held it awkwardly in the moonlight, though he was not quite sure what he was expecting.

That's strange. The moonlight did not glitter off the blade as it had the dew upon the leaves, or even the large green stone. The metal seemed to absorb it, and the curious blade glowed and shone fiercely.

He slipped it back into the sheath. It whispered and clicked as a sword readily used and cleaned. Arnaud pondered this, but he knew very little about such weaponry. He wrapped it again with great care, pausing for a moment as he reached the hilt and the glowing green stone, then packed the thing away with his satchel.

He stretched out across the path, resting his head in his hands, and quickly fell into dreams thick with roast pork, and swords, and trees.

***

Arnaud awoke to the symphony of wood larks and starlings and the soft patter of rain. The sky visible above him was grey and big fat drops were skipping over the wide sheltering leaves, and running gently down to splatter him. He rose creakily and found that his muscles were stiff and reluctant to move without protesting in the form of sharp pains. Sleeping on packed earth was not something Arnaud had had any reason to become accustomed to. He took up his pack and swaddled sword and began walking again, but more slowly and awkwardly.

His muscles stretched and softened considerably over long hours. The rain continued to dance ceaselessly upon the roof of leaves overhead, which provided adequate enough shelter so that Arnaud was thoroughly dampened rather than soaked. Only from the occasional gap above did a steady rain tip through, and he skirted around these with little trouble. The light of the clouded sun brilliantly displayed the shades of the muted, moss-grown land around him. It looked to Arnaud a place from a different world and time. He caught himself staring intently around, as if expecting the blue glow of fairly lights to spring out from the green. But if such magic ever truly lived, it had been too long ago for this young forest.

The thick of the wood began to thin before the sun had too long begun its descent into the west. And as the trees grew steadily further apart, their leaves no longer provided the thick layer he could take shelter under. Arnaud began to feel harshness in the rain and a fierce wind from the east. He pulled his cloak up over his face in an attempt to ward off the nipping and scratching of the storm, but it did little good. The wind whipped up and around, and if he were to truly block it out, he would not see where he was going.

The storm had grown so fierce by the time he entirely left the trees, that Arnaud did not know he had stepped into the outskirts of a city. He kept his eyes fixed firmly upon the path and when it began to take a more definite form and paved itself with cobbled stones; he stopped abruptly and squinted up around him. His eye caught sight of a chipped blue sign swaying angrily back and forth in the gale. He could not quite make out the words painted onto its front. He ducked inside the door.

Arnaud could see without lowering his hood that he had stumbled upon an inn. He could smell the bite of pine wood floors, tables and rafters and seasoned ale; and he could hear the low gurgling of conversation. Upon his entrance this gurgle dimmed to a trickle and then stopped. Arnaud removed his cloak from his head and stared around the wide room. Twenty- four eyes stared back.

"Can I help you?"

Arnaud turned to the voice. Its gruff and portly owner looked over at him from behind a grubby countertop. Next to the man stood a barrel of ale twice his considerable size and weight.

"I'm Arnaud of Calais," Arnaud said. His voice seemed to echo around the eerily silent room. "I am looking for work. Any work." He addressed the room at large now, "I'm a skilled sailor and—"

"There's no work to be found here," the man at the counter interrupted him. One in the crowd took a swig of ale from his oversized mug, never taking his eyes from the scene.

Arnaud was unable to keep a smirk from crawling up his lips. "But surely—"

"Trust me, boy, I would be first to know if any were in need of hiring. Now, can I help you with anything else?"

"Well, no, but—"

"Then you'd best be going."

Arnaud bit his tongue. He had to control his temper. If he faced even half the number of men in the room he might have pursued the matter, but twelve large drunk men was no easy fight to win. A shiner would be no aid in finding employment.

Without a word he turned towards the door, pulled his cloak over his head, and stepped back out into the darkness and pelting rain, fighting discouragement. In a city twice the size of Calais, there must be work. Perhaps he would visit the parish when the rain calmed. He had hoped to find work on his own, but his first attempt had proved useless and he had not the luxury of time.

He set his boots in the direction he had come; for the cover of trees until the storm passed. Great puddles formed in the uneven surfaces of the road, and Arnaud's concentration shifted from direction to avoiding pools. He couldn't afford to wet his boots and feet any more than he already had.

Therefore, when he peered out from under his makeshift hood, he was surprised to see no trees. He could see little of anything at all. He turned cautiously on the spot, searching for any form of shelter. Rain popped up from the cobblestones and bit his arms and face. He caught sight of a door in a giant building and made toward it. It was devoid of a swinging sign, so it was sure to at least be a separate establishment from the unfriendly one he had recently left. He shook the rain from his shoulders as he stepped inside.

The thick scent of hay and horse struck him immediately. A stable. Arnaud had hoped for a residence of some sort or an inn, but a stable would do. Perhaps a stable's better anyway, he thought, I doubt horses will question my presence. The light was very dim, almost nonexistent but for a single lantern hung upon a peg half the building's length a way. Arnaud's eyes slowly adjusted to rows of stalls, few of them occupied. Those few nibbled at hay nets and quietly ignored his sudden presence.

Shuffling echoed around the stalls. Its likely origination was the stall adjacent to the lantern. Arnaud took a few cautions step toward it. The horses turned back their ears at the scratching of his boots but continued eating.

But before Arnaud quite made it to the light, before he could look around inside the stall, he sensed something: an object flying at him. He dodged out of the way. Swinging around, he seized the wide shovel from the attacker's grip and used it to push him up against the wall, pinning him weaponless and useless. Arnaud had often found the need to defend himself among rowdy sailors, but even so he was surprised by his reflexes.

"Who are you?"

His demand was met with grunts and struggles.

Arnaud dragged the assailant into the light by his collar. It was a boy with brown hair and freckles. His green eyes could not have seen sixteen years.

"Why did you attack me?" Arnaud commanded, louder this time.

"You're not here for me?"

Arnaud shook his head, "What?"

The boy smiled, clearly relieved. "Nothing. I'm Andre." He held his hand out awkwardly under the shovel for Arnaud to shake, as if they were meeting under normal circumstances.

Arnaud stared at the hand, then back at Andre's face, not removing his grip on the strange boy.

"I'm sorry I came at you like that. I thought you were someone else."

"Who did you think I was?"

Andre tried to wiggle free and Arnaud let him go, not wanting to create too much of a feud with the boy, despite his aberrant and somewhat cryptic behavior.

"So what brought you here?" Andre asked, ignoring Arnaud's question as he strolled over into the lit stall.

"I was just trying to get out of the rain," Arnaud replied, still defensive.

"Oh, is it raining?"

"Do you work here?"

After a thoughtful pause Andre replied, "You might say that. You might say other things too."

"But what would you say?"

Andre smiled, "I would say . . . I come here to get away from things."

"Things or people?"

His smile dropped off, "I don't think I like where this is going."

"Well, I don't like how it started. Why did you attack me? Are you expecting someone?"

Andre's smile spread wide. Like a jester he could just take it off and put it back on again.

"You're not from around here are you?"

Arnaud didn't reply, but he knew the boy could see his answer.

"Why don't we start over?" The boy held out a grubby hand again. "Andre Landon."

Arnaud considered this and then shrugged. It would probably be better to know someone in Boulogne anyway. "Arnaud Lemarin. I hail from Calais."

"Calais? Never been there. A fishing village, right?"

Arnaud nodded, "A fishing village with no fish."

"You'll be here looking for a job then," Andre commented sitting down in the corner on fresh hay.

"Do you know of any?" Arnaud sat across from him in an opposite corner, attempting to tuck his soaked bag and swathed sword out of sight.

"Not any honest work. And you seem like the type who'd only go for honest work."

"Well I'm not going to steal or anything if that's what you mean."

"Then no, sorry."

Arnaud appreciated Andre's frankness despite its bad news. But what would he do now? If there was no honest work to be found, would he have to resort to dishonesty?

"Is thievery common in Boulogne?" Arnaud asked already suspecting Andre's involvement in such crimes.

"Fewer fish, fewer jobs, more thieves. It's gotten to a point now where only the pickpocket's pockets are safe 'cause they know who and what to look for. That is, unless you carry a weapon." He glanced pointedly over at Arnaud's packs and then back at him. "Such as a sword."

"I take it your pockets are safe," Arnaud said refusing to feel threatened. He'd already proven he could overpower this little twit with no warning. In the dark.

Andre smiled at the insinuation, "Perhaps." He leaned his head back against the stall and closed his eyes.

They sat there in silence for an indescribable length. Long enough that Arnaud wondered if the boy had fallen asleep.

I can't take to thievery; Arnaud decided, wondering how he could ever have considered it even for a moment. It was wrong. Dishonorable. Though he didn't quite know who he would be dishonoring. Letting his family starve seemed more dishonorable anyway.

No. There was no point even thinking about it. He would find another way.

"You don't have any food do you?" Andre asked suddenly.

Arnaud sighed. It had been almost two days since he'd eaten. "No."

***

There was darkness. And then there were trees. Shorter and darker than any he had seen. Their leaves were of an odd pointed shape. Shadows between them grew shorter and thicker. With each step he drew closer to darkness and further from the trees, always in a pool of dim light, or dim awareness.

He closed his eyes and when he opened them he was in a cabin, a log cabin. It was empty but for a few chairs and a blanket and a horse. No, two horses standing on the dirt floors, flicking their tails and staring around contentedly. And a boy, maybe seven or eight years old stroking and silently consoling the gentle beasts. A man's voice boomed, but it was indistinguishable and far away. It grew fainter and fainter until it disappeared.

***

Arnaud didn't realize he'd fallen asleep: the consequences of exhaustion from two days of travel, malnourishment; and lack of sleep from the hard ground and a running mind. He rubbed his eyes and looked around, surprised at his surroundings. Andre was gone. This worried Arnaud though he couldn't immediately grasp why. The grogginess of sleep still clung to him, clouding his thoughts and reactions. He stood to his feet, brushing away straw. He yawned and reached for his things.

The sword. It was gone.

Without even waiting to blink, Arnaud grabbed his bag and began running through the other unoccupied and occupied stalls. When he found them empty, he flung open the barn door and strode out into the busy street and the fresh morning air, brisk after the storm.

How could I let this happen? How could I let myself fall asleep in the presence of a thief? It had been obvious the little rat was a thief. I shouldn't have sat down in the stall. I shouldn't have entered the barn at all. I should've just kept on walking until I reached the forest.

Arnaud stomped over the cobblestones, his eyes darting about, furiously looking for Andre or his sword, but knowing deep down that he wouldn't find them. Regret surged through him with exponential force and power.

What was he going to do now? His backup was gone. He could have sold that sword for more than a year's food for his family. It would have saved them from the cruelty of starvation. Arnaud ground his teeth. It was maddening. Because he had dozed off, an heirloom that would only be sold in the direst of circumstances for only the highest price was gone, lost.

Bumping past people he didn't see, making his way steadily deeper into the intricate cross-work of side streets and alleyways, he scoured the city streets, searching for any sign of Andre. By mid-day he honestly didn't think he could walk anymore without nourishment.

He stopped at the entrance of a boulangerie and dug through his bag, looking for anything that might be tradable. Luckily Andre hadn't taken the bag or even rifled through it for valuables. Not that there were any valuables. Arnaud pulled out a long knife he used for gutting fish. He stared at it a moment, recalling memories of his father teaching him how to use it. It would be a sore loss, but Arnaud had little choice. The knife was truly the only thing of value he carried, and starvation was close at bay.

So he traded it. For three loaves of bread. He was soon a loaf fuller than he'd been in months.

In melancholy Arnaud walked the streets of Boulogne, musing how quickly objects holding memories of his father were disappearing. It was as if the world were wiping Mathieu Lemarin from existence; making it difficult for those closest to the fisherman to draw up memories of him. Arnaud sighed. It was a foreboding and gloomy thought; the consequence of regret and disappointment.

But regret faded with rest and disappointment was replaced with determination.

When Arnaud awoke the next morning in a cramped alleyway far from the forest, where he'd once planned on staying, he decided that dwelling on past mistakes would do him no good. He entered the first business he saw and asked for work. When he was denied, he proceeded to the next and the next. He soon recognized the truth in the barman's and the thief's words. There was no work. Not for anything. Even though Boulogne was a farming town as well as fishing, the fishermen out of work had snatched up any available work. This city's state was only slightly better than Calais' and in many ways worse.

But Arnaud's determination was not so easily snuffed out. The next day and the next he continued from shop to shop, asking owners if they might be hiring, or if they knew of any work. Any kind. Anywhere. But those who didn't throw him out immediately when they realized he would make no purchase regarded him with suspicion, even fear.

Crime stared Arnaud in the face down every street, at every corner. It was an organized disease eating away at the city and its people, causing a dark cloud of suspicion and fear to reign over their days.

Twice in the three days Arnaud had been there, attempts were made to snatch his bag and he was forced to physically beat the culprits off or run them down and take it back.

It was after the second of these exertions to regain his belongings that Arnaud slumped down on the steps of the cathedral with defeat heavy on his thoughts. Thunder clouds had been gathering over the city all day, hastening darkness before its time. Such was the season, though these storms seemed unusually strong. Arnaud could feel bruises forming on his arm where he'd had to tackle the bag snatcher. Focusing on the pain helped clear his thoughts.

He would just have to move on. Go to another town; one further inland where out-of-work fishermen were not an issue. The difficulty was that he knew of no other towns. Boulogne had been the only other name he'd heard mentioned because it lay so close to Calais. He would need to ask for advice and direction.

Which was why he sat now upon the steps of the Boulogne parish, hesitant on whether he should bother Pere Estienne. It seemed foolishly waiting at God's doorstep was turning into one of Arnaud's regular activities.

The cathedral lay near the outer edge of the town and Arnaud could see the tree tops of a forest opposite the one he had come through a few streets away. He rubbed his bruised knuckles and stared at branches swaying violently in the gathering wind. He would need to find some sort of shelter tonight, and soon, the storm was moving fast.

"Are you waiting for Pere Estienne?"

Arnaud turned around and saw an older man in a habit standing in the cathedral doorway.

"I – yes, is he here?" Arnaud stumbled.

"I'm afraid he is out. Last rites."

Arnaud nodded. It was uncanny to think someone was dying right now.

"Will he be back soon?"

"I'm sorry, I could not say. Is there anything I might help you with?"

"Thank you, no," Arnaud said standing, "I'll come back at another time."

He felt distinctly cowardly as he walked away. The man was probably a bishop or some other higher member; he would be as help as any.

A figure walked toward him up the street, head bowed against the sudden rain, cloak pulled up over his face, arms wrapped protectively around a long thin package. Arnaud would recognize his sword anywhere.

Looking back, shouting was obviously the wrong thing to do. But strong emotions harbor no reason and Arnaud's combined anger would be classified as a strong emotion.

Andre took off the moment he recognized the owner of his prize and Arnaud bolted after him. There was no way that thief would get away this time. Down streets, up alleyways, around corners, even when Andre took difficult and intricate shortcuts Arnaud followed, coming always nearer and nearer. The freezing March rain, sloshing puddles and dim light might not have existed, for all Arnaud noticed them. He had one goal: to regain his sword, and nothing else mattered.

Even though Arnaud was a stranger to these streets, he gained on him. So when Andre, desperate, turned to the forest for refuge, Arnaud was not ten feet behind him. And when he hesitated a moment at the barrier of foliage, as if he might've changed his mind, as if he were afraid, Arnaud was within an arms breadth. But when Arnaud stepped after and reached out to snatch the thief by the back of his cloak, there was no cloak. There was nothing. Nothing but darkness, and pounding rain, and clawing branches.

Arnaud snatched blindly around him, hoping Andre would still be near, but his hands met only with rough bark and sharp twig. Anger and frustration boiled over and Arnaud cursed the little thief with the harsh language of sailors. Punching the black air he stepped forward and tripped over what must've been a large protruding root.

As he lay there in the mud with any empty stomach, no hope, and the rain beating down on him, Arnaud was struck with an intense feeling of revelation. But revelation of what he could not say. And he began to laugh. At the injustice of life and all the little mistakes he'd made that God seemed to find severely punishable. He was tired of working so hard. Tired of trying. Just tired. Laughing seemed to help.

Then he woke up.

The sun was bright and hot overhead, causing the mud to dry quickly and cake all over him. Arnaud groaned and stood creakily to his feet. Yet he felt better than he had in a long time. It seemed he had reached the utter bottom, and it was time to move up.

He would forget about the sword and about revenge on Andre. He would swallow his pride and speak to the priest of the Boulogne parish. Somehow he would find a job, any job, no matter where he would have to go to get it. For some reason there was hope now.

And trees, lots of trees. Arnaud looked around him at the short, dark trees and knew that he was lost. He stared around him, directionless, his new hope fading just a little bit. How was it possible? He couldn't have taken more than five steps into the trees, but every way he looked the forest only seemed to get thicker and

darker. Shadows between the trees became steadily
longer and deeper until the sun could no longer
penetrate them. But these shadows were different from
those Arnaud had trod through on the way to Boulogne.
They seemed more *alive* somehow. He felt that just
beyond the corners of his sight, the darkness was
jerking; crouching; spinning, and it filled him with not
fear, but dread.

Time wore on, eroding numbly into Arnaud's
mind. The darkness and thickness of the forest, and the
sharp edges of the land slowly ceased to unsettle his
mind. Eventually, he felt strangely as if the hidden
venue had given up staring him down and decided him
harmless.

But though the fact that his surroundings were not
hostile was good news, Arnaud was still lost.
Uncertainty had never been familiar with him, and he
resented it. Still, there was no logical or rational
decision concerning which direction to walk in, and the
irrepressible indecision stepped in.

He stood staring for a long time, losing himself in
the frozen void of unthinking. He could have spent a
long while there in suspended thought and motion if he
hadn't been interrupted. Movement— sudden and
unexpected in the trees and the darkness ahead. But
when he went forward to investigate, the trees were bare
and there was no sound, no movement.

It was possible, probable, that he had imagined it.
Nevertheless it was something. It gave him direction
and he began to walk.

The darkness so reminded Arnaud of being under
water that, in spite of himself, he took several deep
breaths just to ensure that the air was thin and clear.
His eyes slowly adjusted to the absence of light until he
could at least see the outlines of the wide trees, their

41

thick pointed leaves and their winding roots snaking over the uneven ground.

But as he went deeper into the shadows the silence pressed close around him like a mothering blanket, tighter and tighter until he felt it become harder to more or think.

He stopped to breathe again. This place reminded him of drowning; he could think of no worse feeling. But there was no turning back, not now. He'd already walked several hours, and though it appeared he had not chosen the correct direction for Boulogne, it was too late. He might only end up further twisted in the trees, and he was no woodsman. There were no stars in here to guide him; they were hidden too far in the leaves.

So he continued on a steady course into the pressing and deafening shadows, hoping he would meet civilization before he started to --

He stopped.

A cabin stood not ten yards away, staring blankly at him with deep soulless eyes and a door-less mouth. Derelict and decrepit, Arnaud could see it had long been abandoned to decay, but it was a sign of civilization and at this point he would take anything.

But this house was different. Arnaud was far from superstitious, but he knew he had seen this place before. He had dreamed of it only a few days ago. The night Andre the thief had stolen his family's sword. Anger came up quickly as if it had stood close by waiting to be called.

There were horses inside the house, Arnaud recalled as he walked closer to the gaping doorway. He had passed it off as an odd and meaningless dream, and lost in anger had not thought of it again. But perhaps it had meant something. Here was the cabin, after all.

As he stepped inside, he knew there would be no horses. He knew the house would be empty. He was wrong.

There were no horses but Andre sat in a corner staring blankly into the air. Arnaud's sword sat next to him, unwrapped and gleaming in what very little light there was.

The moment Andre spotted him he was on his feet and scrambling out a back way. Arnaud saw clearly the heels of his retreating boots and the sword. He'd left it. Arnaud stared at it a moment, surprised by the boy's actions. Hadn't he come all this way, hidden out for days, tramped through muddy woods, for the sword? Why abandon it now?

But Arnaud stood there only a moment. He strode swiftly through the cramped cabin and out the door taking up his sword and slinging it over his back as he went.

He felt a drop of rain as he stepped back into wilderness. The house was in a small clearing opened up to the now dark heavens. Another storm, angrily approaching fast. None would be out on the sea in this coming tempest. Yet even now Arnaud would be more adept on the water than in the trees.

Andre was his hope now. The boy must surely know these woods. He had known the cabin. He must know the way back to Boulogne. Arnaud hurried into the shadow-infested trees where they boy had disappeared, and the rain followed.

"Andre!" Arnaud shouted again and again, "Andre Landon!"

The wind drowned his voice. But even if it hadn't, Arnaud could not expect the boy to come forward. He'd hunted the boy far enough and long enough for Andre to surrender the prize. Why would he willingly give himself up now? But Arnaud couldn't give up;

43

even though he walked deeper and deeper into a wooded grave; even though the storm's intensity rose higher and higher.

Lightening sprinted across what Arnaud could see of the sky in purple slashes, each throwing into jagged view sharp slicing raindrops. Thunder crashed so deafeningly Arnaud could think of nothing but the next wave of painful sound. It would be impossible to find the boy in this. He could barely keep his eyes open for more than a few seconds, and when he could see, darkness championed.

Exhaustion began to crowd in again, but Arnaud fought back this time. He needed to get out, away from the trees. He needed to follow Andre. So he continued on for what felt like hours in the rain and the slippery mud, until at last an illuminating flash of lightening suddenly revealed the back of a worn coat up ahead. Arnaud moved cautiously toward the boy, though there was no need, with the storm there was no chance of detection.

He was mere feet away, debating between force and manipulation when suddenly Andre was gone. Disappeared. Arnaud sprang forward, refusing to let him get away again; and lost his footing.

The earth crumbled beneath his feet. He tried to step back onto firm ground, but his left food slid and jolted off a sharp muddy corner. His heart flew up into his throat as he fell away from the cover of trees. He felt a table of wind pushing up on his back and hard rain pelting his face, and then he felt nothing and knew nothing.

***

Chapter Four

It was morning in every sense: grey, reflecting a sadly aged world; and the overwhelming hopelessness of a young man standing with his toes aligning the outmost edge of a cliff. His hair was flaming red, but his face was as colorless as the sky. Water boiled up at him from the roof of the cliff.

He gazed deadly out at frosted waves farther out to sea. They never ended; they jutted up for days until they lapped the sky. An icy wind howled and hushed at him and whipped about his flaming hair and his cloak.

Fear, hatred, hopelessness, grief: his face was horribly lined with bitter emotion; and breathless frustration swelled out into rigid arms and neck, but his eyes were utterly dead, beyond saving. He dropped. Like an old stiff tree, forward over the cliff. Down, skimming endless meters of orange shale until the sea leapt up and swallowed him. It's glacial grey stung and bit, and he could not breathe, but he did not want to. He clung to death, physical death; he welcomed it beside the deaths he had already faced.

He prepared himself for a great leap into relief from mourning, but instead flinched from the shock of strong hands gripping his arms. He saw a flash of blue scales and then the water fell away beneath him. It dripped from his hair and his face in little streams, and his lungs pulled in frozen air even though he tried to stop it. The hands released him and he collapsed on the rocks, retching and gasping pitifully.

Every bone splintered and ached as he pushed on his hands looking angrily for his executioner. There. A man – not a man – out in the water with a snowy mane down to his shoulders. Black buzzing crowded his eyes and ears, and not death, but darkness took him.

All was black, and then stairs appeared laid out before him, stone with a crimson carpet running up them in a great stripe. They climbed up and up and then blended into an echoing hallway hung with vibrant paintings as tall as the mast of a ship and as wide as its mainsail. Faces in them stared ever fixedly down upon the carpet and the crowns of the heads of passersby. And again, there were stairs. These were small and quick and wound in a wide spiral, wrapping around the core of a high tower. There were no paintings here, nor windows; only steps and more steps that seemed to go on and on into the cloud, until suddenly they ran into a doorway. Its door hung wide.

It was like entering a symphony. Like becoming one of the notes, blaring brilliantly. Or perhaps like gliding into a great dance, for there was no sound. The room was brimming with something that could be neither seen nor heard, but felt. It was like a breeze heavy with life, blaring and gliding.

And in one corner there was a window. A full moon hung in it as the faces had in the paintings: gazing down into the room with something more than polite indifference. Its beams hung in the living air as the final note of a grand concerto, trembling evident, but transparent.

The blue light illuminated a bed, pushed up to the wall under the window, and in it laid a young woman. She was sleeping, as still as marble and as pale as her glowing companion. She was robed in a white gown with gold trim, and white and gold ribbons were laced into her long dark hair, and she was the most beautiful creature he had ever seen. Even to stand before her, she would be far away; near in the leaden breeze that caressed her cheek, but as distant as the stars in the velvety heavens.

***

The chirp of water lapping on rock gently pulled
Arnaud from unconsciousness. For several moments,
he only listened to the familiar sound, resisting
awareness in his other senses. The tranquility of the
sleeping woman hung behind his vision and briefly
sheltered him from reality. But screaming thoughts
could not be restrained for long. He opened his eyes
blearily.

Arnaud could feel now that he was lying on uneven
stone, and that its edges were spiking into his back and
side. He tried to move, to sit up, but he had not gained
a centimeter before his body jolted back involuntarily
and he let out a sharp gasp. The sudden pain made his
breath jolt in the shallows of his chest. He involuntarily
twisted his body toward his aching ribs attempting to
shelter them from another attack of agony. His eyes fell
upon a still form lying beside him on the jagged island.

Andre had been badly injured. Arnaud could see
only his hands and face, but they were deeply bruised.
A single jagged gash ripped across his forehead just
before his left temple. Blood had gushed from the
wound and now caked his cheek and ear and brow. The
boy was a thief, possibly worse, but Arnaud couldn't
know enough to pass harsh judgment. He couldn't just
let him die. He wouldn't let him die.

Arnaud drug himself over loose and uneven rocks
to Andre's side, paying no heed to his own aching
ribcage. He took the hem of his own shirt into his
hands, ripped a large strip off, and pressed it upon
Andre's wound. Andre made no sound or movement.
Only the fractionate rising and falling of his chest
detached him from the dead.

It took several endless moments for the trickle of
blood to clot, and Arnaud had to take another strip of
cloth from his shirt. André looked no longer human.
Such pallor was reserved for those who had crossed the

River Styx. But Arnaud felt a slow pulse under his burning skin: *life*. He clung to it, holding Andre's head in his arms and delaying thought beyond the boy's survival.

Arnaud guided his eyes slowly across the water for restless ripples or any sign of what had wakened him to Andre's aid. They lay in a cove, spacious with cliffs hunched over it like a wizened man, bones twisted with age. Arnaud could see far out across the sea; moonlight tipped the soft tide with silver.

He noticed that Andre's pack had remained miraculously strapped to his back. His own was gone, far beneath the waters now. Arnaud attempted to remove Andre's, but was unsuccessful. He would not take his hand from halting the flow of Andre's blood.

Time passed too quickly; for the blood clotted, but the wound would not be stopped entirely. Arnaud clung to the faint hope that help might come. His thoughts had been mercifully dulled, yet he grasped vainly at this hope through long hours, not daring to reach for it in earnest.

Resting his aching back into a crevice in the jagged rock boulder, Arnaud stared up at the vast sky. Stars almost entirely lit it, one great beam shattered into countless, endless pieces. Under Arnaud's stiff hand, Andre's pulse was slowing further and further, but Arnaud's thoughts and emotions remained suspended without movement. He sat as ice upon the rock.

Arnaud sensed movement in the water around them before he heard it break the surface. He sat up as quickly as he could without jostling Andre's head. He found himself facing the form of a woman. Her head and shoulders only could Arnaud see above the rock. Her long dark hair flowed about her like smooth waves. Her eyes held deep urgency. Suddenly the head and shoulders of a man appeared beside her. His long hair and beard were harsh yellow and knotted, and his eyes glowed with dangerous ferocity.

Arnaud attempted to drag Andre's still form further into the safety of the rock island, but the woman held out her hand and lay it so gently upon Andre's boot that her skin barely touched it. This gesture calmed Arnaud, but he still would not remove his eyes from the barbaric-looking man. They watched each other tensely for several minutes. Only the beat of waves spraying over the rocks broke the rigid silence.

Andre suddenly twitched and groaned faintly from deep inside his chest and then stilled once again. This was the first movement he made since Arnaud had regained consciousness. Instead of heartening Arnaud, it disquieted him. For a second, he broke his gaze with the peculiar man to examine the boy's face. It was paler than Arnaud would have thought possible, but the boy's skin vibrated with heat under his touch.

Something grazed Arnaud's arm. He twisted around, his cracked ribs sending daggers into his muscles and back. The woman had moved from the man's side to stare beseechingly up at Arnaud. She slowly stretched her arm out and set it gently down upon Andre's shoulder. And then she spoke, but Arnaud could not understand her words. The sounds, strange to him, resonated in her throat and glanced metallically off of the waves. Like her eyes they carried deep urgency. The wild man's head and shoulders gradually split the water beside her and ended even with the plateau on which Arnaud lay, clinging desperately to Andre's life.

The woman's brown eyes did not leave Arnaud as she placed her other hand on the shoulder of her perilous-looking companion. Arnaud stared for a moment, and then nodded once, gently sliding Andre's

49

head from his lap, cushioning it with his cloak as he did so.

The man swept over in one powerful movement. He stared severely down at Andre for a long moment and then removed Arnaud's bloody cloth from his forehead. The wound was wide, and had taken on a twinge of green among the purple bruising. Arnaud's heart fell when he saw the infection, but the preternatural man's face held its stony demeanor. He produced a small conch shell from somewhere Arnaud could not see for the rock, and dipped his rough fingers inside of it, and the set it aside. A thick yellow paste dripped from his fingertips as he smeared the substance into Andre's cut. The patient jerked restlessly and then lay still.

The wild stranger then placed his palms roughly on either side of Andre's head and closed his fierce eyes as if in deep thought. Moonlight reflected from each bulging muscle in the man's arms. Arnaud realized how easily this stranger could crush Andre's head and began to move forward in protective protest, but again it was the woman who stopped him with an urgent sound that Arnaud could not understand. She glared at him for a moment and then dived down under the water, a great fin following a tail with a thousand earthy scales into the depths.

A bolt of lightning seemed to shock up Arnaud's spine when he saw this. She had been other than human! To truly see a legend that had haunted the tales of seafarers caused his thoughts to both freeze in utter disbelief, and to race all at once.

How was it that he got to truly see with his own eyes these creatures' sailors had christened 'mermaids'? They had seemingly swan to him through the mists of children's stories and drunken tales. *Can I no longer trust my own eyes?* Arnaud wondered.

He looked over at the merman whose large hands were still wrapped around Andre's head. He could now make out the dark green scales spiraling around the man's lower waist that must end in a powerful tail and fin beneath the waves. *What else is true that I have believed false?*

Feeling a gaze upon him, Arnaud turned. The dark haired mermaid had come again and was quite close to him. Arnaud's gut gave an uncomfortable twist as he saw her through his fears and cautions and realized that she was more beautiful than any woman he had seen on land barring his dark-haired dream. But her eyes were utterly solemn, and looking into them Arnaud thought she must be very old. Perhaps older even than the cliffs he had fallen from.

The sky was becoming noticeably lighter. The mermaid was much closer now; not a foot from Arnaud's face. He could distinguish each eyelash and the wind softly tossing little curls on her forehead. He was beginning to back away when she lifted a long object from the waters. She held it out to him, dripping with the ocean and glowing in the moonlight.

Arnaud stared at his sword for a moment and then reached out for it. The mermaid studied him carefully as he laid his hand upon the hilt and lifted it from her palms. As he did so, light from the emerald sliced through the dawn like a dagger and then dulled to its proper sheen.

The merman had finished with Andre and the mermaid had swept over to stand by him. One glance at Andre was evidence enough that he would live. A little color had returned to his cheeks, and his chest was rising and falling, slowly and evenly as the tide.

Arnaud held his hand to his breast in thanks to the merman who had saved the boy's life. Instead of offering the same or like, the stranger opened his hand

and held out a cut of thick cord and a heavy hook. He placed them roughly upon the rock near Andre's head and then dove beneath the waters. The mermaid, however, clasped her hands together in warm salute and smiled before following her companion to the depths of the sea as the sun's yellow orb rose over the waves behind them.

Andre mumbled incoherently and his eyelids flickered as Arnaud reached over and took up the rope and hook. A new salty wind wiped through his hair. He realized with a sudden jolt what had been cutting the nets and banishing the fish of the coasts, and had brought ruin and despair into the lives of many who depended upon such things.

***

The sun steadily broke the horizon. Within a few moments, Andre had regained a healthful pallor under his freckles and his heartbeat was sound and steady; his breathing deep and even. Arnaud watched in disbelief as the gash on the boy's head sealed itself under the yellow salve, leaving behind only a wide, fresh scar and a pool of cracked blood along the side of his face. Arnaud shivered involuntarily. It was so blatantly magical, how could one sanely believe otherwise? But he did not believe in magic. Nor did he believe in mermaids, though that was easier.

Perhaps the fall has broken my body and this has all been a hallucination. Or has only broken my mind; I might have jogged my head upon a rock.

The notion that he might be trapped inside a phantom of his own thoughts sent an eerie shock up Arnaud's spine that spread out to his fingertips and toes and crawled around his scalp. His gaze fell upon the peaceful sleeping form of Andre.

If none of this was real, then what of the thief—Andre?

A sound suddenly echoed off the cliffs above and around them. It was not loud, but was greatly magnified by rock and water. Arnaud recognized it immediately, for he had heard it nearly every day of his life. It was the hush and drip of paddles stewing thorough calm water. It sent a thrill through him, but whether of joy or dread, he could not tell.

"Who's there?" the voice echoed off the cliffs, but Arnaud could not see its source. "Speak now, or breathe your last upon that spot!" It commanded.

"I am Arnaud of Calais," Arnaud said, trying to raise himself up to peer over the jagged rocks. He could see movement from around the corner of the cove in which he sat; a blue shadow crawling steadily with the lapping waters.

"We fell from the cliffs during the storm."

The shadow crept further out and then draped from the bow of a skiff. One man sat at the front. A cross bow was loft in his thick arms and his left eye was cocked in aim.

"How many are you?" he demanded.

"Only my . . . companion and me," Arnaud replied hastily. "He has been badly wounded."

"And you fell upon this rock?" the man asked skeptically.

Arnaud did not know how they had come to be upon the rock. He made no movement or reply.

The stranger opened both eyes and studied Arnaud for a moment. His boat had drifted quite close to the rock island before he lowered his weapon. He glanced at Andre, lying utterly still, as he propped one booted foot upon the rocky island. He then glared intently, fiercely at Arnaud for several long moments, though it appeared more that he looked on at the rocks behind him. Arnaud stared at him unmoving, wondering if perhaps he were mad.

Finally the man's eyes rose to Arnaud's face. "And you were not hurt by the fall?" he asked, again dubiously.

"Thankfully, no," Arnaud replied, not taking his eyes from the stranger.

The man nodded once and shifted his back to Andre. Arnaud got the impression that he did not believe him.

The silence expanded once again into a chasm. Waves softly rocked the man's boat. Arnaud was uneasy being at the mercy of this outcomer. But their only other option was to swim along the cliffs for a spot to climb up to the trees once again.

"There are bandages at my camp. I will take you there," the man said suddenly, snapping his eyes back to Arnaud's face. "If you will aid me in lifting your friend into my boat, we will leave at once."

Arnaud nodded and gripped Andre about the shoulders and lifted him as gently as he could by propping Andre's head against his stomach. His ribs felt as if they were ripping from him as boar meat tears from the bone.

Andre lay upon the floor of the boat partially tucked under the cross-board. Arnaud had removed the boy's bag and placed it under his head, and then he sat down, breathing heavily. He pressed his side to stem the flow of pain.

"How long has your friend had that injury?" the man asked as he sat at the helm and took the oars into his hands.

"We fell during that great storm yesterday," Arnaud repeated, "we could not see where we walked." His head was beginning to cloud.

"There was no storm yesterday. It has been two days since last rainfall," the man said speculatively, "but his cut has scarred. If not for the bruise, I would

54

not have believed your story for a moment. Is that an old wound?"

Arnaud stared at the gash on Andre's forehead. The salve the merman had smeared upon it had left no trace.

"Yes, it is an old wound," Arnaud replied, not wanting to speak of the mer-people in case they had not been real after all.

"Whose blood then?" The man's dark eyes clung to Arnaud's features for a moment, and then he said, "It does not matter."

Arnaud was taken aback by this change of inquisitiveness and slightly suspicious.

"My name is Evrard," the man said with a sort of half smile propped upon his face. Arnaud could not prevent a feeling of distrust from sweeping over him.

"Are you not cold?" Evrard asked after a moment. Arnaud noticed that Evrard was wearing a thick cloak over his plain garb.

"No," Arnaud replied. But he did not know why. He'd always needed to dress warmly when first casting from the docks at dawn. He had not felt a chill even in the night when the wind and waves must have cooled to frigidity and he had been still damp from the water.

"Your friend might be though," Evrard said. Even with the strain of rowing, he kept his breath steady and conversation easy, "And to be so would not help his condition."

"I had not thought of it," Arnaud replied, reaching for his own cloak. It lay wrapped around his sword by Andre's feet. Arnaud considered it for a moment.

A tugging at the corners of his mind told him to keep his sword hidden. He turned back to look at Evrard. A look of what Arnaud thought might be contempt fled Evrard's eyes and a farce kindness was hoisted swiftly into them.

"I do not have my cloak close," Arnaud said. "Do you—"

"Under the tackle behind you," Evrard said, cutting through Arnaud's words.

Arnaud slid a thick elk skin from under a simple pole and crude netting. He spread it over Andre, whose clothes had not completely dried.

"So Arnaud, what were you doing out in the Bois Noir? As I hear it, not a soul has entered them in half a century."

"And why is that?" Arnaud asked.

"Haunted," Evrard replied simply.

Does this man truly believe in ghosts? Arnaud thought, yet after what I've seen, how can I know they do not exist?

"Is your camp not in the woods, then?" Arnaud asked, peering above them at the hunched cliffs. The forest was so thick it had spilled over to saplings sprouting along the spines of grooves, sparing the passing boat glances of dark leafy reflections.

Evrard stared at him with an expression resembling anger. Half a moment later a broad grin had cracked his icy stare and a booming laugh erupted from his chest.

"You're right, Arnaud," he said, "but I have good reason to do so."

"Perhaps I have good reason as well," Arnaud said.

"Perhaps," Evrard replied with a nod, "but I will not ask for it, knowing you would not tell me."

Arnaud stared at him, trying to determine what motives lay beneath the surface of his bizarre actions.

"But I do not fault you for it," Evrard continued, "a man who places trust in any passing stranger is a great fool." A curious expression was suddenly kindled in his black eyes. "Particularly if he has something to hide."

"Or protect," Arnaud added, sure they were thinking of the same thing: his father's sword tightly concealed beneath his cloak. "Would you tell me your business in the woods though I will not tell mine?" he asked.

A look fled Evrard's gaze before Arnaud could read it, "I however, have nothing to hide. My colleague and I hunt umbras."

"The term is new to me."

"They would be unknown to you if you are unfamiliar to this forest. Umbras are wolves, but larger and more vicious. Their name is such because they are difficult to track. Like shadows they move." Evrard's body quaked slightly. "Your friend is awake, I think." Evrard gestured toward Andre, renewing the vigor of his rowing.

Arnaud quickly leaned over to Andre's head. His eyes were half-open and bleary. "Are you alright?"

Andre squinted in pain. He opened his mouth as if to speak, but no sound came. He nodded once and then scrunched his face up in pain again.

"This is where we stop," Evrard said suddenly. Arnaud looked around. They had come to a shallow cove that ran up into a wide, rocky beach where cliffs sprung up on either side.

"A path leads from the water behind that ledge, there," Evrard said pointing.

"How far?"

"The path along the cliff is not so steep, but the way is hard. You'll have to help him," he nodded towards Andre, who had closed his eyes again and was breathing deeply and unevenly.

Evrard dragged the oars across the splintered boat sides, stowing them beside Andre beneath the cross boards. At the first touch of rock and sand, both Evrard and Arnaud leapt agilely over the side and lead the skiff onto the rocks.

"You're a fisherman?" Evrard asked.

"Was," Arnaud said.

Evrard nodded knowingly, "It's those damned mermaids," he said.

Arnaud stopped and stared at him. "Then you've seen them as well," he said impulsively.

"They've been tearing nets and plucking hooks all along these shores," Evrard replied grumpily.

Arnaud helped Andre from the boat, who then sat very still upon the rocky beach with his eyes shut and jaw clenched, not far from the peak of the low tide.

"Why do they do this now?" Arnaud asked.

He took Andre's pack and discreetly tried to conceal the hilt of his sword with it.

"Sailors have traveled farther out into what they claim to be their territory," Evrard replied simply. He dragged the skiff, hopping over pits and rocks, behind a wide ledge in the cliffs.

Arnaud's side twisted and throbbed convulsively as he helped Andre to his feet, and they began to shakily inch their way up the path. The way was uneven. It did not climb straight along the cliffs, but seemed to slope widely through them, and, Arnaud assumed, cut broadly up toward the forested plateau.

Giant, jutting boulders sliced up from the earth and an array of shrubbery sprouted from every crevice. Trees hung from above, shading them from the sun. Arnaud and Andre stumbled drunkenly. Arnaud exhausted all of his strength in supporting Andre and hauling his satchel and sword, and could sacredly manage to place one foot before the other.

His mouth was dry and grainy. Dizziness began to set in again, and black spots started forming before his eyes. He was being dragged into a chasm of darkness when Evrard suddenly took Andre's other arm and slung it over his shoulder.

"I'd forgotten you were injured," Evrard said. In his other arm he held his meager fishing tackle.

With the majority of Andre's weight taken from Arnaud's shoulders, he could breathe more easily and the spots disappeared, but his legs remained unsure. And though he was grateful for the help, Arnaud was uncomfortable being so close to this stranger. The man was clearly insane or had at least malicious ulterior motives. But Arnaud felt he had little choice.

Though they had not been to the north, birds, Arnaud noticed, were plentiful in these trees. They chattered and gossiped as they swung down from high branches and swooped up precariously close to the edgy, uneven rock.

As they rounded a turn in the wide path, Evrard turned to Arnaud.

"We're nearly there now." He nodded at something ahead.

Arnaud stared for a long moment in the direction the man had indicated before he realized what he was looking at. It was a pillar of some sort; very cleanly carved of stone in plain fashion. It peeked from the tall cliffs around them so that half of the structure morphed into the cliff side. It was huge; taller than the cliffs, with the cap resting flat on top where trees and grass grew up around it. Arnaud had to crane his neck to range its height.

"And over there," Evrard said, nodding his head toward the opposite cliff side.

Arnaud twisted his head around. An identical pillar stood directly across; the top third had crumbled and little green plants veiled its rocky innards.

"Who—?" Arnaud thought aloud, but the view ahead suddenly hit him with a force that made him stop and stare in amazement.

It was a city carved out of the cliff sides. The buildings towered above; some, it seemed, reaching almost to the clouds. They were efficiently crafted in that doors and rooms and wide windows were plentiful, but there was nothing overly elaborate to the construction. Later, Arnaud believed he might have passed the entire city by, as he would have the pillars, mistaking them for the many turrets of an eroding mountain.

But this close he could see what had once been streets weaving among oversized stone houses, now overrun with flowering vines and scattered bushes. Trees parted the rock-filled clay ground and shot up, never, however, stretching far enough to stroke the shale roofs with their leafy fingers.

A small smile grew upon Evrard's face. "I take it you've never heard of the giant city?"

Arnaud only stared.

"How did you find it?" Andre had apparently summoned enough strength to speak, though his voice was weak.

Arnaud readjusted his stare to his pale blood caked face.

Evrard did likewise.

"None have known the whereabouts of the bergrisar dwelling since the giant wars in the time of King Armand II." Andre persisted, looking at Evrard with a hard expression.

"How do you know this?" Arnaud asked.

"Books," Andre offered no further explanation and Arnaud wondered if he'd stolen said books.

Something like angry bewilderment flashed through Evrards's eyes. He glanced over at Arnaud and then quickly bathed the moment in a booming laugh that made Andre startle from the sharp abruptness. Just as quickly he was silent again, staring intently into the overgrown streets. They were too thick and dark to clearly see more than a few yards, Arnaud thought, but Evrard continued to watch in utter stillness.

Then, without blinking or shifting his gaze, he seized Andre's arm again and began to swiftly lead them towards the leafy darkness blanketing the oversized streets.

"What?" Arnaud protested, but was silenced with a low and urgent

"*Quiet!*"

They had reached the outskirts of the abrupt green, and Evrard crouched down behind a thick oak and peered into the foliage, apparently waiting for something beyond. Arnaud followed suit, helping Andre to do so as well. They remained in this position for several long minutes with only the gay chatter of birds to disrupt the silence. Just as Arnaud was opening his mouth to ask what it was that Evrard had heard or seen, the strange man stood up straight and relaxed. But still he said nothing.

Arnaud aided Andre to his feet again. Andre's face squinted in pain, but he carried himself more steadily than before.

"What is this place?" Arnaud demanded, determined to get some answers.

"Toevluchtsoord."

But it was not the voice of Evrard who answered.

There was no warning of his approach. No rustling of leaves, no crackle of movement, over the twig and pebble-littered ground. Arnaud did not even see him walking toward them. He materialized suddenly and unexpectedly ten yards away, calmly answering Arnaud's question. It was evident that this man was an acquaintance of Evrard. They both wore shaggy black beards and elk skin coats. Evrard showed no surprise at his sudden appearance.

"What?" Arnaud asked, attempting to overlook this phantomlike apparition.

"It was the hidden haven of the bergrisar," the man said, "once named Toevluchtsoord." He turned to Evrard, "I'd wondered why you were not back sooner." He smiled, and unlike Evrard, a fleck of warmth shone through his eyes.

"I'm Damien," he said.

Arnaud and Andre offered their names in reply.

"Were you lost?" Damien asked. They began to walk through the trees, Arnaud helping Andre along over winding roots and under low branches.

Arnaud related their story, again leaving his and Andre's conflict and the mysterious merpeople a blank. Damien, however, filled this gap when Arnaud fell silent.

"But you have said nothing of the merpeople. Or did you not see them?" he asked, "A merman healer has seen your friend here." He gestured toward Andre who looked rather startled.

Before Arnaud could formulate a reply Evrard once again spat his disgust. "Unnatural creatures," he said, "they're inhuman and should be dealt with as such. Along with those damn centaurs."

"It is my belief that the race is nobler than you think," Damien commented.

They passed under a giant red oak leaning over a pointed stone hut. Its branches creaked around the roof, shading the dwelling from the gaunt eyes of surrounding buildings as well as from the sun.

"Your belief is biased," Evrard replied gruffly.

They turned sharply to a small cracked hole in the structure and disappeared within its bleak depths. Arnaud, experiencing minor difficulty in aiding Andre around the wide cramping trunk, followed.

62

The two hunters continued their argument in the dusty black, but Arnaud stopped dead and the words floated by. All but for two fat ribbons pulling from high windows, the place was devoid of light.

But these two sources cast white shadows upon the bulky structures that made Arnaud stop and stare in wonder. They were chairs perfectly constructed with unique carvings upon the back and arms, but they were easily twice the size of human chars. Arnaud would have had to jump up onto them to sit and then uncomfortably.

"Friend," Arnaud turned to the voice. Damien was looking over at him, "Put him over here." He indicated a silvery skin draped over a pile of leaves.

In his astonishment, Arnaud had not noticed Andre's recent unconsciousness. He had been all but carrying him for an undeterminable time; the entire journey through the overgrown city perhaps.

But the moment Arnaud put Andre down, Evrard's already inconsistent behavior took a turn. His stance and his voice changed. His eyes went wild with suspicion and anger as he watched Arnaud closely.

"And what exactly are you doing in these parts, boy?"

"I . . . I told you. The cliffs. Our coming here was purely accidental," Arnaud said guardedly.

He was honestly confused and worried by this sudden alteration. Insanity was clear.

"And I'm just supposed to believe you? We're just supposed to believe you? Consorting with mermaids and the like. How do I know you aren't just going to slit my throat when I'm asleep and clear out my pockets?"

The mad hunter advanced towards Arnaud, who stepped back toward the unconscious Andre, toward his concealed sword.

"Perhaps I should just do away with you both now and prevent any unpleasantry."

"There will be no killing. Not of anybody," Damien interjected powerfully from the entrance where he looked out.

"I assure you we mean no trouble," Arnaud said, "we only wish to return to Boulogne."

"Boulogne?" Damien remarked quizzically. "That's three days journey through umbra and troll infested woods."

"Not to mention the damn centaurs," Evrard added.

"If we could pay – perhaps we could pay . . . something," Arnaud stumbled.

Evrard watched him expectantly, greedily. Damien looked uncomfortable.

"Right," Arnaud nodded, walked over and began digging through Andre's damp bag, praying there was something of worth inside. He wanted to avoid bartering his sword, although it might be becoming more trouble than it was worth.

There was a leather belt, made to fit a sword about the size of Arnaud's but too worn to be of any use to Evrard. Andre must've acquired it to increase the value of his latest item. Arnaud set it aside; it would prove extremely useful. Beside it lay a pair of lace gloves, several soggy but respectable handkerchiefs, a worn book, and two intricate brooches that looked fairly inexpensive, and –Arnaud lifted from the satchel— a necklace. It was the finest unworn silver, winding about itself in appealing little half ringlets all down a rather long chain. But the pendant was what stunned and perplexed him. It was an emerald. A single stone the exact cut and shade as the one adorning his sword, only a smaller size.

"Where did you get that?" Evrard stood over Arnaud, his eyes basking in the jewel.

64

"Does it matter?" Arnaud said harshly, yet wondering the same. Where would Andre get such a thing? Who did he steal it from? He felt suddenly protective of the necklace. He hated to see such a beautiful, delicate thing in the hands of Evrard.

The mad hunter flashed a yellow grin, "No. I suppose it doesn't."

"Then do we have a deal?"

"A deal, yes."

Arnaud held out his hand to shake, but the hunter acted as if he did not see it and walked away to another part of the hut to busy himself with various pelts.

Arnaud grimly took out one of the large handkerchiefs and wrapped the necklace in it and put it in his breast pocket. He loathed the entire situation; being in any way indebted or dependent upon such a man. "Do you know how to use a crossbow, Arnaud?" Damien asked shattering his thoughts.

"No," Arnaud admitted, "I fish for my living."

Damien nodded and preceded to hand him a quiver of black arrows.

"Still," he said, "another pair of ears is always welcome."

***

The light was beginning to fade, casting the world around them in ethereal grey shadows. After having been shown how to do so, Arnaud held the crossbow with an arrow in the notch, feeling rather foolish. He did not know how to shoot it and would surely miss his target.

"You are quite sure it is safe to leave Evrard with Andre?" Arnaud asked bluntly.

"For now yes. He would have no cause to kill your friend when you carry the prize," Damien replied.

"In any case, why did you bring me?" Arnaud asked. "Surely another hunter would be of more use."

Damien spoke softly, his eyes intent to the surrounding. "True. In the event of danger you would be quite useless back there alone. But Evrard must remain with your friend. I wish to speak with you apart from Evrard."

"Danger?" Arnaud asked as he ducked under a low birch branch. The arrow he had been carefully holding in place slipped and he was forced to reset it. "What sort of danger?"

Damien halted and held his hand up for silence. Arnaud aimed the crossbow to the direction Damien stared but could see nothing and hear nothing. They waited for several long minutes with not the shake of a leaf or breath of wind evident to Arnaud's senses. He was about to lower his bow when Damien let loose his arrow. It blurred through the dense forest and met an unseen something with a dull thump.

They moved forward through the trees in apprehension. The kill was much farther from them than Arnaud had guessed, and the arrow, plunged into a hairy silver body, sprung up suddenly at his waist. It was a wolf, but far larger than any he had ever seen or heard of. It was perhaps the height of a small deer. And Arnaud had never seen an animal with such a shaded coat.

"Is this what you hunt?" Arnaud asked as Damien pulled the black arrow from the creature's innards.

"This is an umbra," Damien replied. He took a long knife from his bag, "but it is rather small. Most likely exiled from the pack." He began to skin the animal as it lay.

"The rest are larger than this?" Arnaud said incredulously, "How do you know others are not here around us?"

The light was fading quickly now, and Arnaud did not revel in the thought of an ambush, particularly when he had no weapon he could readily defend himself with, as his sword was wrapped tightly in one of Andre's blankets.

"Their greatest threat is in groups. If others were near, we would never have made it so far into the trees."

Arnaud, still wary, peered into the shadows intently. All was still but for the sounds of Damien skinning the umbra and slicing its meat.

"Is this the danger you spoke of?" he asked after several long moments.

"Take my bag," Damien said, "in it you'll find rolled strips of cloth. Arnaud took them out. "Now help me wrap the meat. And be sure that no blood gets on you."

Arnaud complied without a word. They worked for several minutes, taking long strips of hot pink meat and wrapping it up in rough cloth. Arnaud had skinned an endless number of fish, so the operation did not surprise or worry him. They ran short of strips long before the meat supply had diminished. Damien placed the crude parcels in his bag and slipped the thing on without touching it with his stained hands.

"Take the back legs." Damien said, as he seized the giant forepaws.

They lifted it and again they walked with the carcass pulling and swaying gently between them. The direction they took was not a return from their outward journey and slanted slightly uphill. Arnaud wondered how long they would be out in the dark and unfriendly trees.

"Yes," Damien said after several minutes labored walking, "Umbras are the foremost threat in these parts, and they are why your friend could not stay alone."

"But surely wolves would be unable to get into the . . . giant's hut. Those walls were thick and the windows too high and an animal this size would find it hard to come through the small entrance." A loud shushing suddenly filled Arnaud's ears.

"Wolves, perhaps not," Damien said, "but umbras are not wolves, just as we are not giants."

The shushing grew louder and Damien was forced to shout over it.

"They are much larger, as you've seen, much stronger and they are also smarter and thicker walls they have penetrated. They all but destroyed my village."

Arnaud nodded in acknowledgement of this information, but was steadily going mad from the unexplained noise, until he saw its source and then felt a fool. They slipped unexpectedly from the thick trees and found themselves on the very edge of a great river. If Arnaud had not been paying attention, he would have stepped straight into the bellowing water crowding past.

"On third count, we'll throw it in."

The gentle roar of the sweeping current muffled the sound of umbra remains meeting the angry water.

"The pack would have followed such a strong scent as the blood of their own," Damien explained.

They stood in silence. The moon looking on with glowing curiosity as the skinned umbra flowed swiftly with the current. They watched it until the carcass disappeared around the sharp bend.

"There was one more thing I wished to tell you," Damien said solemnly as he bent down to clean his stained hands in the sprinting water. Arnaud crouched and followed suit.

"You have noticed Evrard's hostile behavior."

Arnaud said nothing.

"He was not always as such. But dragons breed madness. Evrard is mild compared to some I've seen."

He paused and Arnaud wished to say something, to ask what he meant. Surely it was a metaphor. He couldn't mean real dragons.

"Greed is now the dominator of Evrard's life. Self-involvement is easily accessed and embraced to a fevered mind. I am convinced he would take the cloak from my back if he thought it would benefit him. You, no doubt, have recognized his coveting that sword of yours? Do not think he will be content only with your bargain."

A shaking pang went through Arnaud. He had been careful to conceal his weapon.

"Why associate yourself with such a man?" Arnaud couldn't help asking.

"He is an excellent hunter," Damien replied simply. "It would be hard to find his equal. Besides he will not kill me. We are two alone hunting umbras. To kill me would be suicide."

"And hunting is more important to you than self-preservation?"

Arnaud was amazed. He couldn't imagine risking his well-being to fish with a skilled but dangerous fisherman.

"It is my life," Damien stood to his feet.

"Avoid solitude with him, and keep what is precious close to you at all times. I will do what I can for you, friend, but be always on your guard."

"Is it safe, then, to leave him with a sick man?" Arnaud asked thinking of Andre.

"If there is no gain from brutality. For now, I believe your friend is safe."

As they turned and left the abrupt river, Arnaud resolved to sleep with his sword hidden at his side.

"You are injured," Damien commented as they walked back through the wood. There was no sympathy or concern in his voice. He stated a hard fact.

"From the fall, yes," Arnaud complied, "I might've cracked a few ribs."

"You must take care of that, or you will slow us down in travel," Damien said coldly.

Arnaud said nothing. The pain had increased greatly through the day so that now he moved stiffly and his side was too tender and inflamed to touch easily. If now they were to be in danger he would surely be as much an impediment as Andre whose wounds were severe.

"I find it hard to believe you could take such a fall with no more than cracked ribs to show," Damien continued, his voice still monotone.

"It is as much a mystery to me," Arnaud said truthfully, staring at the hunter, unsure if his words had been a challenge or a threat.

Damien caught his glare. "I neither expect nor wish you to tell me your secret, Arnaud, but do not believe you hide anything well." Then he sighed and weariness was evident upon him. "I will bind your ribs when we return."

***

Chapter Five

The night was colorless; bleak; grey but for a snapping, spitting fire that glowed red upon men's faces: faces that were gaunt with worry, pale with fear; and blank with hopelessness.

"We may as well die here tonight," one said dully, "far away from—"

"Not so far anymore," another added.

A dark man walked swiftly through the camps. But though need for haste was great, this man could not pass by such remarks.

"Courage, men," he told the grave group as he passed, "let not such evil thoughts trouble hope."

He could say no more until he spoke to the captain, nor could he pause to hear a reply. But he could see no agreement in their eyes. And for what they knew, he could not blame them their melancholy. But thoughts, even these thoughts, flew from him as he now began to run through the sea of tents and forlorn faces. His news was from the king and it was urgent. But it was of good report and that is why he ran. If it had been yet more discouraging news, as all had been since the regiments' stationing in the cliffs, he might not have had the heart to run.

He approached a tent much longer than those endlessly pitched upon the red shale.

"Captain," he said as he entered, waiting not for admittance or recognition, "orders from King Phillip."

Five grey young men sat in conference about a small table. They raised their heads at his abruptness and stared with interest but little enthusiasm.

"Captain—"

"Wait!" Captain Jaques stood to his feet. He could not have been much the elder of the answering officers about him, but his hair was dusted so to be

71

almost white and lines of worry scarred his countenance.

"Gentlemen, we shall continue this discussion at a later time."

He nodded at them and they began to file out. When the last man had left he stood before the tent opening for a listening moment.

"All news is to be spoken in private to me," he said, dropping polite demeanor, "now, what have you to say?"

"King Phillip has ordered peace envoys to be sent to the remaining giants."

This news would bring life back to the men and, if all went well, would, in a short time, end the war and endless death toll. But the runner was surprised to see the captain clasp his hands behind his back and maintain a severe expression.

"Did the king give you explanation for stopping just shy of victory?"

This reply was inexplicable to the runner. Surely a captain, the head of the King's armies, would desire peace? What else would he be fighting for?

"Ewoud, their leader, has himself offered surrender and peace. They have lost most of their warriors and would rather surrender than further endanger their women and children," he replied.

They stared silently at each other for a long moment as Captain Jaques considered this order. The runner's nerves jumped as he watched for a reply, nervous for reasons he could not explain.

"Their women and children you say?" the captain whispered as a scoffing smile fell upon him. "And what about my men? They too have women and children to protect, many of which have died in their absence under the hands and spiked boots of these monsters. My own

wife and three sons included in their slaughter of innocents, even before the war."

The runner gazed on in mounting alarm. The captain's eyes darted maniacally, his hands shook with uncontrollable passion. The man was mad and as such, was entirely unfit to govern battle.

The captain spoke on, "Only a King who has scarce visited a battle ground, with one child and a faerie queen would order peace on the brink of total victory. How can I abandon years of loss and bloodshed when I am but a step from vanquishing my dearest foes?"

The messenger did nothing but stand and attempt to tame his mounting alarm.

Captain Jaques seized the runner's collar and pulled him close, centimeters from his anger-flushed face. "I ASK YOU! HOW!?!"

"No matter your convictions or mine, Captain Jaques," the runner said severely, "the King's orders are law!"

He removed Captain Jaques's shirt-filled fists. No matter the man's station, he was not one of the captain's soldiers. He answered to King Phillip alone, and he would tell the king straight off Captain Jaques's inconsistencies. Such a man, so emotionally involved and unstable, should be in no position of power.

"What is your name, son?" Captain Jaques said suddenly in a tone polar to the tempestuous shouts that had moments ago shaken the drawn curtains.

"Messenger Ferrand, Sir."

The Captain strolled, alarmingly calm to the door of his tent.

"Ferrand, you are right. You may inform King Phillip that his orders have been carried out. I shall send peace envoys to the bersingr at first light. You may go. Oh, and here," he picked an apple up from a

basket on his table and tossed it to the runner, "you might get hungry on your way."

Ferrand left, feeling more uncertain than he had in his life. He did not trust the captain. A man in his state should not be leading the king's men. As he tramped through rows of heavy tents, past hundreds of men troubled and worried over grave casualties of brothered soldiers, plagued with tragedy, and homesick to distraction, he decided to wait in the camps to see if Captain Jaques was true to his word.

***

Time jumped as ripples in a still pool, Many days had passed in disquiet. Ferrand had not spoken to the soldiers for fear that they would peck and bribe from him what their captain had not said. But the messenger held a dim hope that Captain Jaques would follow his word. Three men had been sent out on the first day, but they had been armed, which was unusual for negotiators of peace; and no hope had been hinted to the soldiers. A pale mist of gloom and despair hung still over the camp. But a change was indeed anticipated, though Ferrand could not identify it.

Odd sounds awoke him at dawn. Croakings and chirpings that he would normally have ignored were eerie under the blanket of tension that muffled the early air. Ferrand stood and immediately hurried to the camps. He'd slept many yards beyond the range in which firewood was gathered, past where voices could be heard in the early morning. He moved swiftly to a run, and his uneasiness intensified with each step.

There were no sounds of camp. The striking of tinderboxes and easy conversation was replaced with the ominous croaking and creaking of empty forest. The campground came upon him as a blur. It was, for the main, empty. The tents remained and a few unsoldiered men lazed before dwindling fires.

Ferrand hurried directly to the nearest, a cook by his looks.

"What has happened!" he asked the man urgently, "Where have they gone?"

"To battle," the cook replied, standing to his feet. "A message came from the King a few nights past . . . but you're the King's messenger, aren't you? Surely you'd know what it said."

"I don't—can you tell me what it said?" Ferrand asked urgently.

"No survivors....something about no survivors."

"That was no message of mine," Ferrand replied angrily, "Can you tell me where they've gone?"

"The Northern overlook of the cliffs."

Ferrand took off for the cliffs without another word. Speed was his ally, but the cliffs were an hour's march from the camp. When he finally arrived, it was too late.

Bloody carnage flooded the ravine. Before their giant homes they were massacred. Men, women, and children that, if only for their size, could have defended themselves if they hadn't been so outnumbered and the docility of prospective peace hadn't been upon them. They were cut down, lifeless before his eyes. None were spared under the mad captain and his corrupt orders.

The sight made Ferrand sick, physically and to the depths of his soul.

The scene faded and another emerged in gentle waves of subconscious.

Crawling, spindly arms snaked up smooth, even boulders. Their appearance was fragile, as if a stray breath would send them coiling down; but thus they had hung for hundreds of years and through hundreds of kings. They veiled the outer walls.

The forgotten castle peeked out at overgrown fields and emptiness.

It was twilight, and the light was such that it could be the rising or the falling.

The decaying side doors responded to touch and swung in with no sound but hovering dust. This same dust, sticky upon the ground, muffled booted clacks to flat thumps. The silence prickled and mocked, but he took no notice. He wandered, searching for something unknown even to himself. Through choking hallways, stale and cobwebby, until he came upon a great staircase. It had once been elaborately carved of gold which now winked from its stifling blanket.

Up, he mutely stepped, and then to a second staircase, and a third, until he was sure to be level with the clouds and still he climbed. And then there were no stairs and no musky halls. Only an open room with an open window and an embellished bed thinly veiled by silk frothing from a canopy above. This room was different from the rusty halls; the only sign of age lay in creeping vines that had slithered over the walls and spiraled around the posts, the canopy, and the solitary soul who lay in the bed, asleep. Brown hair, rose cheeks and a soft smile reflecting the contentment of deep rest. And then a sudden explosion of light and sound and a feeling of stiff hot ice upon his chest.

***

Arnaud sat up, woken suddenly as if someone had shouted in his ear. But there was no one, only fresh light sneaking through corroded walls. He looked around, attempting to slow his racing heart.

"Mab sends you her devilish mares," Evrard leaned against a wall facing him.

Arnaud shuddered to think he had been watched sleeping.

"What did you do to anger her?" Evrard asked his question seriously, but Arnaud had no answer for

76

ridicule. Evrard rose suddenly into a fit of uproarious laughter that made Arnaud jump.

"Prepare yourselves, we will leave now."

He walked out of the hut and into green sunlight.

"That man is crazy."

Arnaud swung around to see Andre leaning up on his elbows next to him. The muscles of his ribs writhed, but Damien's tight binding kept him from twisting far enough for true pain.

"Where are we going?"

Arnaud did not reply. He stood and began collecting his things. "Can you stand? Walk by yourself?" he asked, perhaps more abruptly and harshly than he'd intended.

"Well, apparently I can bleed," Andre commented, rubbing his palms over the side of his face and stared at the crumbled blood.

"Try!" Arnaud wished he could keep the impatience out of his voice. But he still harbored anger and resentment toward the thief who to robbed him.

The natural joy in Andre's countenance seemed to drain at Arnaud's harsh demeanor. He braced himself and stood very slowly, stumbling only once and using the wall for support.

"You think you'll be able to travel all day?"

"I – I'll manage," Andre said, but his demeanor was distinctly ill. "Just a bit dizzy."

Arnaud said nothing. He buckled the empty belt around his waist and slung Andre's bag onto his back.

"Here's your . . . sword."

Arnaud stared at it, thickly wrapped in still damp cloth, and at the shame upon Andre's face.

"Thank you." He took it but offered no consolation or forgiveness. He couldn't keep himself from wanting to never see this boy again.

Arnaud walked out into leafy light, paying no heed to Andre taking his first solitary steps since the fall.

"Is he alright?" Damien seemed genuinely concerned.

"He says he is," Arnaud replied blankly.

Damien nodded, "Just stay close, and when I tell you to do anything: run, crouch, or hide; don't question. Just do it."

"Is that . . . likely to happen?" Andre asked nervously.

"Neither of you are woodsmen," Damien replied hoisting his crossbow over his shoulder, "you do not know how to move quickly. We will likely be heard."

But there was no incident that day. Arnaud spent it watching shadows crawl around beneath the heels of the two hunters and listening to Andre's labored breathing behind him.

***

"We're going back to Boulogne, aren't we?" Andre asked in a whisper when the shadows had made their final round and dawn had sprung again.

Arnaud nodded, "Yes."

Andre stumbled on a protruding root and Arnaud caught his arm, heaving him up to keep him from falling.

"How are you doing?" Arnaud asked, feeling acute guilt. Only a few days ago this boy had been beats away from death. Arnaud should be helping him no matter what he'd done.

"Calais," Andre asked as if he wished to ignore what had just happened, "is it a big city?"

"It's a little smaller than Boulogne, but it's a trade city so there are more people and more ships."

Andre seemed to consider this, but said no more.

"I hope the necklace wasn't an heirloom of yours," Arnaud said with unintentional bite, "it is the price we pay for their protection and guidance."

"What necklace?"

"The emerald pendant in your bag."

"I've never seen an emerald necklace in my life," Andre said seriously.

"Perhaps you forgot you'd stolen it."

"I never steal from a lady," Andre insisted, his voice several volumes louder.

"And that brooch? I suppose you've never seen that either," Arnaud said, attempting to control his rising temper.

"That was in a man's pocket all wrapped up." Andre was almost shouting now.

"Quiet!" Damien whispered back at them anxiously.

Arnaud had not seen them raising their crossbows or crouch and peer intently around; had not noticed the sudden lack of forest music. The chirping of birds along the cliff beside them, the croaks and chirps of misty mud-dwellers, the gentle hush of a slight breeze— all had ceased, leaving ominous silence.

Arnaud had crouched right next to Evrard, or he would never have heard them speak.

"It's a pack," Damien whispered, "I'd say twenty or thirty?"

"They moved in damn fast," Evrard cursed.

"We might manage if we act quickly. I don't think they've fully closed in yet."

"Then this is the perfect opportunity," Evrard said.

"What?"

But Evrard had already grabbed Arnaud's collar with one powerful hand and began pawing around his cloak and shirt with the other.

"Evrard, what—" Damien whispered frantically, "there's no time!"

"We've gotten through worse, "Evrard was feverish with greed. He found the handkerchief-wrapped necklace in Arnaud's breast pocket, but before he could get it out, Arnaud had gained his bearings. He swung back and smashed the man's nose in. The blow pushed the mad hunter onto his back and he lay stunned a moment with blood gushing down over his lips and chin. But it didn't seem to faze him.

"We were alone then," Damien continued arguing, too busy letting loose an arrow into the soft flesh of an umbra out of sight to notice their struggle.

"Exactly," Evrard shouted, springing up at Arnaud, who, unprepared for such an action, was thrown to the mud under the weight of the giant man. Evrard began scrambling through his tunic again.

Arnaud cocked his arm and cracked his elbow down on the man's supporting hand feeling at least two fingers snap, when, out of nowhere, something swung out and hit the hunter hard across his head and he fell unconscious.

Arnaud stared in astonishment at Andre standing over him with his wrapped sword gripped tightly in both hands. The boy stood there a moment, breathing heavily, and then apparently overcome with dizziness, he crouched down beside them.

"Andre . . . thank you," Arnaud said sitting up.

Andre passed over the sword without opening his eyes or saying a word.

"You two. Go. Now!" Damien barked. He let loose another arrow. Arnaud heard a yelp echo behind them.

"But what about—"

"I'll manage, but not with you here. I can't protect both of you and myself."

"But, Evrard—"

"He'll be fine. Just run. Quickly! Or you won't make it! That way." He pointed back toward the cliffs. "There's a cave. They won't follow you in there. Don't go too far in. Wait there."

Arnaud nodded. He seized Andre's cloak and pulled him up. He didn't let go as they made their way through the trees that had only moments ago seemed innocent and inviting, but were now filled with sinister. They moved quickly, but they could not run. Their injuries were crippling and forbade it. Yet Arnaud quickened their pace until Andre was stumbling and wheezing beside him.

They reached the cliff side, the flat base of a small mountain, with no incident and no sign of vicious attackers.

"Where . . . where are they?" Andre asked in a small breathless voice, "What if . . . what if we can't see them and they just pounce at us and we don't even . . . ."

Arnaud was worrying the same thing, but he released Andre's cloak and gripped his arm. "Come on."

They shuffled quickly along the cliff, always within arm's reach, stepping around and over protruding foliage.

"Look for a cave," Arnaud commanded.

He let go his grip on Andre and began quickly unwrapping his sword. It was better than no weapon and he did not see any cave. What he did see were eyes. Many half-hidden, winking and blinking in the shadows behind them. If Damien had been accurate in his description, the umbras would devour them within seconds. But Arnaud wasn't one who would sit and wait for that to happen. He unwrapped, then unsheathed the sword.

"Do you see a ledge, or anything we might climb up on?"

"A—a ledge? No—no, I—oh, God, they're coming! I can see their eyes—"

"Focus, Andre! A cave. A ledge. Do you see anything?" Arnaud gripped his sword until he could feel blisters forming on his palm. Growls rumbled from the umbra's hungry throats.

"There! A ledge! Over above that tree," Andre said pointing. "Do you think that will work?"

Arnaud nodded. It was a slim shot, but their only one. He braced himself as five umbras stepped out of the shadows and began closing in. They were huge, half the size of a horse but fierce; their haunches bristling, their razor teeth bared.

"Now!" Arnaud whispered. He seized Andre's arm and pulled them forward while swinging his sword around at the snapping wolves.

Arnaud ran harder than he had ever before, but knew that it could never be fast enough. He pulled Andre along beside him, but though the boy kept up surprisingly well, broken ribs were a leaden weight to their speed. The second they had left gnashing danger, ten beasts were at their heels.

Arnaud could feel phantom jaws around his legs when Andre shouted and jerked him into utter darkness.

***

Chapter Six

For a moment; a fleeting, terrified moment; they believed the beasts had followed them into the cave, and thus kept running. But when Arnaud realized that they had entered into the bowels of a cave their pursuers dare not enter, he seized Andre's shoulder.

"Wait! Wait. We've not been followed."

"They—they didn't follow?" Andre turned around, taking deep, pained breaths. He started to laugh; shallow, nervous giggles. "Let's never—I'm never, ever doing anything like that again! I think I'd rather die than live an inch from *death*."

The last word he emphasized and the cave shouted *death* back at them in echoes. Ominous and sobering.

"Where are we?" Andre asked in a small voice.

The silence following *death* was absolute. They had been sucked from a world of sound, color and rigid panic, to one of numb nothingness. They were left devoid of the senses of parallel planes.

"It looks like you found Damien's cave."

"If this is the cave, where's the entrance?" he asked.

Surely there would be some light; a solitary beam or a few flecks of white shadow. They could not have gone far in.

Arnaud shuffled back and groped along the cave walls for a sign of the opening.

"It should be here," he said, "we didn't go further than a few steps."

But it wasn't there. The walls were jutted with uneven stone all around. There was only one direction to take and Arnaud was sure it led deeper into the cliff side and under the mountains. How is that possible? He continued to examine the walls with his hand. It

83

isn't possible. There must be some small opening I'm missing. But there wasn't. Even when he covered the walls again and again, all he felt was rough rock where the opening should be.

"What's . . . what's wrong?" Andre asked, but Arnaud didn't have the heart to add more worry to the boy's already terrified outlook.

Arnaud said nothing, and Andre didn't ask again. Yet it was another hour before Arnaud finally surrendered hope. He slumped down against the baffling wall and Andre sat next to him. Arnaud closed his eyes wearily, wishing that he would wake up and find it had all been a dream. That he could return to the worries of his life a week ago. He'd almost be happy to face starvation and unemployment next to daemons he could not recognize and could not see.

"Why can I see you?"

Arnaud opened his eyes. "What?"

"You're green," Andre elaborated. He held out a hand and stared at it. "I'm green."

Arnaud looked down at the yet sheathed sword sitting upon his lap. The emerald was glowing. He held the ting up to look more closely. Even as he looked, the light was fading. They stared as the mystifying glow drained, draining their hope along with it.

"Why did it do that?" Andre asked.

"I . . . I don't know. Maybe the stone momentarily absorbs light? I'd never really had the opportunity to look closely at it before."

"Why not?"

"Never thought much about it. Then when I did have the opportunity . . ." he shrugged.

Andre lowered his eyes. "I'm . . . I'm sorry, Arnaud for taking it. I would never have . . . I mean if they found out that I had it and didn't . . . and I was already on the line with them."

"Wait, who are you talking about?"

"Monsignor Serge. He helps some of us. We acquire valuables for him and he sells them and gives us food and a place to sleep. But I've acquired more debt than most."

"Why?"

Andre's lips pursed into a very thin line.

Arnaud nodded; he didn't press the subject. But he couldn't help feeling a surge of violent hatred toward men who would do that, who would take advantage of children even younger than Andre.

They sat vacantly in the darkness for several long minutes.

"Your city, Calais, will you take me there?"

"You wish to try your luck in another city?"

Arnaud could sense the boy's nod beside him.

"Your luck at thievery?"

"No, no," Andre said quickly, "no. I want to get away from all that . . . if I can. I want to try."

Despite himself Arnaud believed what he said, "I cannot guarantee any success, but, yes I will take you there. Once we quit this place."

"Well how—how are we going to do that?"

Arnaud stared ahead at the black and endless chasm. He stood to his feet nursing inflamed ribs.

"If we cannot go back, then we must go forward."

"But there might be no end," Andre said.

Arnaud knew this was likely. "Our only hope waiting here is a slow death of starvation. I'll take the bag."

Andre gave it to him.

"Hold on to it," Arnaud said as he slung it securely onto his back, "Don't let go."

He unsheathed his sword and held it out in front of him. With Andre gripping on to him and his sword held aloft before him, Arnaud led the way out into the void.

The black did not end. If anything it increased, becoming denser and denser until Arnaud feared they would drown in it.

They moved very slowly, tentatively testing each step and feeling along the rough sides as they went. But still Andre had difficulty and began to limp and wheeze behind him.

It might have been days later when they finally stopped, and still darkness suffocated.

"It's like we haven't moved at all," Andre said as he slumped wheezing upon the icy ground.

Arnaud agreed. Their surroundings were precisely the same and the way had offered no turns.

"What if we never get out?" Andre said limply from the ground. "Maybe there is no way, maybe a dead end lies buried deep under the mountains.

Arnaud remained quiet and they sat long in the suffocating black mute. Everything was calm, as death or as the pause before a booming storm.

"We're a long way now from Le Bois Noir," Andre said.

Arnaud said nothing. He knew that walking back to Calais would take months even if they were able to find it directly. But he had not the heart to impart this on Andre. It would do no good to encourage low spirits.

Silence grew heavier and heavier upon them, smothering and crushing until they slowly drifted to sleep.

***

When Arnaud opened his eyes, he was not sure he'd actually done it; the darkness seemed denser around them. Arnaud could hear Andre's deep breathing by his side, but he did not wake him. He just sat in the endless black and battled darkness within. Would he see his family again? Would he see the sun again?

He'd been dwelling upon these thoughts for a time he could not determine when he noticed a sound gradually growing in intensity and rapidity. It was faint and would easily have been overlooked if any other had challenged it; but as it was, Arnaud could hear it clearly between Andre's breaths. It was the gentle dripping of water upon stone. It plunked steadily, methodically, and once recognized, Arnaud could hear it louder and louder.

"Andre," Arnaud shook the prostrate from beside him. "Andre."

"I'm awake, Arnaud, what is it?" he still lay on the ground. Arnaud assumed in pain.

"Do you hear it?" Arnaud asked quietly.

All was silent again but for the drip dripping.

"Water?" Andre asked.

Arnaud nodded and then remembered he could not be seen through the black. "Yes."

"What has it to do with us?" Andre asked wearily.

"We've likely gone a far way under the mountains," Arnaud replied, "and if the water is any good, we might not get another opportunity to drink. "

André said nothing.

"I'm going to get around and look for it, but we shouldn't separate in this or we may never find each other again, alright?"

Andre began a sigh but cut it short. "I won't be able to go far," he said, "my ribs seem to grow worse each day rather than better."

Arnaud could relate, but his thoughts had been too occupied of late to notice the slightly lessening pain.

Still, he felt a bit guilty for not guessing Andre shared the same or worse pain that afflicted him.

"I swear in daylight I will wrap them," Arnaud replied, "but we haven't the time or the means now. The longer we wait the less chance we have of . . . of getting out," he added, feeling he should explain his reasons for not lessening the boy's pain.

But Andre had already risen to his feet as Arnaud spoke.

As they groped around in the darkness, Arnaud realized that the tunnel had grown wider so that even after several tentative steps he could not reach out and touch the rock walls.

"We must be in a wide cavern," he said and his voice echoed hollowly. But he was not cheered by this. It was easier to get lost in a cavern, and slithering and crawly things widely inhabited them.

"The sound is louder out that way," Andre said, pulling Arnaud's sleeve.

He felt very vulnerable now with no wall to guide them along. Arnaud skid his sword upon the ground ahead so that they were not swallowed by holes or beaten by jutting stalagmites.

But as blind men they did not walk for long. Soft light began again to illuminate their surroundings and at first Arnaud believed it to be coming from an unknown source in the cave, but a glance proved it to be his sword growing brighter and brighter. The result was a clearer view of their henceforth invisible surroundings.

The cave was huge. So wide the light was unable to reach out and graze the walls and so tall the high ceilings remained a black cloud over them. They were a tiny blip of green light in a world of darkness. All they could see was sharp and contorted and evil-looking. Stabbing, razor-edged domes pierced up from the ground and slime-covered rocks and boulders piled over their uneven way.

And creatures; little beasts with no eyes and too many legs, scuttled out of the light. Occasional black wings swooped around them and away. Yet all remained frozen and eerily silent. They'd been outnumbered by black fauna this whole time and not known it. What had crawled over and around them in the night while they slept unaware? Arnaud could feel Andre tighten his grip.

"Oh," Andre shuddered, "I can't do this."

Arnaud could feel panic rising in the boy next to him and apparently the cave-dwellers could too, for they began to scurry in their own panic, but not necessarily away. Arnaud watched two beetles the size of his palm, scuttle past a slimy black centipede longer than his arm, wound about their feet.

"So . . . so everything in your bag," Arnaud conversed, attempting to take Andre's and his own mind from the so far harmless cave-dwellers, "everything was to go to Mon—"

"Serge. Yes," the boy's voice shook, but he was going along with it. He was calm enough to think and to answer. "But I swear I've never taken any necklace."

Arnaud slipped his hand into his pocket and pulled out the handkerchief. He placed it in the boy's hand. "That was in your bag. Tell me I'm the liar."

Andre stopped to unwrap it, and Arnaud watched. He witnessed the awe and surprise on the boy's face.

"You found this in my bag?"

"Yes."

"But I've never seen this before. I'd never seen anything this valuable, before your sword, that is."

Arnaud nodded but he still had doubts. The boy was a thief. He was likely a practiced liar as well.

Andre seemed to suspect Arnaud's speculation. "Here," he held out the necklace, "take it."

Arnaud continued to study the boy's expression as he reached out for the pendant, but he saw no shame there. Worry, anger and frustration, but no shame. Perhaps he was wrong. Maybe the boy hadn't stolen it after all. Or maybe he wasn't ashamed of his actions as he'd implied, only angry Arnaud had found his prize relic.

But the moment Arnaud touched the chain of the necklace all suspicions were forgotten. The pendant began to glow brightly as his sword did, and the cave was suddenly illuminated as if filled with thousands of candles lit with green fire. Hundreds of gargantuan insects scuttled away from the burning light. Arnaud promptly dropped the thing in surprise.

"What did you do?!"

"I—*nothing*," Arnaud was utterly bewildered.

Andre bent down and retrieved the jewel, "You're what's making them glow."

"How? I've done nothing!"

Andre held the stone out again and the moment it touched Arnaud it shone fiercely. "Are you . . . are you something . . . else?" Andre asked with due timidity.

"Am I *what*?"

"Like those mermaids I heard you speak of. Are you a . . . sprite or something?"

"Of course not!" Arnaud said angrily, "it can't be me doing this. There has to be some logical explanation."

"You make things glow when you touch them. You survived a two hundred meter drop with not a scratch to show," Andre argued. But his tone was subdued, as if afraid of Arnaud's reaction, or of the cave-dwellers hearing.

"Don't be ridiculous," Arnaud said. Such preposterous accusations were surprisingly calming to his temper. "Here."

He held out the sword. More than one light source would obviously be useful, but it seemed despite Arnaud's protestations, the light would only respond at his touch, and dimmed to a slim circle around him leaving the rest a black, crawling unknown.

No further pondering would escalate their escape, so they continued on, praying the light would last until they found refuge in the brush and trees. They hurried through the cavern, moving more quickly now that they could see, but it was hours before they reached the end of the echoing mountain hall.

"Can we—"Andre wheezed, "stop a while?"

Arnaud felt guilty, wondering why he never sensed these things. Andre was much shorter and Arnaud had been taking long, determined strides. It might've been hard for the boy to keep up, even without his numerous injuries.

"Yes," he said, "we need to stop anyway."

They had reached the end of the cavern, but there was no one clear path to take further; there were two. They were not clean-made tunnels, only rocky slits to squeeze through, but the emerald light already revealed paths leading further into the mountains, or further out of it.

"You don't have any food do you?" Andre asked feebly. He was leaned up against a wide rock, his eyes closed and his face paler than Arnaud believed possible.

He didn't. The last they'd eaten was two day past; umbra meat the mad hunters had cooked over the fire.

"I seem to recall you asking me this question before," Arnaud joked, attempting to draw Andre's thoughts away from his stomach to Boulogne and happier times.

Andre chuckled weakly, "Your answer was 'no' then too."

Arnaud attempted a laugh to keep the mood up, but it sounded hollow and nervous.

"That was such a long time ago," Andre's breathing was yet labored.

"It was only a week." Andre began to laugh nervous laughter, but Arnaud wondered if it were closer to crying.

"No, it had to be longer. I was healthy then, I wasn't trapped in the dark." He opened his eyes. "Maybe I'm not here at all. Maybe the wolves got us and we died back there in the . . . in the canyon."

"If you're dead, then why am I here?" Arnaud asked, genuinely worried about the damage of the boy's head injury.

"I—I don't think I was good enough to make it to heaven." His voice shook. "You must be a daemon. My head couldn't hurt so badly in heaven. It wouldn't be so cold."

"You're not dead," Arnaud said firmly.

"Well, if we're not dead now we will be soon. And what a grave."

"Enough. You're not going to die. Not here. Come on; stand up." He grabbed the boy's arm and pulled him up. "No more wallowing," he commanded, "it does no good. Here, help me decide which path to take."

He'd been always staying to the right, hoping they were inching closer to an eventual way out. But this path, it felt wrong. The whole area gave him an eerie, chilled feeling that made the hair on his arms and neck stand up. Yet it was the logical choice. It was the only path that might lead them out; to go left would only take them further into the mountains. But still, Arnaud was wary. There was something down the right path, something evil.

"What does it matter which path we take." Andre said. "We'll likely be eaten by wolves if we get out."

Arnaud pinched him hard on the arm, the one place he knew the boy wasn't already bathed in pain. Andre's exclamation echoed through the cavern.

"I said no more talk of death and hopelessness. I don't care how ill you are, next time I'll make it hurt."

Anger flooded Andre's eyes, an improvement over dormant defeat. He didn't whine of their eminent doom again.

Arnaud helped Andre squeeze through the opening of the right-way tunnel. He couldn't justify following his gut and staying away from the darkness because he'd made a poor decision. Particularly if that decision had a foundation of cowardice.

So they walked down the right tunnel more quickly than they had been, for Andre seemed to have gained some strength, or purpose at least.

But Arnaud's wariness against the place only increased. He made the boy walk behind and kept his glowing sword at the ready in his hand. His eyes and thoughts darted about, searching for the cause of his caution. But he couldn't keep his mind from wandering to Andre's forebodings. What would they do when they got out? They had no food, no shelter, and no means of navigation through hostile woods. He was determined to get them out of these caves, and he would find a way if it killed him, but what after? He couldn't afford to be short-sighted.

"Arnaud, did you hear me?"

"What?"

"Do you see a light up ahead? Or is it—is it just me? Oh, God. Do you think—is it too late to repent?"

Arnaud turned to glare at the quaking boy. But he was so genuinely terrified, Arnaud tried to add reassurance to his words. "I see the light, Andre."

It was blue. Powerful it seemed, but the light did not reach out to them. Its glow was limited to some source, and as they followed the path around a corner they spotted its originator. A pedestal, the light made them believe the pedestal itself were shining.

"What is it?" Andre whispered.

Arnaud shook his head. It must be extremely powerful to glow so under mountains. With each step, intense curiosity raced through and burned his chest.

They walked forward and as they entered into the light they realized the light source lay inside a stone basin atop the pillar, not the pillar itself. Liquid crystal it seemed to be, the essence of stars; its shine was concentrated and blindingly powerful but it winked and flickered like candlelight or the mirror of gentle water.

It was beautiful, but though he did not know why, Arnaud was revolted by it. His spine crawled and he was over swept with instinctual disgust, as if an unbearable scent had been thrust upon him.

And then he saw it. Blood. It was smeared upon the walls all around them, all around the pedestal; in crude, barbaric runes. Arnaud knew they were evil, he felt it though he'd never seen anything like them before.

"We need to get out of here. Now. Andre?"

For Andre had offered no reply. Arnaud watched the boy with growing alarm. Andre's face contorted with fearful insanity. His eyes were wide, almost popping from his skull and dartingly fixed upon the glittery substance in the basin.

And suddenly Arnaud saw the snippings of memories that were not his. Red hair – the man from his dream. But he was not dreaming now. The man had been here, long ago, Arnaud thought, but he pushed it aside. It wasn't important now.

"Andre, we're moving on!" Arnaud shouted taking his arm and shaking it.

But the boy wasn't listening. He extended his arm toward the serum in its basin, muttering and mumbling under his breath and paying no heed to Arnaud.

The icy burn that had twanged Arnaud's chest moments ago now stabbed him through his heart.

"What are you doing?" Arnaud shouted.

His voice echoed at them from the high spanning walls. He seized Andre's arm and, despite Andre's struggles, dragged him from the basin back into darkness.

Arnaud had accidently loosed his grip on the sword during the struggle, and again they could see nothing. But he would not release Andre until the boy stopped struggling for the light. It was a few desperate moments before Andre half-collapsed and his breathing grew suddenly labored as if he'd been running moments before.

"Thank you," Andre whispered when he could manage it. "How did you resist it?"

"Resist what?" Arnaud asked, extremely concerned.

"The . . . voices."

"Voices?" Arnaud asked.

"Did you not hear them?" Andre was scared, Arnaud could sense that.

They fell silent again for several minutes.

The pain on Arnaud's chest had receded a little, but the pressure upon his heart had not. They were still far too close to the dark pillar for any sort of hope or comfort. He lifted the green stone from under his shirt and let it sit icily in his palm.

So this is the cause of pain. Arnaud mused, staring at its feeble light. He used it to locate his sword, just outside the ring of blue light. The emerald fire that blared around them was warm, like the sun in that cold place.

"Stand up," Arnaud commanded.

Any time for compassion was over. Besides hopelessness and starvation, there was evil in this place. Death was nearing upon them, closing in. And if they were not quick enough, they would be caught.

Andre, spurred by Arnaud's tone, climbed quickly to his feet and they went on, leaving the blood-writing and blue pedestal to the darkness.

***

They did not speak. There was no room for words. Arnaud was spurred on by some horror that chilled him and made the emerald glow bright, but he could not see it. He did not even know if they approached or fled it. It didn't seem to matter; he could not turn back. He quickened their pace again and again until they were almost running; until he could hear Andre wheezing behind him; until the horror showed its ugly face.

At once and without warning, a thousand red eyes popped into existence around them. They were all of one size: large and unblinking, and they lurked behind the emerald light, staring from every side.

Arnaud slowed as fluidly as he could manage, afraid of what any sharp movement might do. Andre stumbled into his back.

"What—?" he panted, but as he realized their plight his question turned into a whimper. "Wha-what do we do? What do we do?"

"Stay quiet and keep close," Arnaud commanded.

So they continued on, unspeaking, unfaltering in their course, on into a blackness now watchful and menacing. Arnaud could only trust Andre to remain in the circle of light. He could not turn to see him or make any more sound for fear of startling the lurking eyes that drew always closer and closer in around them.

But he could no longer hear the boy's shaky breath in his ear. This concern grew greater and greater in his mind until he could bear his thoughts no longer. Slowly, Arnaud turned his head and peered over his shoulder.

There was nothing there. Nothing. The protecting light that surrounded him seemed now to do only that, and no room had been left for Andre to walk in the glow. He was gone. The shock stayed Arnaud's steps.

"Andre?" he called.

The name echoed back at him followed by a loud silence. Even the burning, menacing eyes had left him, and Arnaud faced a solid wall of darkness.

His thoughts dodged and scurried. Before, he had feigned his confidence that they would find a way; he had blindly trusted to hope and chance and somehow salvation had always found them. Damien had happened upon them upon the mermaid's rock, the tunnel had opened at their elbows at the peak of danger from umbras, light had come to them in the darkness; but not now.

Nothing came to pull Arnaud from despair. He was alone. And where the watching eyes had taken Andre, he could not know, and knew not how to discover. He could easily be strong for others, but not for himself alone. There was no redemption from this pit.

Arnaud, a solitary ray of emerald light piercing through the black sea, sat down upon the earth, unable to decide whether to continue on into obscurity or to turn back to where Andre had disappeared. But he knew not how long ago or far the boy had been taken.

"Either fate or God is set against me," he spoke in deep hopeless melancholy.

He lay his head back against the stone wall and willed his mind into numbness. He had not slept in what must be many days and the clever ferryman twitched and flicked and implored his mind, but Arnaud wouldn't fall under such spell in this watching darkness.

Arnaud was not one to surrender to despondency, but only one thought crowded his mind and he could not push it aside. He had failed. He'd failed his family by their need to resort to beggary to live, and now he'd failed his friend. Confidently, he had led Andre deeper and deeper into the darkness, and now they were each apart and lost.

He sat still in the semi-darkness for countless long minutes wallowing and contemplating nothing. He mused at his life and his misfortune and wished the darkness would swallow him.

For perhaps hours he sat in the obscurity. And the weight of his self-incrimination pushed him down further and further into darkness. He might've been lost. He might've slowly withered under guilt and starvation under the cold mountains with only hunger pains for company. He might've, if he weren't so absolutely strong-willed and pigheaded.

I can fix this. I will fix this. Arnaud thought at long last. Andre may not be so far gone. He shuffled to his feet, the sound of pebbles crunching under his worn boots echoed up at him. He began to walk back the way they had come. He held his sword before him and began to vigorously search around for Andre. He called the boy's name, realizing the echoes that followed him for many steps. What better way to find him than to be taken by the same fiends.

He called out again and again, and his voice ricocheted back at him from the rocks. All weariness forgotten, he wandered for hours far into the darkness, taking random obscure tunnels with the simple goal of locating the eyes. And in all that time not once did he come across another living creature. No eyes, no wings, no scuttling cave-dwellers. But his determination was heartily steadfast and he continued on, shouting and searching.

But eventually, though he bartered no thought of surrender or defeat, weariness began to creep back in, and the effects of days without rest or nourishment lay heavy on his eyelids and his feet. Even as he was shouting Andre's name Arnaud stumbled upon an oblong object, hollow from the clanking it made as he fell over it. He waited upon the ground in the darkness and attempted to slow and silence his breathing. He had dropped his sword when he fell and the light extinguished the moment the hilt had left his hand. The emerald pendant he had still, but he was laid flat upon it and the glow was muffled. But Arnaud's chief concerned was not the light; for all around him there pulsed a heavy, steady breathing.

Lungs that breathed so long and deeply could not belong to a human. The very air surrounding him whipped and scurried and scattered Arnaud's hair and heated his face with every inhale and exhale. The creature, whatever it was, must be of gargantuan size, and Arnaud must be very close. He could smell the rancid residue of bleeding meat and hear the deep grumbling of sleep in the creature's chest.

Though, no doubt the source of such pulmonary proportions would possess the stature and strength to crush Arnaud, he was not afraid. He was more clear-minded and fearless now that he had been throughout the abyss of darkness. He swiftly sorted his options and fixed upon his first action: regaining his sword. Cautiously, he pushed himself up from the floor, carefully concealing the luminous pendant at his neck. But he could not entirely shield the brilliant light, and the darkness was partially unveiled.

Immediately, Arnaud recognized what had caught his foot and caused his fall. An obvious war helmet sat unassuming in aged dust. It was long with plates growing down past the jaw and silver wings pointed several centimeters above the head. The metal was smooth but ground with dirt and age.

Arnaud stooped and took it into his hands. He had seen it before. He knew he had, though he couldn't quite place it; he hadn't time now. He reached back and tied it quickly to his bag, egged on by the chilling, heavy breaths of the unseen.

Arnaud turned back to the place he had fallen and the pendant illuminated a wider berth. His sword was there; it had fallen not a meter from where he had lain, but Arnaud did not attempt to retrieve it.

It had fallen only centimeters from the keeper of such deep and stirring breaths. The creature was broader than the light could reveal, and was entirely hidden in an endless mane of brown fur. Arnaud saw the features of its head for the thing had tucked itself into a colossal ball. But a paw lay out upon the mountain floor and Arnaud could make out claws as long as the span of his own palm grown from a paw the size of his torso.

Never in his life had Arnaud seen an animal of such proportions. He had once seen a bear in the woods near his home, but is size was incomparable to the mass before him now, blocking the passage of both air and foot.

He would've backed down the pass from which he had come and try another way, but for his sword. He would not leave his father's sword.

He watched the steady rising and falling of bristling fur until sure of the monster's deep sleep. It had not stirred at his noisy fall; surely lifting his sword from the ground would make too slight a sound to disturb. He crept over, leaned down, and grasped the weapon at the middle, very careful to not let the blade scrape upon the ground or touch the creature fur, paw, or hide. But as Arnaud touched the blade, the emerald light of the hilt-stone erupted into being, much brighter now than it had ever been.

This explosion was the sun and stars constrained to a box of rock walls. It frightened all shadows from their deep corners with emerald brilliance. Its strength was enough to penetrate the beast's subconscious and Arnaud stepped back in horror as the thing huffed and began to rise.

Arnaud could see now the monster was indeed a bear, a grandsire of bears; its size at least twice that of one already larger than its kind. Arnaud did not pause to see the thing rise to its full height. He gripped his sword by the hilt and began to edge past the beast that had not yet recognized his presence. But he did not get far before the great bear had put its nose into the air and caught the scent of human flesh. The thing turned its head and Arnaud froze.

The bear had red eyes, angry eyes; they pierced through the emerald light, and burned through him. And Arnaud could not move. It was as if his feet were rooted into the ground. The beast snorted at him and Arnaud could see streams of dust cloud from its fur and the ground below like smoke from a dead fire. A bass rumble growled deep in the bear's chest as it registered Arnaud stiff against the rock wall. But Arnaud had turned entirely to stone, all but the springing, buzzing terror that flapped through him.

The monster started forward, growing to mountainous heights as it came closer and closer. Its putrid scent thickened with each pounding step. All Arnaud could think of, cornered by terrors he'd never imagined, was how frustrating it was to be so easily cowed. This anger at himself broke through the fear. He gritted his teeth and lashed out at the beast with his sword, feeling acutely the black slicing through thick flesh, the hot blood splattering across his chest and face.

The monster's roar was deafening. It seemed to shake the cave around him as Arnaud dodged to the right attempting to flee the death-trap. But the cut had not been deep enough and the roar seemed only one of irritation. Again the beast came at him, blocking his way. Again Arnaud felt the intensity of those crimson eyes, now burning and bloodied with anger. And again Arnaud was paralyzed with terror, realizing now some devilry the beast owned.

Arnaud closed his eyes to block the treacherous reds of the monster. But the thing was too near. The odds too great. He was sure now that he would die, sure that at any moment he would feel the pierce of foot long claws and the rush of his soul fleeing his mutilated body. His only comfort now was in his last thoughts of raven hair and red lips. But instead of the sure-coming pain, a light brighter than the sun penetrated his lids and burned deep into his eyes. He shut them to bar out the pain. A shrieking wail rose up and filled the cave with vibrations that pierced Arnaud's eardrums. He grated his teeth and tried to hide his ears, and realized it was the bear.

He tried to open his eyes to see where the beast stood to formulate an escape, but he couldn't. They had swelled shut against the light and pain. But even loss of sight could not cripple Arnaud to abandon opportunity. He groped along the wall with his right hand, slowly gaining speed, tentatively stepping on uneven ground littered with bones picked clean. He held his sword out before him and could yet see its green glow faintly through his watery lids.

He halted suddenly, nearly slipping on smaller loose bones, and gripped a jut of the wall. Here, the light was white with blushes of blue and yellow. It almost silenced the powerful green, and Arnaud was sure it must be the spring of the sun at dusk or perhaps dawn. Again, he tried to open his eyes, but they only watered through the swell and stung horribly. Arnaud kept on, determined to reach the open air, sure now that life and light were within his reach.

He made only a few steps farther and then was carried off with loose rock and bone underfoot. He lost the wall and did not bother in the attempt to regain it, concentrating on gripping his sword. If lost in blind shadows there would be no way to recover it with damaged, unseeing eyes.

The rolling current carried Arnaud down and down, kicking up ancient dust that swept into his lungs and caked his face and fused eyes. He tumbled and slid on and on, out into twilight and further – down a wide hill or, by the length, a short mountain. Stones and dead branches sprung out at him but did not bite or claw, and Arnaud felt relief at what should have been ghastly pain, but was not. And then it ended.

Arnaud sprawled out beside what must've been the rough trunk of a tree – that which had numbly broken his descent. He lay still for a long while coughing mud from his lungs and carefully trying to prize open his eyes. Most of his attempts ended in his shielding his face from the harsh, welcome sun. But when he could again breathe deeply and had accepted his failed attempts at sight, he stood shakily to his feet only slightly sore. He began to walk with his hand stretched out before him, but immediately sat again realizing he would get nowhere under cover of blindness.

Where was he? He could be at any point along the mountain range – still on the side of the sea, or the opposite which was, to him, unfamiliar land. Arnaud realized with dread that where he sat was likely upon land where umbras were populous and any other imaginable creature might have infested as well. The mermaids and giants of childhood tales had been real. Perhaps ogres and trolls lurked, even now, behind his eyes.

Arnaud gripped his sword until his hands chaffed the leather and old blisters were reborn in fire. He heard nothing but gently cooing wind and whispering trees. He sat still as he felt the sun's heat age. It had been dusk when he'd escaped the caves, and now night was rushing in. And though darkness in the strange is unwelcome, Arnaud was grateful for the relief it brought from searing sunrays pressing through his weak eyelids.

He was exhausted, more weary than he could recall being in his life. At least two days had passed since he had slept and almost three since he'd eaten. The moon tolled, and creeping reveries swooped down and submerged him in blissful unknowing.

***

Still wind filled the room; wind that fluttered sheets and ebony tresses and long eyelashes. Pink dawn floated through the yawning window; the breeze illuminated into thousands of dancing sparks that glittered on pale, beautiful skin...

***

It was true. The witch stared out from under cloak of darkness pierced by blades of moonlight. There was the sword, wretched thing, and a boy in tote. Young, very young; and likely unaware of what he held with him: the cursed blade.

"Here, for your troubles," she pointed her bony hand at the ground and up sprang two field mice chittering around in the dirt. A large raven that had hence perched upon a high branch let the squeaking meat run for a desperate minute and then swooped and snatched a bloody dinner.

"Oh," she shuddered, "I cannot touch the thing, not yet; it still reeks of her magic."

She stepped toward Arnaud's slumped, subconscious form. Her black hair rebuffed pure moonlight yet her head glowed blue with the nights reflections.

"But I cannot let it leave. A new king would not suit us at all, would it?" she crooned to a second bird, larger, sitting in the tree beside her. "We must take the boy. But they seem to be at my doorstep far too often. Three is too many. Perhaps we should snuff him."

She stared long at Arnaud, who was helplessly unaware of his danger.

"But wait," the witch moved even closer as she spoke, "my fears are perhaps unfounded. He is obviously no king. And if he will pass this to me willingly, I'll be at liberty to destroy the evil device, or even take it for my own! Just magic is easily overcome by wicked magic."

Seeing only the great power the sword might be, she hungrily reached down and touched the blade lightly with her fingers. Immediately she was thrown off with a shock and a violent green *pop*.

"That filthy hag!" she screeched, nursing a badly burned finger. She turned to the bird staring menacingly down from its perch. "It was once only kings who gained protection. She must've counted my threat as an exception, hideous leech that she is. Or," she turned a menacing eye upon the fowl, "perhaps my messenger has gone astray?"

The raven stared unflinching.

"He is under my sleep," the witch said harshly, "Put him in with the others."

The raven cocked its head to her now.

"And be wary of that sword. It has powers you do not know."

***

He walked on, heedless of cold and darkness. The moon threw again a shower of pearls, this time briefly on a large black raven. Its feathers glinted deep blue and then became again the darkness, leaving only two red eyes as a marking. The man did not care for the creature's presence and walked by without a glance. He walked silently for many minutes until this same beast of the sky swooped down upon him and drilled its pointy beak into the man's forearm.

He cried out in pain and anger at the winged devil, and then carefully examined the puncture. There was more than only blood there.

"Your poison will not work on me!" the man shouted to the watching trees, the listening air.

He waited in silence, confident of a reply. But none came. His fury was met with stillness, and he continued walking.

"I know what you've done," the watcher and listener said suddenly.

The man halted, "I have come to ask a favor of the great Sorcha."

The disembodied voice cackled in mock amusement, slicing the air as with a thousand daggers, "A favor! I hear no favors from mortal men . . . or immortal if you prefer, and never from the bloodied hand of a wretched king." She spat her words with intense disdain. "Be gone!"

"It is because of those very elements that you will want to hear mine." He dare not move or blink as she considered his words.

"Come further in."

The man followed and the raven swooped after. The figure of a lady moved behind a cloud and then nothing could be seen.

All faded into strange voices.

"Sire, do you not think this path unsafe?"

"I would hope no path unsafe in my kingdom, Captain."

"But just the same, sire, this may be . . .unadvisable."

Laughter; rich, wholesome laughter resounded, "Shame to any king who avoids simply unadvisable ways, Captain Jaques."

Another voice, higher and sweeter than the kiss of dawn, "Are you well, Captain? You seem troubled."

"I'm quite alright."

***

Chapter Seven

It took Arnaud a few moments to realize that he could see again. The dirt chamber in which he found himself was so dark that he could scarcely differentiate the opening of his eyes from the closing. But then they hooked onto something: two glowing black coals, red in the center; inhuman eyes, boring into him.

"You carry the sword of my king. Who are you?" A voice, cracked from disuse, unraveled from not the red eyes, but another's, half-hidden behind darkness.

"It was my father's," Arnaud replied, moving to gain a better view of the man. The stranger had red hair and a beard.

"That cannot be," the man said. "The king's line is ended. I broke it myself."

His voice bore the quiet sadness of regrets pulled from far past.

Arnaud watched him for several minutes and then asked, "Your name is Jaques, isn't it?"

The man looked up sharply, "How came you by that name?"

His appearance was alarmingly wild with outgrown red hair and wide flashing eyes. His apparel was shredded from time and use.

"I've . . . dreamt about you. And what you have done, and what has been done to you," Arnaud said, at once deciding not to conceal truth or suspicion. He suspected falsehood would prove no advantage in this situation.

"Who are you?" Jaques said again, his tone conveyed distrust.

"I am, I think, the fourth heir to your line."

The man stared fiercely at Arnaud, in an apparent attempt to make him coil back in discomfort. But Arnaud stared back more fiercely, never one to be

108

intimidated or outdone. They held a stationary battle testing wills, until Jaques suddenly burst into a maniacal laughter. It was long before he was calm enough to speak.

"And how came you to this conclusion?" he asked, his tone more amused now than threatening.

"Before she took a husband, my grandmother's name was Jaques and she came to Calais from the far North."

"Your grandmother, you say?"

"Marion was her Christian name. She had flaming hair and spoke of her father once being a great general," Arnaud said, watching the man closely. But the man's expression concealed any possible recognition.

"But you haven't aged since last I saw you. In the dream, I mean," Arnaud said. "It must elongate life, then."

"What?" Jaques visibly flinched.

"The potion under the mountain," Arnaud replied, "on the blue pedestal. We were there not long ago, and I know you have been there too, but many years have passed since then."

"Did you drink it?" Jaques demanded, suddenly tense.

"No."

"Lucky man. How did you resist?"

"I . . . felt its evil."

"As did I, but I couldn't stop myself. She made it so . . . enticing."

"She made it?" Arnaud wondered.

"Yes. She." He did not elaborate.

"And the drink has blessed you with long life. I saw you commanding troupes in battle against giants, but I was there, at the colony where it took place and I found it in dusty ruins."

"Do not say blessed!" Jaques said bridling anger. "It has been the greatest curse. I idly wait for death, trapped always reliving my grief, my wrongdoings. The crooked cloak will not grant me my desire.

"How long have you been here?" Arnaud asked after a minute of calming silence. He peered around at the black walls and earth floor of the large dungeon.

"Fifty years, perhaps longer," Jaques replied. "And each moment I regret and despise. Neither the giant claws of a bear, nor any great fall can crush this unnatural life, this breathing hell."

Arnaud suddenly recalled where he had seen the battle helmet. He reached over; feeling the tender pull of yet bruised ribs, and detached it from his satchel.

"This was yours." He handed it to Jaques.

When the man reached out to take it, Arnaud caught the unmistakable sheen of moonlight on old scars. Hundreds of them, crossing and interweaving throughout his skin.

"Yes, it was mine," he confirmed sadly. "I wore this proudly through many a battle. I had no right to it. How did you know?"

"It is a general's," Arnaud said. "It's made to hold feathers. And I remember you wearing it in the dream. Blue feathers. I found it in a bear's cave. Were those the great claws you spoke of?"

"How came you to be in that cave?"

"Through accident, I assure you. And I almost did not come out again."

"You fought the beast?" Jaques said incredulously. He began to laugh. "The great legend Orson, whose very eyes are paralyzers. You are far more courageous than I ever was."

"But you were there yourself," Arnaud said, confused.

"I, however, went in search of death. I had hoped the beast's supernaturalism might combat her evil potion. I was wrong. I walked out with much pain and many scars, but alive. You fought for your life and won. Incredible."

Arnaud didn't think stumbling blindly away from an enemy could accurately be construed as 'incredible,' and he said so, not wishing to take praise for any misconception.

"Courage has little to do with it," he said. "This sword that which you say belongs to your king, it seems to be . . . helping me."

Arnaud never would have expressed such an unanalyzed, ludicrous thought if he wasn't sure this man could provide some insight. He needed to know how powerful this weapon was that had lain so innocently years in his home; if that power could truly be controlled.

"Tell me all you know about it."

***

Jaques stared a moment, seemingly ready to challenge Arnaud's brisk tone. But he changed his mind, fascinated by how like the boy was to himself so many years ago: the same red temper, the same high spirit. But I had not his courage or his command of respect, general though I was.

He glanced at Arnaud's boots almost worn beyond patching. Why has he not risen above his station?

"It's a unique make; crafted especially for the king of France by the faie centuries before I was born. I don't recall any special power . . . stay, the once my king fought in battle he shone like the sun, yet it may have been the sun I saw, it was so long ago my memory fades."

Agitation suddenly gripped him. "I seem to remember . . . recall, recall!" Jaques pressed his hands

111

upon his head and Arnaud stared, opened mouth. "Her madness is like an infection, and I've been here so long!" Jaques explained, anguish filling him.

***

Arnaud could see it. The man's whole countenance changed as if taken over by another. One moment they had been talking, the next Jaques was apparently unaware of his presence. He got lost somehow, in his thoughts or in himself, and he stared blankly ahead in a waking nightmare.

They sat many minutes in the darkness. Arnaud's loud thoughts blocked the heavy hush, and Jaques neither moved nor spoke.

"You said . . . then that your family had been killed by the giants. But not Marion. Why?" Arnaud asked preparing himself for a wild lashing out or the disappointment of a cold stare. But the question drew Jaques back instantly.

"Marion was only an infant," Jaques choked and strained over the words. "Claire, my wife Claire sent her with a friend, away from the attacks." He slipped back into memory, and Arnaud watched his face, waiting. "I've . . . I've wondered about her these hundred years. Is she well?" He seemed afraid of an answer.

"She . . . died," Arnaud replied as gently as he could. "I do not remember her. I was only a small child."

Jaques chuckled with mad irony, "My last child rests, and I sit here, praying for peace and being ever denied."

They fell silent again.

"Do you regret what has happened? What you have done?" Arnaud asked finally.

This was a heavy question, one he needed to know the answer to. If such merciless blood-lust, such

112

absolute revenge was in his line, he himself might be capable of the same.

"I have had my revenge upon the fiends responsible for the deaths of my family. And now my anger has cooled, leaving only dust and cold tears."

"But that revenge is what I speak of," Arnaud said, "do you regret innocent blood upon your hands?"

"Innocent!?" His eyes suddenly filled with madness. "Innocent for splintering entire villages and stopping rivers and outlets to the sea? For murdering my family and the families of countless others?"

At this last, he collapsed onto the filthy floor and alarm died down into silence. After all that time he still clutched at bitterness and utter grief, and Arnaud pitied him.

He left the withered man to his grief for a time, many hours at least. Until at last he drew himself from his own thoughts and began to peer more closely at their jail.

"Who is it who brought me here against my will?" Arnaud asked.

"Sorcha," Jaques replied, subdued. "A sorceress hag fallen from the faie."

Arnaud recognized that word, faie, but he did not pursue it. There were more pressing concerns.

"Is it so hard to escape her dungeons?" Arnaud asked.

"Escape?"

"From this cell. You said you've been here fifty years. Why haven't you escaped?"

"I was not captured and taken here as you were. I admitted myself."

It took Arnaud a moment to register this. "Why?"

"There are few who are able to grant me death. She only, I think, would grant it. And it is the home of my last and worst offence. I pay penance by suffering to re-live the memories of my treachery."

"What . . . do you mean?" Arnaud asked, unsure of whether he wished to hear the crime regretted by a man who felt triumph, not remorse, at the innocent blood of hundreds, perhaps thousands.

"It was here I pleaded the death of my king and of his family."

"You killed them?" Arnaud hated the question as it left his lips. He could not be descendent to a man so treacherous. He could not.

"I did not turn the knife, but I might as well have. You must understand. I was mad with grief. I would take my revenge upon any and all. I was—I was so angry. If King Phillip had only taken a stronger stance; if he had only pushed for victory early in the war instead of wasting years on peace convoys and worthless treaties, many lives could have been spared. My wife and children's lives could have been saved!" His voice was pleading for affirmation that Arnaud refused to give.

"So you asked the help of black magic," Arnaud finished, shaken.

The sword that he held had belonged to this king. It may have been in his very hand when he was stabbed in the back by this man before him.

"If this was once the king's, how did it come to be in my father's possession?"

"If I had not asked him to protect it for me, he would not have died," Jaques replied miserably. "I—I remember now. The sword was blessed with the power of protection. No known enemy could remove it from his hand. I was King Phillip's greatest general, his military advisor. He did not know that the face of his greatest enemy was mine. He trusted me. He entrusted the sword to me. And he is dead."

114

"But the sword. What did you do with it?" Arnaud asked. "Why do I have it now?"

"I—I hid it. I would never tell her where it was. I had seen what she could do, what she had done to my king and my queen. I knew what she might do with such a weapon if she bent it to her will. She was—she was angrier than I'd ever believed," Tears now teemed in his maddened eyes. "She—she slaughtered the king's hunting party. All of them. One by one. She made me watch, made me listen to their screams, and then she took them back here and pinned them to the outer walls of this place with their own swords." He choked. "When the birds had cleaned the bones I got many scars burying them. But I—I couldn't get the—the skulls off, or the blood. They wouldn't come off."

Arnaud was disgusted by this story, but wouldn't be sidetracked. "But where did you hide it?" he demanded with clenched fists. If this man, this pitiful man had hidden the sword with his infant daughter, as Arnaud suspected he had; if he'd put his child in the way of such merciless evil, Arnaud believed he would pound him, no matter his shame or pity.

"I—I can't remember. I was afraid to remember."

He broke down and wept for several minutes. Arnaud felt sorry for him, for drilling this man, hunched under crushing guilt and sorrow. Arnaud wondered if he was the first to speak to him as a human in half a century.

"I—I wished his family dead. He'd done little to prevent mine from slaughter," Jaques pressed, wanting Arnaud to understand, to perhaps condone his crime.

But it was hard for Arnaud to look at this man; his own ancestor.

"You destroyed the crown. That is why there is no king; why all are at the mercy of any power-mongering fool who can claw their way to the top. Had he no sons

115

to challenge you, or did you do away with them as well?"

Jaques shook his head, quite calm now, the grief of his morbidity unsuitable for weeping. "A daughter, but I did not pursue her. I'd had my taste of revenge and found it bitter and unsatisfying."

Arnaud considered the man before him; his great-grandfather who looked not twenty years his senior. A wilder, more broken man he had never before seen. He waited for Jaques to continue.

"Betraying the trust of a fellow man is my foulest regret, boy. For that I pay penance in the dark and wait for sweet peace that will never come."

He spoke as if imparting advice, but Arnaud had no reply. The words had fallen hard on him and pressed even more upon his urgency to find Andre. But he could do nothing until he broke free of the hag and her dungeon.

"Do you know of any way out that you have not tried before?" he asked.

"You are so eager to leave, then?" Jaques asked, suddenly animated. His entire spirit and countenance had swung so high Arnaud had no option but to attest it to the insanity. But he had already wasted too much time searching for answers. He hadn't the luxury to wait out the madness.

"I am in search of a friend who was lost in the caves," Arnaud explained, "and each moment that passes narrows my chances of finding him."

"It is not so bad here, you know," Jaques plowed on as if he hadn't heard a word. "I have gotten a loaf nearly every day. And there is a window where the sun counts my endless days before my eyes."

Arnaud saw the opening construed to be a window. The moon and stars shone their brightest. A finale before the dawn.

116

"Besides that, you have already found your friend, I think." Jaques gestured to a deep shadow in a far corner. "He came two days past, and has not moved."

Arnaud stood and entered the darkness.

"He had not the smell of a corpse so I let him be." Jaques said, as Arnaud reached out for a wall enrobed in shadow.

Unwilling to leave the instrument behind with Jaques, he brought the sword, but its own light was dim and self-contained. The cell was much longer than he'd anticipated. Before he could gain the opposite wall, Arnaud's boots stumbled into what was unmistakably a body.

"Andre?" Arnaud asked into the murky darkness.

There was no reply. He crouched down and felt the sightless ground. His hand brushed a rough cloth, perhaps Andre's cloak. Arnaud seized it and dragged the prostrate form across and back into dimming night light.

He was dead.

His body was stiff and lifeless and cold. His skin was paler than the moonlight, ethereal on the dungeon floor; and his eyes stared lifelessly beyond, into worlds where walking men could not follow.

Arnaud was overcome so suddenly and powerfully that he could not move and could not speak. He stared on, almost as lifeless as his friend.

"He is not dead."

Arnaud heard only the faint static of shock and grief.

"Boy, he is not dead. Look." Jaques pointed to Andre's chest.

It rose up and down more slowly than the sea at low tide. Arnaud put his ear to Andre's chest and could hear the steady pound of a funeral drum.

"But his eyes," Arnaud said. "They're dull. Dead."

117

"He's been poisoned by her birds, their beaks," he said gesturing. "I have seen it done many times."

"To me?" Arnaud asked tentatively. Poison might have run through him, might still be in him.

"Not to you. Others have been here."

"And for days they've been as one dead?"

"Not days, no, hours. Until they're given her antidote. But sometimes she forgets about them," he added, not seeming to notice the affect it had on Arnaud. "And I am left to bury the body."

The opening of the cell door broke his poorly-timed comment. One small loaf was placed roughly upon the dirt floor and an open jug beside it. Their warden left without entering the room. Jaques walked over and took the stale bread offering it to Arnaud. Arnaud stared at it.

"It looks as if she has forgotten about you. Take it. I cannot starve to death. I've tried."

Arnaud nodded and took the bread. Jaques stared off into another time while Arnaud chewed in silence. After a three day fast he felt he'd never tasted a thing so wonderful and delicious.

"I am sorry for what I said before, boy," Jaques said suddenly, "about her being likely to kill you for the sword."

Arnaud stared. The man had said nothing of the kind. He must've confused his waking-mares with true life.

"If I can help you I will. To protect the sword."

Arnaud had no reply to this. He nodded and Jaques leaned against the wall and closed his eyes. Arnaud sat in the growing light for many minutes contemplating their predicament, struggling to find a solution. He reached over and closed Andre's staring eyes. Open wide, they were like death; closed, he was only sleeping.

***

He was in the same place. The same choking dungeon. And it looked the same, but Arnaud knew it wasn't. Two tall barrels of black water stood against a wall, and there was a girl in the corner. She was maybe fourteen years old, had long black hair, and was very small and skinny, like she'd been starved. Her eyes were closed and her body stiff. She looked dead, but when the door opened she quickly sat up and tried to push herself deeper into the corner, as if to make herself disappear.

Three men barged in. One tall and straight and dressed all in black, the other two shorter and in the manner of peasants or servants. Without a word the servants each grabbed a bucket and dipped it into the water. The girl's expression was one of utter terror.

"Please. Please, I'm ready now," she pleaded her voice high with fear. "I haven't slept. I promise."

The tall man moved his hand very slightly and the two servants began emptying the buckets on her. Continuously, one by one, scooping them into the black water and splashing it onto her tiny frame. She writhed and screamed in agony.

For several long minutes the man watched in apparent disinterest. His face blank and relaxed, even when her screaming rose to a shriek and her body began to shake uncontrollably. The servants began to sweat with exertion.

"Use it," the tall man said quietly.

A second later one of the servants dropped his bucket. He then reached up and wrapped his thick fingers around his temples. Choking out a cry of pain, he crumbled to the ground, twitching and writhing.

The tall man, still utterly blank, twitched his fingers and the standing servant dropped his bucket.

119

"Better," the man said without emotion. He twitched his hand again and the remaining servant followed him out of the cell.

The little girl folded herself down into the corner carefully not looking at the convulsing body. She trembled and cried softly.

This horrifying scene dissolved into powerful light...

Arnaud's dreams grew thankfully scattered, pathless, yet with similar ends; a divine light and divine face surrounded in gentle brown ringlets.

She was alive, awake, and they were no longer in a dusty room. They stood together in a lush and deeply colored garden. She spoke and he replied, but he knew not what they said. It was as if he spied on someone else's dream and could not catch the detail. Or could only catch the details. He saw each little loose curl around her face and neck and he saw light dancing in her eyes as he pulled her close. He felt the softness of her skin as he took her hands and placed them around his neck. And he kissed her.

He would always remember the kiss.

Always.

***

"She wishes you to wake," Jaques said nudging him with his foot.

Arnaud opened his eyes, groggy and irritated at being pulled from heaven back into hell, choosing to only remember the pleasant part of his dream. Jaques stared gauntly at him from the opposite wall.

"Isn't the worst outcome of provoking her anger hastening your . . . death? Is that not what you want anyway?"

Jaques did not acknowledge this logic. He shook his head slowly, "I can still feel pain."

Arnaud stared at him and nodded, scanning the dim
room and failing to prevent his eyes from observing
Andre unconscious on the floor.

"If she is as powerful as you say, why does she not
just kill me?"

"Perhaps she cannot," Jaques replied, his eyes
rested on Arnaud's sword.

They sat mutely for a while, Arnaud staring blankly
at Andre.

"It's just as well," Arnaud said. "I must plead for
an antidote, and all I have now is words. Perhaps I can
convince her to give it to me."

"Or bargain," Jaques said quietly. But before
Arnaud could reply the heavy door creaked open.
"You'd better go quickly. You will not want her in an
evil temper if you are set on using words alone."

Arnaud gripped his sword and walked to the door.
There was nothing there. Nothing but the total black
that Arnaud was still yet uncomfortable in. He stepped
through.

More so than under the mountain, Arnaud felt an
utter unbeing. He could see nothing and feel nothing,
not even his feet upon the ground. In a moment, he
could not determine direction and felt confused and
sick. And then he saw a light, a single beam shooting
out towards him in the darkness. It came closer, but it
was the light that moved, not him. Arnaud gravely
wondered if he'd died and was now entering a bleak
afterlife.

The darkness evaporated and Arnaud found himself
in a room brightly lit, though eons from cheerful.

"Sit down." Her voice was thistles coated in bitter
honey.

Arnaud did not move. Sorcha was not as he'd
expected. She was not hunched and grey, twisted and
wizened as in the tales Arnaud knew. She was not

beautiful, but she was young. And she was tall, almost his height, and straight to the point of stiffness.

"Sit," she said again, and Arnaud sat in the stiff chair.

He looked around at walls covered in bowls of squirming maggots and dirty jars of large eyeballs trailing pink nerves and veins.

"I have a proposition," she said, sighing down into a chair opposite. She seemed eager to appear open and pleasant. "You give me my asking, and I will set you free to go your way."

"And what is your asking?" Arnaud was calm, but, if possible, more on his guard than before.

"Oh, only some expendability; say that sword you hold so tightly in your hand. What need has a fisherman for a sword?" She smiled stickily. "I can even offer you a dagger, which is a more practical blade, in return for your miniscule loss."

She procured a long sturdy dagger from somewhere about herself and held it out for display, but Arnaud wouldn't look at it.He stared at her for a long moment; her false grin never wavered.

"And what of my friend. You have poisoned him."

Arnaud watched her steadily. He had no intention of giving her his sword. It was possible she might reveal the antidote as she had the dagger. But she did not move or procure it from her black robes.

"You know, Arnaud." Arnaud shuddered hearing his name pronounced by such foul lips, "You are hardly in position to bargain. I am offering mercy. I could take the sword through unpleasant force."

Arnaud smiled. "You underestimate my knowledge of this weapon," he said halfway bluffing, "and its powers."

He could see he had hit it right on. Her painfully pleasant demeanor dropped off and she immediately looked more like the lecherous hag she was.

"Perhaps you are the one in no position to bargain."

And then he could see clearly the woman's insanity and he wondered if maybe he should have been more delicate in revealing his stance. She began to shake with fury, and seized great fistfuls of her own hair and began pulling it out. She shrieked wildly at the top of her lungs. And then she looked very suddenly at Arnaud as if throwing something at him.

He opened his eyes.

He was standing in a room. A wide room that smelled of freshly cut oak and pine. It was a storage room that Arnaud remembered very vividly, but he couldn't quite place it. His mind raced. How had he gotten here? Had she sent him somewhere? How would he get back to Andre? The boy would die there without him.

"Who was that boy who just left here?"

Arnaud heard voices coming from the next room. He recognized them, he remembered them, but how was that possible?

"It must've been Arnaud, my apprentice," another replied.

He suddenly remembered. This was M. Gerner's shop. Where he'd been apprentice for almost a year. It was an unusual thing to do outside the family, but his father could be very persuasive.

"Apprentice!?"

"A special favor," M. Gerner replied.

"Well, I like him exceedingly. He has a certain quality about him."

"Yes, Arnaud can be very charming when he chooses."

"Yes. Well, in any case I'm glad to say it has won you my business."

"Excellent!" M. Gerner said with enthusiasm, "then we'll start on the paddock next week?"

Arnaud remembered listening to this conversation while he looked for hand-wrought nails, but he also listened intently as if it were the first time he'd heard it. He was a spectator to his own fifteen year old emotions and reactions, yet he felt them all acutely.

He knew what was coming next, but he couldn't prepare himself. He couldn't soften the shock.

"Arnaud, there's a young lady come to see you."

He walked slowly out to the front of the shop. Anais was waiting there; eleven years old and already she was serious and grave. When she saw him she hurried over and buried her tear-stained face in his shoulder.

"Anais, what's wrong?" But Arnaud knew what was wrong. He remembered it all too well.

She didn't look up. "It's—it's father he's . . . he's dead."

Arnaud closed his eyes as this news crashed down upon him like a bone-crushing wave.

* * *

When he opened them the scene had changed, the memory had changed. A breeze floated by thick with humidity and salt. He could hear sails flapping and water lapping gently against the creaky ship. It was dark, only the stars lit his way, but Arnaud knew where he was. He knew exactly what was coming, but he couldn't keep his feet from taking him to the place it had happened. He would have to live through it all again. He couldn't stop it.

He strolled leisurely across the deck. As one of the newest members of the crew, he'd been assigned night watch with a lieutenant named Guichard; a flighty man prone to disappearing for hours at a time. But Arnaud wasn't looking for him. He enjoyed the quiet. It gave him time to think. He leaned against the rails and stared out across the moonlit water.

This serenity was soon broken.

Arnaud heard faint scuffing towards the foremast and thinking it might be gulls trying to nest again, he went lazily forward with an idea to scare them away. But as he came closer he heard low voices.

He stopped, thinking it might be the captain berating one of the men. He might as well throw himself overboard to interrupt that. Then he heard a shout and a slap and the unmistakable sound of someone being repeatedly beaten.

He hurried forward into a sprint trying to follow the crack of meat and bone and low groans and pleading. Arnaud recognized the pleading voice. Dreu, a cabin boy not twelve years old who'd been aboard this ship longer than half the crew. He willed his conscious self to move faster to turn sooner. But his memory found the voices hard to follow, and he had to back track until he finally came to a cabin door. He flung it open and the sight that hit him would never fully leave.

He wouldn't have known it was Dreu if he didn't recognize the boy's garments and small stature. His face was so swollen and bloody, so marred by heavy beating it no longer looked human. Arnaud felt sick; he wanted to walk away, to go curl up somewhere and forget the face that was no longer a face. He was so horror-struck it took him a moment to register the man hunched over the boy's body, still administering those blows.

Arnaud felt anger flare inside of him. Rage like he'd never felt before in his life. His hands balled into fists. He leapt forward and pulled the man away throwing him over against the wall, catching the strong scent of rum as he did so.

The boy wasn't moving. He wasn't moving.

In his mind, the mind that was reliving this memory, that wanted to change things but couldn't, he knew the boy was dead. He knew that later he would discover this was not the first time this man boatswain Renier had battered the cabin boy in a drunken fit.

It only made him beat the man harder. It only made him detest his pleas, his slurred reasoning, the more. It only made the white rage embraceable. Arnaud scrunched his eyes, trying to clear the boy's mangled corps from his mind.

When he opened them again the rage was gone. He was sitting beside a bed. A familiar bed. He stared blurrily at the coarse sheets, rubbing them between his fingers trying to remember something. Trying to remember . . . what? Then he realized why his eyes were blurry, why he was trying not to cry and he remembered. Anhault. This was his little brother's bed. This was where he . . .

Arnaud slowly moved his eyes over the sheets. He didn't want to see. He couldn't bear it, but he had to.

The boy was so small, even for his seven years; shriveled with sudden illness. Arnaud felt fresh tears well in his eyes. He remembered this, all of it. Only a few weeks ago his brother had died. But maybe all the rest, leaving Calais, all of it, maybe that wasn't real. Maybe he'd dozed off and it had all been an uncannily realistic dream. Maybe Anhault wouldn't die. It was all too much to hope, but Arnaud desperately needed hope.

Anhault groaned weakly.

Arnaud read the pain and the fear in the boy's fevered face and quickly swallowed his tears. He placed a calming hand on Anhault's shoulder.

"It's going to be alright, Anni. Everything's going to be alright."

Arnaud stayed by that bed for hours, unaware of his mother and sisters' sobbing of their walking in and out of the room. And he felt every pain, every acute awareness of his inability to help. To do anything. All through the night he did not move his arm. Not after Anhault's breathing became labored, and then shallow, and then stopped altogether. Not even after his skin turned pasty and cold.

The sun was rising. Arnaud took one last look at his little brother, still on the bed. He stood to his feet and left for a day of work on the sea. He stepped outside and shielded his eyes from the sun. He opened his eyes.

"And how are you enjoying your happy memories?"

The hag's eyes twinkled as she spoke. She had apparently regained some of her composure.

"I can make them last forever, you know. I can make you feel that pain over and over and over again." She came and stood over him, as close as she could get out of range of the sword. "It's funny how people are always dying around you. And now this friend of yours. You could even save him." She shook her head. "All for a silly sword. You know, I think you and I are a lot alike."

"Go to hell," Arnaud said passionately.

A sinister smile crawled onto her face. "Do you have any idea what I could do to you? What you are doing to yourself?"

"You can't touch me."

Her smile grew. "Not you."

***

Chapter Eight

Once more Arnaud opened his eyes and found himself in a familiar place. His home. He was on the front path looking back at the little house, the sagging barn, the empty garden. He knew what memory this was; he thought of it often. The day he'd left. Yet this was different. He was sitting yet in the hag's chair, his sword lying across his lap gripped tightly in his hand. There was another him, the memory-Arnaud; bidding his family farewell.

He watched as Clarice tried vainly to suppress tears, as Anais nervously wiped her hands repeatedly on her apron. As his mother spoke to the memory him. He watched himself watch her disappear into the house for the sword. He looked impatient. Arnaud didn't remember feeling impatient.

Mother returned with the package and gave it to the memory-Arnaud. She stood close to him as she explained what it was. Then everything changed. The memory-Arnaud lovingly unraveled the sword. Arnaud had never done that.

Mother clutched his arm as he did so; crying and pleading, but Arnaud couldn't hear her words. He tried to stand up out of the hag's chair to go help her, to hear what she said, and found that he couldn't move. It was as if he were bound to it, but there were no ropes or knots. He tried again and again in vain as his mother's incoherent pleadings rose more desperate.

The memory-Arnaud finished his slow unwrapping of the weapon. Arnaud looked on in powerless horror as he inch by inch unsheathed the blade. His mother backed away, quivering in terror. He watched himself swing the sword and slice his own mother's throat.

128

Arnaud struggled violently to go catch her as she crumbled to the ground; to stop the memory-self— the wrong memory— from following Anais and Clarice into the house. But he couldn't move. He could only sit and listen to his sister's screams, watching his mother's blood soak the garden path.

The scene changed. A different garden, a different time. But this wasn't a memory. This was his dream, or like his dream. She was here, her radiant smile, her brown hair catching the sun. Arnaud found himself watching her, forgetting what this was, what was going to happen.

He looked on as the dream-Arnaud snuck up behind her and covered her eyes. She laughed and stood on her toes and gave him a quick kiss which he returned more enthusiastically. Arnaud watched her chat animatedly, throwing her head back to look into his face.

And then he saw her sweet, trusting eyes turn suddenly startled and fearful. Arnaud had been so caught up in her he'd paid no attention to the dream-him. The look on his face had turned maniacal, murderous. Arnaud tried to stand, to prevent what would inevitably happen, but he was yet in the hag's bewitched chair.

As he watched her struggle desperately to get out of his arms, anger rose in Arnaud. He wouldn't watch this. He wouldn't watch her die like this. Not her.

He focused his red anger on the chair. Every ounce of his will and determination was focused on getting out of it, on getting to her and saving her. His muscles burned and perspiration clung to his skin. He wouldn't watch himself hurt her.

And just as his dream-self was placing his hands around her neck, Arnaud sprung forward from the chair, naked sword in hand. He slashed at the dream him, but he was gone. Everything was gone.

He stood in the witch's room facing her; listening to her terrifying shrieks beating in his ears. He had only time to register a deep slash on her am and the livid look on her face before he opened his eyes and found himself standing in the cell with Jaques staring at him.

He was breathing heavily, trying to quell the residue anger in his heart. He began to pace, sword still clutched in one hand, sheath in the other.

"How does she know?" Arnaud asked urgently, "can she . . . read minds?"

"Whose blood is that?" Jaques asked shakily.

"How does she know?" Arnaud demanded. "How does she know about . . . my family?"

"She is an apprentice to the devil."

Arnaud stopped pacing. "What?"

"His daemons are at her call. Or so she's led to believe. I've heard her muttering to herself about it. But she knows only that they cause pain. I don't believe she can tell the nature of the pain."

Arnaud considered this. She must know more than Jaques believed. How else would she know each painful memory involved death? Yet, if she could read minds she would've discovered the sword's location long ago.

"Come with us," Arnaud said suddenly. "It can do you no benefit to stay here."

"You're leaving?" Jaques spoke as if he wouldn't advise such rashness.

"Yes. Immediately." He had already sheathed his sword and walked over to examine the open window. It was about shoulder height.

"That sword is not rightfully yours from the first, boy. It belongs to the Kings of France, and if you are truly of my line, then you are no king. Why don't you just give it to her? Save your friend."

Arnaud longed then to tell the man exactly what he thought of him. That he was pathetic and self-concerned. That he had no honor and deserved no more than what he had now, the low life of a prisoner. But it would only waste time, and time he did not have.

"Are you going to help me?" he asked. "At least to lift Andre out?"

Jaques looked surprised. "You'd have a hard enough time of it as it is. There's little chance of your making it through alone. Impossible if you add burdens."

"All the same, I will not leave him here." Arnaud thought he would take Andre back to the mermaids. They had saved him once. But he did not tell Jaques this; it was possible the man was actually loyal to the witch.

Jaques did not move from his seat. "You will not make it past her birds. If you are not beaked to death, you will be poisoned."

Arnaud closed his eyes to think and to calm his temper. There was only way to keep his life, Andrews and Jacques, and it was through that window. He would not be deterred.

"Why don't you just give her the sword, boy?" Jaques said again, quietly.

"Because there is something . . . more about this sword, and I will not hand it over to evil."

"It is not our lot to protect the world."

Arnaud gritted his teeth. "I, however, will not be the one who hands it to destruction." He took a deep, steadying breath.

Jaques remained silent, either in thought or indifference. Arnaud paid no heed. He took into consideration Andre's size and weight and the time it would take to lift him through the window alone. He took hold of the boy under the shoulders and began to drag him over. He'd only moved a few inches before another pair of hands came to aid.

Jaques took up the boy's legs and together they lifted Andre onto the dirt sill. Arnaud glanced at the man but did not put his gratitude to words. He placed his sword upon the sill and climbed into the window, pulling Andre through after him.

"I thank you for your help, Jacques," Arnaud said, turning back to his great-grandfather. "And I must ask your help further in delaying Sorcha's knowledge of our escape."

Jaques nodded gravely but said nothing until Arnaud had turned away. "I am glad to have met you, Arnaud." Arnaud looked back, crouched outside the sunken window. "It is a great consolation to know that my line has risen from the poor state I left it."

"Come with us," Arnaud pressed again. "The way will be hard. I can already see her sentry in the trees, but there is time yet for you to amend your judgments and seek forgiveness."

Jaques smiled sadly. "I have seen too many years of this place to leave it now. But one day we may meet again under brighter circumstances."

"I hope for it," Arnaud said sincerely.

"May God and chance protect you, Arnaud. Now go quickly. The sun soon rises."

Arnaud nodded and turned away from his forefather and the dark hole.

He swept his eyes over their surroundings. They were now under shadow of the great building beside them, but the way ahead was open and dimly lit by starlight, and Arnaud could see long black feathers shining blue in it.

It would be best to delay their going; to study and consider the path least guarded and under best cover. But Jaques was right; the sun would rise soon. They must move now or go back through the window and face the consequences there.

Even as he thought this his eye caught the glint of starlight on metal not three paces next to them. It was a long sword thrust up through a pale, gaping skull and deep into the wood of the building. Beyond that there was another and another, and on the other side, the same. Arnaud suppressed a shudder. He had hoped the man told tall tales, that his description had been a grotesque whimsy of insanity. But he'd spoken truth.

Arnaud took a deep steadying breath and hoisted Andre onto his back. He stepped forward, away from thought and shadow and into the doomed clearing. Red eyes instantaneously sprung; the same that had vexed the tunneled mountain.

Arnaud avoided the sinister glares, moving forward under his burden, his sword unsheathed in his vice-like grip. With each step the winged evils came more restless; they ruffled their feathers and crowed piteously, but Arnaud did not concern himself at this. The glowing barrier had erupted once again from the sword in his hand putting Andre within its protectorate.

It didn't take long for Arnaud's steps to weaken under the strain of fatigue and hunger. How far must they go? The clearing could be managed, but what if they were followed into the cover of trees? And with Andre on his back he moved frustratingly slow; like a boat with no oars on a calm sea.

The ravenous crows suddenly dived down at them from lofty perches, beating their wings and squawking agitatedly as they drew away from the impenetrable barrier. Arnaud refused to hear or heed them. He focused determinably on the cover of trees ahead, out of this perilous field of waist high dying grass he now waded through. The moon was out and shining on those trees; their leaves reflected moonbeams like still water. Arnaud concentrated on that welcoming glare of lights like warm candle-lit windows during a raging storm.

It took him many long minutes to gain the lights; and when he did he almost cried out in despair. The crows did not stop when away from their mistress's home. Undaunted they swooped down through branches and continued their attempts to slice through the protective magic. Disappointed Arnaud realized it was too much to hope the winged devils would abandon their pursuit just because they'd left sight of the witch's blood-stained shack. His worry now was that Andre would somehow fall out of the protection of the sword; that even a hand would return mutilated beyond use by angry beaks.

There was no refuge, no escape, only forward; away from what he knew to be danger, into a land likely wrought with dangers. It was a bleak and hopeless prospect, but Arnaud had no other.

Several hours passed in numb, blind moving forward. The sky shed its pink hues for oranges and yellows as if eager to be rid of them. And as the sun came brighter, it seemed to glean its power by draining Arnaud's.

By the time he could discern showers of points that were the leaves and bushes around them, Arnaud could no longer lift his leg to step, and he collapsed into a jumbled heap. The surety that they would be fallen upon directly filled Arnaud's chaotic mind. His sword had slipped from his hand as he'd fallen, abandoning them both from its protection. Andre, who had slipped off his back, might already be beyond saving from the subjection of a hundred beaks and talons.

Arnaud waited in horror for the dull thumps of plunging beaks and the rip of flesh being torn away under slashing claws. But he waited in vain. All was silence. Arnaud raised his head slowly; unwilling to witness the horror that surely waited. He opened his eyes and his heart jumped deep in his chest. Andre lay whole beside him with not a feather in sight. Had the birds left them in the woods, too far out of their mistress's domain? Or had it all been a phantom of the mind? A trick to return them to her cell. There was no sign of them; of a single bird or any animal at all. They were alone.

The sun had fully risen now above the mountains at their back. Arnaud reached over and picked up his sword. He stared at it. That was strange. The glow of protection generally extinguished immediately upon the exit of danger. Yet even in the bright air he could see the emerald's light. But Arnaud lacked time to ponder this. Andre lay as stone, mere feet away; already he might be beyond saving.

Arnaud scooted over and felt Andre's hand. It was chilled, but not yet by death. But though Arnaud was far from giving up, fatigue had drawn him to a point that offered no easy thought. Short of receiving a neat bottled antidote in his hand, he could think of no means for revival, even in the most complex and unlikely forms.

The wasted despair of simply waiting fell upon Arnaud. He could do nothing, nothing at all to help his friend. Only wait for eternal cold to grip the boy and draw him beyond any futile efforts.

Arnaud sat against a tree and gazed about the green forest feeling beyond feeling, seeing fully his insignificance and utter inability to restrain or motivate life. His eyes rested upon their sack, unopened since they had fled the hunter Damien five days past. He took it up and emptied it on the not yet warmed grass. The same items he had counted when bartering with the mad hunter fell out. Lace gloves, brooches, a watermarked book, and handkerchiefs. There was no mysterious vile of antidote, and there was no food.

Arnaud leaned back against the tree and closed his eyes. They could be anywhere, farther from known civilization than they'd been on leaving the mountains; on the wrong side of Sorcha's dungeons by many miles. Further from home than they'd ever been, and without nourishment of the smallest kind to be had or found. Reviving Andre would be pointless, even cruel, if only to waken him to their lack and misery.

The sun was higher now, laughing down from directly above. Arnaud could feel its heat on his face and could now hear birds busily twittering. He hadn't heard bird song since they had walked through the giants' ruins. He opened his eyes. Gloves, handkerchiefs, book. He took up the book indifferently, wondering who Andre had stolen it from and if they were missing it. He opened it.

The writing was very cramped and difficult to decipher, but it was at least in common French. Arnaud flipped through the cracked pages and held it up in the sunlight.

. . . *suffers from an aching in the bones. Suggest a poultice of rhamella leaves, honey, and water. To mild success . . .*

He glanced over at Andre and flipped the page.

. . . *Patient suffers from high fever. Leaching has proved unsuccessful, will try---*

He stopped. Had Andre actually stolen the personal notes of a physician? It was far too convenient to be possible. Yet as he turned the pages filled with patients' ailments and treatments, Arnaud found it to be the most likely explanation. He was seized with a sudden urgency. Perhaps one of the patients had been poisoned.

Arnaud dove into the journal and devoured its contents, unwilling to stave off hope. But even after hours of shuffling through pages until his fingers were chaffed and raw; after the sun had dipped down low in the sky, he could find nothing that immediately pertained.

High temperature . . . considerable swelling . . . blocked breathing . . . nothing about poison. And the man's scrawl was hard to decipher. Arnaud scanned through it cover to cover one time. And then again. And again. And when the sun fell below the horizon he waited impatiently for the moon.

He stood to his feet and paced, rapping his hands and shaking his head, anything he could think of to ward of sleep. Even if he weren't fixed on finding some cure for his friend, he needed to watch for any dangers the strange wood undoubtedly offered.

It took him a moment to realize that dropping temperature proved a masked danger, but a danger still. He crouched down and felt Andre's hand. It was cold, much colder than it had been, and Arnaud desperately hoped it was the result of mountain chill. He thrust any alternative aside and removed his own cloak, wrapping it securely around the boy's still body. Pacing became a necessity for warmth after that.

The moon rose and he walked back and forth, shivering and chattering, straining his eyes on the untidy scrawl for anything that might help. Anything at all.

There! No. Reoccurring aches did not even remotely apply.

It was getting harder to turn the pages. His fingers were stiff and numb. He realized his pace was slowing and immediately picked it back up, but he couldn't raise his drooping eyelids no matter how hard he tried.

He stopped. *Internal complication treated with a poultice of rhamella leaves and wine.*

That was it! As close as he could find after making it through the book four times. And Arnaud even dared to believe he knew the appearance of rhamella leaves. He thought he'd seen them in the village apothecary as a boy.

His mind had been so occupied these last hours he had failed to notice the emerald light creeping alive. He saw it now. Its brilliance lit the pages and its warmth thawed his frozen fingers. Its warmth. He had never known the sword to produce heat. Perhaps the cold threw its powers into sharp relief.

But Arnaud didn't care just now how or why the sword was acting this way. There was heat! Glorious, delicious heat! And that thought inspired more hope than any leaves could.

He hurried over to Andre's still form, removing the sword and sheath from his belt. He sat down next to the boy and laid them both across his body in the same fashion a warrior would receive in a funeral rite. He sat there for a long while, his back propped against a tree trunk, his hand always on the sword so that its power might warm his friend.

And yet, as he sat there, shivering in the moonlight, he almost missed the intense cold. Its numbing had masked other ailments, and now that it had lessened to mere discomfort he could feel his injuries acutely. Hunger and aching tiredness had dulled into a low background hum, but there were plenty of other marks to remind him of pain.

He stared down at his free hand. The cuts and bruises on his knuckles were still healing from his beatings of random thieves in Boulogne, perhaps even from scaring off Anais' suitor: the slimy Alphonse DeGaule.

It felt so long ago, years and years at least, since he'd seen his family, since he'd only had boding destitution to worry him. Now he had the dangers of the mountain forest, starvation, poison, and time to fight against; and his body was too weak to go on. He wished now that he could go back to simpler times.

***

Arnaud groggily lifted his heavy eyelids.

He'd fallen asleep! How could he have fallen asleep! He cursed his weakness in that hysterical frustration that only comes with incredible fatigue. There was too much to be done; too much he hadn't tried yet! Andre might die because he'd let himself doze off.

And then he heard it. The sound that had woken him.

A howl: rich and throaty and not so far away. Arnaud stood to his feet. He had feared this. That umbras had claimed these woods. The world was dark still; almost black now that Arnaud had taken his hand from the sword. He crouched down and picked it up off of Andre's chest. The emerald glowed brighter than it had before. He took two handkerchiefs from the ground where he'd left them and tied them around the emerald, hiding the unnatural light as best he could. Perhaps danger was nearer than he thought. The howl had sounded at least a mile off.

Adrenaline pumped through him as he made his way through the trees, keeping always in sight of his invalid friend. Arnaud determined to meet the danger head on and preferably away from Andre. He detested the thought of being cornered or crept up on, and wolves may not be the cause of the glow. The possibilities for hostility in a dark forest were endless.

The moon shone very suddenly down upon him like a spotlight, its grand entrance from behind a group of blue clouds. Feeling suddenly exposed, Arnaud quickly ducked behind a tree. If he had not, ho doubt death from the rabid beasts would be slow and painful and ugly. He peered out through leafy, moonlit branches at the most horrifying creature he had ever seen.

It was tall; half the height of the great surrounding pines, lanky and spindly. Its grey skin stretched tight over tendons and sinewy muscles. It was built like a man with twice the length of arm and leg but it did not move like a man. Like an insect, or a spider, Arnaud thought, long and jerky yet quick movements. From this angle he could not see its face, but its head was unnaturally small for such wide shoulders.

A chill spun up his spine and Arnaud shivered. The thing would've seen him if he'd not moved so quickly. He quietly crept around one tree to the next; following the creature to be sure it would not trek back to them. But it seemed to be heading off toward the mountains. Arnaud stayed, weapon ready, and watched the creature until it was far away and out of sight.

He involuntarily shivered again and made his way back to his makeshift camp, wishing he had not seen what he had. He spent the rest of the long night chattering in the cold, with one hand upon the sword to warm Andre. He started at every creak of the forest, and was sure the dawn would never come.

But it did. Slowly at first, and then the sun shot up over the mountains and Arnaud sat blinking and shivering in its fierce light. He waited several moments for the warmth to reach him, to remove the chill from his aching bones and give him energy. He stood unsteadily to his feet and attempted to shake numbness from his legs before gathering Andre's bag and then hoisting the boy onto his shoulders.

It hurt more than he remembered. The weight pressed down on his yet healing ribs, and he'd obtained several large and painful bruises on his back when he'd slid over rocks and branches down the mountain slopes a few days ago. But he set his jaw against the pain and his mind upon rhamella leaves, and they moved forward through the morning woods.

Arnaud was not immediately discouraged. It was a large forest, and as far as he knew rhamella leaves were fairly common and widespread. But he could not be certain he remembered precisely their appearance, and at every large cluster of underbrush he found it necessary to put Andre down so that he could closely examine the leaves. It grew harder and harder to pick him up again.

By the time the sun was high above them Arnaud struggled for several minutes to lift the boy up. The muscles in his back and arms and legs screamed in agony, and his head swam; yet he managed to somehow lift him again onto his back. But he only made it a few steps before his side seized up and buckled, and he stumbled to the ground panting.

Arnaud waited for the muscles to relax to a searing throb and then he stood up and tried again. But the moment he began lifting Andre up his side cramped and buckled again so that he cried out and his eyes watered in pain. He waited longer, several minutes at least and tried a third time, but it was no use. He wouldn't be carrying Andre again for a while.

He continued his search on foot.

He'd only walked a few steps before he saw it. A cobbled well stood ahead through the wide trunks, decrepit and forgotten. All matter of plant life, large and old, grew up close around it, and strange vines with wide silver leaves sprouted up the stones and wound around the beam handle. It had been subject to disuse for well over a century, or such growth could not have been possible. The back of Arnaud's neck prickled as he walked closer. The silver vines had grown over the mouth as well, and when Arnaud looked down into the dark hole, he could see them trailing down and vanishing far into the black.

Any expectance of water fled Arnaud's mind as a sudden breath of wind sighed into his face from the unseen underground. It could not have been a huff of the breeze that blew spontaneously above, for that was warm now, almost hot, and this had been pleasantly iced with cold. It caressed him into a hypnotic lull; into a state of conscious dreams and intoxication. He could see her, wisps of golden brown hair, and skin, pale to rival the moon. She was there, asleep as she'd always been; but this could not be a phantom of nocturne mares. He could see her, now, down to detailed, star-flecked eyelashes, but he could also see the snowy leaves and cobbled basin of the well. And here he could catch music, faint and mournfully sweet, where his dreams held only silence.

And then she was gone, and Arnaud was left alone with the feeling of a thousand fleeting starlings alighting from his shoulders. He stared down into the empty well, involuntarily attempting to regain that feeling, to see her again, but instead he started in shock. The well was not empty. A sheen of water lay below that he was certain had not been there a moment ago. He stared at the innocent ripples in horror and then shook himself. What was more natural than water in a well? Hunger and lack of sleep must be catching up with me.

He began walking back to where Andre lay pondering some way to move the boy over to the well. The dipping bucket was cracked and holed and would not carry water far. He didn't know what water might do for his friend, but maybe something. Maybe—

But the moment he caught sight of Andre, twitching and convulsing on the ground, he abandoned this train of thought and ran, sprinted as fast as he could to the boy's side. He stood for a moment helpless and unsure of what he could do, what he should do. He kneeled down and placed his hands on the boy's shoulders, holding him down on the ground, attempting to calm him. And even he was not expecting it, but Arnaud's heart called out to God. His last hope, the only thing he could think of that might give the boy a chance or at least peace.

After a moment Andre's body lay still and Arnaud was sure he had died. He felt energy leaving his own body through the palms of his hands and wondered if that was what happened when you touched a man as his soul left his body. He slumped down on the ground and stared. Not quite comprehending this, not wanting to comprehend yet another death.

Andre's eyes flew suddenly open. He rolled over and was sick on the ground at Arnaud's feet. When it stopped Andre laid very still, breathing unevenly, shallowly, contrasting his poisoned state solely by opened, staring eyes, unnaturally wide. Arnaud, hardly able to control his exaltation, dragged him gently away and propped him carefully against a tree. He pulled a handkerchief from the bag and tried to put it in his hand, but realizing Andre was too weak to even grasp it, he cleaned the boy's face himself.

"You're alive," was the first he could think to say, still disbelieving his eyes. "Is there anything I can do?"

Andre was unable to do anything but close his eyes in peace. For a long time Arnaud only stared, not daring to attempt help for fear of causing harm. After the first joyful moments had worn off, his mind ran again to their poor predicament. No food, no shelter, lost in the woods far from any known civilization. How long would it be before Andre was well enough to travel? Would he ever be that well again? He attempted to thrust these nagging doubts aside, but it was difficult. There was nothing to offer the boy if he should ask.

Water. Andre's lips formed the word, but no sound left them and his eyes remained closed.

Arnaud gripped the boy's shoulder and said, "I'll try."

He did try. Several times he lowered the cracked and bleeding bucket into the well, but by the time he'd pulled it up again the water had drained but for a cup or two. And when he attempted to untie the bucket and carry it the hundred yards back to Andre it was dry within the first few steps. As he'd suspected there was no hope for it but to move Andre to the well.

"Andre," Arnaud said gently, laying a hand on the boy's arm, " I'm going to have to drag you. It isn't far."

There was a pause of silence and then Andre groaned, Arnaud hoped, in assent. He grabbed the boy under the shoulders and, ignoring his own protesting body, lifted the boy as high as he could and dragged him through the trees and underbrush, carefully attempting to not jostle or upset him too much. By the time he reached it, his head was spinning and he had only the energy to place Andre gently back against the cobblestones before he slumped over himself breathing heavily.

Yet he was up again in a moment, doing his best to ignore his own ailments. With shaking hands he pulled up a leaking bucket of well-water and using a concave bit of tree bark lying by, he scooped as much of it as he could manage into Andre's mouth. The boy surely did the best he could, but most of it dribbled down his chin and tunic and Arnaud had to pull three more buckets before he'd had a decent drink.

"Okay?" Arnaud asked.

Andre opened his eyes slowly and ever so slightly nodded his head. Otherwise he lay still against the cobbled well, and Arnaud was sure of life only by movement of his eyes. Arnaud leaned back and shut his own more from fatigue than deficient rest. But they had scarcely closed before they sprung open again in alarm.

A growling moan echoed through the trees to where they sat, carrying the overwhelmed anger and frustration of a wild animal. That sound could not have protruded from the throats of humans. Arnaud sat up and rose slowly to his feet. It was close, far too close to ignore.

"I'm going to look into it," he said turning to Andre. "Just . . . stay here; don't move." He stared at the boy a moment and then made up his mind.

"Here." He pulled the emerald necklace over his head and put it over Andre's. "I don't know if it will help, but it might."

Andre seemed ready to protest, but still no sound would leave his lips, and Arnaud was grateful for it. He turned and unsheathed his sword. The stone shone dully from under the handkerchief as he set off toward the agitated moaning.

He walked slowly, attempting to avoid the rustle of leaves or crack of twigs. But it didn't seem to make a difference over the groaning that became incrementally louder, and he had not moved far through the tall high-branched trees before the creature was in sight.

It was a bear towering high above on its hind paws. Its back was to Arnaud, but he could tell that its size was equal to that of the monster he had met in the mountain caves. Its fur was black as a moonless night, but was dusted with the snowy silver of time.

Arnaud blessed the sun and its mask over his glowing weapon; the creature did not notice him or turn to regard his presence. It padded great paws toward a nuisance or threat that Arnaud could not make out. The beast growled deeply in frustration and anger and swiped its massive blade-tipped paws.

Arnaud crept carefully behind wooded pillars to snatch a look at this doomed victim; it had made no attempt to flee.

It was a man.

Arnaud endangered his obscurity in a fit of unequaled astonishment. The man was tall, though only half his opponent's size; the hair on his head lay almost white, but he was young and fit. And the man's sword, still in its sheath, glowed deep red; its blood color matched the monster's fiery stare. The man held a long bow in his hand, and as Arnaud watched he loosed an arrow at the beast. Arnaud heard its dull thump as it entered flesh and the bear roared wildly, but did not seem too affected by the wound. It glared fiercely at the man who suddenly stopped refitting his bow as if transfixed.

The bear suddenly boxed its paw around and knocked the man violently over. The bow flew out of the white-haired stranger's hand as he fell. He quickly reached for the sword at his side, but the beast had swung again and its long claws slicked into the man's side, digging deep flesh out with them. The sword's fire immediately flicked out as he dropped it in shock and pain.

Arnaud sprang out from behind the trees as the bear stumbled forward for another killing swipe. By the time the wounded man had fully collapsed onto the ground, Arnaud was close enough to slash out at the monster. He sliced a great gaping wound across the bear's face. Dark blood poured forth, splashing onto the ground and

Arnaud's arm. The bear stumbled back and roared in agony. It turned its head and glared at him for a long sizing moment, angrily regarding this new challenger.

Arnaud stood between the beast and the unconscious man and stared. It was the same beast from the cave. It had to be. A great gash across its chest was fresh and healing. It had to be the blow he'd delivered only days ago. But he knew the creature's powers now. He grasped his blood bathed sword painfully and it shone fiercely around him, ready to fight, to run the animal through if it should move.

The bear glared fiercely at him and Arnaud fought it, staring back just as fiercely. And when the beast realized its trick had no affect, its anger mounted to an absolute fury. It sprang down on four paws and charged grunting furiously.

Arnaud waited until the thing was near enough and then leapt to the right. He thrust his blade deep into the creature's chest as it rose up to swipe. Arnaud felt the claws wrap around his back as the beast fell, pulling him down as well. The bear's last breath huffed hot on his face and immediately Arnaud tried to stand up, to get away from the dead animal, but even the smallest movement made him shout in pain. The bear's massive claws had shredded flesh out of his back and even after death one claw was still wedged in his muscle. His back twitched and spasmed as he cautiously tried to wriggle free, biting his lip until it bled to divert his mind from the pain. He finally reached back and ripped the thing out; his shouts echoed through the trees.

Arnaud lay still on the ground panting, feeling warm blood ooze down his back. The bear's corpse was so close; disgustingly close. He could see little droplets of its brown blood clinging to blades of grass near his face. And he could smell its hair and blood thick on the humid air. He had to get away. He

147

couldn't lie so close to fresh death. He reached out and yanked his sword unevenly from deep in the animal's chest. An array of innards spilled out with it. The stench was unbearable.

Arnaud began to drag himself weakly away through the grass barely lifting his legs at all, but he couldn't seem to escape the beast's blood. It was everywhere. Yet, as he moved, it was different, a lighter hue than that which had poured from the bear.

He swung around. The man lay there still, slumped into a twisted heap of white hair and rough brown cloth all doused and splattered in his own blood. Arnaud crawled over and seized the man's shoulder forcefully turning him over. The gashes were four and horribly deep. Arnaud could see ripped muscle and two of the man's lower left ribs clearly through a flood of clumpy red. And yet he was alive.

The man moaned weakly and then fell silent. His head flopped back useless, and his face was as pale as dead winter. Arnaud swiftly ripped off the man's cloak, tore it into long strips and began tying them around his warped torso, pausing only to tie one as best he could around his own waist before loss of blood could cloud him. The deep gashes restricted his movements and made even breathing excruciating, but Arnaud continued to wrap the stranger's wounds until all the strips were gone. Then he pressed down on them and waited.

* * *

Chapter Nine

The white haired man was alive. His heart was beating and his breath was shallow but existent. He was alive even after a long hour of watching and waiting, but he did not seem to be improving. Arnaud had not moved him, had not even touched him other than ensuring blood had not soaked through his makeshift bandages. But it would not be long before the sun set, and Arnaud must think of Andre as well, who could not defend himself against beast or plague of any kind.

He leaned over to check the stranger's wound again. The outer cloth remained clean and dry, but the gash had been so deep; Arnaud wondered if his help was just a stall, and how long he would be able to keep stalling.

The sun glistened ruby into the corner of Arnaud's eye as he sat back. He looked and saw, not three meters from him, a sword. The stranger's sword that had been knocked from him. Arnaud stared at it and then crawled over grimacing and grunting and took it into his hands. It was a good weapon, well and equally made with a plain hilt and a slightly curved blade as a scimitar of the east. But what kept Arnaud's eye was the stone set in the hilt. It was of a similar size and shape to his own emerald, only this was a deep ruby. He ran his fingers lightly over it expecting it to flicker into life. But the ruby remained dormant. Arnaud dragged it back with him to the stranger's side.

He reached over and slid the sword into the sheath at the stranger's immobile side and was surprised to see it suddenly emit the warm red glow he had before expected. Interesting, but he was unable to ponder it now. The gashes in his own back had long begun to bleed through the cloth. He could feel warm blood trickling again over his skin. Arnaud tried to reach back and press on it with his hand, but the pain was blinding and he would be unable to apply any pressure. He looked around for something, anything else he could rip into bandages, but there was nothing. The beast's gigantic corpse, the dying man, the trees.

Arnaud pushed himself up onto wobbly feet and stumbled over to a tree. He pressed his back hard up against the trunk, focusing on the pain, the unbearable sting, to clear his thoughts.

That man, sparring now with death, had to come from somewhere, some civilization. But how far away? He was apparently a hunter as Evrard and Damien had been. This man could've traveled days before finding himself here.

Arnaud's eyes began to cloud and he shook his head to clear them. If the man was a hunter he must have supplies, food, a bag to put them in. Arnaud squinted and looked around for it, his last hope; he daren't leave the pressure of the tree without some bandage. But this stranger might have a camp. Might've left the camp when he heard a noise as Arnaud had, and all his things behind. It was likely and a useless conclusion. How far away might this camp be? And in what direction?

Arnaud pulled his eyes back into focus. His tunic. It was torn and too thin and worn to do much, but it was something. He tried to lift it off over his head, but quickly gave that up and tore it off from the bear-class shreds. He folded it and pulled it as tightly as he could manage around his bare waist.

He could move now. With great difficulty and pain, but he was no longer bound to the now blood-stained tree. Arnaud moved on impatiently to the next obstacle. Already the sun was setting. He needed to return to Andre and he needed to bring this man with him. He was unable to lift anything so he began to drag him through red grass toward the well.

He moved slowly, very slowly, but he ground his teeth through the pain. His head spun and this stranger felt heavier than anything he'd seen or heard of, but he groaned and bit his lip and didn't stop moving. He was disoriented and would've dragged the man right past the well if Andre hadn't spoken.

"Did you do that?" the boy asked weakly. He spoke with difficulty but evident horror.

"No," Arnaud replied, just as weak. He dropped the stranger's arms and attempted to sit, but fell over before he could.

"Good," Andre said between heavy breaths. "'Cause I don't think . . . I don't think. . . we could be friends anymore."

Arnaud chuckled, lightheaded. None of this was real. The world was spinning in and out, very close then very far away, and then it disappeared altogether.

***

They were sitting together. Alone, by a stream. Arnaud could feel her next to him; her calm and gentle presence, but he didn't look at her. He watched the water run past them, listened to its murmuring trickle. Everything was right, in order, taken care of. Everything was calm. He turned, but before he could see her, it all turned strange and chaotic. What seemed to be wind beat up against him on every side, and he felt out of breath, like he was choking. A whisper, desperate and urgent entered his ear. Help me.

He opened his eyes. They were out of focus, but he could blurrily see that he lay in a strange place. He attempted to stand, but the gash in his back tried to split open when he moved. He sucked his breath in sharply and laid still.

151

Four walls, chairs, paintings, and he lay on a soft
bed with lush quilts. Where was he? And where was
Andre? He began to scoot carefully out of the bed but
suddenly stopped. They, whoever they were, had
removed his clothes. He wore nothing now but a fresh
bandage about his middle. His eyesight had cleared
considerably and he peered around the room for them,
but there was nothing besides furniture, strips of clean
cloth, and an extra quilt. However, there stood a long
desk with a drawer in the corner. Arnaud pushed
himself up and was in the process of going to look
inside when the door opened.

He froze as a short and extremely robust woman
backed into the room humming gently to herself. She
turned widely around and when she saw Arnaud,
standing in the middle of the room, quickly pulling the
quilt around his middle, she gasped.

"What are you doing?!" She started forward and
began to force him back toward the bed. Her hair was
pale as the stranger's had been, but Arnaud suspected
this woman was older. "I spend a week putting you
back together and at the very first chance you get you
upset everything!"

"Where is my sword? And my clothes?" Arnaud
said trying to stand his ground, but she was a large
woman with surprising strength.

"What you've been doing I can't even guess!
Mauled, poisoned, botchy mermaid healing! Where
have you been, I wonder?"

Arnaud grasped onto this quickly, and collected his
strength. He stopped suddenly and stood against her
pushing and prodding a foot from the bed.

"My friend, the one who was poisoned. Tell me
where he is."

She tried to push him again, but finding he wouldn't move she went around him and busily arranged the bed.

"My guess is that you're the last survivors of a village the dragon has consumed, or of a shipwreck. Am I right?" But she didn't even pause for an answer. "Floris said you're likely travelers from the north, but I think my theory is more exciting."

Arnaud grabbed her arms and looked fiercely into her face. She glared at him in mock outrage.

"My friend! Tell me where he is. *Right now.*"

"Tell him what he wants to know, Grainne," a voice said from the door.

Arnaud turned and saw a young woman standing regally in the doorway. Unlike the others she had black hair, as black as his, and utterly pale skin.

"He saved the life of your king. Treat him as a guest of honor, not a prisoner."

King? Arnaud thought, bewildered.

"And bring him some clothes," the woman added before she turned away.

Arnaud blushed as he realized he'd dropped the quilt when trying to force an answer from the old woman.

"Scandalous," Grainne whispered as she thrust another quilt at him and huffed out of the room.

The clothes she gave him were of very fine material. Soft and smooth and extremely comfortable, but not at all durable. They wouldn't have lasted three minutes on any vessel or tramping through a forest. He would've much preferred his own clothes, but Grainne insisted they'd been burned. Arnaud suspected she was bluffing and merely did not want them, bloodied and soiled as they were, in her painfully neat rooms.

Arnaud was quick to discover Grainne to be a stubborn woman not above resorting to trickery to get her way. And she was just as quick to realize he was even more stubborn than she.

"My friend. Where is he?" Arnaud repeated later as she entered the room with a tray.

"He is alive and he is safe," Grainne replied without looking at him.

"But where is he?"

"Take this broth," she said and laid the tray on his lap. "All of it. Then I'll tell you."

"No," Arnaud said, though his stomach burned with hunger. "Tell me now. Then maybe I'll think of taking your broth."

She puffed up like an angry squirrel. "I'll pour it down your throat."

"You can try."

She bristled at him a moment and then shook her finger. "It will be difficult controlling you, I see."

"I make it a point not to let anyone control me."

She mumbled something he could not catch and turned away, busying herself refolding some towels. Her movements conveyed anger, but Arnaud thought he saw her smile.

"He's two doors down. On the left, and he's resting," she insisted, as if Arnaud had proposed a boxing match. "He'll need a lot of rest to recover from whatever it was you put him through."

Arnaud bowed his head pointedly, picked up the spoon, and took a large mouthful. She watched him swallow, and then wobbled dramatically out of the room.

"It's very good broth!" Arnaud shouted after her. He grinned and took another mouthful.

But not another bit of information did Arnaud receive from Grainne. She did not stay away from his room. In fact, she was there constantly; puffing, folding, cleaning, bringing broth, changing bandages;

154

but she kept her mouth shut. She was either afraid of saying too much, or she was bitter at the failure of her manipulation. At first he didn't care. Generally, Arnaud preferred the quiet. It gave him time to fully consider his options once he and Andre had fully healed. It was a silent room but for when Arnaud occasionally tossed the nurse a dashing smile and she chuckled at him.

But after a few days he became impatient. He wanted answers, detailed answers. He couldn't make any definite decisions until he had information.

***

"May I come in?"

Arnaud startled at the unfamiliar voice. A very tall, very thin and composed woman stood at the door. It was the regal, black-haired woman who'd watched him argue with the nurse a few days ago. Arnaud did not think her particularly beautiful, but something about her drew the eye.

"Am I disturbing you?" she asked, still standing motionless in the doorway.

He'd been thinking of Jaques. Wondering how long the man would remain in his dungeon. But he preferred not to think of it anyway. He couldn't change anything.

"No, no, of course not. Please, come in."

"I have brought you your sword," she said, sweeping across the room. She laid it on the table by his bed. "And pendant." She held it out and Arnaud took it. "Your friend insisted I return it to you."

"He probably didn't want me to think he was stealing it. How is he doing?"

"Grainne informs me that he will be many weeks in bed, but he is rapidly improving. He has you to thank for his life."

"I couldn't just leave him to die. No one could have," Arnaud said. "And the other man? How is he?" Arnaud suspected he had died. He'd seen men die from far less.

"My husband is . . . also improving." She stood up a little straighter. "In truth that is why I have come; to thank you myself for what you have done."

Husband? That was unexpected.

"You are, of course, welcome. But I did no more than any other would have in my place," he insisted.

She stared at him a moment, and then shifted her gaze to the sword. "Where did you obtain this weapon, Arnaud?"

Hearing her speak his name when he had not given it her, when he did not know hers, was disquieting. Naturally she learned it from Andre or Grainne, but it still put him on guard.

She sensed his wariness. "Please understand, I don't mean to probe you. I'm only curious."

Arnaud nodded. "I am quite willing to answer your questions, uh—?"

"Brighde," she said.

"Brighde. If you'll answer mine."

She stared at him and then nodded. He got up, walked across the room, retrieved a chair then carried it over. "Please, sit down."

"I see you are healing rather quickly," Brighde said as she sat.

"Yes, I'm very grateful," Arnaud replied in an open and inviting tone, trying to cover for any suspicion she'd sensed. He sat on the bed across from her.

"Do you know why?"

"Why I'm healing so quickly?" He shrugged. "Probably the same reason I've not been so badly injured as I might've. Something to do with this sword."

He picked it up and the stone glowed brightly. He looked at her. "This is what you wanted to ask me about isn't it? But I think you know more about it than I do."

She smiled at him, and then looked around the room. She quickly stood to her feet, obviously aware of the indecency of the situation. As Arnaud had healed enough to move about the room, she no longer sat alone with an invalid, she sat with a stranger. "Do you think yourself able to walk?"

"Yes," Arnaud nodded catching on to her thoughts.

"Let us go into the gardens. They're beautiful this time of year."

Arnaud took the sword with him. He suspected Grainne would move it if left unattended in his room.

Neither spoke as they walked through long winding halls, passing countless elaborately, embroidered doors. Arnaud looked carefully around him at the structure and carvings so different from any he had seen before. Grainne had forbid him from leaving his bed, but truthfully he had not been able to move without splitting his cuts open until today. Even now each step was uncomfortable, but he didn't let it show.

They finally wound out under the softly lit sky. It was green, bright and clear, and trees stood like giants all around them.

"It is a beautiful day," Brighde commented, breathing deeply.

"These are the gardens?" Arnaud searched about, looking for flora. There were only towering high-branched trees here.

"Yes," Brighde said simply. And then reading his confusion, she pointed up to the skies.

Arnaud followed her direction and realized no need for flowers upon the ground. Birds, thousands of them, covered the branches, as thick as the leaves upon them.

Their feathers cast the rainbow in all hues as bright as the sun and as deep as the black sea. Their plumage envisioned a garden of the skies. And the sound. Arnaud did not understand how he could've overlooked it. Sweet melodies mingled into thick, soothing music.

"You are intelligent, Arnaud. That's easy to see."

"Thank you," Arnaud replied, unsure of the reason for the comment.

"And I believe I am right in thinking that you've been educated, which is unusual for your position." She stared directly at him, and Arnaud could feel the pierce of her black eyes. "Was there opportunity for you to notice the similarities between King Eochan's sword and your own?"

"King Eochan?"

"Yes, my husband. The man whose life you saved."

Arnaud was startled. "I am sorry, Your Highness. I didn't know." She nodded. He continued, "There was."

So that was it. These swords belonged to kings. It was clear the queen wanted to tell him more. He took a deep breath to prepare himself for the rest of the story.

"Perhaps I should begin father back, with the coming of my people to these lands." She tilted her head. "Have you heard of the faie, Arnaud?"

"I recognize the word."

"We are a people who've come from the North, over the sea. We have . . . qualities that were unappreciated, envied even. That was a thousand years past, and the sword, King Eochan's sword, was before our journey. It has been passed down among kings for generations. King Eochan being the eighth of those—"

"Eight kings in a thousand years?" Arnaud interrupted.

"Our lifespan is longer than yours. It was once twice the length, but has since been lessening." She watched him, waiting for a response.

"What are these qualities you speak of?" Arnaud asked finally. "Are you not human?" He would once have been disbelieving, skeptical of such a notion. It now only produced surprise, as in the unfolding of a story.

"We are human," Brighde replied. "But we are the long descendants of the god Alaunus, and part of him, a very small part, remains. In some his part is stronger and produces . . . *abilities*, greatly weakened through generations, yet still godlike."

"You would have me believe you are gods?" Arnaud was amazed. This was ridiculous. And what did it have to do with the sword?

"Not at all," Brighde said, shaking her head. "I merely wish to explain that we are not quite like you, and that fact can prove dangerous." She paused. "You have seen merpeople, the descendants of Poseidon? You know they possess qualities you do not: healing, the ability to lift curses, discernment, and prophecy." Arnaud nodded. "Poseidon was a much more peaceful god than Alaunus. The faie, too, some of us, have the ability of discernment, prophecy and healing. But we have also the ability to wield enchantment."

"You can . . . cast spells on people?" Arnaud said, disbelieving.

"Only some of us. And as blood spreads out through generations those abilities grow weaker. Eventually they will die out completely. But then, when we first came to these lands, and even now, it has been a great problem, a danger."

"Because you can't defend yourselves or fight back?" Arnaud said.

Brighde nodded. "The King and Queen of the faie have passed down these powers in a powerful form by way of a sword and a pendant. To ensure they would always have reign over their people; that none with a surprisingly strong power could threaten their rule. We quickly learned that the same would need to be done for each race in these lands, especially the native peoples."

"So, you made an enchanted sword for each race?"

"For the King and Queen of each race," Brighde corrected. "Emeralds for King Charles. Aquamarine for the merman king Tarsius, Jade for the giant king Aunid. Sapphire for the centaur king Corbus. Jasper for the faun king Deru, Opal for the naiad Suri. Pearl for the dryad Cleptis. And ruby for the ruling faie ruler King Aidan."

"And I assume one could not simply steal the enchanted gems?" Arnaud asked. "That would prove more dangerous than having none at all."

She smiled at him and nodded. "These powers only react to descendants of their original recipients, and the spouse that they choose. I am sure you have an idea of what I am going to suggest."

"I am not a descendant of King Charles." Arnaud met her eyes.

Queen Birghde nodded. "I know." She looked back up at the plumage-filled sky. "I knew King Phillip and his wife Alana. And I knew their only daughter Genevieve. Never before has there lacked a son or daughter to receive the emeralds and take the throne." She looked at him. "You have seen many of the dangers that threaten these lands, Arnaud. They are numerous and terrible. And your people are leaderless."

Not liking the direction the conversation was taking him, Arnaud asked, "Where is your pendant? Are you not Queen of the faie?"

"It was lost." She stood up straighter, pushing her shoulders back. "I have given you much to consider. If you have any more questions, tell Grainne and she will get me. I will answer as truly as possible."

She turned and left him alone in the garden.

Arnaud remained there a long while, trying to let the busy chatter of birds soothe him, but it didn't work. There was no escaping what Queen Brighde had said. What she'd suggested.

Your people are leaderless. She expected him to lead them.

How different it was here. He had no work in Calais, not even as a deckhand on board a fishing vessel. He struggled to keep his family from starvation.

Here, they wished him a king.

He had to admit it was an enticing prospect, to lead the people of France; to be their commander, their guide to a brighter, safer future. And the power that would inevitably come with it was undeniable.

He could act against the injustices of this land. He could fight against the Lord Gualhart of Calais and his tax collectors; against Andre's M. Serge and his reign over Boulogne, against the witch Sorcha and her strange strength over the minds of others. To have the power to prevent and defeat the reign of tyrants over men who could not defend themselves drew Arnaud in a way he could not understand. And because of this sword, he would be able to provide for his family.

Because of this sword.

Arnaud shook himself from these visions. How could a weapon choose a king? Even if it were possible, if what Queen Birghde had said was true, this sword was old. Time might have reduced its abilities. It could be wrong.

Arnaud walked back into the hallways of the building. He would think of it no more. Even if he

161

wanted to, was able to, how could he possibly lead these people? He had no training. And why would anyone follow an out-of-work fisherman when they already had a king?

***

Arnaud went directly to the room two doors left of his own, where Grainne had said Andre would be. He wanted to see himself how his friend was. He pushed the door open slowly, careful not to make a sound in case the boy was sleeping. Arnaud peered inside and saw the room was very similar to his own; small and plain and very neat. Several large chairs sat about, empty but for quilts and towels draped over their backs. A long bed filled up a corner and Andre lay upon it dressed in similar garb to that Arnaud had been given. The bed quilts had been pushed back as in agitation and his deeply sunken eyes were closed, but he spoke as Arnaud drew closer.

"Did you get the pendant?" he asked. His voice was much stronger than it had been the last time Arnaud had heard it, but it was still pained and weak.

"Yes, I did."

Andre opened his eyes. "I didn't want you to think I was trying to steal it."

Arnaud smiled. "It didn't seem to do you much good anyway." He looked at the boy's pale, drawn face. "How are you doing?"

Andre waved his hand in a feeble gesture of discredidation. "Apparently I've been worse. Or so they tell me. They also tell me I should be dead." He continued thoughtfully, readjusting the position of his legs. "The nurse tells me that a lot. I'm beginning to wonder if it's a suggestion."

"Grainne?" Arnaud laughed. He pulled up one of the chairs and sat. "She's pretty grim isn't she?"

Andre smiled weakly. "Boy, she loves you though. Always going on and on about how you saved my life, and that other man's: King Eochan she calls him; how brave you must be. Won't shut up about it."

"Really?" Arnaud was surprised. "I was sure she disapproved of me. Never says a word. She must be trying to teach me some kind of lesson."

"Be thankful," Andre commanded. "I don't know how she expects me to get any rest when she never stops talking." He sat up a bit more on the bed. "She's right, though. I'd have been dead long ago without your help."

"It was nothing," Arnaud said, again feeling uncomfortable. How many times would he have to sit through demonstrations of gratitude when truly he neither wanted nor deserved it?

"I remember it, Arnaud; parts of it anyway," Andre said gravely. "It wasn't nothing. You saved my life. Several times I think. And if there's ever anything I can do for you, just name it."

They stared at each other a moment and then Arnaud nodded, realizing that before Andre could fully relax, he'd needed to thank him; that his own belittling of the situation was only making it more difficult for his young friend.

"You're welcome," he said sincerely.

They sat in awkward silence. Arnaud watched the boy rub one arm and then the other as if nervous or irritated by something. "You know, after all of this excitement it'll be hard to go back to the humble life of a petty thief." Andre said, looking sideways at him. "I'm thinking of trying something different."

"What'll it be then? The monastery?" Arnaud joked.

But Andre remained serious. "You're a fisherman, right? What made you choose that?"

"Well, my father was a fisherman," Arnaud replied.
"But I was apprentice to a carpenter before he died and
I suddenly had mouths to feed."

Andre bit his lip. "How did he die?"

Arnaud stared at him and then said, "He was
arrested and executed for conspiracy against Lord
Gualhart for refusing to pay his tax."

Arnaud wasn't ashamed of this. Countless times
he'd wanted to do the same thing, and in fact, had
almost done the same. Lord Gualhart was a leach on
the economy of Calais. Arnaud was sure, as his father
had been, that if the oppressed men would band
together, something could be done to change things. It
had been difficult to watch the fruits of a hard-labored
day: eight fish out of ten— go to the tables of the Lord,
his spies and collectors. But if Arnaud had been
arrested, there would've been no one to provide for his
mother and sisters.

Andre looked uncomfortable; about to say
something, but instead he swallowed hard and rubbed
his hands together. "Where are we? Do you know?"

"I'd rather hoped you would know," Arnaud said,
"Grainne talks to you."

"For all she says none of it's of any use. And I can
never get a word in to ask a question."

"It must be a large city. Large enough to have
royalty anyway. And they call themselves the faie, or at
least some of them do."

"Huh," Andre commented still rubbing his hands in
agitation.

"It doesn't matter anyway," Arnaud continued.
"Once you're well enough I'll get you back to
Boulogne. I'm sure you have someone there worrying
over you."

Andre looked down into his lap. "It might . . . be a
while, you know," he said quietly. "Grainne says I

164

must rest for several weeks at least. But who knows? It could be longer."

"I guess not all of her chatter is useless then," Arnaud said lightly, but he was pondering the boy's demeanor and his words. Was it self-pity? Or did he truly wish to stay away from Boulogne? Perhaps there was no one there for him but that conductor of robbers, M. Serge. It was a depressing thought.

"You said your father was arrested for breaking the law?" Andre ignored Arnaud's last comment, looking up from his wringing hands. Arnaud nodded slowly. The boy snickered in sudden apparent carelessness. "Well then, we're more alike than I thought."

Arnaud watched him a moment and then decided to go along with this strange turn of conversation. He smiled as if he found Andre's words amusing. "Oh? What did your father do?"

"He . . . bartered suspiciously acquired horses."

"A horse thief?"

"Well . . . yes, I suppose that's what it was," Andre nodded, apparently enjoying himself. "He would hide them at a cabin in the woods near Boulogne until he could sell them."

"But they found the cabin," Arnaud suggested, recalling the dream he'd had long ago, before all this had happened.

Andre looked sharply at him, and Arnaud realized that though his tone was light, this was a grave subject. Andre was ashamed, and after meeting Jaques, Arnaud felt he knew something of the sting of family dishonor.

"Did I already tell you this?" Andre asked. "I'd never spoken of it before."

"No," Arnaud said seriously. "I remember the cabin, when I followed you there. It was empty," he said, deciding not to speak of his dreams.

Andre nodded and was quiet, remembering.

"Listen," Arnaud said, "you don't have to tell—"

"I want to," Andre interrupted. "I want to . . . explain something."

Arnaud nodded and waited, but it was a long time before Andre continued.

"I was eleven when my father was taken." He breathed deeply. "My brother, Raulet, was five. We were left there in the cabin. I didn't know what to do so we waited. But after a few days, Raulet was still crying." He dropped his gaze, not looking at Arnaud. "So I picked him up and brought him to a man I thought was one of my father's friends in the city."

"Serge," Arnaud guessed.

Andre nodded, still avoiding his stare. "He said he had liked my father, and that he would find someone to take care of Raulet, but it would be a lot of work, and I'd have to pay it off."

Arnaud nodded. So this was how he'd become a thief.

"I knew it was wrong," Andre continued. "My father never wanted us to become like him. He wanted us to do honest work, like my grandfather who was a foot soldier in the armies of King Guilham. Father wanted us to do something we could be proud of. But I . . .I didn't think I had a choice." He looked up. "I'm sure you would've found a better way."

Arnaud stared hard at him. "You were protecting your brother; I can understand that. You did what you felt you had to do. But it's not necessary to feel guilty anymore. Raulet is safe now, isn't he?"

Andre nodded sadly.

They sat in silence for several moments before Andre said, "Say, why are you doing so much better than I am?" His voice was suddenly jovial again, but he grimaced and reached across to scratch his shoulder. "I was sure you were closer to death than I was."

"Apparently it has something to do with this," Arnaud replied lightly, holding up the sword.

"Well, whatever it is, I wish I had one," Andre said in exaggerated agitation. "Grainne isn't the only reason I can't sleep. She tells me that poison's still in my blood. And it itches and burns and stings like anything all over."

"Here, let me try something," Arnaud said. Brighde had said with the sword he could heal, that already it had helped Andre. He laid a hand on the boy's shoulder and immediately the emerald began to glow stronger.

Andre sat very still for a moment and then his fatigue-lined face lit up. "It's almost all gone! I'd nearly forgotten what it feels like with no pain!" He chuckled in relief, "It's a pity you had to catch me, Arnaud. That sword is by far the most valuable thing I've ever stolen." He leaned back and closed his eyes in exhaustion. "But I'm glad you did anyway. I'd still be a pickpocket in Boulogne if you hadn't." His eyes shut.

Arnaud waited quietly for Andre to drift off to sleep. He stayed long after, sitting by the bed with his hand on the boy's shoulder, with the hope he would get at least a few hours of painless and peaceful rest.

***

Arnaud left the room hours later, what must've been late into the night. He felt drained and exhausted, which was strange because he had only sat calmly in the chair with his hand on Andre's shoulder. Perhaps it was just everything catching up with him; sleep deprivation, starvation, and exertion. He shuffled down the hall with an idea of going directly to bed and sleeping well into the next day. Grainne would love that; plenty of rest.

"Hey! What're you doing in here?!"

He was jolted by a sudden shout and someone seized him by the arm. He sucked in his breath at the sudden flame of pain shooting across the rips in his back and side.

"No strangers are allowed in the Great Hall. Ever. Especially at this hour." The speaker was a man about Arnaud's height, but his extreme thinness made him appear much taller. His hair was the same unusual white Arnaud had been seeing so much lately.

Arnaud was about to say, ' I'm not a stranger, ' but he actually was.

"Well, who are *you*? What are *you* doing here?" he asked instead, mimicking the man's harsh tone, and shaking his hand off his arm. He was tired, exhausted, and irritated by the fresh pain in his back.

"I'm of the King's Guard, and it's my duty to keep peddlers, thicves, assassins, and the likes of you, out of here." The man grabbed his arm again, and again Arnaud shook it off.

Assassins?

"I was told I was a guest here. Or have they changed their minds already," Arnaud said, clenching his teeth against another wave of pain.

"A guest? But you're . . ." the guard's eyes lit up in comprehension, "but you must be *him*. I must say I thought you'd be older. You only look about my age."

Him?

"I'm . . . not sure what you mean."

"The slayer of the great bear, Orson. You saved the king's life! I've heard talk of nothing else for two weeks."

"Two weeks?" Arnaud asked, ignoring all else the man had said. It couldn't possibly have been two weeks!

"Well, it feels like two weeks anyway," the guard complied, "but you are him?"

"I'm Arnaud." He held out his hand and the guard shook it enthusiastically.

"Theobus. It's a strange name; I know."

"Well, I'm glad to meet you, Theobus, but if you don't' mind, I'll—"he gestured to the door of his room.

"Oh, yeah, sure." Theobus moved out of the way.

Arnaud waved his hand as if in farewell and entered the room, but he was surprised to find Theobus follow him in, apparently ignorant of his unwelcome.

"My, you do seem to be doing well, especially after having faced Orson. That beast has devoured more innocents than I can think of, for centuries."

"Centuries?" Arnaud said skeptically. He walked over and placed his sword discretely on the floor between the bed and a table. Thankfully the guard seemed to have not noticed the weapon.

"Well, a long time anyway," Theobus agreed. He sat down in a chair and spread his long legs out comfortably.

Arnaud stared at him and almost laughed. He went over and sat on the bed, succumbing to the man's intrusion. He rubbed his face wearily and then looked suspiciously at his hand. Someone must've shaved off his growing beard. That was odd.

"So, you're a guard then?" Arnaud didn't think he'd ever seen a man who looked less like a guard.

Theobus nodded , pointing to his clothing. It must've been a uniform, but Arnaud couldn't tell.

"My aunt got me the job. She's a nurse here. She said she was one of your nurses in fact. She told you were badly mauled, but you look okay to me. What's your secret?"

"Your aunt's name is Grainne, isn't it?" Arnaud asked.

"Yes. How did you know? There must be many nurses in and out of here. Or maybe not, as you're doing so well," Theobus said, hardly pausing for breath.

"Resemblance," Arnaud said. "You both . . . have the same . . . ears."

"Really?" Theobus reached up and felt his ear. "Most people can tell because we both talk a lot."

"Well, there's that too," Arnaud scoffed, now running a hand through his hair. He was so tired. "A guard, huh? Are there many of you here?"

Theobus shrugged. "Twelve maybe. Besides me. I was specially assigned to guard your room."

"From what?" Arnaud asked, indignation rising. "To keep me here?" He'd already sized this man up; even in his present state he was confident he could defeat him if the need arose.

"No, no, nothing like that." Theobus held his hands up in reassurance. "You're quite free to leave whenever you choose. You're something of a hero here now. A big crowd gathered when they brought the beast's hide in this morning. There should be a great feast to honor you once the king is recovered."

"Then why? Why is a guard assigned to me?" Arnaud asked.

"For protection," Theobus said simply.

"Against what?"

"Not everyone is . . . appreciative that you saved the king's life. Some believe you should've just let him die. And they're quite angry about it."

"But that's—*why*?" Arnaud asked, confused.

"Don't you know this?" Theobus asked. "I thought you were from here?"

"No. We're—I'm from the north," Arnaud said. If there were truly any danger he'd rather not bring Andre unnecessarily into it.

170

"Really?" Theobus sounded surprised. "You don't look like a northerner. They're usually kind of short, aren't they? You're pretty tall, even for here. And I've never seen a northerner with black hair like that."

"Nevertheless it's true." Arnaud had grown up hearing those very things, had wondered them himself, but now that he knew his mother's ancestors were not native to Calais it seemed to make more sense. "Why would someone want to kill the king? To kill me?" He said drawing the conversation back.

"Politics," Theobus said, waving a hand as if to dismiss the topic. "I try not to get involved."

"If someone is going to try to murder me, Theobus, I want to know why."

"Not going to try," Theobus insisted. "Might try. And you'll have a guard outside your door all the time, so it's not going to happen anyway." Theobus yawned then said, "I'm pretty sure I'm not supposed to say anything about the dragon."

"Dragon?"

"Well, since you asked." Theobus sat up and leaned forward, his eyes twinkled conspiratorially. "That monster seems to be an absolute blind spot for King Eochan. No matter what complaints or reports come in, he won't hear them. Won't have anything to do with it."

"A dragon? What . . . kind of dragon?" Arnaud asked.

"Well, I've never seen it myself. It lives further south of here. But I hear it's a red dragon, fire-breathing, and it's huge, probably bigger than this building."

"But a beast of that size must cause considerable damage."

"You wouldn't believe the stories I've heard." Theobus shuddered horrifically. "We've got more

coming in every week who've lost their homes and
entire families to a wave of fire or bloody jaws.
Terrible. And not only that, but the beast's territory
seems to be spreading. Sightings of it are closer and
closer to Ardgal."

"And . . . and your king just ignores this?"

Theobus nodded several times. "It's odd, right?
But you heard none of this from me." He held his
palms up innocently. "He is my king and my employer.
And speaking of these things is frowned upon if not
downright prohibited."

Arnaud exhaled wearily and nodded. "What you
tell me is the truth?" He had to ask. He wouldn't put it
past this man to invent such an exciting tall tale.

The guard sighed. "Unfortunately it is."

Arnaud nodded again and rested his hand on the
bridge of his nose. He stared at the sword hastily
concealed next to the bed, trying not to think about
anything.

"Grainne warned me not to bother you 'on pain of
a real hiding,'" Theobus quoted, standing to his feet.
"I'd better get back to my post before someone sees I'm
gone." He strolled towards the door.

"Will you do something for me, Theobus?"
Arnaud asked, before Theobus reached the door.

"Anything you want, Arnaud."

"Keep any eye on the room two doors left of here
as well."

The guard saluted. "Sure thing." And he left.

Arnaud lay back on the bed. He stared up at the
ceiling, attempting to block his thoughts; to avoid
dwelling on all he had heard today. Why did everyone
choose this day to thrust their unpleasant information
upon him? He hadn't asked for it. He didn't want to
know about the dragon or about their hapless leader
who refused to do anything about it. Nor did Arnaud

have any desire to save lives or prevent others from being taken by the dragon. He sighed.

But, on the other hand, there was nothing more for him in Calais but his family. And they could be easily moved. With very little trouble...

Arnaud shook himself. What was he thinking? If Theobus was right, the old kingdom would be half destroyed by the dragon. Its people massacred or uprooted. There would not be enough land or people to be ruled. Plus, taking the throne would not mean removing the faie king from his.

"I'm too tired for this."

He rolled over and willfully directed all his thoughts to her. To the calm he felt when with her in his dreams. And he fell uneasily into sleep.

***

A room. A very long room with echoing wooden pillars running down along either side, and a raised chair at the end. A beautifully carved and positioned chair, a throne.

The throne was empty. The room was empty but for a girl waiting patiently by one of the pillars. She had very long black hair and she stood erect, postured with discipline. A door opened along the opposite wall and the girl stepped forward as four men walked through it.

Their words echoed records of the harvest and of the depleting umbra population. The girl waited quietly until one of the men spotted her.

"Sire," he said, pointing.

The men stared for a second and then one of them walked forward. He was a tall man with the white hair trademark of the purer blood of the faie. He held a certain quality that was not so much confidence and respect as swaggering ease.

"What can I do for you, young lady?"

"You are King Eochan, the new ruler of Ardgal?"the girl asked.

The king smiled and nodded, "Yes, I am he. Can I help you with something?"

"I wish to speak privately . . . if that is permitted." She glanced at the other three men.

King Eochan followed her gaze back to his advisors. "Well, as you can see now I am very busy. However, I believe a king should spare time for the various concerns of his people. I can give you a few minutes." The king raised his hand at his advisors. "Wait outside. There is still much to discuss." The men exited through the door.

"Now," he said, turning to her, "what is it I can do for you?"

"Sire, I wish to continue my studies in the ways of Alaunus."

"Continue your studies?" King Eochan was clearly confused.

"I was a student under you father, the late King Ailean."

"What is your name?"

"Sorcha Conmidhe." Her mouth smiled up at him but her eyes were dark and detached. "I am from a family whose bloodline can trace directly back to the gods with little deviation. As a child I showed great potential in the ways of Alaunus, particularly in enchantments. King Ailean was teaching me to strengthen and wield these powers."

King Eochan stared in amazement. "Did the king say why he was teaching you these things?"

"To preserve our great culture."

King Eochan nodded. That sounded like his father. "Well, I am very sorry, Sorcha, but my plans for the faie are very separate from those of my father, and I will not be continuing your lessons."

"But I am one of the few left with natural powers! You will abandon the heritage of your people?"

"I will not continue to put barriers between the faie and the people of France." King Eochan tried to calm his temper. What need had he of explaining himself to this strange girl?

"That is evident by your choice of wife."

King Eochan was outraged. How dare she? "Out! Get out!" The king seized her arm and dragged her to the door. "If I see you again near this place you will be taken into custody!"

The advisors on the other side were shocked. Why was their new king so angry with this young and innocent looking girl?

King Eochan was furious at himself for his anger, and at the girl's obstinacy and sense of entitlement. There was something distinctly wrong about her. Why would his father help increase the powers of one obviously unstable?

"Cathal," King Eochan said calmly, "you were speaking of the time estimated until the umbra population would be under control in these parts."

The scene faded and then a different appeared.

The same place. The same room, yet altered. It was dark. No light shone in through the high, unshuttered windows, and the place seemed disused. At the time of the new king's coronation the hall had been polished and gleaming; now it was cold and dusty, as if forgotten.

It was hallow, empty but for a single person. A woman sat lazily on the throne playing listlessly with her long black hair. She stopped when a door opened along the wall.

A man strolled in, apparently deep in contemplation. His hands were folded behind his back and his snowy head was bowed down, facing the floor.

He did not notice the woman or her presence on his throne until she spoke.

"I thought you might come here to rethink my offer," she said conversationally. "It is, after all, the place of our first meeting. You remember? You refused to guide me and I was forced to take my extraordinary talents elsewhere."

King Eochan stared at the enchantress Sorcha in pure loathing.

She laughed. "You know, if you had an enchantress in your employ, as I'd wanted to be, you might've prevented much of this; as the French King did." She laughed uproariously. "How ironic!"

The king watched her in mounting wrath.

"Oh, but let's not dwell on the past," she continued, "I've taken my revenge. We're even now."

"You murdered my wife! My son!" King Eochan physically shook with rage. "You dare to show your face here! To sit upon my throne!" He stepped forward, hands outstretched as if to strangle her, but the witch held up a hand and he stopped.

"You would not teach me then. I will teach you now. Do not cross me!"

She suddenly appeared serene. "Besides, you seem to have moved on rather quickly. The first wife was unfit for you; you have chosen better this time." She stared at his yet quivering form as if posed to strike, and then smiled. "You seem happier now anyway." She laughed, a cold, heartless laugh. "If I were you, I wouldn't do anything to disrupt that happiness." She twitched her hand and King Eochan stumbled back, gasping for breath. "Just because she's a purer choice doesn't mean I can't kill her too."

***

Chapter Ten

Arnaud awoke the next morning, or afternoon, feeling just as tired as he had when he'd fallen asleep. He knew he had dreamed. That he'd been disturbed by those dreams, but he couldn't exactly recall them. They were shattered into fragments and pieces; a phrase here, a face there, and those pieces were slipping away.

"Sit up a bit so I can change your bandages." Grainne stood over him with fresh cloth and a grim expression. "I'm glad to see you've slept a long while, but it doesn't seem to have done you much good."

Arnaud pushed himself up with a groan. It felt like every muscle in his ribs and back had been pummeled in the night.

"How is Andre?"

"He is surprisingly improved," Grainne said, wrapping a thick white bandage around his waist. "But he'd slept some, so that must be why."

Arnaud decided not to tell her he'd sat with the boy. He was fairly sure that despite the positive outcome she'd disapprove.

"How long will I be in these bandages?" he asked as she tied a knot.

"A week. Maybe less. It's hard to tell with that sword around." The old woman stepped back and admired her work. "I have some food for you," she said, retrieving a tray she had evidently brought in with her, "and you are to eat very slowly and take very small bites."

"Real food?" Arnaud asked. He'd had nothing but broth since he'd awoken here, and he was extremely tired of it.

"Very small bites." Grainne repeated sternly, laying the tray on his lap.

Arnaud stared down at a plate of steamed green vegetables and a soft slice of bread. "There's no meat here."

"You've all but starved for who knows how long," Grainne insisted, "be glad I give you this."

Because the nurse watched him closely Arnaud took a small bite. He savored the feel of solid food in his mouth. "Can you tell me how to get out of this building, Grainne?" he asked taking another bite, larger because her back was turned.

"And why would you need to know that?"

Even though it'd only been a few days, Arnaud was tired of being cramped up in a room. He'd never been long idle before and he found it immensely difficult. He wanted to learn more of this city, how far it was from Calais; and he wanted to talk to the people, hear their stories for himself.

"I'm not a prisoner. I can leave when I wish," he reminded her gently.

"Tramping around dusty streets will do you no good," Grainne said, "and that cut hasn't healed. It's very likely you'd get a horrible infection and die a painful death."

Arnaud could tell she was getting angry. There was nothing to clean so she darted about refolding quilts.

"Keeping me cooped up will do no good either." He liked the old nurse. He didn't want to upset her too much. "I'll be back for you to make sure I don't die without a decent 'I told you so.'"

She gave him an exasperated look and seized the used bandages. "I'll send my nephew to show you the way."

"Ask him to bring my clothes too!" Arnaud called before the door shut behind her.

***

"Your shirt was in shreds. Looks like your boots are as well." Theobus held up a boot and stared at the peeling leather. "Sure you don't want me to get you a new pair?"

"No thank you," Arnaud said taking the boot from him and pulling it on. They'd cleaned and pressed everything and given him a new shirt. He didn't care whose life he'd saved, this was all the charity he was going to accept.

Arnaud picked up his sword and began to strap it on, fairly certain that now it had ceased to glow, none would recognize it to be anything but an ordinary long-sword.

"I would leave that here if I were you," Theobus said pointing at it. "People might recognize you by it. Or try to lift it off you if they don't. It is a pretty thing, besides the fact that it belonged to the olde French king."

Arnaud stared a second in amazement and then began to remove the belt. "Does everyone here know so much?" he asked, setting it down reluctantly. He still wore the pendant but Arnaud felt safer with the sword at his side. Whether safer for himself or the weapon he was not sure.

"You forget our own king has one," Theobus explained as they left the room.

Arnaud was glad of a guide as they wound through curving hallways and made endless turns. Apparently many additions and improvements had been added to the Great Hall since it was first built, and the result was a maze of corridors. Theobus explained this all to him in great detail as they walked.

"Well, here it is," the guard said as they rounded a final corner and walked suddenly into sunlight, "the great city of Ardgal." He held out his arms in grand introduction.

The Great Hall had been built upon a wide hill and the city spread down from there into the valley of the mountains. It was green and flourishing with countless trees grown close together so as to make a canopy. Arnaud couldn't help comparing it to the dusty trade city that was his hometown, and find Calais severely lacking in beauty.

"Would you like me to take you somewhere?" Theobus asked. "I know of an inn, the White Horse Inn, that has the best ale you've ever tasted in your young life."

Arnaud turned to him and said very seriously, "I would welcome company, Theobus, but I neither need nor want any bodyguard."

"I'm off duty," Theobus said gesturing to his clothing.

Arnaud could see little difference in this garb and that he'd worn before, but he accepted this explanation.

"To the White Horse." He gestured for Theobus to lead the way.

***

They took two seats at the bar of the inn and waited for someone to serve them.

"It's the richest you've ever tasted, I guarantee it." Theobus told him with wild hand gestures.

"What'll it be gentlemen?" A bartender had come up to them, but Arnaud didn't reply. He had no money. He couldn't recall a time when he did have spare coins for such things. His pay went to feed his family and pay the bills.

"Uh," Arnaud pulled out a handkerchief, one that Andre had stolen, and was about to suggest some sort of trade with it when Theobus, who'd been strangely distracted, said, "Two pints of your finest, sir, if you please." He stared at the handkerchief. "You don't need that."

180

"I'll pay you back," Arnaud said, putting the handkerchief back in his pocket.

"Don't worry about it, friend," Theobus said jovially clapping him on the back.

"No. I'll pay you back."

"Alright. You'll pay me back," Theobus conceded heartily. "But there's really no need. This is my place; I have a tab here, and I'll surely forget about the whole thing."

"You come here often?" Arnaud conversed drinking from the mug placed before him. It was good ale.

"Quite often," Theobus said, turning and looking out at the people seated at tables. A group of dark men whispered together in a strange tongue at one table. At another, two very old, grey men and three considerably younger sat together playing some game involving dice. A large group of grubby, weary looking men sat smoking and chatting and occasionally laughing uproariously. An array of empty mugs cluttered their table and they called for more. An attractive barmaid appeared with a tray and distributed fresh drink.

"Do you know many of these people?"

"Huh?" Theobus said, suddenly distracted again.

"Do you know these people?"

"Oh, you know… some." Theobus cleared his throat and turned back to the bar. "That group with the cloud of smoke over their heads are farmers."

"What sort of farmers?"

"Uh, grain maybe. I'm not sure. So what about this sword of yours?" he whispered, abruptly changing the subject. "Are you here to reestablish the French throne or something?"

"I'd rather not talk about it," Arnaud said. Why would this man advise him to leave the sword behind and then bring it into conversation? And why was he suddenly so distracted?

"Right, sorry," Theobus said, taking a deep swig. "Don't know why I brought that up." He cleared his throat again and looked over his shoulder. "So what do you do for a living, Arnaud?"

"I was a fisherman," Arnaud said, watching him suspiciously.

"A fisherman, eh? That must've been . . uh, interesting." He took another swig, already emptying his pint.

"Fairly."

"So what brings you to these parts?"

"Another?" The attractive barmaid interrupted, taking Theobus' mug.

"Thank you," Theobus grunted inaudibly and gazed down at the table, his face a deep red. She set down another drink then left.

Arnaud stared at him and then sniggered, taking another drink, "Is that all?"

"Is that all what?" Theobus asked.

"You were acting so sneaky, I was sure you were going to murder me or something."

"I don't know what you're talking about." Theobus blushed more deeply.

"The girl. The girl!"

The only other man seated at the bar nodded. He was thickly bearded and thickly built, and extremely drunk. "I see you in here . . . all the time . . and you never . . . even talk to her," he slurred and giggled wheezily, slopping drink down his front. "Go for it man!" He spread his arms wide. "While there's still time left for you!"

"Shut up," Theobus mumbled into his cup. He turned to Arnaud, attempting to change the subject. "A fisherman?" Arnaud nodded. "How does a fisherman come to know swordplay?"

"I don't," Arnaud said simply and took another drink.

"Then how could you possibly—" he peered around and dramatically whispered, "—take down that huge bear. And I hear it's got abilities on top of its size that make it even more formidable."

Arnaud shrugged, "Luck?"

"That's a lot of luck." Theobus suddenly tensed again as the barmaid came around a second time. She placed a fresh mug in front of the drunk sitting beside Arnaud.

"Thank you, Rosemary, my dear," the drunk said sweetly, and then gave Theobus a hearty wink.

Theobus mumbled and grumbled and gulped down the rest of his second pint.

"Do you know that man?" Arnaud had to ask.

"As you can plainly see he's a drunk and a bum," Theobus said brutishly.

"And . . . he's after Rosemary, the barmaid, as well?"

"No. No, he's just trying to bait me," Theobus explained taking a deep breath. "He's one of those men I told you about. Lost everything to the fires of the dragon. He was one of the first to come in; probably ten or eleven years ago when the dragon just appeared. He's been sittin' at this bar ever since."

Arnaud glanced over at him in a new light. This man had experienced terrible things, seen terrible things. And without the drive for anything, even revenge, all he could do was try to drown them out.

"Sad, isn't it?" Theobus commented, and then forgetting his mug was empty he brought it to his lips but was interrupted.

A low whistle soared through the room, followed by hysterical laughter.

Arnaud swung around to find the table of drunken foreigners poking at Rosemary the barmaid, and then laughing at her reaction.

Rosemary appeared to keep herself composed. She had the air of one who had dealt with drunks before. But when one of the men shouted something in his strange tongue and pulled her onto his lap, she began to struggle in earnest.

"Theobus." Arnaud looked at him expectantly but the guard only stared in shock. "Why isn't anyone doing something?"

Arnaud's eyes swept over the room. The other men were either burying themselves in their game or their drink. Rosemary continued to struggle as the forcigners laughed heartily.

"Fine!" Arnaud spat, suddenly disgusted with the lot of them.

He strode up to the man restraining her and laid a heavy hand on his shoulder, knowing that if he spoke the man would not understand. But he would understand the look on Arnaud's face. The foreigner looked at Arnaud with an amused expression on his face. He passed Rosemary to one of his friends and stood up to face Arnaud.

"Let her go," Arnaud commanded, pointing at the girl, hoping that would make his point.

The man gave Rosemary a sweeping look and then laughed. "We'll share," he said in thickly accented French.

Without another word Arnaud punched him hard in the face, sending the man reeling to the floor. Rosemary screamed. Her captor tossed her aside and prepared to fight with the others. Arnaud found himself outnumbered six to one. He raised his fists and prepared himself for a heavy beating. Boy, would Grainne be happy.

They were on him in a second. At first, Arnaud hardly felt their meaty fists contacting with his cheek, his back, his ribs. He could tell the carefully mended claw rips in his back had reopened and were bleeding again. But he stood his ground and managed to level at least two of them before a couple whoops of excitement announced two of the younger men at the game of dice were in the thick, swinging wildly. Before Arnaud could blink, every man in the bar was beating on the offending foreigners. And when they were down, the men turned on each other.

Arnaud watched the mob of men steadily knocking each other out, and was strongly reminded of life aboard the Nitona. But he didn't have long to reminisce. One of the first men to join him in the fight swung around with great momentum and got him right below the left eye.

Arnaud heard a very distinct, "Oh, sh—" and then he hit the floor.

***

"Arnaud. Arnaud!"

He opened his eyes heavily and saw Theobus standing over him with a brilliant black eye.

"Arnaud, I have . . . unfortunate news." He helped pull him up into a sitting position.

"Is— is about this pain in my head? Because I already know." Arnaud peered around him. He'd never seen this place before. A small and rather dirty room with fewer furnishings than sleeping bodies, on the floor. "Where am I?"

Theobus ignored his question. "King Eochan has given orders to remove you from the Great Hall."

"Remove me?" Arnaud tried to grasp on to this. Did it have something to do with the brawl last night? "Why?" he asked gruffly.

"Blast if I know why. The order was given this morning. Here, I snuck this out for you." He passed Arnaud his sword. "I still wouldn't take it into public though. Extremely recognizable. People were pointing at me on my way here."

"You're the one . . . moving me out?"

Theobus looked at Arnaud as if he were an idiot. He swept a hand gesturing his clothing.

"Don't do that! Your clothes all look the same to me!" Arnaud snapped. The pain, no doubt from the blows to his head, seemed to be mounting.

"No. I'm not on duty," Theobus explained. "I just thought you'd like to know you and your friend were being removed. Grainne didn't seem at all happy about it. Do you have another place to stay?"

"They're making Andre leave as well?"

"The king is, yes."

Arnaud was on his feet and out the door in a second. "Can you take me to him? To the king?"

"Uh, I can try," Theobus said, hurrying to keep up with him. "Are you going to argue it? I don't know if it'll do any good. He's known to be extremely stubborn."

"So am I."

***

Arnaud would have barged right into the king's office without introduction if guards had not been standing outside the door.

"Arnaud . . ." Theobus trailed off. He did not know Arnaud's last name. "Arnaud to see King Eochan on urgent business."

The guards spoke to one another and then one entered the room. Arnaud was irritated, but the delay gave him a moment to calm down; to collect his argument. There was no way he was letting them toss a sick man out into the streets.

The guard returned, nodded to him and then held the door open.

"Good luck!" Theobus whispered after him as he walked into the room.

It was a rather wide, high ceilinged room with many closed shuttered windows and a second door further down on the same side. There were no paintings or furnishings of any kind but for a long oak desk and four large chairs pushed up to the wall behind it.

But the first thing Arnaud noticed was the people. Four men were around the desk with only one of them seated. Even without the bandages Arnaud would've known it was the king. He recognized the face that had then been spattered in blood. In calmer circumstances and up close, Arnaud did wonder now if the man's white hair was an effect of age as well as race.

The king stared at him a moment and then said something to the others in a low voice he could not hear. They left the room eyeing Arnaud as if he were about to turn and strike them down.

Arnaud waited for the king to speak, assuming that was some sort of protocol, but the man only stared with a distinctly angry look in his eyes. That anger transferred very easily.

"What right have you to remove an ill man from his bed?" Arnaud tried to keep emotion from his voice, but he couldn't help dousing his question in accusation.

"Ill?" the King scoffed. He turned his eyes to something on his desk as if this was wasting his time. "You look a little beaten up, but I'm sure that was of your own doing."

"I speak of the other who was brought here with me. Andre. Your own nurse believes him unfit to leave her care."

"And why am I obligated to aid any friend of yours? Last I checked I was still king."

Arnaud could hardly believe what he heard. This was a power struggle? He stared at the man before him.

"I am not challenging your authority. I'm only concerned for a sick friend."

"Your very presence is a challenge to my authority!" King Eochan slammed a hand on the desk. Apparently his temper was very short. "You think I don't know about that sword?" He glanced at the weapon at Arnaud's side. He'd ignored Theobus' advice and wouldn't leave it in a strange place. "What it means? That I don't know what information you must be gathering?"

Arnaud stared at him.

"Do you deny any right to what's left of the French throne?"

"I neither accept nor deny anything," Arnaud said, not quite following, but refusing to be bullied. He was a northerner. This man was not his king.

"Then I have every cause and right to remove you from my home and my city. Especially if you are, as I suspect, her new—"

He was interrupted by the sound of the door being opened. Arnaud turned and found Brighde entering the room. She strode regally over and stood next to her husband. He did not finish what he was going to say, and Arnaud, who was confused by it, addressed the previous statement.

"Perhaps you have cause to remove me if you feel so threatened," he plowed on, aware of the insulting affect this would have. "But Andre is innocent of any offence you can conjure up."

King Eochan looked livid, and Arnaud wondered if the king would've walked over and started a fistfight with him if he hadn't been so seriously injured. The king took a deep breath. "You claim he is a friend of yours. Perhaps that is offense enough."

"Or it is reason enough to aid him. Apparently I saved your life. Consider it repayment." Arnaud pulled all punches. He had no money, no place to go. He could do nothing for Andre without some kind of help. He wasn't leaving this room without the result he wanted

King Eochan stared at him, and Arnaud found it difficult to read his expression.

"I did not ask—" Queen Brighde laid a hand on her husband's shoulder, interrupting him. He looked at her a moment and then turning back to Arnaud said, "You will leave the Great Hall immediately. You will not be permitted to enter again under any circumstances. The moment your . . . friend is well enough he will be told the same. If ever you or your friend is caught near this building, you both will be thrown out, regardless of the circumstances. Are we clear?"

Enraged, Arnaud did not wait to be dismissed. He did not bow or show any kind of courtesy. He turned and walked out the door.

***

"You actually got what you wanted?" Theobus asked incredulously as they maneuvered down the twisting hallways to Arnaud's former chambers.

"More or less," Arnaud replied shortly. He was still angered and perplexed by the king's unfounded hostility. He took a deep breath and forced himself to calm. Theobus had nothing to do with the king's decree. "Andre's allowed to stay until he's well enough. But he seemed to think I was . . . spying on him or something. Do you know why he might think that?"

189

Theobus shrugged. "The king's been like that longer than I would know. He was the one who added guards to the Great Hall. And then later increased their number. Maybe that's what happens when you live so long."

"Live so long? Why? How old is he?"

"Well, he's been king for . . . wow, he's been for more than a century. Can't believe I missed that festival . . . "

"That's impossible," Arnaud insisted.

Theobus shrugged again. "It's in our blood. And those enchanted swords." He pointed to Arnaud's. "I wouldn't hope for an early death if I were you, Arnaud. Here we are."

They'd arrived at his door and found it open. Two men were inside rifling through Andre's bag of stolen goods, no doubt searching for evidence of some kind.

Arnaud immediately strode in and with authority said, "Your assistance is unnecessary. I will pack my own things and show myself out."

The guards stared at each other and then at Arnaud and left the room.

"That was . . . impressive," Theobus said entering the room. "I'm sure they were ordered to stay with you until you left."

Arnaud ignored his comment. "Perhaps he believes I am one of those who you said conspires against him," he said, still trying to figure out a cause for the king's strange behavior. He began stuffing things back into the bag.

Theobus looked doubtful. "Maybe, but the conspirators aren't really organized enough to make such a bold attack. I think he's just generally paranoid."

"So there's no actual threat from these . . . dragon people?" Arnaud halted his gathering and stared at him.

"Not yet. But they grow in number and anger each time the beast strikes," Theobus said sitting on the bed.

"So you weren't sent to protect me from some attack. You were sent to spy on me."

Theobus looked up, startled. "Not spy."

"Keep me from doing anything suspicious."

Theobus looked uncomfortable, but didn't deny it.

Arnaud tied the bag and pulled it over his shoulder. "Huh. Well at least you didn't lie about being a bodyguard." He was surprised at how little he cared about this new development.

"But, I'm not really—"

"Honestly, it doesn't matter," Arnaud interrupted. It was disappointing that he could no longer fully trust this man and that he knew no one else in this part of the country. But Arnaud had never fully relied on others anyway. "I'm going to go see Andre; explain all of this to him." He paused, "Unless you need to show me out or something."

"No," Theobus said quickly. "But I do have a shift today. I should probably go." He stood to his feet and walked slowly to the door. "You're welcome to stay at my place if you have nowhere else."

"Thank you, but I'll find something." The last thing Arnaud wanted was to be under constant surveillance.

"See you, Arnaud." Downtrodden, Theobus exited.

***

Arnaud walked alone down busy streets. The third time in this short year he'd done so. Each time in a

191

different city with different shops staring back at him.
Each time searching for a place to stay or a job. Two
jobs now. But he couldn't focus.

This city was beautiful. Actually beautiful.
Yellow canna sprung up right alongside the road and
purple bougainvillea grew in places as thick as grass.
Trees tall and wide enclosed half of the city in perpetual
shade. And birds flew thicker in the trees than Arnaud
had ever seen. Their song was constant and reminded
him of being deep in a forest.

But the people were different. They hurried
through the streets with heads bowed and items held
close, but they did not appear to be protecting their
items, like the people of Boulogne had. This had the
feeling of avoiding contact with others; a sense of
wariness seemed to hang over them. This behavior
contrasted strongly with their paradise-like
surroundings.

Arnaud attempted to sort through this as he
walked, occasionally stopping in a shop, only to be
rejected for work. Their behavior must have something
to do with the king. Perhaps there was a law
forbidding conversation in the streets in order to prevent
conspiracy from spreading? No. That was ludicrous.

Perhaps it had something to do with the threat of
the dragon. Many of the faces he saw appeared
frightened, like they could be anticipating burning
destruction and devastation at any moment. Arnaud
pondered. Were these people without defense? Had they
no means to fight back, to prevent the death and terror
from dragons spreading? No one could stand behind a
leader who refused to acknowledge a problem such as
this. Arnaud looked at the faces and felt the frustration
of the people, defenselessly waiting by for an attack;
waiting for the moment when they would be filled with

screaming horror, and then either die or be left alive and abandoned. Something must be done to change that.

"Whoa, look at that shiner! Nice work Marc."

Arnaud lifted his head from these despairing thoughts to find he had wandered onto a familiar street. He could see the White Horse Inn a block down. A crowd of about eight men were walking up the street toward him conversing, laughing and roughhousing. They were young, all within ten years of Arnaud's age and each had a long bow slung over his back.

"Thanks, Gaspar, I can still feel it." A second man separated from the group and joined the first, rubbing his knuckles and staring at Arnaud's face. They were shorter and stockier than he was and had light brown hair. It was obvious they were related. The same mixed expression of awe and humor lit their faces.

"Sorry about that," Marc said to Arnaud. "I swung before I recognized you."

"Do you know me?" Arnaud asked, eyeing the others who were obviously interested in the conversation, but avoided eye contact. And then he remembered where he had seen them. These were the first two men to step in to fight at the inn the night before.

"Only from the epic bar fight yesterday," Gaspar said. "Battle scars." He gestured at a black and purple bruise on the side of his chin. "That dunce Pierre snuck a left hook while I was distracted."

This comment elicited a snicker from the other men. "Why don't you admit you lost to a farmer, fair and square?" One of the men called.

"Are you headed back to the White Horse?" Marc asked Arnaud, ignoring the group.

"I wouldn't try it," Gaspar said before Arnaud could reply. He laid a hand on his shoulder and turned him to speak away from the others. "Old Estiene isn't too happy with what we've done to the place. Says we cost him business."

"We had to give him your handkerchief to shut him up."

"My handkerchief?" Arnaud felt his pockets.

"But it actually just made him louder," Gaspar elaborated. "He insists that if you're able to afford a gentleman's handkerchief then you're able to afford to pay for damages."

"So I wouldn't go back for a while."

"That is unless you have a bag of gold to throw at him, which I doubt you do."

Arnaud stared at them a second, wondering why people who never stopped talking always seemed to find him. He glanced at the remaining group who now seemed generally uninterested.

"So what's your name, friend?" Gaspar asked.

"Arnaud."

"Well, Arnaud, superb fighting by the way— great form," Gaspar said, clapping a hand on his shoulder. His voiced lowered, "By the by, you don't happen to be missing something, do you? Something valuable?"

Arnaud stared at him, not following. There had been nothing in his pockets other than the handkerchief.

Gaspar stared closely at him. "Something shiny and green?"

Arnaud pawed through his tunic with a pang of shock. The emerald necklace was gone. "Where is it?" he demanded, wondering how he always managed to attract a city's criminals.

"It's safe," Gaspar said mysteriously.

Arnaud was in no mood for their games. There was nothing more valuable than the pendant except the sword. He seized the man by the collar and pulled him to within an inch of his face.

"Where is it?" he repeated loudly enough for the others to hear. Gaspar giggled nervously and Marc moved forward to help but was at a loss as to what to do.

"He's only joking. We'll take you there now if you like." Marc laid a hand on Arnaud's arm.

Arnaud stared at him and then released his brother, patting the man's tunic down to show all was forgiven. Gaspar pulled uncomfortably on his collar.

"Who're your friends then?" Arnaud gestured to the group.

"Hunting party," Gaspar said high-spiritedly, clearly forgetting any hostility. "Just returned. We were to buy the drinks this time around but the White Horse won't admit us."

"It's just as well. We're broke."

Arnaud nodded, then gestured for them to lead the way.

"Next time!" Gaspar called over the group's mute protestations as they left.

"You should know we didn't steal it from you," Marc said as they walked down darkening streets. "We prevented it from being stolen."

"By one of those shifty farmers," Gaspar added animatedly.

"You prevented it from being stolen by stealing it yourself?" Arnaud tried to sort out this reasoning.

"We would've given it to you immediately if you hadn't run off in such a hurry this morning," Gaspar argued.

"I see."

"Since Marc here was the one to knock you cold—"

"Mistakenly," Marc interjected.

"—we carried you to Nicolas' place to recuperate."

"It was either that or leave you in the street," Marc explained.

"We're good people," Gaspar said grinning widely.

"Nicolas?" Arnaud drew them back.

"He's our –" Gaspar traded a look with Marc, "guardian."

"Yea, guardian sounds right. But not really anymore, considering our age."

"You'll always need a guardian, you infant."

"But more importantly," Marc said firmly, "he is chief hunter. You will report to him for parties and duties."

"I'm not a hunter," Arnaud explained, sensing they were insinuating something.

"That's not what I heard," Gaspar mumbled.

"Are you a farmer, then?" Marc asked more loudly.

"No."

"Good. I didn't think you looked like a brutish idiot." Gaspar sounded relieved.

"Farming would make me a brutish idiot?" Arnaud was curious. Farming had always been considered a respected profession to the north. It was a steady job.

"Well, the occupation keeps les faible anyway," Gaspar offered.

"Lumbering about on nothing but brute strength," Marc added, "there's no skill, no excitement."

"They're just big and," Gaspar felt his chin tenderly, "unfortunately very strong."

They turned a corner onto a darker, narrower street. The quickly darkening sky could barely be seen through thick, intertwining branches overhead. Arnaud pondered this apparent prejudice between hunters and farmers. It was unfortunate, dangerous even, to allow two strong and vital groups to be at odds in one city. He was surprised the king had not attempted to dissolve it. Without a strong leader, the people were clearly divided.

"Voila!" Gaspar gestured to a small and somewhat worn looking house.

Arnaud could vaguely recall rushing down that front step this morning on his way to the Great Hall. He hadn't bothered to pay attention to where he was at the time. "We're here?"

"Indeed," Gaspar said, as Arnaud followed them tramping up the step and barging inside.

They entered the dark and slightly furnished room where Arnaud had awoken that morning. A single table sat in the middle of the room with a single candle on top. Two chairs were occupied by gruffly bearded men, one large and lean, the other shorter with a round belly.

"—be able to find you something. But any tardiness or flippancy will not be tolerated, and obviously neither will intoxication." The taller man was speaking when they walked in. Marc and Gaspar interrupted with a loud greeting.

"You will be extremely pleased to hear, Nicolas, that I successfully shot not one, but two enormous bucks," Gaspar crowed.

"And successfully missed not four, but five easy shots," Marc mocked, giving him a little shove.

The taller man opened his mouth to speak, but was cut off by the other who, upon catching sight of Arnaud, shouted, "There he is! That's him!" He strode quickly over, seized Arnaud's hand and began to shake it vigorously. "We need more like you around here. Real guts! Real fighting spirit! Inspirational."

Astonished, Arnaud stared at the man. He'd never seen him before – wait – he looked again. He did seem familiar. And then a light turned on. The drunkard from the inn who'd teased Theobus. He looked different sober; almost respectable even.

"Are you a hunter?" the drunk asked. He turned to Nicolas. "Do you think I might join his party? You may recall I was once quite good." The man did not cease his enthusiastic, almost painful grip until Nicolas came up behind him and laid a heavy hand on his shoulder.

"We will speak more of this later, Martin." He smiled at the man and Arnaud thought it looked a little sad.

"Yes, yes, of course. You're busy," Martin said, giving a final shake before walking toward the door, staring at Arnaud the whole time. "I'll . . . be off then. We'll talk later."

Arnaud stared after him as he left. Arnaud shook his head, trying to understand. He could honestly see nothing extraordinary in what he'd done last night. Nothing to deserve such esteem from Martin, anyway.

"Crazy old man," Marc commented as he and Gaspar, seeming to forget the cause for Arnaud's presence, strolled over and lounged in the vacated chairs.

"Never thought I'd see that," Gaspar said, throwing his feet up onto the table. "Old Martin give up drinking and become a respectable hunter?" He acted as if he couldn't believe his ears.

"Do you think he'll really do it?" Marc asked.

"I would very much like to hope so." Nicolas glanced at Arnaud who was still standing beside the door. His expression was curious, but instead of addressing him he turned to the brothers. "Two bucks?"

"Five if you count Marc's," Gaspar corrected.

"And already you've stripped and cleaned_five? That's especially quick for you."

Gaspar put his hands relaxingly behind his head. "Our extremely hard work was interrupted by one Arnaud, a very distinguished guest." He gestured to Arnaud.

Nicolas gave them a hard look. Gaspar sighed and the two stood and gathered their things. Marc winked at Arnaud as they passed him, leaving the house.

The room felt empty and silent for a moment. Surprised by this sudden turn, Arnaud stared at Nicolas, apparently an important man in this city, and decided to refuse to be intimidated by him. He would get the pendant back no matter what it took. He stepped forward.

"I've come only for an item that was taken from me. Your . . . Marc and Gaspar had said it would be here."

But Nicolas either did not hear him, or ignored what he'd said. "Reckless boys." He gestured to the door. "Well, not boys anymore," he admitted, walking over to a cabinet in the corner. "Can I get you something to drink?"

Arnaud, who had had nothing to eat that day except a small loaf when visiting Andre, held up a hand in passing. The sky was nearly black, but if he could get the pendant immediately there might be time to find some sort of shelter. Even the slightest intoxication would hinder this.

"You're much younger than I thought you'd be," Nicolas mused, sitting in the chair Gaspar had sat in. "Those two might even be older than you."

He set his dirty glass of what Arnaud thought might be whiskey on the splintery table. He gestured for Arnaud to sit, as one used to having his orders followed. Arnaud returned the directive with a cold stare, prompting Nicolas to smile.

"I have heard a lot about you... Arnaud, was it?" Arnaud nodded. "There hasn't been a fight like that in – well, in a very long time. Especially with foreigners. Affects trading relations, you see."

Arnaud watched him closely, wondering if the man were about to lecture him. "I don't know what authority you have, Nicolas," he interrupted before the man could continue, "but I will not apologize for what I did."

Nicolas stared a second. "Naturally." He gestured to the chair again, this time invitingly. "Please, sit. I wish to speak with you on something."

Arnaud hesitated. Why couldn't the man just hand over the pendant so he could be on his way? But it would do no good to be short or rude. He'd already made an enemy of the king. Or rather the king had made an enemy of him.

He sat. Nicolas appeared much older from this distance. His brown beard was flecked with grey and succeeded in concealing many deep lines. The look on his face suggested him tossing an idea around and then dismissing it.

"You would be a very skilled hunter if presented with proper training," Nicolas said, taking a sip from his glass.

Surprised, Arnaud said, "Are you recruiting?"

Nicolas chuckled with more tiredness than mirth. "In a way. I've examined the hide of Orson," he explained. "Very accurate strikes. It would be difficult to defeat that creature with only a sword at such close range."

Arnaud wished the man would just get to the point, but he forced himself to be patient. If there was any chance Nicolas was offering him a position, he did not want to blow it. Perhaps after a time he could request a long range hunting party like Damien and Evrard and bring his family back here. Or something. Now was not the time to work out details.

But Nicolas changed the subject.

"It is obvious that you are not from here, Arnaud, though you rather look like the people."

Did the man expect him to elaborate on his origins? What business had he to pry into that? Calm. Calm. Arnaud's temper seemed to be unusually short today. A result of all these unexpected turns.

"I am from the North, and I believe you are not from here either," he said after a beat.

Nicolas chuckled again. "You are right indeed. I am not originally of the faie. My city was Caen, many miles south of here. Once larger and more prosperous than Ardgal."

Arnaud could tell where this was going. Nicolas was about to tell his tragic story, but he couldn't figure out why that would be important information right now. It doesn't matter, he told himself. Patience.

"It was the first and largest to be burned to the ground," Nicolas continued sadly. "Thousands died. Bodies everywhere . . . charred beyond recognition." He took another much deeper drink, and took his time swallowing it, gazing off at something Arnaud couldn't see.

"So was Martin from Caen as well?" Arnaud asked, feeling he should say something but not wanting to ask the wrong question on an obviously distressing subject.

Nicolas stared at him and then collecting himself said, "Yes. Yes, Martin and I came here together." He drew a hand over his beard. "I suppose I would have turned out very much like him if it weren't for those boys."

201

"Gaspar and Marc," Arnaud clarified.

Nicolas took another pull and nodded, his face tight with the bitterness of the drink. "Picked 'em up as we were leaving the city. Clinging to each other all covered in ash. Just little boys; eight and ten I think. Don't know how they found each other." He pushed himself up and strode over to refill his glass.

Arnaud knew it must be painful for him to remember such things and wondered why the man felt a need to tell him.

"Are they not brothers?" He asked trying to lead the conversation onto possibly brighter paths.

"Look like it, don't they?" Nicolas commented, filling the glass full this time. "No. No, I don't think they knew each other before that day. They were the only two left in that section of the city." He paused and swirled his glass, standing beside the chair. "But they are a pair, though," he said heavily and took a sip. "I remember coming back from a trip... they couldn't have been more than thirteen, just really learning to hunt. They'd—" He began to laugh, deep rich laughter, "—they'd taken one of my spare bows, gone practicing. I walked in to find Gaspar with an arrow sticking out of his leg." He held a hand over his own leg to display how high the arrow stuck out. "They were trying to hide it from me; cover it up." He gave in to the laughter and Arnaud joined in.

He could understand the man trying to forget a horrifying memory by covering it with a pleasant one. It seemed as if he'd been doing that a lot lately; thinking of her— the woman in his dreams— to ward off physical pain, or thoughts of the suffering his family must be going through.

"I've been dealing with things like that often though, these days." Nicolas wiped his mirth-filled eyes, "More so than I ever did before, that's for sure."

He took another pull of his drink. He seemed to have relaxed considerably since Arnaud had first entered the room, but he didn't appear intoxicated.

Arnaud felt himself relax into the man's friendliness. Hearing about his problems seemed to help divert Arnaud from his own, and though he would rather resolve them, this was a great diversion.

"And why is that?" he asked, leaning back in his chair.

"Oh, it's all these kids I've been teaching." Nicolas waved a hand noncommittally. "Before I'd always had some aged men, you know, with real experience. Not anymore. Just a bunch of young boys learning from scratch."

"So what did you do with all the seasoned hunters?"

"They're all gone." Nicolas waved his hand again and took another drink.

Gone? Gone where? But Arnaud didn't ask. "Well, I'm afraid I don't have much experience, but I'm a fast learner," Arnaud said, hoping to perhaps draw the man's thoughts back onto a job.

They hadn't actually established anything. But Nicolas only nodded and stared into the distance. Arnaud got the distinct impression that he was again considering and reconsidering something. It was curious. Why did this man feel so inclined to impart difficult memories?

Nicolas continued to stare and to nod. Apparently he hadn't heard what Arnaud had said. "After . . . the first attack, many people sent their children north. So suddenly I've got a hundred young 'uns ready to learn and no one to teach 'em." He sounded almost bitter about it.

"Well, I would think you'd rather have it this way than reversed," Arnaud commented. "A hundred men to teach and none to learn. The young would learn quickly and your problem solves itself."

"They certainly are eager . . . and sprightly, but that doesn't make up for experience, not when up against the sort of things infesting these lands."

Arnaud watched him take another long drink and his stomach growled with hunger. "What about men like Martin? He can't be the only one left."

Nicolas stared at him and swirled his glass. "No. No, to be sure he wasn't." He took another sip. "At first we had a lot of skilled, very angry men here in the city. Good for nothing in their state but fighting. And when that – that coward of a king would do nothing, they went out themselves after the beast." His relaxed mood was suddenly tense again. He threw the glass back and drained it quickly.

Arnaud didn't have to ask if any of the men came back.

"Lord, it's been . . . it's been eleven years since the dragon appeared, and that man is still king," Nicolas said more to himself than to Arnaud. Bitterness was etched his features now.

Arnaud suspected this was the sort of man Theobus had referred to. Conspirators against the king.

"He's truly done nothing?"

"Acts as if there's no problem. Won't hear any pleads or complaints. Nothing. He's either blind or bewitched."

Bewitched. This seemed to trigger something in Arnaud's mind, but he couldn't recall what just now.

"Is he a fair king otherwise?" Arnaud asked, genuinely curious.

"He was, I think, in the beginning. He had all these ideas about uniting the people of Faie and France to dispel prejudices. Well, the dragon did that for him," he said bitingly. "Lately he concerns himself only with this city; hardly even does that right, and what good will it do if the dragon just comes and burns it into the ground?" He scoffed and shrugged a shoulder. "Maybe I can't judge him as a man. I should know losing a wife and son changes you. But the last thing we need now is an indifferent and cowardice king."

Arnaud said nothing. He agreed with Nicolas, but didn't want to openly take sides in a dispute he knew so little about.

"Well, you apparently saved his life. Has he told you anything? Or for that matter what he was doing alone in the forest that day?"

Arnaud did not detect any anger or regret in the man's voice. He must not be one of those who despised him for saving the king's life. "Is there no obvious reason he might do such a thing?"

"None that I can think of. I heard that he was once fond of troll hunting, but that's strictly night sport." He shook his head. "Whatever he was doing, it was damned stupid. Besides wild animals, any of us could've killed you or the King and not known it 'till we went to retrieve the arrow." A sneer grew on his face. "That's just fine. We've got a King who hunts for sport but won't lift a finger where it counts." He rubbed the back of his neck and peered up at Arnaud. "In the one day you've been here, you've inspired every man you've met to take action where it counts."

Arnaud stared at him, confused by the sudden change of subject. Then he realized it wasn't a change.

"All we need is someone like you," Nicolas said. "Someone men will follow. We'd have a fighting chance against the dragon if we could band together under a strong leader."

Arnaud could tell this is what Nicolas had been aiming to say the whole time. "And no leader has arisen in all this time?" The thought was incredulous.

Nicolas shook his head. "The city's gone weak. There are no more fighting men and mothers will not give up their sons."

Arnaud leaned forward. "What about you? Don't you command all huntsmen of the city? You're a strong leader. Men follow you."

Nicolas shook his head. "Not like you. My men might follow at first, but they won't stay when the outlook turns bleak. And the farmers wouldn't come at all. You, on the other hand— there's a certain quality in you. I can see it now. Something that commands respect."

It wasn't the first time Arnaud had been told this. Years ago, before his mother's bout of illness, the captain of the Nitona said the same thing. He'd been all but promised the position of first mate in a year's time and eventually the captaincy. Arnaud knew he could charm people, but he didn't want to now. Not when the lives and livelihood of half a country were in the balance.

"Besides," Nicolas continued, "I'm too old for such a thing."

He got up and walked over to the cabinet, presumably to refill his glass, but instead he wiped it and put it away; seemingly disappointed by Arnaud's reaction to his intimations.

Arnaud carefully weighed his words. "They wouldn't . . . listen to a stranger." Ever since his conversation with Queen Brighde about the dragon, this issue had been on his mind. But it wasn't his problem. He didn't live here. Right?

"This city is divided," Nicolas stated quietly, still facing the cupboard. "It is something I hate to see, and perhaps might've prevented, but alas, it has happened." He turned and faced him. "These people need an outsider to unite them; to show them how to channel their anger and resentment against a common enemy instead of towards each other."

Arnaud stared at the scrubbed table. This was too big to commit to without deep contemplation, and he couldn't do that here.

"Arnaud." Nicolas's tone was very grave, yet somehow desperate.

His last card, Arnaud thought.

"I can't pretend that I don't know what that sword means."

Arnaud looked up slowly and studied the intense expression on the man's deeply lined face.

"It's a sign. And even if you don't believe its meaning, I can tell you my young men do. They'll stand behind it." He gestured vaguely. "The farmers I couldn't say."

Nicolas watched him for a long time and Arnaud knew he wanted his commitment to the situation, but Arnaud wouldn't give it. Not yet. Not until he was absolutely sure.

Nicolas heaved a great, weary sigh. The deep sadness returned behind his eyes. "You came here for this." He reached into his pocket and pulled out the emerald necklace. "Do you know who it belongs to?" He held the stone delicately in his hands and studied it with a professional air.

"The Queen of Caen," Arnaud replied, remembering Queen Brighde's words. He stared at it. "I claim it, as she died long ago."

Nicolas watched him silently for a long time, as if contemplating whether to give the necklace to Arnaud or not. He suddenly passed it to him across the table.

"Before you decide anything, I want—I *ask* that you speak with M. Maeve Conmidhe."

"Who is that?" Arnaud asked taking the necklace, feeling its familiar warmth and weight.

"She will have something to say to you which I am certain you will want to hear."

Arnaud nodded and pulled the pendant over his head, tucking it into his shirt. He liked Nicolas, his heartfelt sincerity, his selflessness in placing his own pains aside to help others. And Arnaud believed what the man had said. Nonetheless, there were many things to consider. His family for one. Yet, he wanted to offer some reassurance that he would at least consider the man's words.

"I will speak with her," he said, "and I will make a decision, Nicolas, but I cannot promise it will be the one you want."

Nicolas nodded. "Well, I guess that's what I'll have to take, then." He slapped his hands on the table and pushed himself onto his feet. "You need a place to stay." He pointed to Arnaud's bag. "You're welcome to stay here. I don't expect Marc and Gaspar will be back tonight. I'll tell them to take you to Madam Conmidhe when I see them tomorrow."

Arnaud nodded his thanks and Nicolas left the room in the same forlorn state he was in when Arnaud first saw him.

***

Chapter Eleven

"Good morning, sunshine!" Arnaud opened his eyes blearily to find Gaspar's grinning face swimming hazily above him. He blinked a few times until it came into focus. "It's a beautiful day!"

Arnaud peered around at the room he'd slept in. It took a moment for all the details of the previous day to organize in his thoughts. He caught sight of Marc standing over him as well.

"It is a beautiful day," Marc said seriously.

Arnaud sat up gingerly, extremely aware that the slices in his back had indeed reopened during the bar fight and were taking their time re-healing.

"And we're wasting it," Gaspar insisted impatiently. "Thought we'd start your training today."

"Training?" Arnaud swung his feet carefully over to the floor.

"You're to be a hunter, right?" Gaspar asked, and then without waiting for a reply commented to Marc, "Training is the best, isn't it? Just hand 'em a bow and shove 'em out there. Hilarious."

"But we won't laugh at you," Marc said.

"Of course not." Gaspar clapped Arnaud hard on the back and he couldn't help wincing in pain. Neither seemed to notice. "But we're wasting daylight. Let's go!"

Arnaud blinked at them. Now that he looked closer, they didn't exactly look like brothers. Marc was a few inches taller and had much sharper features than Gaspar, but both had the exact same shade of light brown hair. That must've been what threw him off.

"Sorry to disappoint, but you'll have to find another poor trainee to laugh at today," Arnaud said pulling his boots on slowly. "I'm supposed to speak with someone called M. Maeve Conmidhe. Nicolas said you'd take me to her."

Gaspar stared. "That doesn't sound like him."

"Are you sure he said Maeve Conmidhe?" Marc asked.

"Yes." Arnaud stood to his feet and began strapping his belt on. "Why?"

"She's scary." Gaspar admitted unabashedly.

Arnaud couldn't help snickering. "What do you mean?"

"I mean she gives me the heebie jeebies."

"The spinner never leaves her house," Marc said in a mysterious voice. "Just spins cloth all day and night, like a spider spinning a web."

Arnaud half expected him to howl like a ghost for effect. "The spinner?"

"Well, that's what we call her," Marc replied casually.

"Fondly." Gaspar added.

"And that's why she frightens you? Because she never leaves her house?" Arnaud managed to refrain from laughing again.

"No," Marc said. "Because she's an enchantress; an old one. One of those faie with pure blood or whatever."

"She could turn you into a toad in the blink of an eye. No one would ever know."

"They say she worked for King Phillip over a hundred years ago."

"Plus, you've got to admit, it looks a bit dodgy to stay cooped up in your house all the time."

"Wait! She worked for King Phillip?" The sword he wore at his side had once belonged to King Phillip. Was that Nicolas' plan? To try and get him to familiarize himself with the previous king? It was a weak strategy.

Marc nodded. "And no one's seen her since his untimely death, save a select few who bring supplies or sell her yarn for her."

"Wait. I've seen her," Gaspar said.

"You have not."

"Yes, actually, I have. Really, I have." He looked at Arnaud.

"When?" Marc asked in a disbelieving tone.

"You had that fever that one time, remember? And I was tired of sitting around so I went for a walk." Gaspar squinted his eyes, as if trying to remember. "I was strolling down that deserted street over by Speleain's, minding my own business, and suddenly I saw her. She was coming towards me from the opposite direction."

"What did she look like?" Arnaud asked, wondering if she was an old woman like he pictured her, or younger looking as Jaques, Sorcha, and King King Eochan were. All of them had lived an extended lifespan.

"I couldn't see," Gaspar replied. "It was dark and she was wearing a hooded cloak."

"Of course she was," Marc said. "And I suppose she spoke to you? Told you something incredibly meaningful?"

"No. I skirted to the other side of the street before she could hex me or something."

Marc rolled his eyes. "You probably just saw Madam Despensier on her way back from the sick house."

"Don't roll your eyes," Gaspar said angrily. "I know what I saw and it wasn't Madam Despensier! Plus I felt all . . ." He cringed and rolled his shoulders. "Strange when she passed. I bet that magic just clings to her. Swept over me as she walked by."

"Well, I bet it was the fever finally coming on to you," Marc said. "As I recall you got it only a few days later."

"Shut up! It happened."

"Either way." Arnaud interrupted before Marc could retort. He didn't think he could handle any fistfights right now. Not with the state his back was in. "I'm to speak with her. So let's head out." He waved his hands gesturing for them to leave the room.

***

"Well, here it is," Gaspar said.

Arnaud found the little cottage on the edge of the city to be a bit anticlimactic. They stood before a very small wooden home that had been painted bright red with a door and shutters as yellow as the hundreds of large daisies sprouted over the ground, covering it like a blanket. But despite its extremely innocent and cozy appearance, Marc and Gaspar looked as if they would prefer to be hiding behind the bushes.

"Hey, Gaspar," Marc whispered in a mocking tone. "Maybe she'll recognize you and invite us in for tea."

Gaspar hit him on the arm. "So, there it is," he said, quickly turning to Arnaud before Marc could reply in kind.

"Wait, you're not coming in with me?" Arnaud teased.

Both shook their heads warily. "You're on your own, man," Marc said gravely. "Good luck."

Very slowly and dramatically Gaspar added. "And stay alive."

Comforting words before they turned back down the street, Arnaud thought with a chuckle. He strode boldly up to the yellow door and knocked. After several minutes there was still no answered so he opened the door slowly and called "Hello!"

He didn't want to startle the old woman who appeared to not receive many visitors, but no one answered. Surely she was at home. Where else would she be? He stepped inside and called out again.

"Hello?!" Nothing.

He looked around the small place. The inside was as pleasant as its exterior with bright colors and little vases of flowers situated generously and strategically about. He seemed to be standing in a sort of entryway, but the house was openly built and from where he was Arnaud could see into several quaint little rooms.

"Hello?!"

He crept forward through the shadowed hall. The cherry wood was shaded black and gave the appearance of a tunnel winding out to bright little rooms. The first was empty.

"Is anyone here?"

The second room was pretty and charming and just as empty, but the third presented a clutter of un-hung paintings, loose wool and thread and a large spinning wheel at the center of chaos. A middle aged woman with long black hair streaked with grey hunched at the wheel, entirely involved in spinning vigorously. He hovered outside the doorway, unsure if he should enter the room or not. It seemed rude to just stand out here and watch her, but entering might pose a hazard. He could see himself tripping over something and running headlong into that wheel.

"Hello. I don't mean to—" Arnaud began, but was interrupted by the woman's jump and shriek of surprise. The shrill cry caused Arnaud to flinch, causing a shock of pain to travel through his back.

"What do you mean startling someone that way?!" she said, holding a hand to her heart. "And in my sickly state!"

"I'm very sorry, but—"

"Are you Madam Despensier's boy? What happened to your face?"

Arnaud raised a hand to cover his swollen cheek. He kept forgetting about that.

"Where's my wool?"

"No," Arnaud said firmly, somewhat annoyed by the woman's interruptions. "Nicolas asked me to speak with you. Perhaps I should come back at another time."

But she didn't seem to be listening to a word he'd said. She was staring at the emerald sword, twinkling in the sunlight from the room's window. Arnaud laid a protective hand on it as her eyes filled with comprehension.

"Ah." She rubbed arthritic hands together. "I'll tell you the same thing I told King Eochan. I'm retired." She gestured her point. "Absolutely retired and I'm not coming out of it again." She continued more softly. "You must understand, it's not personal. Performing enchantments is just too great an emotional strain. Too much for an old woman." She shook her graying head. "You'll have to find someone else to help you with . . . whatever it is you need help with."

Arnaud had so many questions regarding this long statement he hardly knew where to begin. Come out of retirement again? And why had King Eochan needed the help of an enchantress? He gaped and she blinked sympathetically.

"Uh . . . no. That's not what I'm here for. For some reason the hunter Nicolas wanted me to speak with you. But if it . . . bothers you I'll leave at once." He moved a foot back into the dark hallway to make his point.

"Just to speak with me?" She sounded disbelieving. "I can't think of anything I might know the king of France wouldn't."

Arnaud shook his head. "I'm not the king."

She glanced at the emerald. "Then what are you doing with his sword?"

"I'm—"

What was he doing with it? Last night he'd told Nicolas he claimed the pendant and sword as there was no one else to claim them. On reflection that hadn't been entirely accurate. Yet, if he wasn't actually going to try to help these people, shouldn't he hand the sword and the pendant to someone who would? After all, they deserved a chance to find a man willing to lead them. Right?

But he couldn't do that. Arnaud felt strangely connected to the sword. He realized with a pang that he could never give it up willingly. Maeve stared at him a long time with large round eyes. Arnaud thought she looked like a bird.

"I see," she said. Her manner and tone became solemn. "And the dragon is still flying? Murdering? Terrorizing?" Arnaud nodded. "I see," she said again.

She stood slowly to her feet. Arnaud was surprised by her considerable height. She'd sat crouched like a little old lady at the wheel. "Let's go sit at the table."

She moved with the slowness of age as Arnaud followed her out of the room, pondering her total change of disposition. At first impression she had seemed very loud and spirited. But now that the shock of his sudden appearance had worn off she was quiet and watchful.

They entered a sort of kitchen, bright and sunny yellow, now contradicting her grave demeanor. She took a seat at a small square table in the middle of the room and Arnaud sat across her. His eye caught on a tray of scones sitting by the window and his stomach growled. He wished she would offer some and then dismissed the thought. He took an empowering breath and studied the woman to direct his thoughts away from

215

hunger. She had the appearance of a middle aged woman, but he could tell she was much older. Her brown eyes were deep wells, carrying the spark of many years.

"I'm afraid I have not properly introduced myself." She pulled a little shawl around her shoulders as if she were cold, though the temperature with the sun streaming in through the windows was quite warm. "I sometimes forget these things when the pain in my joints is unbearable, like it is now." She gave him a wry smile while rubbing her hands. "My name is Maeve Conmidhe. Though perhaps you are one of those boys who like to call me 'the spinner'. I hear some of them go so far as to say I prick my victims of enchantment with a spinning needle." She sounded amused rather than offended by this. "Ridiculous. Though I did prick my own finger on it the other day. Quite a nasty cut, too."

Victims of enchantment? "I have not heard it said," Arnaud told a polite half-truth.

She nodded with a twinkle in her eye, insinuating she knew he had.

"I am not from here." Arnaud explained. "My name is Arnaud Lemarin."

She stared at him a moment with her round eyes. "Well, Arnaud Lemarin, I rather think I like you already." She folded her long hands formally on the table. "I will try my best to answer any questions you may have."

Questions? Was he supposed to prepare questions? He didn't even really know what he was doing here. "Well," he said pulling the emerald pendant out from under his tunic, "Nicolas was holding this when he told me to come see you. Do you know anything about it?"

Arnaud could see her eyes fill with recognition, then joy, then sadness; all in quick succession. She gestured impatiently for him to pass it to her. He pulled it over his head, watching her face closely.

"Where did you find this?" Maeve asked. Her voice brimmed with remembrance and her eyes pooled with tears.

"I . . ." he shrugged. Arnaud knew Andre had stolen it, but who had he stolen it from? And where had they gotten it?

"I threw this into the sea." Maeve's voice quavered with emotion. "To the mermaid's, for safe keeping. She wouldn't dare follow it there. It was my last act before coming back home." She ran her fingers lovingly over the chain and jewel, lost in memory.

"This was in the mermaid's care?" Arnaud asked. Could it be possible that the mermaid he'd seen, or the merman that had healed Andre, had slipped it into his bag when they were stranded on the rocks? An amazing wave of guilt swept over Arnaud. It was possible that Andre had been telling the truth when he said he'd never seen it before. And Arnaud had stubbornly never considered believing him.

Maeve nodded, still staring at the emerald. "I shudder to think what my niece had planned for this. This was my queen's jewel. She wore it proudly about her neck all those years. I couldn't let her take it."

"Your niece is an . . . enchantress as well?" Arnaud asked, trying to follow the woman's clipped memories.

"A family trait, unfortunately," Maeve said. "There are just a very few of us left now." She paused, staring off into nothing, absentmindedly caressing the chain of the necklace.

Arnaud gazed over at the fireplace. A beam of sunlight shot directly into the ashes and the dust floated

217

up like a shimmering wall. "And the woman who lives near the mountains," he asked, looking back at her, "Sorcha. She is . . . one of those few?"

"How do you know my niece?" Maeve demanded. "How do you know where she lives? Have you been to see her?" She was urgent, angry. Her big eyes grew even wider.

"Not intentionally," Arnaud said a little confused. Her niece? He had obviously made it through Sorcha's clutches intact and with both emeralds. Was there some other danger of his having been there that he was unaware?

"You made no deals? No bargains?" Maeve pressed, still urgent. "She made no undeniable threats?"

"I—she threatened my family, but I was assured she had not the power or means to locate them," Arnaud replied, now experiencing urgency and anger himself. "Was I wrong in believing this? Can she . . . read minds or something?"

He was prepared to dash out the door and set out immediately for Calais if her answer spoke otherwise. He would never forgive himself if his family came to harm where he might've prevented it. Memories of the vision Sorcha had invoked, of his mother and sisters dying painful, bloody deaths swam dizzily before his eyes. Was he so foolish to believe Jaques' word?

"Not that I know of," Maeve said and Arnaud almost sighed with relief. "Yet, she was not blessed with the gift of long life and somehow she obtained it." Her thin lip curled in disgust. "A terrible, unnatural version defying the gods themselves." She shook her head. "Who would want it anyway? A lonely life filled with the aches and pains of age."

"And how did she acquire it?" Arnaud asked. Was not the capability to read thoughts obtainable then if immortality was?

"I couldn't even guess the science of it," Maeve said, shaking her head. "She must've learned it from that warlock she went to study under when the king refused her education."

This last comment seemed to spark some remembrance in Arnaud, but it was fuzzy and he couldn't recall exactly. Why? Why couldn't he remember?!

"This . . . warlock," he asked, attempting to quell his sudden frustration and move on. "Was he a tall, thin man with a grey moustache?" The man he'd dreamed of while fitfully sleeping in Sorcha's dungeons; who'd tortured the little girl with black water. Could it be him?

"The man you describe is an extremely power-hungry warlock," Maeve said. "I suspect he was behind much of the . . . terrible things Sorcha did." She looked mournful, ashamed. "That was his cabin in the mountains, before she did away with him, too." She swallowed hard and stared down at the emerald. "She was a sweet little girl at one time; curious and very proud, but never power-hungry or evil. That didn't happen until she went to the mountains."

Birds chattered and argued in high voices out the open shuttered window. Their cheery melody contrasted with the conversation. A black thunderstorm would've suited better.

Maeve heaved a deep sigh. "But now, I don't know. She has committed unforgivable crimes."

Arnaud thought for one frightening moment the woman would break down into tears. He didn't know what he would do then. But instead she passed him the necklace over the table. "This belonged to my Queen Alana. A woman of my own blood. And I loved her dearly." She took another shuddering breath. "You will try to get it to her daughter, won't you? She would've wanted that."

Arnaud took the pendant. "But . . . her daughter is dead." He told her as softly and considerately as he could. Was he truly the first to break to her this news? Even if the princess had survived Sorcha's blood bath, almost a century had passed. She would've died of natural causes.

"The—the dragon?" Maeve was dangerously close to tears now. Her voice was broken up with small, scattered sobs of emotion. "I had hoped—prayed— that my enchantment was strong enough."

Wait. What? "Enchantment?" Arnaud asked.

"My sleeping enchantment," Maeve said. "King Phillip had paid me to protect his daughter. But there are so few . . . so dangerous are dragons. They have capabilities I know not." She placed a hand despairingly over her face. "It must be why Sorcha called up the beast. Oh, vengeful girl!" She pounded a fist weakly on the table.

"A sleeping enchantment? That would last against time? Against anything else?"

Maeve seemed to realize that all he'd said was conjecture and visibly calmed down. She wiped her eyes with the palm of her bony hand. "Against a dragon? I don't know."

But Arnaud wasn't really listening. She was alive! She was alive. Arnaud thought he had always known it was her, the princess. Nothing else could do her justice. It had just never quite registered in his numb, preoccupied mind until now. And she was alive, somewhere, waiting for him!

"Where is she? Where did you perform the enchantment?"

"The castle," Maeve said, her wide, puffy eyes fixed on his face. "They'll all still be sleeping in the castle if my work has held. And if—"

"And how do you break the enchantment?" Arnaud cut her off.

"The emeralds." Maeve gestured to the pendant gripped too tightly in Arnaud's hand. "Only the emeralds can dispel the sleep."

"Why?" That seemed a dangerous countermeasure. What if the sword had never been found? The pendant had stayed lost to the sea? Or if Sorcha had succeeded in obtaining one of them? Would she be lost forever in dreams, or murdered by the same enchantress who had destroyed her parents and her kingdom?

"It was King Phillip's orders to protect his daughter. Only his presence could awaken her. All else who tried to enter the castle would fall into the sleep themselves. I've often wondered if going up there, falling into the sleep myself, would have helped my state."

"Protect her from what?" Arnaud asked urgently. Ye gods, trying to get answers from her was like pulling teeth!

"Sorcha's, or rather that warlock's threats." She shuddered. "I was present for one of them. Delivered by a peasant whose ear had been maimed and eye had been gouged out in some sort of punishment or practice." She covered her face, once again mournful. "Oh little Sorcha…" She moaned.

"So this enchantment was how he protected her?" Arnaud felt anger rise within him. This man had been a king! He should've sent her away from any danger, out of the country! He should never have left her alone, guarded only by some flimsy magic! He took a deep breath. Calm. "The castle. That's where the dragon is,"

221

he said slowly, forcing himself to sort out the facts he knew. He realized now why Nicolas had sent him here.

"They're drawn to magic. I—I don't know …" Maeve faltered. She wiped her eyes again and then gestured to her tear stained face. "I'm sorry. The emotional strain. It's . . . somewhat permanent." Sighing again she said, "I do hope the enchantment's held. Genevieve is a darling girl." She closed her eyes as if in pain.

Arnaud nodded slowly. He bit his lip, somewhat regretting how harsh he'd been with the centuries old woman. "I apologize, Madam Conmidhe, if I have caused you any pain." He spoke gently and then stood to his feet, impatient to leave; to take action. "I will leave you now. But I hope to visit again sometime, if that's alright."

She smiled genuinely. "If my health allows, I would like that very much."

***

Arnaud forced himself to take slow, steady steps through sunny streets. He was aware of people pointing and whispering as he passed, while others were too busy in their moment's work to spare a glance for the heralded emerald sword. Arnaud wished they were all as preoccupied, but he did not let it distract him. His mind ran over the old woman's words again and again, as he passed quiet, little houses, processing information.

But really, only one thing the elderly woman said mattered to him. She was alive! Genevieve. He said her name softly. Everything else was trivial in comparison; just an insignificant blur.

She should be alive. She might be alive. He told himself firmly. Any number of things could've happened to break the enchantment. But he could not deny the hope that was swelling in him, or the joy, or the fierce determination to find some way, any possible way, to release her from this spell.

It was indeed a strange compel for a woman he had never actually seen. And yet it did not feel strange to him at all.

He switched over to the facts and logistics of the situation. He must somehow get past the dragon. No. That wasn't right. He must kill the dragon. It was the only way to completely ensure her safety. But kill a dragon? Arnaud had never even seen a dragon. He knew he couldn't do this alone. He knew that the young men of Ardgal would join him as Nicolas had suggested. But it would be misleading to establish himself as their leader only to abandon them when his own desires: the death of the dragon and the safety of Genevieve, were met.

His stride had lengthened, quickened, and had brought him back to Nicolas' house, now deeply shadowed by the setting sun. He walked past. Marc and Gaspar's good-humored prattle and Nicolas' pressings would be a difficult environment to process everything he heard this day.

But he was finding it difficult to process anyway. How could he guarantee the results he wanted? The simplest, most logical solution would be to fall into the role of king. But he couldn't do that lightly. His conscience wouldn't allow him to accept that role unless he was absolutely certain he could follow through with it.

Could he be the man the people of Ardgal needed at this uncertain time? Could he lead them in their fight to overcome an oppressor, and then successfully guide them in rebuilding a city and restructuring a government? Such a thought was daunting. In truth, he had little more than charisma to offer them.

He twisted through the darkening city, brooding. Each turn displayed deserted streets, hushed but for soft wind and the pad of his worn boots. He looked up to find stars popping into existence through the bountiful leaves of intertwining branches.

His thoughts drifted back to Genevieve. No matter what he had to do, he wouldn't leave the city without her.

"Monsignor! Monsignor, did you know—" A tall someone gripped Arnaud's shoulder and pulled him around. "Arnaud!" A pleasantly surprised Theobus exclaimed. He grinned widely with recognition. "Hey, Monsignor!" He teased then pulled on Arnaud's shirt. "You're bleeding through your shirt, Arnaud. Did you know?"

"Theobus!" Arnaud was also surprised to see the man again so soon. "What are you doing out so late?"

"I should be asking you that. No one's trying to kill me, I don't think." He tried to hide a mischievous smile. "I've just been to the White Horse."

"Oh, they let you back in there, did they?"

"Of course they did," Theobus said as if he'd already forgotten the brawl. His black eye hadn't forgotten. "You're really bleeding though, Arnaud. Come on. I'll take you to Grainne's place. She'll fix you up." He pushed on Arnaud's back to propel him along. Severe pain ensued.

"No, really, I'll just rewrap it myself later," Arnaud said, gritting his teeth against the pain and digging in his heels. Grainne and Theobus were worse than Marc and Gaspar for gabbling. He would never be able to think and sort his thoughts out there.

"Do you want to bleed to death?" Theobus demanded, pulling on his arm. "Well I don't want you to, and Grainne's likely to bludgeon me if she finds out I met you in this state and let you go. Besides, your friend is there with her already, the annoying stubborn one."

"Andre?" Arnaud said surprised. "Shouldn't he still be at the Great Hall?" It had only been a day. He himself had obviously not even healed completely.

"I was just following orders," Theobus said.

"The king's orders?" Arnaud asked, trying to keep anger from his voice. King or no king, they'd had an agreement. Arnaud had half a mind to go break in to the Great Hall and steal some important documents just to spite him.

"Who else?" They began walking, Arnaud picking up speed in his anxiousness to see Andre. "Hey, slow down, Arnaud! You don't even know where you're going!"

After a quick jaunt they arrived at the small house. Arnaud's first impression of Grainne's home was clean. Small and clean. It was one story with four rooms, housing very little furniture, but there was not a cobweb or speck of dust to be seen.

Arnaud let Theobus lead the way to the kitchen where his aunt was. Arnaud hoped the familiar sight of her nephew might soften the blow of his current state: bloody and bruised. Her outrage was more considerable than he'd expected.

"A bar fight!" She scolded in a tone dangerously close to screaming. "What were you thinking?!" She bullied him painfully into a bedroom, very un-nurse like; and proceeded to pull his shirt off and thrust it at Theobus before he could even protest.

"Man, you go through these," Theobus said, starting at the bloody rag.

"Look at this! Cuts and bruises all over! And half-starved again, I see! Ribs sticking out everywhere." She pushed Arnaud down on a bed. "You sit still. And don't get any blood on my quilts!" She huffed out of the room, leaving him breathless but chuckling at her hilariously fiery temper.

He looked around the room, leaning forward so no blood would drip on her precious quilts. There were two beds.

"One day. I can't leave you alone for one day without you getting into some kind of trouble."

"Andre!" Arnaud smiled. The invalid hardly looked like one anymore. His face was still a bit pale under a shock of brown hair, but his breathing was normal, his voice strong. "How are you doing?"

"Better than you," he said, eyeing Arnaud's back. "What happened?"

"Well, what happened to you?" Arnaud asked seriously. "Did the king say why he made you leave the Great Hall?"

"They caught him wandering the corridors." Theobus strode into the room with a fresh shirt. "I'm to say you won't get any more after this." He tossed the shirt on the bed beside him. "Grainne hopes it will inspire you to behave."

Arnaud nodded to Theobus and examined the fresh shirt. "Add it to my tab."

"Tab?"

"I still owe you for that drink." He turned to Andre before Theobus could reply. "Wandering the corridors?"

"I was restless . . ." Andre protested apologetically, "I didn't think going for a little walk qualified—"

"Andre." Arnaud shook his head in mock shame. "All the work I went through . . . and weren't you supposed to be sick?"

"Oh, you're off starting bar fights and I can't take a little walk?"

"I'm much healthier than you are." Arnaud laughed.

"Well..." he gestured to Arnaud's oozing back and purple bruises. "Clearly."

"Hush!" Grainne bustled into the room with an armful of clean bandages. "You need rest." She pointed an angry finger at Andre, "And quiet!"

"I know," Andre mumbled, clearly chastised.

Grainne grumbled extra loud as she cleaned and rewrapped Arnaud's wounds, but he suspected it was largely in part due to her frustration at him for reopening wounds she had so carefully nursed.

"Now," she said tying the last bandage extra tight causing Arnaud to flinch. "You are going to lay there and rest for a week. Yes, a whole week!" She scolded before Arnaud could even catch his breath. "I'll get a guard if I have to. Those swords don't ward off infection. King Eochan made that mistake a couple years back and almost died. Lay down! Whatever it is that's so urgent with you will have to wait until you're healed... *Completely* healed," she added, as if to cover all her bases. "I'm not doing all of this again, and I don't mean to start having patients die on me. Especially not you."

"I'll let Nicolas know," Theobus said as he stood to leave the room.

"Why? How do you even know I've met him?" Arnaud asked.

"Everyone knows," Theobus said matter-of-factly.

"Gossipy town." Andre added.

***

Chapter Twelve

That week would have been torture, complete torture lying on that bed, staring up at the ceiling, if Andre hadn't turned out to be surprisingly good company. The poison seemed to have aged him several years. Or perhaps Arnaud had just never paid proper attention to the young man before.

"So are you going to do it?"

It was Arnaud's fifth bedridden day and Grainne seemed happy with his progress. Hopefully happy enough to let him out a day early. He felt like a prisoner again, cooped up away from fresh air.

"What, the spice trade?" Arnaud asked, confused. They'd been tossing an apple back and forth and discussing French economy.

"No, the . . . dragon thing." Andre seemed uncomfortable, like he wondered if he should be asking such a question. "Gossip, you know. Theobus was saying something about that sword and the dragon and the king . . ." He tossed the apple.

Arnaud caught it and examined it in his hand. He hadn't actually made a decision yet, despite constant pondering. There didn't seem to be a right decision. He stared at Andre and decided he could trust him.

"I don't know," he said, tossing the apple up and catching it. "I kind of wonder if we haven't been through enough: if you've been through enough, if my family's been through enough. Maybe we should just settle down here and live quietly, while there's still work to be found." He tossed the apple to Andre, adding to himself: after I've released Genevieve from that enchantment. "Let someone else deal with all of that." He watched Andre carefully, wanting to gauge his reaction.

Andre caught the apple looking even more uncomfortable. "But—" He threw the apple back.

"What?"

"Look, what if . . . what if all of this, all of the stuff we went through with the mermaids and the bear and everything, what if all of that happened just to get you here?" He spoke quickly as if he'd been thinking about it for a long time and just wanted to get it over with.

"How do you mean?" Arnaud asked, trying not to sound skeptical. He tossed the apple.

"I mean everything you've told me. It all . . . fits," Andre said. "You were forced to leave Calais; you made it out of that witch's place alive, you just happened to save the king's life." Andre sounded amazed himself. "And how many times did we almost die, but didn't?"

"But that was only because of the sword." Arnaud argued.

"Yes, but the sword, Arnaud. What are the chances that you would find the sword and the necklace, and end up in Ardgal at this time?" Andre pressed. "Even the bar fight and running into Nicolas… It all fits too perfectly."

"What are you saying?" Arnaud asked, feeling like he should understand but didn't.

"I'm saying what if . . . what if God brought you here to help these people? You can't ignore something like that."

"God?" Arnaud held the apple. God was a big, all powerful, omniscient being. You had to go through channels to reach him. He might deal with a priest, but Arnaud had guiltily avoided churches. Still, he wished he could believe what Andre was saying. That God knew what he had been through; that there was such a purpose in his life. "You know I was joking when I suggested you join the monastery. Have you become spiritual since the last time I saw you?" He tossed the apple.

"Don't say it that way," Andre said and rolled his eyes. "But yeah, kind of." He continued without shame. "Listen, you fought death, Arnaud. I faced it square on. It slapped me in the face, hard, and sent me back." He threw the apple hard. It stung Arnaud's hand. "You can't go through something like that without changing . . . or questioning at least."

"But if it was God, why would He be so cruel?" Arnaud posed honestly. "To put us through all of that? Surely he could find an easier, quicker, less painful way to get us here."

"None of the important things are ever easy." Andre said. "And maybe . . . well, we do know this country's problems first hand now...I'm just saying neither of us should be alive now. But we are. And everything feels . . . planned." He tossed the apple. "Just consider it, will you?"

Arnaud could tell he was serious. And maybe he was right. There were an awful lot of coincidences; far too many to ignore.

"I'll think it over," he said solemnly, nodding.

"Thank you." Andre seemed genuinely relieved. "Hey! I was gonna eat that!" He protested loudly as Arnaud took a huge bite of the apple.

***

Arnaud did think it over. For the next two days he couldn't stop thinking it over. Every time he tried to push it aside, regard it as false or ridiculous, the idea came back stronger. If God did know about him, He wasn't leaving him alone.

But it was a reassuring idea. Extremely comforting to believe someone would always be with him, by his side. If it was real. If he could actually believe it. And he badly wanted to believe it. With God and

Genevieve, Arnaud knew he could go through with it.
He could rule these people. He could bring the country
back to order. It would be difficult, a struggle all the
way, but he could do it.

And so, early in the grey morning of the eighth day
he'd spent at Grainne's, he decided to. He'd healed
beautifully, she said, and Arnaud believed it was high
time he moved on. With the sword at his side, he
stepped out into the street, ready to leave. It was as if a
path were laid out under his feet. That in itself was
entirely reassuring. He knew what he needed to do.

***

"M. Bhain sent me here. I'm looking for work."
Arnaud stood out under pouring skies, holding Andre's
old bag over his head as a makeshift shelter. But the
rain was so heavy it did little good.

"M. Bhain?" The burly young man at the door
asked skeptically. "You don't look much like a
farmer."

"I'm not," Arnaud said, blinking rain water off of
his eyelashes. He shifted his weight, hoping the man
would invite him in. The rain was surprisingly cold.
"But I'm strong and a fast learner. I desperately need
work. M. Bhain said you were looking for a hired
hand."

The man eyed him suspiciously, his gaze resting on
the still red mark under his eye. Arnaud stood his
ground, hoping he wouldn't label him as a hunter. The
sword was well-hidden anyway.

"Let him inside, Lucas, before he catches cold," a
feminine voice said from behind the man, but Arnaud
couldn't see who it belonged to.

Lucas turned back to glance at the girl, whoever
she was, and then moved aside to let Arnaud in, still
scowling.

"Thank you." Arnaud stepped inside after shaking the water from his cloak and wiping his boots. He ran a hand over his face to wipe excess water off, flinching when he accidentally pushed on his left cheek bone. Why did he keep forgetting about that? It was still quite sore.

"Not at all," the feminine voice said. Arnaud looked up. An extremely pretty girl with long blond hair and bright blue eyes stood alone in the room. She smiled at Arnaud, but upon catching sight of Lucas's grim face, turned and walked into another room.

Arnaud was surprised by their melee, but said nothing. "You are Lucas Adamar?"

The man nodded once and then gestured to the doorway the girl had disappeared through. "My sister, Collette."

"Arnaud Lemarin." Arnaud held out his hand, and after a second's hesitation Lucas shook it, a suspicious expression still plastered on his face.

"You came late, Arnaud." Lucas said, striding over to sit at a table that reminded Arnaud of the one at his home in Calais. He followed and sat down. "I have most of my plowing and seeding done already. I'll be able to use help nearer the harvest, but that won't be for several months."

"There must be something I could do until then. What about your winter crop? You will be readying the plow for that soon. I can get it ready. What about weeds and animal care?" Arnaud pressed. He didn't much care which farm he worked on, but he had a good feeling about this place, despite Lucas's suspicious scowl. "You might use an extra pair of hands."

"Possibly... if I knew what sort of skills you possessed. Were you a hunter?" The man asked flat out. But Arnaud could detect no hatred or disdain in his voice. Perhaps the feud was mainly one-sided. That would certainly make things easier.

"I was a fisherman," Arnaud said just as bluntly. "And at one time a deckhand. Unless there's a lake of fish somewhere around here, I don't think my finer skills will much matter. But I think you'll agree strength and agility are generally useful assets."

Lucas made no reply in ascent or descent. His expression remained a blank. "What are you doing here?" He asked, and the rephrased the question. "What's a fisherman doing in Ardgal?"

"There was no work in my hometown," Arnaud said honestly. He sniffed and waited for another question, but Lucas only stared at him calculatingly. "I've come here to find a way to support my family back home." Arnaud hoped to help his case by relating to the man in some way.

"And where is 'back home'?"

"Calais."

"Calais is hundreds of miles from here." Lucas's tone implied he didn't believe a word Arnaud was saying.

"Hundreds of miles and no work to be found. Likely caused by the dragon." Arnaud tried to study his reaction without appearing to do so.

Lucas only pursed his lips and silently studied him. There was a slight reaction to the dragon, but the farmer wasn't buying it. This was business and Arnaud could tell the man was skeptical of him though he had (mostly) told the truth. A northerner looking for work must be unusual in Ardgal. No man would intentionally move closer to the dragon.

"I can't pay much," Lucas said at last. Arnaud sighed, feeling like he just passed an extremely complex test. "At least not until after the harvest."

"Right now I'll take anything I can get."

Lucas studied him again, and then glanced at the door Collette had gone through. "You'll sleep in the barn."

The barn turned out to be nicer than Arnaud had expected. Lucas and Collette were poor by Ardgal standards, but compared to what Arnaud possessed, they were rich. There were three barns, one for housing the wheat or rye once it had been dried, one for the livestock, and one much smaller that was used for storage of tools among other things. More like a shed than a barn, Arnaud thought.

But it must've once housed livestock. There were six dusty stalls and one of them was entirely cleaned out but for a very small, worn cot. Perhaps where previous hired hands had slept.

Arnaud was too used to sleeping on muddy, rock-filed earth so wasn't picky. He slumped heavily down on the bed (but not too heavily to disturb his even yet tender back) and tossed his bag and newly wrapped sword on the dirt floor. Moonlight shone through a rugged hole in the roof at the far end of the building. He stared around at the dusty clutter of the unused, barely lit room. It would work.

He lay back, exhausted, and tried not to focus on anything. He stared over at the unplanned sky light. From this angle he could see stars poking through slowly separating clouds. It would likely be clear skies tomorrow...

***

He was outside in a bright garden at a wedding; a very small and intimate wedding, with only fifteen or twenty guests. Arnaud couldn't recognize the guests, couldn't exactly see their faces. But he could see the bride, a very pretty girl he didn't recognize, and he knew the groom. It was Marc.

Arnaud felt like laughing. Why was he at Marc's wedding? He didn't think he really knew the man that well. Nevertheless everyone seemed happy. Marc and the bride were certainly smiling. He might as well join them. It felt like a while since he'd smiled.

***

The work was much harder than Arnaud had anticipated, but he refused to let Lucas see this. From dawn each morning he was out in the fields, walking along lines of sprouting rye, crouching down to uproot unruly weeds. Up and down, up and down the long rows of the square fields, until the muscles in his back ached and his legs and arms were numb from sheer repetition. Those first few nights Arnaud suffered the hot pain of discovering sore muscles he never knew he had. But the work got steadily easier and not all of it was foreign to him.

Collette took care of their two horses, numerous chickens, and tended the garden by herself. Arnaud grazed the oxen and set traps for little animals that might come along to nibble the green rye. Sometimes he skinned the voles and rabbits found in the traps, or butchered and de-feathered a chicken for dinner. Once he ran an errand in town for Collette, but that was more a favor than part of his work. It gave him a chance to see Andre, hear how his early training as a hunter was progressing, and speak with Nicolas.

But no matter what he did, Lucas worked alongside him just as hard or harder. And though the man hardly ever said a word, Arnaud could tell he didn't regret his decision in hiring him.

"Here." Arnaud stared at Lucas's outstretched hand, more than a little surprised.

The three of them were sitting down to a dinner of trap rabbit and potatoes. Lucas hardly ever spoke during meals, and then it was only to comment on

235

something his sister had said. The only time he said anything to Arnaud was in the fields when he was giving a direction or command.

"Two francs," Lucas said as Arnaud held out his palm to receive the coins. "I said I wouldn't be able to pay much at first. I'll make up for it after the harvest."

"You can just wait until then if it'll be—" He was going to say 'easier' but he knew that would offend Lucas. "I mean, I'm not in hurry or anything."

"Send it to your family," Lucas said, watching him closely.

Arnaud nodded. He wanted to. Not an hour went by that he did not think of his mother and sisters and the hardship they must be going through. They would have expected some earnings, or even just word of how he was doing. But all trade and travel had long been cut off between Ardgal and Calais due to the dangers of the lands. There was no way to get it there.

"Yes, I'll . . . try." He picked up his fork and speared a potato.

"Or you could use it to go buy a new pair of boots," Collette said to make a point.

She'd been leaving comments about his boots every day for a week now. She was right. They were ridiculously worn to the point where Arnaud could almost feel his toe sticking through the leather. But spending money on a new pair was not something he was about to do.

"Fine," she said a little huffy. "I'll patch them for you."

She stood up from her dinner and walked over to the door where Arnaud's mud-caked boots lay. Lucas and Arnaud paused their eating and stared at her.

"I was hoping you would ask me to patch them, but I see you're just as stubborn as Lucas." She picked them up gingerly, touching as little as possible, and carried them into the next room. A moment later she reappeared and sat herself at the table as if nothing unusual had occurred.

"But . . . my feet," Arnaud said still staring. "What will I wear to the barn?"

"It's a warm night," Collette said coldly, taking a bite of potato.

Lucas looked at him and shrugged.

***

There were few leisurely joys to be found on the farm. Arnaud spent the entirety of the day with exception of meals, doing hard labored chores and working in the fields from dawn to dusk. Sleep became sought after not only for rest, but for looked forward dreams of Genevieve.

However, the southern country was almost beautiful enough to make up for the painstaking and repetitious work. Arnaud stared out one day over the flat rye and barley fields. Multiple shades of fresh green stretched out for miles until they hit the sweeping hills and grey mountains. Arnaud leaned against the livestock barn taking a small break before heading off to check the traps. He wiped sweat from his brow and took a deep breath of the cool breeze. He could get used to this. If only the dragon hadn't come to these lands. He would go waken Genevieve and they would live quietly together somewhere like this. Growing rye, planning for the harvest, just living simply, happily.

"Taking a break, are you?" Collette trotted up on one of their brown horses. "You know those traps won't reset themselves." She teased.

Arnaud stared at her in shock. He didn't know why he hadn't noticed it before. He recognized Collette from one of his dreams. She was the bride in Marc's wedding. Her hair had been different; down and

237

flowing rather than braided as it was now, but it was her.

"Why are you looking at me that way? Is something on my face?" She reached up and rubbed a cheek.

"No. No, it's nothing." He couldn't help smiling. "Hey, you look pretty good on that thing."

"'That things' name is Blanche," Collette said, feigning anger.

"Well, excuse me." Arnaud held up a hand and strode over. "Hello, Blanche." He petted the horse's neck. Blanche arched her neck and nuzzled into his chest.

"Whoa, she likes you." Collette laughed as the horse moved closer to Arnaud. "Have you ever ridden?"

Arnaud shook his head. "I've ridden a donkey."

Collette laughed. "That doesn't count."

"A cow? Is that closer?" Arnaud laughed as well. "She's older, isn't she?" He commented, noticing the wealth of grey hair flecking the brown.

Collette nodded. "She was my mother's." She stared at him a second, her smile fading a bit. "I could teach you. To ride."

"Well, you know, those traps won't reset themselves." Arnaud grinned.

Collette rolled her eyes and laughed again. She reminded Arnaud strongly of his sister Clarice. "After your important work of course. Oh, do let me," she said. "It's not as much fun riding alone. And Crespin hardly ever gets ridden."

"Maybe." Arnaud patted Blanche one last time before going off to check traps.

But Collette didn't give up so easily. She spoke to Lucas that evening about the horses, and continually reminded Arnaud for a week and a half, until he finally gave in and got on a horse. Marc is going to have his hands full. Collette is one determined lady, he couldn't help thinking as he climbed onto a jittery Crespin's back. But then remembering what Marc and Gaspar had been like, she would have her hands full too.

"So, we'll take it slow, okay?" Collette circled him on Blanche. "We'll just—"

And then Crespin's growing agitation suddenly climaxed. He reared up onto his hind legs, throwing Arnaud backward onto the ground. Collette doubled over in stitches of laughter.

"I'm sorry," she said still giggling. "He hasn't been ridden in a while."

Arnaud sprang up and climbed right back onto Crespin's back. By god he wasn't going to be shown up by some horse!

"There, see?" Collette smiled. "You're doing well already."

It was a challenge, bending that horse to his will, but Arnaud reveled in a challenge. Especially in the weeks to come when they were to begin the tedious work of preparing the winter field for planting. Lucas was able to borrow a new plow with the promise of loaning his oxen, and Arnaud found himself many hours in the field either pushing his weight down on the handles to dig the blade into the earth or steering the oxen while Lucas was at the plow. Arnaud was grateful for almost daily pre-dawn rides through the pasture to loosen his muscles and clear his thoughts. Collette often joined him, claiming she had little to do while her bread dough rose.

"Wow, you're pretty good on him," Collette said one morning as they stopped to give the horses a break after a good run.

They sat on the animals looking out at the mountains, breathing deeply the cool thin air. Arnaud appreciated that air. Though the coming day would be hot and thick, the morning was pleasant. Cooler than it had been a week ago.

"Well, you know, I had a good teacher." Collette bowed dramatically and awkwardly on the horse's back. Arnaud chuckled. It looked ridiculous. "And a good horse." He leaned forward and patted Crespin's neck.

"He is a good horse." Collette agreed. "My father was just breaking him in before— Anyway, Lucas finished breaking him." She readjusted Blanche's mane. "I can't ride him, though. He won't listen to me."

"You taught me on a unruly horse?!" Arnaud asked incredulously.

"He's not unruly! He's just stubborn." Collette said. "He only listens to Lucas." She gestured in exaggerated graciousness. "And now you."

Arnaud narrowed his eyes. He shook his head slowly at her, and Collette tried to suppress a chuckle. They fell into silence staring out at the mountains, the light of the not yet fully risen sun spanning out around their jagged ridges. The horses huffed and stamped impatient to move now that they had rested.

"I guess I just can't see Lucas riding a horse," Arnaud said, patting Crespin's neck again. The man was so grave, and riding was such a leisurely thing.

"Oh, he's very good," Collette said. "Always used to beat me in races. Of course," she scratched Blanche behind the ear, "Blanche is such a sweet old girl she probably let him win." She sat up straight, smiling. "He's a fair swordsman too. You should ask him to demonstrate."

Arnaud stared at her. "A swordsman?"

She nodded. "He's probably out of practice now though."

Arnaud's mind spun. Why would a farmer need to know swordsmanship? Where would he have possibly learned it? And when would he, considering their strenuously filled days.

"My father taught him." Collette read Arnaud's bewildered expression.

"Do . . . many of the farmers around here know swordplay?" Perhaps that was the farmer's common mode of defense in these parts.

Collette shrugged. "Some. But Lucas was going to be a soldier before father and my older brother David died and there was no one else to take the farm."

"A soldier? Under King Eochan?"

Collette nodded as if this were obvious.

"But, King Eochan—"

"The king doesn't keep armies anymore. He keeps guards," Lucas said.

He had walked silently up behind them through the trees of the pasture. Arnaud detected anger in his voice and wondered if it was directed toward the king and his increasing passivity; or Arnaud and Collette's conversation. Lucas strode over and laid a hand on Crespin's cheek.

"There's someone here to see you," he said stroking the horse's face. There was definitely anger there now. "They're waiting by the barn." He glared up at Arnaud who nodded and dismounted.

"See you later, Collette."

He hurried back to the buildings, wondering who would be here to see him and why. His mind wandered to Andre, the only person he actually knew well enough in these parts.

"My god, you've gotten big!"

Arnaud reached the house to find three men standing together waiting for him. Marc and Gaspar gazed on him with dropped jaws. The other he did not know.

Marc spread his arms wide and exclaimed, "You're huge!"

Arnaud smiled proudly. It was true. He had gained some muscle since the last time he'd seen them.

"What're you—" He stopped and stared at the third man with them. "Andre?" It was his turn to gape.

"Boy's kind of shot up a bit, hasn't he," Gaspar said proudly, clapping his arm around Andre's shoulder. He had to reach up to do so. Where Andre had been a few inches shorter than Marc and Gaspar, he was now a few inches taller. He looked older, much older than he had a few months ago in Boulogne, even a few weeks ago at Grainne's.

"I honestly didn't recognize you." Arnaud walked up to him. Andre was still shorter, but gaining. "Does it make it harder to camouflage?" He joked leading them into the tool barn. He was fairly sure now that their presence was what had put the anger into Lucas's voice, and he didn't want to make his mood worse. Arnaud had to work all day with the man.

"He's damn sneaky," Gaspar said as they entered the dusty stalls. "And he won't tell us how he got that way; moves through the woods without making a sound."

Marc and Gaspar stood together and stared at Andre, as if imploring him to tell his secret. Andre glanced at Arnaud. If the boy hadn't told them what he'd done for a living, Arnaud wasn't going to.

"His arm still needs a lot of work though," Marc said.

"How've you been, Arnaud?" Andre asked, changing the subject. "Any luck recruiting?"

"Haven't lost any brains since you've been here, have you?" Gaspar asked seriously.

"Well, I'm gaining trust anyway," Arnaud said, ignoring Gaspar and walking over to open the shutters of a small window. The sun must be rising fast now, already the barn was stuffy. "I've spoken with several other farmers and they all seemed open to the idea." He watched the three of them: Marc gazing out the window, Gaspar examining the clutter of dusty objects, and Andre leaning against one of the stalls staring back at him. "Why are you here?"

Andre opened his mouth to reply, but Marc cut him off. "Who is that?"

Arnaud glanced out the window and then back at Marc. "That's Collette. And that's her brother."

"I didn't know they had . . . Collette's *here*?" Marc was at a loss for words

Gaspar walked over to see Collette climbing down from Blanche and leading her into the barn. He snapped his fingers in front of Marc's face. "Focus."

"Nicolas sent us to tell you something," Andre said as the other two were preoccupied.

"Tell me what?"

"The boys want to hear what you have to say about all of this." Gaspar left Marc by the window and joined Andre and Arnaud.

"Hear what I have to say?" Was he supposed to make a speech or something?

"We've been doing our best to recruit, but they want to hear it from you," Andre said.

So he did have to make a speech.

"Apparently we don't inspire them enough," Gaspar said with a hint of bitterness. He pulled a rusty training sword out of the rubble. "Hey, what's this doing here?" He clumsily swiped it through the air.

Marc, who had torn himself from the window when Collette disappeared into the barn, strode over and removed the old weapon gently from Gaspar's hand. "You'll hurt yourself."

"When?" Arnaud asked. "Where?" He'd never had to speak to a crowd before, but it didn't sound too difficult.

"The harvest feast would be a good time," Andre said. "They'll all be gathered then: hunters and farmers all together."

"Hunters go to the harvest feast?" Arnaud asked. That seemed a bit unusual.

"Well, this year we're sort of crashing," Marc said.

Arnaud stared. "You're what?"

"King Eochan didn't call our feast or *your* feast rather, for the slaying of Orson," Gaspar said. He waved a hand nonchalantly. "So we're going to combine them."

That really didn't sound like a good idea. Nor for what they were trying to do.

"Don't be nervous," Gaspar said, misinterpreting Arnaud's expression. He patted his arm. "You'll do fine."

"Look, if you don't normally attend the harvest, now is not the time to start," Arnaud said sternly. They needed numbers for what they were going to do. Any man in Ardgal who would be willing to volunteer. The last thing they needed right now was a rekindling of the feud that seemed to affect both parties.

"Oh, we normally attend," Marc said.

"We just don't normally display a ten foot bear," Gaspar said, grinning.

"Then don't start." Arnaud pleaded.

"Nicolas has discussed it with a few respected farmers," Andre said.

"How could you possibly know that?" Gaspar demanded, disbelieving.

Andre shrugged his shoulders. "Sneaky."

244

"Alright, well, tell the men I'll be at the harvest feast," Arnaud said moving them back toward the door.

He'd spotted Lucas outside the window leading the oxen to the field. They had only maybe a day of plowing left. Two now, considering how late it was already.

"I'll answer any questions they have then."

Just after the harvest would be an opportune time to leave for Genevieve anyway. Much of the hard labor would be done, stores would be plentiful. He'd lay his plans on the table for them at the feast, and then give them a few days to process his ideas. Arnaud didn't want anyone signing up who was influenced by ale or high spirits. These men needed to know what they were getting in to.

They walked out of the dusty barn into the bright sun, already halfway up the sky. It would be a long, hard day trying to make up for lost time.

"I don't know how you do it, Arnaud," Gaspar said, gazing out at the fields. "Working in a place like this with—"

"That stops right now." Arnaud cut him off.

"What?"

"Your comments about farmers." Arnaud turned and stared slightly downward at the two of them. "I won't hear them anymore."

Marc and Gaspar studied Arnaud's expression with some shock. After a moment they nodded.

Arnaud nodded back. "I'll see you all at the feast then."

The three of them turned to leave. Arnaud clapped Andre on the shoulder as they went. "Take care of yourself, Andre."

"And you."

***

Lucas did not say a word to Arnaud for an entire
week. The work was long and tedious as they finished
up the winter planting. But Arnaud suspected the real
reason for the man's silence was anger. About what he
couldn't tell.

"I hope I didn't get you into any trouble." Arnaud
sat in the livestock barn milking the cow one morning.
Collette walked in.

"Trouble?" Collette's voice sounded confused.
From around the cow's considerable mass he couldn't
see her face, but heard her digging in the log pile behind
the cow.

"The other day, when we were speaking about
Lucas and his equestrian abilities."

Staring at the cow's fur patterns Arnaud could hear
Collette chuckle.

"And sword fighting abilities," she said, walking
over to his side of the animal looking disheveled. She
wielded a squealing kitten with black and white fur. "I
thought you were going to ask him to show you."
Arnaud raised an eyebrow. "I used to like watching him
practice." Collette explained.

"Then why don't you ask him?" Arnaud replied,
laughing at the kitten flailing its little legs in terror.

Collette folded its legs into her hands and held it
close under her chin. "I'm too busy," she said.

And what do you think I am? Arnaud thought,
considering their respective duties at the moment. "Too
busy rescuing kittens?" he said over the methodic buzz
of milk hitting the tin bucket.

"A vital task." Collette laughed, and again Arnaud
was reminded of Clarice. They were both ridiculously
stubborn and they laughed the same way and often. Or
Clarice used to anyway. He wondered if his sisters ever
laughed now. "Maybe he can teach you and you can
have sparring matches." Collette held the kitten against

her cheek and nuzzled it. The animal squeaked its disapproval. "I know Luc would like that."

Arnaud had considered this. Learning how to wield the sword would be an obvious advantage, though he wasn't sure how much it would help against a dragon. Still, stumbling upon one of the few farms that housed a swordsman, even an out of practice one, was quite a coincidence. Or not a coincidence, Arnaud thought to himself, thinking of Andre.

"I'll think about it." Arnaud's tone clearly stated 'don't interfere.' He patted the cow's rump and carried the half-full bucket out of the barn.

But he never got the chance to talk to Lucas until later in the afternoon. "Arnaud, someone's waiting to see you."

"Who is it?" Arnaud asked standing up from his work. The wind whipped his hair and tunic around wildly.

"She's waiting in the house," Lucas said, "Best hurry."

She?

"I'll finish this." Lucas gestured to the traps Arnaud had been emptying and resetting. Arnaud nodded, trying to read his expression but he couldn't. It didn't sound like Lucas was angry, but his tone was still a bit . . . off.

"Thanks," Arnaud said deliberately. Lucas must at least be peeved that visitors were drawing him away from his work again. What a great hired hand he was, always receiving visitors!

As he walked, Arnaud's mind sifted through the women he knew in town. Grainne was the only name that came to mind. Maybe she'd come to check up on him. Make sure his back was alright, that he was eating properly. It sounded like something she would do.

It wasn't Grainne.

247

Collette was sitting at the table with Queen Brighde chatting animatedly over a cup of tea. Well, Collette was chatting anyway. She reminded Arnaud of a nervous squirrel.

Queen Brighde stood to her feet when she saw Arnaud.

"Hello," Collette said breathlessly, standing as well. She looked very nervous.

"Hello, Your Highness." He bowed slightly. "You wanted to see me?" Arnaud tried to guess why she was here. He suspected it had something to do with King Eochan. Somehow the King had heard what Arnaud was doing, saw it as a threat to his position, and had sent the Queen to talk him out of it. The idea disgusted him.

"Yes." Queen Brighde glanced at Collette. "I was hoping we might take advantage of this weather. May we walk?"

The weather was nothing to want to take advantage of. Arnaud knew she was trying to spare Collette the humiliation of being asked to leave the room in her own home.

"Of course, Your Highness," Arnaud said and opened the door for her. Collette curtsied as they left.

Queen Brighde didn't speak right away. They walked in silence, out toward rolling pastures. Strong winds periodically whipped about their hair and her skirts. Arnaud glanced at her, wondering what she was thinking, what she was going to say. The last time she saw him he was arguing with the king.

"I am sorry about your friend having to leave the Great Hall. His name is Andre. Am I correct?" Queen Brighde finally began.

Arnaud nodded.

"I was glad to hear Grainne took him in. That he was taken care of." She sounded apologetic. Arnaud wasn't sure how to reply.

"I've . . . heard about you." Her tone was utterly grave. They were well upon the first hill, the little house just in sight below. "What you are planning."

Here we go, Arnaud thought. "Your Highness." He turned to face her. "I am sorry if what I'm doing offends you. But I won't stop. Something needs to be done to protect the people and I think—" He fell silent. He had been going to say: 'I think King Eochan knows that too,' but it would serve no use to enter into an argument at this point. Instead he said, "I'm sorry."

Queen Brighde stared out at the tall grass, flowing in the wind like the rolling sea. "You misunderstand me," she said quietly, tucking a loose curl behind her ear. She turned and looked steadily at him. "I want to help you."

Arnaud furrowed his brow. He shook his head slightly. "Help me? But your—"

She nodded, her proud gaze meeting his.

"You know what this will do. What it means if we are successful?"

"I know." She continued to look up at him steadily. "But this is important. And I don't think . . . he can." She shook her head and swallowed, obviously in great agony.

Arnaud bit his lip. He hated to interrogate her in this state, but there was a great chance her answers could prove helpful. "Forgive me, Your Highness, but I have to ask. Do you know why King Eochan won't go after the dragon? Is there anything I don't know? Anything that he might've kept from the people?"

Queen Brighde blinked several times, attempting to ward off forming tears. Arnaud pretended not to notice. "He . . ." she swallowed again; her voice was almost a whisper, its tone almost lost in the wind. He could sense her great pain. "There's something he's not telling me. But I don't think it has to do directly with the dragon. King Eochan wouldn't let all those men go blindly to their deaths if he knew anything that might help them." The tears were gone before they had fully come, and her voice was stronger now, clear and deliberate. She stood very straight with her shoulders back, composed.

Arnaud nodded. Then perhaps they did stand a chance.

"Is there something, anything, you can tell me about the beast? Any physical traits? How large, how far it can spit fire . . ."

He could tell by the look on her face she didn't know. That was unfortunate. He would need facts to form some strategy. It was suicide to face an opponent, especially one so formidable, without researching it first.

Queen Brighde shook her head slightly and looked away, down at the little white house.

Perhaps she could get him audience with the King. King Eochan likely had statistics of the beast whether he chose to use it or not.

"But I know ones who would have that information." Queen Brighde continued to stare at the house. Collette was chasing chickens away from the garden. "You remember I told you there were others who were given enchanted gems, other races of beings?"

"Yes."

"In times of . . . widespread crisis, where more than one race is affected, the High Council may be called to discuss options; band together if necessary." She glanced at him. "The last High Council was held a century ago, after the death of King Phillip. I can call a

High Council but you must preside. King Eochan will not."

Arnaud watched her for a long moment, regal and proud. He wondered how much her help to him would affect her. How would King Eochan react when he found out what she'd done?

"Is there any way I can do it? Could you show me how to . . . call the High Council?"

Queen Brighde shook her head. "You are not yet a leader of your people. They would not acknowledge you."

"Then why would they acknowledge me as presider?" Arnaud asked.

"You will have to convince them. You have the sword and the pendant, after all."

Arnaud tried not to look concerned for her. He hated to come between the king and his wife. "You're sure they will be able to help in some way?" If there was any uncertainty he would forget about the whole thing.

"I am sure that without the help of the High Council you will have very little chance of success."

Arnaud bit the inside of his cheek and stared out at the rolling green pasture. Lucas had let Blanche and Crespin out into the field to roam.

"Alright." Arnaud nodded at her. "I accept your help, Your Highness. Thank you."

Queen Brighde smiled sadly.

They began walking back toward the house in silence. Thick clouds had formed, making it look and feel like night was nearing, though it was still early in the day. Arnaud entered the residence deep in thought; contemplating what he'd gotten himself in to. Everything rested on him: convincing the men to fight, convincing the High Council to acknowledge him as their leader, procuring aid for the struggle. It was a heavy weight to bear upon his already weary shoulders.

"You are here to gain the confidence of farming men?" Queen Brighde asked, her tone now lighter, if it could ever actually be considered 'light.'

"Yes," Arnaud replied. "I spoke to an elder farmer about the situation and he sent me here. Apparently Lucas is . . . a very respected man."

Queen Brighde nodded. "I've seen him several times in the castle as a representative reporting crop yields. He is a very proud man." She took a deep breath, "Forgive me for contradicting your methods, but I believe you're going about this the wrong way."

"In which way, Your Highness?"

"The only way to gain M. Adamar's respect and confidence is to be straightforward with him."

Arnaud had often thought this. It was how he would want to be treated. The facts up front; no tricks or secrets. But the man who'd sent him to Lucas had warned him to gain the farmer's trust before imparting who he was and what he planned to do. He told Queen Brighde so.

"You doubt me?" Her clear eyes stared at him.

"I must follow what I think best, Your Highness."

Despite the king's heated threat about Arnaud entering the castle again, he offered to walk her back to the Great Hall. Collette offered to fetch one of the horses for her to ride, but Queen Brighde refused every courtesy. She left them the way she came, alone and on foot. From the house they watched her go. Then Arnaud gave Collette an exasperated sort of smile and exited the front door to finish his chores.

He suddenly changed his mind and yelled to Collette. "Collette, where is Lucas?" He'd decided to take Queen Brigade's advice to be straightforward with Lucas and ask for his help.

252

"Why?" Arnaud could tell Collette was desperate to question him about the queen, but managed to hold her tongue.

"I want to speak with him."

"I believe out in the barn, sharpening scythes."

Ah, perfect. Arnaud stepped out of the wind into the crop barn warily. Lucas was a quiet man, but he sensed the farmer would murder for something that meant enough to him. Would Arnaud's omission of information qualify?

Arnaud forced these ridiculous notions out of his mind and took a deep breath. The air smelled of stale hay and dirt. He didn't see Lucas until he came striding up to him out of the dim shadows cast by a large lantern.

"I want to speak with you," Arnaud said immediately. He was surprised to see Lucas's expression more relieved than expectant.

"I already know." He said turning back to the lantern and the table of freshly tuned tools.

What?! "You already know . . .?"

"I'm not an idiot, Arnaud, like your hunter friends think I am." Lucas looked squarely at him. "I know who you are. What you're doing. I've known since you first came here."

Arnaud stared. He'd known? "Why didn't you say anything?" He immediately regretted this question. He himself had said nothing.

Lucas shrugged and turned back to the lantern. "It's your own business."

Arnaud was so surprised he hardly knew what to say. "If you know what I'm doing then you know how important it is."

Lucas finished hanging a newly sharpened scythe on the barn wall and turned to look at him. Just look at him.

"I know it is a lot to ask for your help," Arnaud said evenly. "But I am asking."

Lucas stared at him a second longer and then turned to hang another tool. "What is it exactly that you want me to do?"

"Help me win over the farming community," Arnaud said frankly. "We'll need every man we can get."

"You're talking about going up against the dragon?"

Arnaud nodded.

"In defiance of King Eochan?"

"Yes."

Lucas scoffed and shook his head in bemusement. He turned, grabbed another tool, and walked over to hang it. "What else?"

"Teach me to fight."

Lucas immediately stopped what he was doing and snapped his head over to stare at Arnaud.

"Collette told me you know swordplay."

"She did, did she?" Lucas tried to act like this didn't bother him and continued to hang the tool. "Collette knows I haven't touched a sword in years. I'm in no condition to fight myself let alone teach someone."

"Anything you could show me would be helpful." Arnaud argued.

Lucas took his time walking back to the table, rubbing his hands together. "Wouldn't archery be more useful in this case?"

"Unless you will teach me both, I haven't time to learn archery."

"And you have time to learn the sword?" Lucas raised an eyebrow. "You underestimate its complexities."

"I work for you. I said I would stay for the harvest and I will." Arnaud explained. "Besides, I think I should learn to use the weapon that means so much to everyone here."

Lucas stared a long time at him; either studying his countenance to determine sincerity, or considering within himself. Well over a minute passed and Arnaud stared back at him, silently praying. If Lucas refused him then Arnaud had wasted two months of precious time. Three. He would keep his word no matter what and stay on for the harvest.

"How long would I have?" Lucas asked eventually.

"I hope to set out in two months."

"Two months!?" Lucas shook his head again in disbelief. He rubbed a hand over his chin. "I can't guarantee anything."

Arnaud nodded. "I know."

Lucas took a deep breath and nodded his head distractedly. "We'll start tomorrow. Before dawn."

***

Chapter Thirteen

It had been seven years since Lucas had held a sword, so Arnaud's daily lessons twice a day were filled with long breaks and mute pauses as he tried out different movements and methods. Sometimes he closed his eyes and mumbled to himself, attempting to remember different stances. A result of Lucas's rustiness was that he and Arnaud both felt the pain of training. Muscles strong under the strain of the plow were weak when it came to the movements of the sword. Balance and grip had to be entirely relearned as well as physical and mental dexterity and deftness. Their reflexes were tested again and again.

Both practice swords were broke within a week. After that, sessions became significantly more dangerous as they were forced to use real, sharp-bladed swords, and Arnaud could not use the emerald sword due to its protective powers. Lucas managed to dig two heavy broadswords out of the shed and fit both with old leather over the points and blades, so when they accidentally hit each other it only felt like being bashed with a club. Yet there was always the danger of the weapons poking through.

"Last night I remembered a technique David showed me." Lucas walked up to Arnaud fitting the leather strap onto his old sword. They'd begun practicing in the pasture when Collette voiced worry over her chickens in the yard. "The Posta Brina? No the Posta Breva . . .?" He shook his head. "Doesn't matter. You hold the pommel close to your body, blade vertical, and bend your knees." Lucas demonstrated. "To parry or thrust."

The morning was chilly, almost freezing. The light was still grey, not yet pink from the sun. Arnaud beat his hands on his legs to shake out numbness. It hurt like hell.

"Here, let's try it." Lucas raised his sword. "Swing at me and I'll parry away."

Arnaud nodded, lifted his sword, and swung out.

He could tell something was wrong before the blades contacted. The leather Lucas had strapped over the edge of his blade was swinging loose.

"Hey!" But it was too late.

Arnaud's blow knocked the cover completely off. Lucas thrust forward and Arnaud was too distracted by the leather to move out of the way. He gave an involuntary shout of pain as the blade entered his right arm above the elbow.

Lucas stepped back and stared, his mouth hanging open, his eyes wide with shock. Blood was smeared on the tip of his blade. The leather strap lay useless on the ground.

"Your—handkerchief! Quick!" Arnaud said.

He'd slapped his left hand over the wound and was pushing hard on it. He looked over and saw blood flowing out between his fingers. Blast! It hurt.

"Here." Lucas dropped his sword and ran over. He moved Arnaud's bloody hand and thrust his handkerchief over the cut. "Come on!"

Arnaud continued to press on the wound as Lucas grabbed his arm tightly and pulled him toward the house.

"Collette!" Lucas shouted as they came closer.

It took a moment for Collette to poke her head out the kitchen window.

"Bandages!"

Collette stared a second and then scrambled back inside. She was standing in her dressing gown with a pile of bandages sitting on the table when they entered the house.

"What happened?!" She asked with horror.

Lucas ignored her. He pushed Arnaud down into the chair and seized a bandage.

"I was stabbed." Arnaud told her with a wink. Lucas removed the handkerchief, now soaked in blood. "How bad is it?"

Collette leaned in close to peer at the gash. She clicked her tongue worriedly.

"I don't know," she said seriously. "We might have to cut it off."

Lucas laid a hand on his sister's shoulder and gently pushed her away. After he carefully examined the cut, he began to laugh softly. Arnaud had never heard him laugh before.

"I thought I'd killed you," he said as he tied the strips of cloth painfully tight.

"Worried you'd be short one for the harvest?" Arnaud forced a grin. It hurt almost as bad as the bear claws. Almost.

"I was worried what the people might do to me if I accidentally killed their champion," Lucas joked.

Arnaud managed a chuckle. He glanced over at Collette who was watching Lucas's dressing intently.

"I thought girls were supposed to be afraid of blood," he said.

He could remember once coming home with a bloody nose and Clarice running off in disgust. She'd been much younger though.

"Where did you hear that?" Collette challenged, putting her hands on her hips.

"Done." Lucas interrupted. "Can you move it alright?"

Arnaud tried to move his arm. It was extremely painful. "I'll manage."

"Good." Lucas stood up. "We have much work to do."

***

Arnaud walked leisurely through the gardens; alone with iris, lilies, and orange bumblebees darting among them. The sun shone brilliantly upon fluffy sheep-clouds, blazing down upon grass and trees weighted with melodious birds. He inhaled the clean air. This was the most peaceful place. It was like heaven.

To his knowledge, Arnaud had never been there before. But his feet walked the worn paths like they knew where they were going. He let them lead and allowed his mind to wander and soak up the serenity. For several minutes just listening to twitter and hum.

His feet stopped. He looked around to find he had wandered into a more contained garden, flourishing within its boundaries. He could see a stone wall smothered in ivory and beside it a white stone bench. And on the bench Genevieve sat watching two little boys chase each other among the flowers. Her dark hair was braided over her shoulder and tiny loose curls fell over her face as she leaned forward. One of the boys, a black haired fellow of maybe five had scampered up and was whispering in her ear. He looked very much like Anhault had at that age. Genevieve leaned back and smiled at the child, brushing a loose curl out of his eyes.

Her smile grew when she caught sight of Arnaud walking toward them. The little boy leaned in at her beaconing finger and she whispered back into his ear. And as Arnaud came closer, close enough to touch them, they both turned their heads in unison and winked purposefully.

Arnaud laughed deeply. Five years old and she'd taught his son to wink.

He opened his eyes. Stars were still poking through white clouds in the hole in the roof.

My son?

259

***

It rained the next day and the next. A fact which clearly agitated Lucas. The harvest was due to begin less than a week away, and the crops needed heat and air to dry. Unable to do much in the fields, they spent their time in the barn, cleaning out the stale hay and preparing the place for full stores. They also practiced in the barn's open space, out of the rain, away from Collette's animals.

"How old was Collette when your parents died?" Arnaud was considering how everyone he'd met in the past few months was orphaned. He'd been more interested in how old Lucas had been, but felt he couldn't actually ask that question.

"She was . . . eleven," Lucas said between blocks. "Hold your arm up a bit more."

Arnaud had been having a little trouble with the strength of his grip due to the wound. It made his left arm work much harder in cleaning out the barn and it made it work harder now. He grimaced in pain and tried the parry again.

Eleven. That was quite young. As young as Anais had been when their father died.

"What is going on between you and my sister?" Lucas asked very seriously between thrusts and slashes.

"Uh...*what*?"

"I mean what are your . . . intentions?" he rephrased.

Intentions? "I . . . don't know what you mean," Arnaud said truthfully. He gripped the sword with both hands and attempted a downward thrust Lucas had tried to show him. It was clumsy with only one grip.

Lucas looked surprised and confused. "You spend hours alone with her every day." Lucas halted mid-swing and stared. "What are—what are you doing?"

Arnaud stared back. "I . . . hadn't thought of it." Had he given the impression that he meant to court Collette? If so, it had been absolutely unintentional. As far as he was concerned she was Marc's wife and Genevieve was his. He'd somehow forgotten that wasn't yet common knowledge.

"I don't know what your customs are in Calais, Arnaud, but you have something to learn of Ardgal if you believe you can take advantage of a girl with no father and no chaperone." His face was flushed and angry and his hands shook.

He was referring to the horseback riding, and the ridiculous conversations he and Collette had when Lucas was still out in the fields.

"That was never my intention. I am sorry if I gave that impression." Arnaud said with feeling.

Lucas only continued to glare, his expression livid. He glanced down at his left hand grasping the sword too tightly. He visibly forced himself to place the sword on the median between remaining stalls.

"I will talk to her if—"

"Just leave her alone." Lucas snapped.

"She is like a sister to me." Arnaud explained. "In fact she reminds me of my own." He decided not to mention Marc. He had no idea how Lucas would react.

"You have sisters?"

"I have two sisters."

"Then you know." Lucas turned and walked slowly out into the pouring rain, leaving Arnaud feeling sick. He knew how he would react if the same were done to Anais or Clarice. He dropped the sword and ran an agitated hand over his face, thoroughly disgusted with himself.

***

At one time every available man in town was required to help with the harvest. Now, considering the prejudice of young hunters who refused the unintelligent labor, and the prejudice of young farmers who wouldn't have a bunch of wild vagabonds touching their crops, it was up to the farmers to harvest their own.

They worked in groups of ten, traveling from farm to farm. On a good day they were able to cover three fields. It was hot, hard work and yet satisfying to enter a cool house when the day was done. A great meal was laid out by the owner whose fields were worked that day, and Arnaud had a chance to speak with several of the men on trivial topics and to meet their families. At least they would recognize him when the time came to ask their help.

But he had no time to speak with Collette. To explain that any confusion he might've caused was accidental and to apologize. In fact, he scarcely saw her for the next ten-day, until the harvest was complete and the celebrations were due to commence.

They walked to the Great Hall where the festival was held. It would serve no purpose to take the horses when there were only two mounts and three of them. It began with a quiet walk in which Arnaud spent the time wondering if King Eochan's threat still stood. Being publicly tossed out of the festival by the king might cripple his cause.

"Ho, neighbor!"

Arnaud turned to see a man, his wife, and their three young children coming up behind them. The Fourniers whose farm they were now passing.

"Headed to the festival?"

Lucas, who was bearing Collette's basked of baked goods, nodded in ascent.

"We'll walk with you."

They waited for the little legs of the children to catch up. M. Fournier handed their own basked, a smaller one, to his oldest, a boy about nine, and picked up his youngest, a curly blonde headed girl of about three. He struck up a conversation with Lucas about a new plow that would save time and energy due to the use of wheels. Madam Fournier was busy with her two boys, smoothing down their hair and brushing off their dusty clothes.

Arnaud glanced over at Collette, checking her own pressed skirts for dust as they came closer to town. "Collette, I—"

"Don't." She gave a nervous little laugh that sounded more like a sob, and looked quickly down at her boots. Her complexion turned a bright cherry red. "I mean, you don't have to say anything. Lucas was just overreacting."

Arnaud nodded, and put his hands in his pockets. He didn't want to make her feel any more uncomfortable than she already did.

They walked in silence for a while, a more awkward moment Arnaud had never known. He'd never been in a situation like this before. Since his father's death he'd devoted himself entirely to work and taking care of his family. Not a thought or second to spare for girls. Not until Genevieve and the dreams, that is.

"I've never been to a festival," Arnaud said, attempting to lighten the tension. "What's it like?"

"Oh, there's food, and music, and dancing. It's quite a big thing."

He could tell she was falling back a bit into her easy manner. Perhaps he had not so much imposed upon her.

"Food and music is all very well," Arnaud said. "But I've never danced a step in my life."

"Oh, I'm not much good either, but it's fun," Collette said. "I'll defiantly join in if someone asks."

263

She suddenly blushed again. "I . . . didn't mean to insinuate that you—"

"I know," Arnaud said. Why did she have to read into things so much? Even her own words? Awkwardness had taken reign again, and the short remainder of their journey was solemnly mute.

Entering the Great Hall where the feast was to be held was like coming from a lifeless desert into a rainforest. Noise and bustling activity were the norm of the day. The room had floors enough for dancing, and walls and banisters enough for colorful drapes, flags and banners. People stood in groups, laughing and chattering loudly, signifying lightness of heart. It was a crowded and chaotic scene, but one Arnaud enjoyed immensely.

"Bring it to the table. Over here!" Collette said to Lucas, pointing to the heavy basket. Arnaud followed them through the winding crowd, mesmerized by the number of people and their general rowdiness.

"Ah! Lucas! Collette!" A middle-aged woman with a kind face walked out from behind the table of food, seized Collette and kissed her forcefully on either cheek. "How've you been holding up?" She leaned back and looked into Collette's face.

"Well, I had a question about that stitch you showed me."

"Lucas!" A gruff man seized Lucas's shoulder and turned him away from the table. "How've you been?!" The man didn't wait for him to answer. "Come on! The men are all over here." Lucas set the basket on the table by Collette. "Come on, Arnaud," he said.

They pushed their way again through the crowd. Arnaud, who was half a head taller than most, was intrigued by the number of pure white heads and pure black heads. Such hair colors were almost unheard of

264

in Calais. His own black hair had often been stared at and commented upon as a boy.

"Well, here!"

"Here's Lucas."

"Lucas, what do you think?"

A group of about ten farmers of various ages stood together in a group.

"What do I think about what?"

"About impertinent hunters," an older man with a scraggly beard said.

"What do you—?"

"Look." A younger man with a heavy black beard put an arm over Lucas's shoulder and pointed.

Arnaud followed their gaze up to the great skin and head of a bear pinned up on display. He immediately recognized Orson.

"Those boys are trying to get their part in the harvest festival," the old man said.

"Or take over," another said.

Arnaud stared at the skin, angry with Marc and Gaspar. Had they been lying when they'd said Nicolas spoke with an elder farmer?

"I see no problem with it," Lucas said calmly.

"You don't?" The farmers sounded surprised.

"They were awarded no feast in their honor of defeating this large standing threat. I for one believe it was deserved."

The men glanced at each other; a few of them were beginning to nod their heads.

"And Arnaud here is deserving of it," Lucas said, bringing Arnaud forward and clapping him on the back with more warmth than he'd shown in the past few days. "He rid these lands of a beast that snatches your sheep, Martin, and mauled your ox, Gilles, and your prize dog, Guiot."

Arnaud held his tongue, unsure if he should say anything. He hadn't known that he was helping these people when he killed the bear. He was only thinking of a stranger's life—the king's— and his own.

Apparently Lucas's opinion counted for a lot. The farmers stared at Arnaud now with new light in their eyes. They were nodding, agreeing; their gaze focused on the emerald sword.

"You're the one who wishes to speak with us after the festival?" One of the men asked.

Arnaud said, "Yes." And was relieved neither fear nor apprehension was detected in his voice.

"You will want to hear what he has to say," Lucas said seriously.

They nodded at him again, staring.

"One of the men spoke up with a hint of admiration. "So you slayed Orson? How did you manage—"

"You started that fight at the White Horse," another said, talking over him. "I was there. Got a nasty bruise too."

"Yes, yes you did, Colin." Arnaud recognized Theobus's voice before he saw the man coming up behind the farmers. "I believe I was the one to give it to you." Being a bit taller, he cuffed his arm around the man's neck.

"Heh, not likely," the young farmer said, removing his arm and tossing Theobus an annoyed look. But there was no hostility in it. Apparently Theobus, a member of the king's guard, was a neutral party to the young men's feud.

"Someone wants to speak with you," Theobus said pompously to Arnaud, ignoring the farmer's reaction. "I have come to steal you away."

Arnaud smiled. "Excuse me." He nodded to the farmers, feeling their eyes on his back as he left.

He and Theobus pressed through the crowd of laughing, chattering people watching twirling dancers.

"It's Marc and Gaspar who wish to talk with you," Theobus said, through Arnaud had already suspected.

When they finally reached them, Marc asked, "Was he soon enough to save you?" They moved to a corner, away from the dancers.

Arnaud felt incensed. "Remember what I said about your comments about farmers!"

"Alright, alright." Gaspar raised a goblet of wine in salute. He drank deeply.

"Hey, you came with . . . Collette?" Marc asked, standing on his toes to peer over the crowd.

"Yes," Arnaud said. "You should—" He started to say 'You should ask her to dance,' but Marc handed Gaspar his cup and walked toward the tables before he could finish his statement.

"Must be some girl." Gaspar shrugged.

"Some girl." Theobus agreed distractedly, looking through the crowd. "You know, I think I might ask Rosemary to dance."

"Oh, dear *lord*!" Gaspar cried.

"What?" Theobus asked wide-eyed.

"Will you *ever* stop talking about her?" Gaspar's face turned red. "Ask her! Quick! Before I do just to shut you up!"

Theobus squared his shoulders, thrust his drink at Gaspar and set off across the space of dancing.

"Here, Arnaud, take some of these." Gaspar handed two of the goblets to Arnaud. He drank from his own. "Looks like it's just the two of us now. That is, unless you've got your eye on someone," he said tactfully, peering into the crowd.

"No. Not here." Arnaud said.

"Not here? You've got someone back home?"

"Plenty of pretty girls here." Arnaud diverted the conversation, not even glancing at the crowd. "Sure you won't dance? I'll bet half of them only came because they heard you would be here."

"Well, they can't help themselves." Gaspar flexed a bicep with a wink. "Devastating physique." .

Arnaud couldn't help laughing. Compared to half the men here, Gaspar was positively puny.

"Here." Gaspar thrust his goblet at Arnaud and sidled off along the wall after some girl, leaving Arnaud alone with three half-full cups of wine. Arnaud started to yell at Gaspar to take his drink back then sighed and set all three goblets down on a table next to him.

He stared at the clapping, skipping and whirling crowd, not watching the dance, but instead counting the men. How many would join in the fight? Fifty? Twenty? He knew many of them would stay to protect their wives and children, and Arnaud couldn't begrudge them of that. Yet if their numbers were too few, they would end up like the parties of ten years ago and simply never return. Arnaud suddenly felt anxious to get started, to find out how many men were favorable to the idea of fighting.

"Take it easy, Arnaud!" Andre walked toward him along the wall. He took one of the goblets. "Don't you have to make a speech later? No one will take you seriously if you're drunk."

Arnaud clapped his friend on the back then said, "Hey, how tall are you now?"

Andre stood up very straight and managed to look Arnaud in the eye. A heavy tan nearly hid his freckles.

"Six feet one inch the last time they measured me. Nine inches in four months," he said proudly. "Grainne threatens to beat me if I don't quit growing and she has to tailor my trousers again."

Arnaud laughed. They stared out at the crowd for a moment as the musicians ended one song and struck up another.

"So, how is everything coming?" Andre asked seriously, turning to look at him. Arnaud was immediately struck by how much his friend had changed since they'd first met in Boulogne. He seemed so much older now, more serious. It was like looking at a different person.

"Well," Arnaud said. "We'll find out tonight. Any idea how the hunting men will react?"

Andre shrugged. "It's likely they will be with you. They're young, wild; few of them have any family at all."

"Nicolas said they would follow the sword if they followed nothing else."

Andre looked uncomfortable. "Some of them, yes, but I'm not sure about the deeply blooded faie. Their rightful king is of the rubies, not the emeralds. And I'm not sure how much the sword will count for anyway. King Eochan's been a rather poor example."

Arnaud bit the inside of his cheek and nodded. Andre was right. He couldn't rely too much on the sword.

"Of course, I don't pretend to know more about Nicolas's men than he does," Andre said.

"But I agree," Arnaud said seriously. "The last thing we need is an argument over the swords distracting from the purpose of the meeting."

And who knew which side would be right? Perhaps the enchanted swords were poor choosers of leaders. Old doubts began to creep back into Arnaud's mind, but he pushed them forcefully away. What did swords matter anyway? Genevieve needed help, and he would get to her one way or another.

"What about this feud?" Andre asked. "How serious do you think it is?"

"I don't know," Arnaud said. "Lucas, the man I work for, didn't seem to take part in it himself. But he was well aware of it, so there must be some prejudice among the farmers."

"Well, the feud is very strong among the hunters," Andre said.

The people crowded and whirled and drank, unaware of Andre and Arnaud's serious discussion in the corner. A group of three young women passed them, staring at Arnaud, whispering and giggling loudly.

"Have you heard anything about what might've started it?" Arnaud asked. "I have a hard time believing such hatred could rise based purely on a preference of profession."

"It has something to do with land." Andre took a conservative drink from his own remaining goblet. "I think perhaps hunters trespassed into the farmer's fields in pursuit of prey. Each party believed they were in the right. I tried to get Nicolas to explain it to me once, but he was extremely drunk and his view is likely biased."

Arnaud nodded thoughtfully.

"It's mainly the younger hunters who hold the feud strongest." Andre added.

"Those whose entire families were lost." Arnaud clarified. "They're angry at the dragon and at a king who will not protect them. They have nowhere to go with their anger but turn it on each other." He was remembering Nicolas's words.

Andre nodded but did not reply. He took another drink from his goblet.

A lilting jig ended its tune amidst a whooping and applauding crowd. M. Doraig, the fiddle player, and also city barber, took a bow and struck up a slower tune.

Arnaud could see Marc and Collette on the left side of the dance floor. He wondered how Lucas would react when he found out his sister had danced with the hunter three songs in a row and counting.

"So has your aim improved?" Arnaud asked lightly, half teasing.

"Yes, I am quite a prominent hunter these days," Andre said grinning. "Archery's really not as difficult as you might think. Would you like me to show you? You know, you'll need to be able to fight well if you're going to go through with this."

Arnaud hadn't gotten around to telling any of them about his broadsword training with Lucas. But the farmer had been right when he said archery would likely be a more useful skill up against a dragon.

"Yes, I think I—"

"Arnaud!" Gaspar stumbled over to them as if he'd spent the last three songs getting drunk. "Why aren't you out there dancing?" He wagged his eyebrows at a group of girls as he passed. They giggled at him.

"I'm doing this room a favor by abstaining," Arnaud said good-naturedly. He never learned to dance. There'd been no use for it. "What about Andre?"

Andre shook his head, his eyes wide with terror.

"Well, I know of at least ten girls who wish you," Gaspar said, pointing at Arnaud, "would ask them. In fact," he peered around as if to make sure no one was listening in, "I wouldn't go near Theobus if I were you."

"Why?"

"Because he's just discovered his sweetheart Rosemary fancies you over him."

"Who does?" Arnaud asked, bewildered.

"The barmaid, remember?" Gaspar said. "You started that fight over her."

Arnaud's mind jumped back to a few months ago. "Not . . . over her specifically." He stumbled. "Someone had to do something."

"Well, she thinks you saved her life . . . defended her honor . . . some nonsense like that. Anyway, it's put Theobus in a pretty foul mood."

Sheesh! Arnaud thought. Why did girls always have to read into everything? He hadn't been back to the White Horse once! He wished Genevieve were here, if only to lay any doubts about his availability to rest.

"Arnaud!" Andre gripped his arm tightly.

"Wha—" He followed Andre's eyes into the crowd.

King Eochan was striding toward their corner with several guards behind him. People were bowing as he passed. Gaspar sidled away as the king approached, but Andre remained where he stood. The King stopped in front of Arnaud. Arnaud bowed respectfully.

"I wish to speak with you," King Eochan said to Arnaud without preamble.

Arnaud nodded. "Your Highness." He wanted to say something less reverential but held his tongue.

"Alone." King Eochan glanced at Andre. "Let's go into the gardens."

Arnaud nodded again. He followed King Eochan back through the crowd, in front of the guards.

The gardens the king led him to were those Arnaud had seen before. No flora, only trees and short grass, and at this hour stars were the attraction rather than birds. He liked this place. It was peaceful.

The moment the guards shut the doors behind them, King Eochan spoke passionately. "My wife has called a meeting of the High Council with the idea that you shall be presidor."

"I take full responsibility upon myself, Your Highness," Arnaud said immediately before he could

272

continue. "You should not scorn Queen Brighde or her actions."

King Eochan stared at him. "If you would not interrupt," he said with a hint of anger, "I could tell you that I do not scorn her decision to help you. I agree with it."

It was Arnaud's turn to stare. "If you agree with her, Your Highness, why didn't you do it yourself?"

"I had my reasons," King Eochan replied shortly. "If the people knew them they may not judge my character so harshly."

"I wouldn't know how to judge the character of a man who denies care to innocent or ill men," Arnaud spat.

"I had my reasons for that too," King Eochan countered harshly.

"I would love to hear those reasons."

King Eochan sighed angrily and looked down at the ground. Arnaud could tell he was struggling to control his temper. "I wished to speak with you now of the High Council." The king changed the subject. "To warn you of their likely rejection of you as presidor. The centaur Constantin, and the dryad will be least receptive to your presence."

"Why don't you preside? You are the king," Arnaud said.

"I will not," King Eochan replied. He suddenly sounded sad or disappointed rather than angry. "I will not preside."

Arnaud felt anger at the man before him. "If you believe in this cause, and you won't lead it yourself, then you must help me to get there. You must convince them of my credibility."

"I am trying to help you." Echon stood up straighter. "The fauns, Phynnaeous and his wife Derae, they are your best bet. You will have the faie's

273

unofficial support, and if I am correct, after tonight you will have the beginnings of some sort of army behind you. If you can win over the fauns you may have a chance with the mermen and, if you're lucky, the centaurs may follow. And they, being a warrior race, would be the greatest aid to you."

Arnaud nodded. He didn't know how he was supposed to 'win over' the fauns, but he appreciated any advice. Yet King Eochan was hiding something, and Arnaud needed to know what it was.

"Why won't you preside? What are your reasons?" He pressed again.

"The High Council will be held in three days' time," King Eochan said with finality, ignoring his questions. "Queen Brighde and I will be leaving from here at dusk. We will expect you at that time, as you do not know where the High Council will be held." He turned abruptly and the guards opened the door for him to enter the deserted hallway of the Great Hall. He walked through it before Arnaud could say anything.

Arnaud stared at the now closed door. What did the King really want from him? He threw him out of the Great Hall not too long ago, and now says he wants to help him lead a High Council!

Arnaud closed his eyes; recalling images….He shook his head in frustration. Why can't I remember that dream? He turned and looked out at the trees and the stars. He knew it had something to do with King Eochan. That it would explain so many things. But he couldn't . . . grasp onto it. A breeze floated up and scattered black hairs across his forehead. He ran an agitated hand through them.

"What did he want?"

Arnaud swung around to see Andre coming through the door. He had a giant, roasted chicken leg in his hand. He tore a piece of meat off of it with his mouth.

"He wants to help," Arnaud replied, leaning back against a tree and looking up at the stars. They would always be there, so vast and distant. Looking on, but never caring who lived or who died. The idea was both comforting and disturbing.

"Help? Really?" Andre managed to sound surprised, confused and skeptical all at once. He bit off another chunk. "Are you going to let him?"

"Let him?" This was a new way to put it. "Yes, I'm going to let him. Any help we can get is good."

They stood still, listening to the hush of the changing leaves and gazing up into the milky heavens. There was an incredibly cool breeze floating over from the mountains, but Arnaud appreciated it. The crowded hall had been hot, and the fresh chilled air helped clear his thoughts.

"So how are things in there?" He nodded towards the door.

"Well," Andre slumped against a tree and took another chomp of meat. "No fights have broken out or anything. That is, if you don't count Theobus."

"What did Theobus do?"

"He—" Andre tried to suppress a chuckle but failed. "He punched out some guy who'd been dancing with Rosemary all night and wouldn't let him cut in."

In spite of his troubled mood Arnaud began to laugh. "How is he?" He imagined Theobus with another black eye.

"He's dancing." Andre shrugged. "Apparently she liked it. Looks like you won't have to worry about her anymore." He chuckled then tore another hunk of chicken with his teeth. "So do you have a speech prepared?"

"Not exactly. I know what I have to say. I'm just going to tell them, straightforward and honestly, what the risks are and then let them decide."

"And what if they decide not to go?" Andre asked.

"Then there's really nothing we can do."

***

Chapter Fourteen

The room where the meeting was held was considerably smaller than the feast hall. It was filled with round tables seating hearty men; most of them younger than thirty as the elders had already gone off to face the dragon and failed. Where there was no room to sit they stood, all eyes on Arnaud as he entered the room. With a glance Arnaud could easily distinguish farmers from hunters, hunters from guards, and guards and tradesmen; all based upon their appearance and mannerisms. Each group was clearly detached from the other.

Arnaud walked over to the front of the room and stepped up onto an old platform. How many Kings had addressed the officers of their armies this way? His heart pounded in his ears so that he could hardly think. He took a deep breath. Fainting before the men right now would prove counterproductive.

"Friends." Arnaud forced a strong, confident voice. "You all know why this meeting has been called."

They quieted their chatter and every eye turned to him. Arnaud felt his heart slow a bit. They were all at least listening.

"A terror threatens our lands. Reports of its destruction come in every month. Each time at a nearer location. You all know this. You have met the men who bring these reports. Many hare are those men, whose own cities, own homes, own families, have been burned to ashes by the dragon." Arnaud pressed his lips together ."I won't lie to you. I believe in presenting the facts, letting you decide for yourselves. It is a very likely possibility that most who join this battle to slay the dragon, to rid these lands of its evil reign, may not return." He looked out upon the wary faces of the men. "I cannot and will not say to you that honor and glory lie in store, nor even that victory is eminent. This battle goes uncharted; this foe unstudied and unpredictable. I cannot promise that we will have more success than the noble men who have gone before." He paused to emphasize the verity of this statement. "Yet it must be tried. Something must be done. If we do not go out to confront this evil, death will surely reach our doorstep, as it has with countless small towns on the outskirts, and in the city of Caen."

He stared out at them, letting his words sink in. Andre watched him closely from one of the nearer tables on the right.

"I tell you this not because I believe you incapable of aiding in the destruction of our foe, but because I will not have any volunteer with false expectations of an easy conquer." His eyes rested on Nicolas, then on Lucas. "My wish is to gather a party and set out in two weeks time."

"Two weeks!" A man in the back exclaimed.

"You expect us to fight alongside these hotheaded hunters!?" A young farmer shouted over him, glaring at the table where Marc and Gaspar sat.

"I expect any of you to fight like men," Arnaud said quickly. "Together, without prejudice, against a common enemy." He gave them a threatening look. "If any of you can't handle this I'll ask you to leave now. This conference is not for those who can't lay aside a petty squabble in the face of a real threat."

"And why should we believe what you say?" A young farmer, nearer to the front commented loudly after a moment of silence. "Just because you've got some fancy sword? We've already got a sword-bearer and he's turned out to be a coward!"

"How do we know you won't turn and run?"

Arnaud stared at them a moment. Out of the corner of his eye he could see Andre's eyebrows raise.

"Do you wish to take my place?" he asked. "Do any of you?" He swept the crowd with his eyes. "Sword or no sword, it's been ten years and no man has risen to the challenge. But I would willingly pass the burden of leadership if any of you desires it now."

The men stared back in reticence. A few of them dropped their gaze.

"You all agree that something must be done?"

"But why must it be done now?" A shopkeeper in the corner called out.

"If the prospect is so bleak, why should we go blindly to our deaths?" A farmer asked, lazily leaning back in his chair.

"Would you prefer the alternative?" Lucas loudly addressed the farmer who had spoken. "Would you prefer to be caught unawares? Your fields burned, your families slaughtered before your doorstep? It's happening out there," he continued with feeling, "to good men whose only mistake was living a few miles south of here."

His words brought a chilling stillness to the room.

"We could build up defenses," a hunter offered quietly. "Protect ourselves that way."

"It has been tried." An older man towards the front said sadly. "Defenses do not hold."

"Our only chance is in attack," Arnaud said. "In having the advantage of picking our time and place, in strategy."

"But what about our women and children?" a young farmer asked. "If we are . . . unsuccessful, what will become of them?"

Arnaud bit his lip. "Not all will be able to volunteer. Some must remain behind to protect the city. To keep the fields and to hunt. Yet our strength is in numbers." He swept over the care-worn faces again. "I will not ask for any volunteers now. You will have

279

these two weeks to think it over, discuss it with your families. Any who feel the call of God to help destroy this evil must meet back here at that time."

He stepped down from the pedestal, and after a dead moment the two hundred or so men began to filter solemnly out of the room. Marc and Gaspar however grinned widely as they passed.

"Smashing speech!"

"Sure convinced me!"

Andre came forward to Arnaud's side. "Well received, I think, although it looks like you spoiled their high spirits."

"They needed spoiling." Lucas was suddenly beside Arnaud as well. "It's like they think if they ignore the threat it'll go away. They won't upset their lives themselves."

"So I upset it for them," Arnaud finished gloomily. He didn't enjoy this. Knowing that he very likely led many of these men to their deaths with not even a small guarantee of victory. He wished he could be sure of something— anything. "How many do you think will come?"

"It's hard to say," Lucas replied. "The hunters are your more likely candidates."

"Generally younger, no fields to tend to and it's in our line of work," Andre said.

"I wouldn't expect more than . . . ten farmers," Lucas finished.

Ten plus the fifty or so hunters Arnaud expected was not very many. Hopefully he would be able to convince the High Council to help. And somehow 'win over' the fauns and the centaurs.

They had followed the flow of people back into the feast hall where women were chatting as they packed away their leftovers and their tired children. Many of them would return tomorrow to help finish cleaning up, but now it was well after midnight, and the journey home was yet to be made. They said their farewells.

"What do you know about fauns?" Arnaud asked.

"Fauns?" Andre sounded confused.

"Are they going to help?" Lucas asked seriously.

"I'm going to try to convince them to help," Arnaud said.

"You did well to not mention it tonight," Lucas said. "Many of the men are more prejudice against them than they are against each other."

"Why?" Arnaud asked.

Lucas shrugged. "Perhaps because they look strangely, speak strangely, and because they are very private and keep to themselves. They wouldn't aid the first groups of men who went out after the dragon ten years ago."

"They wouldn't help?" Arnaud wanted to carry this conversation through but Collette suddenly appeared out of the bustling crowd.

She held her basket, now empty, and appeared worn out and tired but happy. She looked at Lucas and Arnaud. "Are you ready?"

***

"Are you ready?"

The days had flown by like a flock of geese across the horizon. Just as Arnaud was beginning to make them out, they were gone. The field work was much less and much easier now that the summer crop was harvested. Arnaud and Lucas spent a good amount of their time fencing in the yard in the cool air. Andre, Marc and Gaspar were also coming by every day. Andre was good to his word and began teaching Arnaud and Lucas to shoot bow and arrow. Marc and Gaspar volunteered to help, though Marc mostly chatted with Collette and Gaspar mostly grumbled

"Are you ready, Arnaud?" Queen Brighde repeated.

She stood before him in a long white cloak that reached down and grazed the ground. King Eochan towered next to her in a traveling cloak, grey with age and use. They stared at him.

"Yes, I'm ready."

The moon was a dark orb; only a sliver was lit at her base but it did little to light the night. For the better part of an hour they walked in grave silence and Arnaud looked up to watch thousands of stars wink themselves alive across the sky. They walked through the woods, crunching over fallen leaves and twigs. The only other sound in that semi-darkness was the clinking of aged leaves tapping together in sudden breezes. Finally, King Eochan and Queen Brighde's steps began to slow.

"Here it is," Queen Brighde whispered.

It was beautiful. It looked very old and somehow sacred. Two glass pools had sprung up from the earth around a clearing. Six giant trees with pale bark and gracefully weaving roots filled the gaps of a large and perfect circle. Arnaud had never seen that species of tree and he'd walked among thousands. It was as if every bit of moonlight was condensed in that air, appearing almost thick and solid. He felt he could simply reach out and snatch some.

"Your place will be there." Queen Brighde pointed out one of the silver trees; tall and straight with jutting roots and high branches.

"You must be firm and claim it," King Eochan whispered. Arnaud thought he sounded angry. "Remember we are all equal in this High Council. None has authority over another."

We are all equal here. Had King Eochan said that to prevent him from lording over others, or to warn him that others would try to lord over him?

Arnaud nodded solemnly at King Eochan's harsh countenance, but behind the man's expression lay concern.

"They are gathering." Queen Brighde broke into his thoughts. "It is time now."

Arnaud followed Queen Brighde and King Eochan through sleeping trees outside the circle and to the giant trees assigned to their race. As they approached Arnaud noticed high chairs carved right into the sides of them that had not been obvious from other angles. King Eochan and Queen Brighde sat stiffly. Arnaud sat next to them, feeling out of place.

Shock soon replaced this awkwardness.

Six of the other places were suddenly filled without Arnaud's realizing. It was as if their occupants had walked out of the air. And they were not beings Arnaud had believed real back in Calais.

The merpeople Arnaud had known. They were there, in one of the pools, their scales glistening in the starlight from beneath crystal water. The mermaid had white hair that mirrored her scales, while the merman's hair and beard were an odd tinge of green blending easily with the forest around him, as it must with the weed and coral of the sea.

But the other members he had never before seen.

A short man and an even shorter woman occupied the places opposite him. Very curly white hair framed their warm wrinkled features. Round hooves, they had, in place of feet, and frosted black hair began at their waists and grown down to cover their goat legs. Little black horns poked out from their aged locks Fauns. Even for all the talk about them, Arnaud was unprepared for their peculiar appearance. But his ignorance was greater concerning the last race.

He knew they were centaurs. They had a man's torso and a woman's torso and the bodies of great

283

horses, but none of the tales Arnaud had ever read accurately described the dignity and solemnity they carried. They stood beside the trees rather than sat and their long shiny tales flicked in the moonlight. Honor and pride shown in every bone and every look. He knew in an instant they would be a fierce enemy.

"Where is the Lady Cleptis?" the male faun asked.

Arnaud studied the fauns and centaurs but they were focused on the merman.

"….Dryads abandoned our waters half a century past." The merman's voice was so gruff and throaty it was difficult for Arnaud to make out the words. He had to follow his lips.

Arnaud glanced at King Eochan. His expression remained hard as he nodded his understanding with the others, but Arnaud could sense this was a great blow to him.

"We are all present!" the male centaur boomed. "Who has called this Council?"

Arnaud could see Queen Brighde nod encouragingly to him out of the corner of her eye.

"I have," he said assertively, though confidence was a feeling far from him. He recalled King Eochan's words: We are all equal here.

"And who are you?" the merman croaked.

"I am Arnold of Calais."

"What right have you, Arnaud of Calais, to call a meeting of the High Council?" the centaur said coldly.

Arnaud held up the sword. "I believe this gives me the right."

They all stared at the sword for a moment. The emerald glowed in the heavy moonlight and as they stared, Arnaud looked at all of them and could make out a glowing stone of some kind and shape on each being. Sapphire in a scimitar on the centaur, jasper set in a short heavy bow on the faun, and aquamarine in a long sharp dagger on the merman. Each female wore the same stone in a differently set pendant around her neck.

"Where did you get that?" the faun asked.

"It was given to me," Arnaud replied, summarizing all that had happened to him surrounding his sword. He wouldn't go into Jaques' betrayal. It was unimportant and would only harm his cause.

"As was this."

He pulled the pendant out from under his tunic and laid it out openly on his chest. The merman spoke quickly with his wife in a low throaty language Arnaud had never heard and then they turned to him and nodded.

"It means very little that he has the sword and the pendant of his race," the centaur said with skeptical amusement.

"It may mean much, Constantin," the faun replied softly.

"How so, Phynnaeus? We don't know where he obtained it or whether the witch Sorcha got her hands on it and tampered with its powers." He pointed menacingly at Arnaud. "He might even be one of *her* spies!"

They all stared again at Arnaud. King Eochan shifted nervously in his chair.

"I give you my word, I am no spy," Arnaud said calmly. "Not for anyone. Not for a sorceress."

"I'm afraid your word means very little in this situation," Phynnaeus said.

"And even if he is not a spy, how can we be certain the sword has chosen him? Can we be sure of its power over him in danger?" Constantin demanded.

"My word counts for more at this point," King Eochan said. "I myself saw the emeralds' strong power. In these very woods it saved his life and mine against the Olde bear Orson."

"Orson is in these woods?" The female centaur sounded surprised. She stamped one of her front hooves nervously.

"Orson is a matter more easily handled than the one currently at hand," Constantin said.

"Agreed." Phynnaeus cut in. "A red dragon cannot be hunted and slaughtered like umbras or bears. Even Orson's intelligence has dulled with time, but a dragon is ever cunning and she wears her armor perpetually."

"Which is exactly why you cannot bring against it a human boy. It will be no more than a hindrance," Constantin boomed, glaring at Arnaud.

Arnaud felt hot anger flare inside of him. "I am confident that I will prove an aid rather than a crutch, especially with a small army at my back."

"And you expect us to approve small armies as well?" Phynnaeus asked angrily.

"I would not presume to expect anything," Arnaud said. "I ask only for any help you might be willing to give."

The faun watched him for a moment and then nodded with a glance at his wife. "Please, continue."

"My presence is most important," Arnaud went on as if nothing had happened, "for the fact that only the emeralds can dispel the enchantment laid upon the palace of Caen, if the battle should turn near there."

"What enchantment?" Phynnaeus sounded surprised.

"Of perpetual dormancy," Queen Brighde said. "It was laid to protect the daughter of King Phillip and Queen Alana when threatened by Sorcha."

"Can the boy not come after the battle and dispel your witchcraft?" Constantin spat.

"Witchcraft?" Queen Brighde said, clearly incensed that the art of magic was classified with the evil practice of witchcraft. She sat extremely still and glared with fire in her eyes. "You will find 'witchcraft' in the sword that has spared your life countless times."

"We cannot know how far the enchantment has spread," King Eochan spoke loudly over them. "More than ninety winters have passed since its foundation. Such spells become unstable with time. A misstep would render any of us useless."

"How has the dragon not mis-stepped in its own territory?" the merman rasped.

"A red dragon's size and armor is resistant to such enchantments," King Eochan explained. "Though the magic would ward it away from the area, it would never fall under the effects of the spell."

"I for one would rather face eternal dormancy than a dishonorable death by the mistake of a child," Constantin said, his arrogance reaching new heights.

"Have any of you the ability to read the future?" Arnaud asked loudly.

Silence rang in his ears. The High Council gazed on. Constantin's look was much of a murderous glare.

"Then even you, Constantin, could not know what use I might be," Arnaud said glaring back.

He half expected the centaur to charge through the moonlight and swipe his head from his shoulders. They pitted gazes for a minor eternity which Arnaud considered might actually be worse than a full on attack.

"Very well, human," Constantin said finally. "But I wonder if you truly know how much, or how little, your worth will be in this matter."

The circle seemed to relax, and Arnaud could've sworn he saw Phynnaeus and his wife concealing smiles.

He'd won. Arnaud felt a leap of joy at this victory. He felt things would be easier from now on.

"Let us move on to other matters," Arnaud said.

Phynnaeus stared at him a moment and then said, "Well put. The true purpose for this High Council has yet to be considered."

"It is my belief," Constantin said before Arnaud could speak, "that the dragon is not our chief concern. We should attack the one who opened the way for such evils. It is Sorcha who has cast a shadow over our lands."

The fauns and mermaids seemed to stop and consider this.

"Over ours as well," the female faun said. "Her dogs and her poisoned birds have been a constant threat to our kind."

"But the dragon has taken more lives," Phynnaeus disagreed. "Our mountains lie closer to its lair. Yet perhaps Constantin is right. First defeating the source of the evil may prove a more effective course."

Arnaud took a deep breath before he spoke. Perhaps this wouldn't be so easy.

"In many cases I might agree, but here that would be a mistake," he said. "Sorcha may have opened the way for such evils to enter these lands, but one has exceeded her in strength and power. Umbras and ravens and even trolls can be hunted and eliminated to extinction, but the dragon, even now, will take our combined strength to a cripple. In as little as ten more years I fear its strength will be beyond us. And such evil likely serves as a void for smaller evils to enter in. We must act now in this matter."

"But how are we to defeat a dragon?" the female centaur asked.

"With sheer number," Constantin boomed. "Even a dragon cannot withstand the strategic ambush of a mob."

"And in so doing suffer the loss of half our population?" Arnaud said. "No."

"With cunning," Phynnaeus said. "Use its strengths against it."

"Yes," Arnaud considered, "but as far as we know dragons are intelligent, perhaps even more intelligent than ourselves. And its strengths are not easily countered. Yet we must use strategy and cunning." He took a steadying breath. "I believe our only chance is in close range. We seven must come in as close to the creature as possible, shielded by the protection of our enchanted weapons, the abilities of which are sharper and more accurate than that of their average counterparts."

"But will they work against a dragon?" the merman croaked.

Phynnaeus glanced at Arnaud. "It is untested."

"I am afraid we must take that risk," Arnaud said. "I suspect any long range arrows or spears would be simply repelled by its armor."

"The risk can be reduced with the aid of prepared enchantments. I can—" Queen Brighde began was interrupted.

"Magic?" Constantin spat. "You think magic and bewitchment will defeat a dragon? I have seen what your magic has done. It has bred darkness in these lands. Its only byproduct is suffering and despair."

"A tool of any kind in evil hands will produce evil," King Eochan argued. "There is no undoing of wrong but by right. It would be a grueling, endless struggle to save these lands without good magic."

A pause grew into minutes of silent thought. Water in the pools rippled. A breeze fluttered by through the leaves. The centaur's tails flicked back and forth, back and forth.

"Then it is time," Constantin said, "that the centaurs abandon this grueling and endless struggle and move on to lands free of witchcraft."

Arnaud never thought he would see King Eochan look startled.

"Then you will leave us to the dragon?" Phynnaeus asked.

Constantin turned his head sharply to the faun and pounded his hooves into the dirt. "It is a long made decision. We make our way to the East," he said. "You and your people are welcome, Phynnaeus, Derae." He nodded to the fauns and then to the mermaids. "Treitus, Alaia."

He looked quickly over King Eochan and Queen Brighde and did not spare a glance for Arnaud. The centaurs turned and disappeared into the darkness, the flick of their tails the last Arnaud would ever see of their race.

The gap that followed this departure reminded Arnaud of a funeral. He could not tell if the feeling of loss was for the absence of another race, or for the remaining members of the dwindling High Council. Their probability of victory had diminished considerably.

"Cannot dragons repel any magic with their armor?" Derae asked into the void.

"It is our only chance," King Eochan replied. He rested his hand upon his chin and the thoughtful malaise continued.

How could seven, where two could not go upon land, defeat such a powerful foe? It was insanity to even attempt, and yet they must try. Arnaud knew they must try. The people of Calais did not yet know of this evil, but the dragon's power and wingspan were quickly spreading. In ten more years or even sooner, all that had once been Arnaud's world would be corrupted beyond saving. And if they did nothing, the dark-haired daughter of King Phillip, the object of Arnaud's dreams, would remain captured in enchanted sleep, never to be woken, an indirect captive of the dragon.

"There are so few of us now," Phynnaeus said despairingly.

"We seek help outside the circle," Arnaud said. "Already volunteers are gathering among the men of Ardgal."

"They will have little or no protection," Queen Brighde said. "They volunteer for almost certain death."

"Casualties are a regrettable but certain consequence of any battle," King Eochan said quietly.

"They know exactly what they're in for," Arnaud said, "and we could perhaps try to use our protection as shields or with magic if possible." He knew very little about enchantments and felt a bit foolish stumbling over his words. But he didn't let it show.

"It is no definite plan," Phynnaeus said.

Arnaud sighed. "There is no definite plan to be had."

Phynnaeus stared at him and nodded. "I will see if any of my men wish to volunteer."

"I had hoped to be more aid to you in this matter," Treiton rasped.

"To dispose of any remains deep beneath the waters would be a great aid." Queen Brighde replied.

"You will not retain the head as a trophy?" Treiton asked.

"No part can remain," Queen Brighde said gravely. "The blood of a dragon, even in its smallest measure can be worked for powerful black spells."

The merman turned to Arnaud. "It will be done." With no further utterance he and his wife disappeared beneath the water without a ripple to show they were ever there.

Arnaud stared blankly at the still pool. "God protect us," he whispered.

***

Arnaud did not sleep that night. He lay awake, staring at the stars through the hole in the roof of the barn. There was no turning back now. They would face the dragon, and many would die. Whether their party was victorious or not, lost lives would be on him. He prayed to God he did the right thing.

The sun donned bright and clear the next morning.

"Hold the bow up more. Yeah, like that, but closer to you. Not that close, a bit further. Further . . . further . . . a bit closer . . ."

"Shut up!" Collette laughed handing Marc the bow. "Why don't you must show me?"

He grinned at her and took it.

"What is going on here?" Arnaud asked walking out of his little shed.

"Lucas agreed to let Marc teach Collette to shoot."

Gaspar and Andre were sitting on stools with the legs propped up in the air, leaning against the shed. They looked extremely bored.

"I'm extremely bored," Gaspar announced.

"Huh," Arnaud said. He was surprised Lucas would allow something like this after what Arnaud had apparently done to her.

"After I leave, she'll need to be able to defend herself," Lucas said suddenly, coming round by way of the livestock barn.

Arnaud nodded. He hadn't really thought of Collette being here alone. They watched as she confidently shot a bow at the target and it swerved, just barely missing one of her precious chickens.

Marc quickly removed the bow from her grip. "That was . . . good. Really!"

She glared at him.

"Maybe we should put your chickens in the coup before we try again."

292

"So, you never told us how it went." Andre plopped the legs of the stool back on the ground and stood up.

"The fauns have agreed to help," Arnaud told them. He watched Marc and Collette chasing chickens around their little coup. "We'll go directly to their dwelling in the mountains when we leave. Phynnaeus hinted it was near to where the dragon lived, and they know the area well."

They nodded at him.

"This is good news," Lucas said, but Arnaud detected a hint of apprehension.

"And King Eochan is helping," Andre said.

"Is he coming along?" Gaspar asked sounding utterly shocked. He clumsily plopped his chair down, upsetting himself.

"I believe so," Arnaud answered.

"He's going to fight now?" Gaspar almost shouted in outrage. "After we've finally got things moving without his help!"

"Apparently," Lucas said.

"Well, of all the dirty . . ." Gaspar ranted to himself.

"Did he give you any reason for wanting to help?" Andre asked over Gaspar's profane mumbling.

"Perhaps because the queen's helping… I don't know for sure. But I do know he's hiding something." He shrugged. "Still, I'm glad of it. Enchantments will be extremely useful and he is a seasoned warrior."

They lapsed into thoughtful silence watching Marc show Collette again how to hold the bow now that the chickens were all safe. He made an endless stream of minor adjustments and then backed away. Collette bit her lip and took aim at the wide target. Her finger slipped and she let loose too soon. The arrow zoomed off again helter-skelter and flew just a hair over one of the near-grown kittens. The feline hissed at her angrily and scurried off, its tail down and bushy. Marc seized the bow.

"Before we try again," he said sternly pointing a finger at her, "you tell me if you're hiding any more animals around here."

Collette laughed and seized the bow back.

"I'm serious." Marc couldn't keep a grin from growing on his face.

"Any idea how many are considering volunteering?" Arnaud turned to Lucas speaking on the subject with feigned ease.

"Well," Lucas replied thoughtfully, "M. Verodart and M. Carthaig have told me they plan to join. I would suspect M. Fournier wishes to as well, but he has a young family. Many want to but won't for that reason, Arnaud. This will make you the enemy of wives and mothers."

"I know." Arnaud voiced his regret.

"Well, you'll have at least thirty hunters with you," Andre said encouragingly.

"Thirty? I thought there were more than fifty of you."

"Nicolas is leaving probably ten good men behind," Andre said, "in the event that we don't return."

"They'll have to hunt for the city. Teach others. That makes sense." But it was quite a blow. Ten men might mean the difference between victory and death.

Collette let loose another arrow. It grazed the very edge of the target before flying ten yards. They both gave whoops of joy and Marc pulled her into a victory hug. Arnaud glanced at Lucas to see his reaction, but he didn't seem to be paying attention.

"So thirty hunters and maybe . . . fifteen farmers?" Lucas said. "That might even be less than what the first groups had."

"We'll make it work," Arnaud said, trying not to sound discouraged.

***

Lucas had been right about his numbers. In the cold and the darkness before dawn, Arnaud waited for thirty-one hunters and thirteen farmers to gather before the Great Hall.

Andre stood beside him, silently gazing upon the men's farewells. It was a moving and depressing sight. Teary kisses and lingering hugs. Arnaud wondered if he would ever see his own family again. He had not known then their parting moments might be the last.

"Huh." Gaspar was suddenly standing beside him. "I didn't know he liked her that much."

Arnaud followed his gaze to Marc planting an unabashed kiss on Collette's lips.

Gaspar turned to Andre who shrugged and then abruptly elbowed Arnaud in the arm. "Look."

King Eochan and Queen Brighde had slipped out of the Great Hall and were moving toward him. A cloak of stillness fell where they passed and all eyes followed, staring.

"What is he doing here?" One of the men demanded of Arnaud.

"They are coming to help us," Arnaud replied.

Their reaction was much the same as Gaspar's had been.

"Help?!"

"Now?!"

"Now, when we no longer need his help!" A man almost spat at King Eochan.

"We need any and all aid we can get," Arnaud told them firmly. He gazed around at angry faces, grey in the softly coming light. "If any of you cannot fight alongside this man, then leave now." How many

ultimatums would he have to give before this was
through? How many men would be lost to them?

But no one moved. They just stared at him and
King Eochan, who stood a short distance from Arnaud.

"Then it is time," Arnaud said, feeling like a
criminal for breaking off everyone's last loving
goodbyes.

***

Arnaud had walked under many trees and traveled
much in silence, but this was different. The silences
had never shouted despair and dread, and the trees had
never seemed to pity him. Arnaud wished for a wind to
come and break the laconism with hushing leaves and
preoccupy the trees. But it didn't come. He was
doomed to dwell in his own morbid thoughts as they
walked and walked and walked.

"Arnaud." Andre, who had been walking beside
him pointed out into the trees.

Arnaud peered at what was evidently the form of a
man walking toward their group through the shadows.
He was nearly upon them before Arnaud recognized
who it was. Someone he had never expected, but once
the man was there he wondered why he had not.

The hunter Damien strode up to King Eochan, who
was leading the party, as Arnaud knew not where they
were going, and spoke with him. King Eochan shook
his head and pointed to Arnaud

"You lead this party?" Damien asked, falling into
step with him.

"I have learned to fight since you last saw me."
Arnaud hadn't intended his words to sound like a threat,
but he didn't mind when they did. At their last
encounter, Damien had sent Andre and him towards the
cave. Had he known the umbras would corner them?
Had he known the cave's strange blocking and endless
perils?

296

"I . . . parted ways with Evrard just after you left Toevluchtsoord," Damien explained. Arnaud knew that was the only form of apology he would get. "I wish to join your hunt."

The ultimate hunt, Arnaud finished to himself. A dragon would be the most challenging prey for any hunter. But even if Arnaud didn't fully trust him, he knew Damien was extremely skilled as a tracker and a bowman. He'd somehow maneuvered his way from the predicament Andre and he left him in, surrounded by a pack of umbras.

"Your skill will be much appreciated," Arnaud said in a way that let the hunter know he was in charge. Skill or no skill, Arnaud was calling the shots.

Damien nodded his complete understanding.

They walked in silence for a while, listening to nothing; no shushing wind or rustling brush, no friendly bird chatter.

"How is your friend doing?" Damien broke the long pause. "The one . . ." he gestured to his head.

"Who, Andre?" Arnaud stepped back so he could answer for himself. Andre gave a little wave.

"That's you? With the . . ." Damien stared in shock at the thin scar still visible on Andre's forehead. "I guess it is. You don't look like the same guy though."

"Growth spurt," Andre said, reaching up to run a finger over his scar.

They did not speak again that day. No one spoke. All seemed to be deep in their own thoughts as they tramped through the forests for hours and hours on end. Arnaud found this maddening. He wished to be free of his thoughts, the foreboding of what they were to soon face. The taciturnity forced him to face their detriments and confront them, yet he always came up short. There was no victory over uncertainty.

They passed that night and the following day under the trees in continued, endless quiet. The forest respected their solemnity. There was only the muted sounds of their footsteps upon rotting leaves.

But on the second night, when their destination lay less than a day away, Arnaud addressed the men. Their camp rested that night in the shadow of looming mountains. This looming sight placed a chill in their hearts and in the breathless air. A fire had been built and the men sat around it. Arnaud watched their faces, the orange shadows of the flame caressing their hopeless and terrified expressions. He wondered if he unknowingly wore the same countenance. Or perhaps he was like Damien and King Eochan, who merely appeared bored.

"It looks to me that we have given up hope before the fight has begun," Arnaud addressed them.

The sound of his voice, any voice, seemed excessively loud in the ocean of silence.

"We cannot let this happen. We must always find hope. What we are about to do, what you are all doing, is noble and praiseworthy." He looked around at them, not quite able to tell what they were thinking. "No matter the odds or the outcome, you have made an honorable decision. I am proud to have each of you at my side." They gazed back at him.

"Do you really think we have a chance?" One of the men asked.

"I do," Arnaud replied firmly, though he really didn't know.

"And," Andre added after a moment, "we will not be alone."

"Yes," Arnaud said, "we will meet with Phynnaeus and his tribe tomorrow."

"Those are our allies?" One of the hunters, a very thin, wild eyed man named Aidan, exclaimed. "First farmers and now goats!"

"Bigotry will not be tolerated!" Arnaud said harshly, "any future mislaid comments will face retribution."

"Retribution!" Aidan shrieked madly. "We will all be dead in a few days!"

"We stand a steady chance against the dragon. A good chance," Arnaud said confidently. "However, none shall survive under my blade." Arnaud glared into the man's eyes, who immediately shut his mouth. After giving the rest of the men a wide sweeping stare, he turned and left, feeling their heavy silence, and hoping to find sleep rather than the ever familiar restless repose he was becoming accustomed to.

***

Chapter Fifteen

Arnaud's dreams that night were vague and restless; fleeting from one scene to the next. Yet a common theme was present: fear. Fear and terror and grief. He felt their despair of no hope for salvation. He could hear the echoes of people fleeing these lands. He saw the terror in their faces as they lived in constant horror of a beast ever growing in power. He could sense their despair of becoming crippled due to huge losses. Such dreams made Arnaud not want to sleep again.

***

As they walked the next day, large white boulders began to litter their grassy path until the ground gradually became an uneven tempest of jutting rock. They had reached the outer base of the mountains.

Now silence was necessary. All concentration rested upon the next footstep and the next and the next. But Arnaud was grateful for even this employ of his thoughts; a droning distraction from greater concerns. This focus upon surer footing lasted many hours, blurring one moment into the next so that Arnaud was surprised when King Eochan stopped him. Arnaud looked up from his boots to see a group of fauns armed with short bows and quivers. This sight gave Arnaud hope. Fauns were hunters and warriors as well. Perhaps there was hope after all.

One with golden hair stood apart and spoke with King Eochan in a strange language Arnaud had never heard. Long vowel sounds were prevalent and he could see how it might at times be mistaken for a bleating goat. King Eochan looked over at him and gestured. The faun nodded to Arnaud and he and King Eochan walked up to him. The top of the faun's head only reached about half way up Arnaud's chest. When he was finished talking with them, he clicked his hoofs on the rock and turned to Arnaud.

"Follow us."

Arnaud nodded and gestured to his group. They followed the fauns into a narrow valley of the mountains. As it had been with giant's dwelling, Arnaud could have passed through without ever suspecting the area was inhabited. But he knew now. A series of deep caves dotted the sides of the mountain with no obvious pattern. As they passed, fauns came out and stood before them, pointing at Arnaud and conversing in an indiscernible tongue, making no attempt at discretion. Where the faie's curiosity had been based upon rumors and conjecture, here the emerald sword seemed to be something of a legend. The fauns continued to lead them far into the valley and then, after a turn, into a dark ground level cave.

"Here you will stay," the golden-haired faun said stiffly to Arnaud. "When your presence be desired you will be come for."

He and the others turned and left the cave without waiting for a reply. Arnaud wondered if fauns were bigots to humans in the same way the humans were to fauns.

The men began to shuffle inside, wearily removing packs from their shoulders. As Arnaud stepped inside after them, he could see it was actually rather homey. The cave was very wide and deep, long enough to house fifty men without feeling either cramped or confined. Thick red and yellow carpets blanketed the floors and the walls and intricate clay candle-holders were generously distributed with fat candles glowing in each. Their light flickered orange shadows across the room and the men's drawn expressions.

"What will your 'presence be desired' for?" Theobus asked, groaning as his bag slipped off his back and landed heavily on the carpet with a thud. "Discussing strategy? Do you think the faun will try and put all men in the front? Don't let him if he suggests it, Arnaud. Keep it fair."

"Theobus! You're giving me a headache," Gaspar whined laying a hand on the side of his face.

"Do you think that's what it'll be about? Strategy?" Andre asked, sitting across from Arnaud on the carpet.

"Very likely," Arnaud replied, wondering what he could possibly contribute to such a discussion.

The fauns knew most about the dragon, most about the area and the terrain. They held all the information in this situation, and therefore all the power.

Don't you start thinking that way. Arnaud shook himself. He wouldn't let any prejudices affect him, spoken or unspoken.

"How long do you think we'll stay here?" Theobus asked.

"A day. Maybe two," Arnaud replied, "No longer than necessary. We'll set out as soon as everything's in order. I can't imagine it taking long."

"And it's maybe a day and a half to the dragon's lair." Nicolas joined the conversation.

"How do you know that?" Marc asked.

"I heard some of the fauns talking about it."

"You understand their language?" Arnaud asked, amazed.

Nicolas nodded. "I learned much of my hunting techniques from a faun named Billius. Caen is much nearer to their dwellings," he explained, "and tensions weren't as high between the races as they are now."

"What changed it?" Andre asked, opening his bag and taking out a large chunk of cheese. He bit into it.

"I think trade decreased when the dragon came. The generations that sprang after that up had no relations with the faun."

"There's also the possibility that they host anger over our previous inactivity," Lucas said solemnly. "We have done little to aid against a beast that is slowly killing them of."

"Aye, there's that." Nicolas nodded sadly.

Arnaud looked out at the forty or so men spread out on the carpets, relaxing, eating, talking with one another.

"King Arnaud."

Arnaud swung around. King What? A black-haired faun stood in the entrance of the cave.

Not king, Arnaud thought frantically. But all the men turned to the faun and no one showed the slightest objection to the title.

"Your presence be desired in the high chamber."

Arnaud nodded and stood to go with the faun. As he left Theobus mouthed with wide eyes, 'keep it fair.' Arnaud had to suppress a chuckle at the man's paranoia.

The faun said nothing as they climbed the steep winding incline of the mountain base. It was carved so beautifully and kept so clean Arnaud had a hard time believing they were out doors. He had to look up at the blue skies above to confirm the fact. They climbed for maybe five minutes before Arnaud caught sight of King Eochan and Queen Brighde ahead.

Queen Brighde said something to her husband and they slowed down and waited for him. Arnaud noticed they had no guide. King Eochan, at least, must've frequented the city.

Arnaud couldn't help being slightly out of breath when he reached them. The black-haired faun had left him without a word when King Eochan and Queen Brighde appeared.

Arnaud stared for a second. "Are you alright?" Queen Brighde was leaning up against King Eochan for support. Had she been injured?

"Yes." Queen Brighde stood up straighter. They began to climb again. "It's just . . . been a while since I climbed the base of a mountain."

Arnaud felt like an idiot for neglecting to understand the difficulty of the journey for the Queen. He was only slightly sore himself.

"You've come." Phynnaeus greeted them warmly.

They entered a very large cave deep in the rocky side of the cliffs. It was as long as the one provided for him and the men. The surrounding stone appeared very clean and cast an orange hue upon a long table and chairs that furnished the room. Six fauns stood nearby staring at them.

Phynnaeus said something in the strange language to the fauns, and five of them left the room, leaving Phynnaeus and his wife, Derae, alone with them.

"How many men, King Eochan, have you brought with you?" Phynnaeus asked looking very tired. Even his voice betrayed exhaustion.

"We have forty-seven skilled hunters with us," Arnaud replied trying to discretely adjust his long legs in the too small chair.

"I have only seven," Phynnaeus said. "More wished to volunteer, but I cannot spare them here. As it is seven is almost too great a loss for our current numbers."

Arnaud nodded, hiding his disappointment. Seven could hardly be spared. Their numbers must truly be dwindling.

"Fifty-four against a dragon. There was a time one would never attempt such a thing with less than two hundred," King Eochan said

"But times are desperate," Phynnaeus countered.

"If only we had the aid of the centaurs," Derae mourned.

"Fifty-four must suffice," Arnaud said.

Phynnaeus said, "Already the dragon is becoming active again. We can wait no longer."

"Strategy often proves more important than numbers," Arnaud said. At least it had in any battle tales he'd heard.

"Then what is our strategy?" King Eochan said.

"King Eochan, I believe you mentioned you knew of something to do with enchantments at the High Council," Phynnaeus said.

"Queen Brighde is a gifted enchantress," King Eochan replied.

"I thought perhaps a sleeping enchantment," Queen Brighde said, "or one of dulled wits. Both are effective."

"Could you do something to make its armor more penetrable?" Arnaud asked.

Queen Brighde shook her head. "No, but there is an enchantment that strengthens armor."

"Could you invoke that upon all of our armor?" Phynnaeus asked.

"It would be stretched very thin. It wouldn't be powerful enough to make much of a difference."

"Which is more powerful?" Derae asked, "Sleeping or dulled wit?"

"Generally a sleeping enchantment is more powerful," Queen Brighde said, "but I've never heard of one invoked upon a dragon. You should know the effects will be uncertain."

"What will you need to do this?" Phynnaeus asked.

Queen Brighde folded her hands and King Eochan reached over and laid his own hand on top of them. "The closer I am to the object being enchanted the better its effect. I need a place I can concentrate. That is all."

Phynnaeus nodded.

"Have you seen the dragon's lair?" Arnaud asked.

"I have," Phynnaeus said. "It is a cave lying at the bottom of a small valley where three small mountains meet. It is very steep and difficult to cross, even for us of sure foot."

"But is it possible?"

"Yes, it is. But the going will be slow. It would be better to coax the beast out of its cave to easier ground."

"Is there a way of doing that?" King Eochan asked.

"Perhaps with bait," Phynnaeus said cautiously.

"Absolutely not," Arnaud snapped angrily. This suggestion might be acceptable if the faun were referring to an animal, but Arnaud knew that by bait Phynnaeus meant one of the volunteers. "It would be better to attack it in the valley anyway."

"Cornering a dragon is generally a bad idea," Phynnaeus said in a condescending way.

"But what about our stones? Our jasper and your rubies and emeralds?" Derae said. "Wouldn't they protect us from the beast's fire?"

"Yes, but not from heat," Phynnaeus explained. "We would be dry-roasted."

Arnaud attempted to block out this imagery. "Yet even considering the fire," he said, "it is much easier and more accurate to kill a confined target; and on cliffs we are upon the high ground. In more open spaces the beast would have the advantage of flight. We would be aiming blindly at a quick target when it swooped down and burned us from above."

They stared at him for a moment.

"It is a good point," Phynnaeus said resting his chin in his hand.

"Are there areas in which to place men along the cliff sides?" King Eochan asked.

"I believe so, yes," Phynnaeus replied. "Especially for the few we have."

"Then we will wait and scope out possible firing points for groups of men and fauns when we see it," Arnaud decided.

"And what about us?" Derae asked. "Will we have a rock-sheltered position as well?"

"It would probably be best for us to face the beast directly. At close range," Arnaud said. "Our weapons have enhanced properties. I am not sure, but our blades and your arrows may be able to pierce the dragon's scales. What protection we have may be enough for our swords to deliver a mortal blow a distance arrow could not reach."

"It seems there is little else to be decided," Phynnaeus said taking a deep breath. All around the table stood. "We have no choice but to enter this battle uncharted." He glanced at Arnaud. "As I am most familiar with the land and the beast, perhaps it would be best if your men reported directly to me. That way—"

"No." Arnaud cut him off. "My men report only to me."

Phynnaeus raised his hands half-apologetically, but it was insincere. The faun rose to his feet and the others followed suit. Arnaud moved more slowly than the rest.

Had Phynnaeus really just tried to take full command of this battle?

"Well, I will let you rest," Phynnaeus said as they walked out of the cave. "The finest accommodations have been prepared for you and your men. And—"

A young, brown-haired faun interrupted in the oddly drawling language.

"Leave him then." Phynnaeus told the young faun in plain French. "But post two at all times."

The faun nodded and left.

"I forgot to tell you," Phynnaeus said turning back to Arnaud, "a man arrived this morning, perhaps one of yours?"

"I'm not expecting anyone," Arnaud replied.

"Hmm. That is odd. He spoke about your hometown, Calais wasn't it?"

Arnaud nodded. Who from Calais would possibly be here?

"Calls himself Jaques Ciaran," Phynnaeus continued. "I assumed—"

"Jaques Ciaran?" King Eochan interrupted on the verge of an outburst.

"You know him?" Phynnaeus sounded surprised.

"How can he possibly be alive? She—" His eyes widened. "Phynnaeus, he's the man who betrayed and murdered King Phillip."

Phynnaeus hoofed the ground several times. "If what you say is true I shall have him executed at once!" He raised a hand to call one of the guards.

"Wait!" Arnaud stopped him. "Wait, I . . ." Arnaud didn't know what to say. Jaques here? What was he doing here? He'd said he would never leave Sorcha. Not alive. "Can I see him?"

"Arnaud, you know this man?" Queen Brighde sounded shocked.

"Yes, I know him," Arnaud replied.

They all stared at him.

"Very well," Phynnaeus said warily, "I will arrange for a guard to take you to him, up in the watch where he will not be moved." He called something to one of the fauns. The guard nodded and began walking and Arnaud followed him outside the cave. "I suggest you bring your weapons with you," Phynnaeus said before they left.

But Arnaud had not gone ten steps before King Eochan was beside him, forcefully gripping his arm and turning him around so they were face to face.

"How? How do you know him?" The man shook him in emphasis.

Arnaud shoved his arms off forcefully. He stared at the king's livid expression and tried to remember something. What was it? That dream. It must be that damn dream.

"We shared one of Sorcha's cells," Arnaud replied calmly. The faun who had been leading him stood aside and looked like he was trying not to listen.

"Sorcha." King Eochan hissed through clenched teeth. "What do you mean you shared a cell?"

"Andre and I were taken captive," Arnaud said quickly. He urgently needed to speak with Jaques. To find out why the man had spoken of Calais. "We escaped."

"You escaped?" King Eochan stared with wide eyes. "You escaped?"

"She's not as powerful as she believes herself to be," Arnaud said, assuming King Eochan was amazed that he had outmaneuvered her. The man looked absolutely stunned. "I will leave you now," Arnaud said, and he turned back up the path leaving the bewildered king alone with his thoughts.

***

The sun had begun its descent when Arnaud started walking the steady incline to the watch, and had entirely disappeared behind mountainous ridges when he finally entered the lookout cave.

The two fauns on duty had built a fire both to ward off darkness and to take the chill out of the evening air. They nodded to Arnaud's guide as they entered the cave, but Arnaud looked past them. The far wall opened out onto a wide ledge, and a withered man sat hunched upon it looking out over the mountains.

Arnaud walked over through the cave and sat next to him. For a long while they said nothing, watching the newly twinkling stars grow brighter under the brilliance of the steadily increasing moonlight. Arnaud struggled with himself. He felt he should say something yet failed to grasp what that something was. And each minute grew longer until it blended into the next and the next.

"I had three sons," Jaques said emphasizing the number. "We lived just beyond those hills there."

Arnaud followed Jaques' gaze and could barely make out the shadows of hills not half a day's journey from where they sat.

"Isaac, Henri, and Joseph," Jaques said. "Isaac was fifteen, Henri eleven, and Joseph was . . . seven, I think. Not yet seven."

Arnaud could see his face now in the moonlight. He could see tears forming along the brims of his eyes.

"And they were casualties of a war, not . . ." He paused as emotion overtook him. Arnaud respectfully turned his gaze to the landscape.

Jaques took a shuddering breath.

"But I am glad they could not see what I've become." His voice dripped with hardened hatred now. "A murderer." He laughed sadly.

"Jaques," Arnaud said gently, not wanting to startle the man, to throw him into a fit of insanity. "You said something about Calais. What were you talking about?"

He giggled mournfully. "And this time, it was committed with my own hands." He spoke as if he found it extremely amusing. He shook his head slowly, his expression bitter. "My family is dead. She threatened to murder yours . . . and mine . . . my only family left. In Calais." He spoke through clenched teeth. "So I took one of her tainted knives, and I followed her into the woods, and when her back was turned, I stabbed it through her black heart."

Arnaud was so shocked that even if he'd know what to say, he wouldn't have been able to speak. He had no idea she'd been that close to murdering his family. He felt sick. How could he have let her get that close?

"I stood there, alone. For hours, maybe days." Jaques continued rubbing one arm, then the other, then the first again. "Then the centaurs came." His lip curled in disgust. "They cut off her head and took it away with them. They left me there to watch her screaming birds feast upon her body."

Arnaud felt a numbness fall on him. The sorceress who had caused so much fear and pain, who had opened the doors for the perils he himself would soon face, she was dead. Destroyed.

"Such evil could not have been left to go on," Arnaud said.

"And who is to decide what is evil?" Jaques asked heatedly. "Will you cut of my head, Arnaud? I have, in a rage, eliminated an entire race. A people, with innocent—" emotion choked him again. "Surely that is a worse crime than any Sorcha has committed."

They looked out over the faun's valley, at the flickering light of fires and candles in a hundred caves. Arnaud said nothing. There was nothing to say. There were no answers.

***

"He has been given an elixir of youth."

Arnaud jumped about a foot. He'd been striding hurriedly back down the path toward the cave alone; lost in the darkness and the songs of some strange stringed instrument being played in one of the caves.

311

The music was melancholy and Arnaud wondered if it was for departing comrades that the music was played. Apparently he'd been passing the cave King Eochan and Queen Brighde had been given, for she stood behind him, further up on the incline outside an entrance.

"What?"

"Jaques," Queen Brighde said. She didn't move at all. Not an inch. He couldn't even see her blink or breathe.

"How do you know this?" Arnaud asked.

"King Eochan," Queen Brighde said. "I know Jaques has tasted an elixir of youth, a forced essence conjured by Sorcha who coveted immortality. But there is hope for him. I can concoct an antidote to this stopper of time. He would begin aging again, living perhaps thirty or forty years, but he would be free from the prospect of endless time."

Arnaud stared at her a moment. The music played mournfully on; low notes winding together like tear drops falling on the ground.

"And you can help him?"

She nodded gravely.

"Why would you do that?" King Eochan had openly loathed Jaques. And for understandable reasons, he had known King Phillip and his wife, perhaps been friends with them. But Arnaud knew Queen Brighde was much younger.

"He has suffered long for his crimes," Queen Brighde replied solemnly. "I believe in mercy."

Arnaud nodded his head in acquiescence. "I'll tell him. Thank you."

She nodded back at him and turned into the cave without another word. The song died on a low note.

***

He was surrounded by rock. A lighter-feeling more jagged rock painted in hues of grey and white. It encased him above and below on either side.

Arnaud turned slowly. Where was he? He knew he was in some sort of cave, but where? The sun glowed brightly at its opening; blindingly bright, but its sheen was not comforting. It felt cold and dead. Everything felt dead. Something grazed his feet and he looked down to find several inches of water sloshing back and forth up against his boots. Was he near the sea? Yet when he looked closer he could see something in the water: flecks of black and grey floating gently in little clumps.

Someone touched his arm and he turned him around. It was Andre. He looked exhausted to the brink of collapse. His face and arms were caked in dirt and soot, and sweat plastered his brown hair to his forehead. A long red burn ran down the left side of his face. It was thickly blistered and swollen.

He spoke urgently and though Arnaud could not tell what Andre said, he instinctively retrieved a long handkerchief from his pocket and handed it over. Andre snatched it with a weary nod and strode quickly over to a corner. Arnaud watched him for a moment and then followed, dread and foreboding grinding into every bone in his body so that they ached.

He moved slowly, wondering why he did so. What he was so afraid to behold?

He peered over Andre's shoulder, rocking and swaying with the motion of his quick-moving arms. Lucas crouched beside him, his hands darting skillfully over a body, attempting to salve and wrap the burns that covered it, to do something for the poor man who lay twitching on the wet ground.

It was Marc. Arnaud felt like he'd been hit in the face. The upper left half of the man's body was entirely covered in burns. His arm was black and withered. Could anyone possibly survive that?

A heavy hand grasped his shoulder and Arnaud spun around to find Damien as worn and dirty as he, speaking indiscernible words to him. Nicolas stood beside his adoptive son's charred body. The overwhelming horror and grief that Arnaud felt mirrored plainly on the man's face. Damien still spoke urgently, forcefully.

This was wrong. Arnaud had seen Marc's wedding to Collette. He'd dreamed it. Marc couldn't die.

He sat up breathing very quickly and shallowly so that his head spun. He said in a cave, the faun's red cave and he could see the forms of forty slumbering men around him on the carpets.

"Arnaud."

He twisted quickly around to see Andre leaning up on his elbow.

"I'm fine."

Andre nodded and lay back down.

It was a dream. Just another dream. Arnaud forced himself to breathe more deeply. His head began to clear.

A dream of what's to come? He glanced over at Marc's snoring outline. How could the dreams be true if he'd seen both Marc's nearing death and his wedding? Had something been done to change the future?

Arnaud lay back down, wearily staring up at the ceiling of the cave. The fauns had carved beautifully intricate designs into the stone. He closed his eyes and tried not to consider the number of men resting around him that would die in the next few days.

***

They left on a cold morning with no herald to parade their departure. Arnaud was not frightened or nervous even. The situation was too surreal to invoke such responses. And he would not allow his mind to wonder to death or the future. Instead his thoughts lay with the fauns. He was saddened by their slow and steady extinction. Of their hunters and farmers who had fallen prey to the dragon or who had tried to face it and failed. Fewer and fewer males lived to carry on their line, and the result was an aging and dying population. Strange that he should discover the existence of fantastical beings when they were all moving or turning obsolete.

The terrain was far more difficult to pass than what they had crossed entering the faun's valley. They were in the mountains now, and even though they passed at a low dip between two peaks, the way was steep and perilous. Arnaud saw King Eochan helping and steadying Queen Brighde much of the way, and they paused more often than they might have for her sake.

The sun slid down the sky much faster than Arnaud ever remembered it doing, and before he could gather his oddly scattered thoughts, they were setting up camp in a sheltered cove. It was then that Arnaud truly began to see the men he traveled with.

The fauns, Nicolas, Damien and perhaps five other volunteers were seasoned soldiers through battles of impossible odds. They were hardened to loss and perhaps to defeat as well. They sat calm and seemingly unperturbed as they mechanically ate venison stew prepared hastily over an open fire. Arnaud had little appetite, but he also ate slowly, one mouthful at a time, to insure his strength and to set an example. None of the other men seemed able to swallow. They stared at the fire with wide eyes and drawn, pale faces, clutching their bowls closely. One man named Maurice shook visibly and Theobus mumbled and chattered at anyone who would listen, apparently his way of coping in distress. Arnaud wished he could say something rousing and encouraging to them, but his mind wouldn't focus.

"How far away are we?" Theobus asked as they began securing tents for the night. Many of the men perked up at the question.

"Do you know where the castle of Caen lies?" Phynnaeus asked.

"I know it lies in the shadow of mountains," Philippe replied.

"It is just over that last mountain to the west. This dragon's lair lies in the close valley of that same mountain, and we are just on the other side of it. Easily we could have made the journey in one day, but our light failed too soon, and dragons can see equally well in darkness."

The men and fauns stared to the west where slumbered a hated beast that may be the death of them.

"We have an advantage if we use the sun," Arnaud said, attempting to raise their spirits. "Wait until it rains down against the beast, when we can see and it cannot. With that and Queen Brighde's enchantment, victory is almost certain."

They all looked at Arnaud, and if he was not fooling himself, a glimmer of hope shone in their eyes.

"I would like to speak with you, Arnaud," King Eochan suddenly stood next to him, apparently having finished with his own tent.

"Alright," Arnaud nodded.

They walked a ways from the camp, using moonlight to locate sure footing on the jutting rocks. There were no trees here to block the sky. They were surrounded on all sides by the milky spill of stars on a black canvas. Arnaud glanced at King Eochan out of the corner of his eye. What did he wish to speak of? Was he going to reproach him for dealing out false hope?

"I was wrong about you, Arnaud," The king said, "and I'm sorry."

Wrong about what? "What do you—?"

"Please, just listen," King Eochan interrupted. He stopped and turned to face him. "I need to say something. I do not want you making the same mistakes I did." He took a steadying breath and placed his hands behind his back, looking out at the dark silhouette of the mountains. "I made an enemy of Sorcha when she was a young girl. I refused to tutor her in the arts of enchantment as my father had before his death."

As he spoke, Arnaud knew this was what his elusive dream had been. He could remember flashes of it, the livid expression on King Eochan's face as he shouted at her, her smug smile when she lounged on the throne.

"I do not regret that decision," King Eochan continued. "She was a proud, vain girl. She had not the discipline and appreciation of the power of enchantment. However, my refusal made her angry and vengeful. It pushed her to the tutelage of a twisted man. I know that he helped her mix the elixir of youth before his mysterious death. The same potion Jaques Ciaran must have taken. A drink that's side effect is insanity."

Arnaud remembered the blood-stained markings on the walls of that tunnel under the mountain. It sent a chill through him.

King Eochan shook his head gently. "Other than that I don't know what that man did to her; used torture as a discipline, murder as a practice. He filled her mind with black spells and her heart with a lust for power and revenge. And she took her revenge upon me." King Eochan paused and appeared to gather himself. "Still a girl, she murdered my first wife, Jacqueline, and my ten year old son, Alaine." He pursed his lips, his eyes burned, attempting to control his anger. "Their deaths were long and bloody. I should have set out the moment I found them and killed her with my own hands. But I was too stricken with grief, and by the time I had gathered enough to seek her out it was too late. King Phillip and Queen Alana met their own ends just two weeks later." He turned to Arnaud. "I did look for her everywhere. But she'd disappeared. I know now she called up the dragon and used witchcraft to weaken the people and the land for her evil purposes."

Though he didn't sound as if he sought Arnaud's support he looked it. Arnaud only stared. King Eochan looked sadly back at the mountains. "It was twenty years before she returned; I'd remarried. Sorcha found me, threatened to do to Queen Brighde what she'd done to Jacqueline if I interfered with her plans."

He turned to Arnaud again. "You may reproach me for allowing her any control, but I do not regret this decision either." His tone was challenging, but Arnaud still said nothing. "My mistake was letting her go after she'd killed the first innocents." He stared gravely. "There is no understanding, no compassion, in the truly evil, Arnaud. Don't ever put your people in danger on the hope that someone will change."

Arnaud stared at his dead expression and then nodded. "I understand." He chose not to openly judge the man's decisions. He could not honestly say what he would do in the same position.

King Eochan returned his gaze to the mountains. "Good." He reached into his pocket. "Now, I must ask you a favor." He pulled out a small strip of leather and began unraveling it. A necklace with a shimmering ruby pendant fell into his hand. "This belongs to Queen Brighde. I'm asking you to give it to her after the battle." He handed Arnaud the necklace. "This is important, Arnaud. I would not trust it to another."

Arnaud stared at it lying in his palm. Hadn't Queen Brighde said it was lost? "Why did you keep it from her?" he asked suddenly.

King Eochan bowed his head. "The same reason I believed you to be one of Sorcha's spies. The dreams. I didn't want her knowing what grief I was causing our people on her behalf. I didn't want her misinterpreting dreams of Sorcha confronting me, as I'd misinterpreted my dreams of her confronting you."

"You had dreams of me speaking with Sorcha?"

"Only parts," King Eochan replied. "They are difficult to use with other stone-bearers. Clipped and fuzzy. I saw only you sitting in a wooden chair conversing with her, and I suspected the worst."

Arnaud nodded and stared back down at the ruby necklace. Everything was beginning to make sense. The pieces all falling into place. "Why don't you give it to her now?"

"Please, don't wait long after the battle to pass it on to her," Was all King Eochan would say.

Arnaud nodded, respecting the man's silence. He pulled the ruby pendant around his neck next to the emerald. They trod back to the camp in solemnity.

***

319

Chapter Sixteen

Arnaud would never forget the smells.

Of smoke. It grew in pungency as they crept closer to the cave. Until they came close enough to feel the beast's hot breath upon their faces. Until they could see the glint of the sun upon black scales. Until Queen Brighde felt they were close enough.

Of burning flesh. When the dragon awoke before Queen Brighde had completed her sleeping enchantment. When it unleashed its hellfire upon the men and fauns hidden among the rocks, their arrows and javelins proving useless against the monster's armor, always missing their target's weak spots. The smell of their burning flesh and burning hair filled Arnaud's senses as completely as their screams did.

Of blood. When the beast felt the ruby encrusted sword slice deep into its side, and then snapped down its jaws, taking the sword and King Eochan's arm and swallowing them both whole. But even then the scent had not reached its strength. Before the wounded and angry beast flew away, it ripped its claws into its attacker's chest, tearing leather and skin and worse. Then the crimson blood and the copper scent overpowered Arnaud.

The blood was what he would remember most. It was there when he went to help survivors bind their wounds: the bone-deep gash in Derae's leg, and other slashes among the handful of remaining men. But that blood, that sight and that scent were easy. Easily forgotten.

Not King Eochan's blood. Splattered on the rocks. Smeared on Queen Brighde's hands and her face as she wordlessly tried to revive him and wept uncontrollably. Smudged on Arnaud's tunic and collar when he had picked her up and carried her away from the body.

King Eochan's was the blood that shook Arnaud. It horrified him. That smell would never leave.

***

Arnaud did not begin actually thinking again until after they had moved the bodies of their companions from the rock valley to the softer side of the mountain, and had buried them. A fire was lit to illuminate their work. They labored through the night, unwilling to wait until morning to bury their comrades.

When at last the final scoop of rocky earth had been dusted over the graves, the nine alive and unwounded men stood still paying their respects. The early morning air was thick with grief; as thick as water. A breath of wind floated past them dispelling the soft connection of sadness between them, and one by one the men began to leave to aid the wounded, to get some rest, or to stare blindly off at the canvas walls of their tents.

Arnaud stood staring at the graves. He attempted to pay respects with the others, but instead he only felt anger: anger that King Eochan had to die and leave Queen Brighde alone, anger that twenty-three men had to be in the beast's fire range, anger that the monster hadn't missed by a fraction and spared even a fraction of their lives. He was tired of always standing before graves.

A cool raindrop fell from above and splattered on his cheek. Arnaud looked up and found Andre standing alone beside him, staring blankly at the graves.

"Did you know them well?"

Andre didn't look at him. He shook his head. "Little more than their names."

"Well, at least you knew that," Arnaud said.

"I wish I'd known nothing," Andre replied.

"Why?"

"Because then this would be easier."

Arnaud watched Andre's drawn expressionless face and nodded slowly. "Yes, it would be easier to lose nameless, faceless men." He turned to the fresh graves. "But these people deserve their deaths to be mourned, even if we did not know them well or at all."

Andre stared at him for a long time and then nodded.

The stood together for several long minutes, gazing out upon the new cemetery. Arnaud wondered whether the fauns did the same now, with their own dead.

"Arnaud."

He swung around to see Lucas standing among the rocks a few yards away, having just come around from the camp. He was covered in blood, but not his own.

"You're wanted by Phynnaeus."

Arnaud nodded. He gripped Andre's shoulder in a supportive way before turning to walk with Lucas.

"Also, another has died of his wounds. Francois Fleureton."

Arnaud tried and failed to keep pain out of his expression. Each death felt like his own doing. "Would you make sure—"

"I'll take care of it," Lucas reassured.

Arnaud pulled up the flap of the tent feeling weary and grimy. He was caked in mud, blood, ash and a sticky substance the dragon had excreted with fire. He desperately wished he could dip in the sea, wash away the filth and the memories. Phynnaeus stood alone in the bare tent looking just as worn.

"You have taken care of your dead?" the faun asked, folding his hands behind his back.

Arnaud nodded. "The twenty-fourth will be buried this morning."

Phynnaeus nodded his white head compassionately. "Your loss is great."

322

"It is."

"I must thank you for saving my wife from the beast's fire. I believe you sacrificed a deadly stroke to do so. I owe you much for that action."

Arnaud bowed his head in welcome. "How is she?"

"Her leg was severely wounded, but she'll pull through."

"I'm glad of it."

Phynnaeus nodded his head distractedly and pursed his lips. Arnaud suspected he had something else to say but the faun seemed unwilling to begin.

"King Eochan's death is a great blow to all of us. He was once a very honorable man."

Once.

Arnaud nodded in agreement.

"Our losses have been heavy, Arnaud," Phynnaeus said abruptly. "You can understand why we will not be pursuing the dragon further."

We?

"The beast is wounded." Arnaud tried to keep sudden anger from his voice. "Now is the time to strike, before it has time to recuperate."

The faun shook his head firmly. "My people have already given too much in pursuit of the dragon." He sighed. "I had hoped our combined forces would make a difference but it is too strong an evil. I am beginning to believe Constantin was right; that my people should leave these tainted lands, rebuild our culture anew."

Arnaud found it extremely difficult to keep frustration and anger from showing in his expression. They were close! King Eochan and twenty-three other men had given their lives to wound the beast, not to mention four of the seven fauns. To not use that advantage would be foolish and would dishonor them.

"I understand," Arnaud said calmly, though he did not. "And you must understand that I will continue the hunt with any who wish to join me, or alone if need be."

Phynnaeus looked at him sadly. Arnaud knew the faun didn't think he could do it, that he was arrogantly going to his death and bringing others down with him. But he didn't care. He was going anyway. He refused to just leave her there.

"I sincerely hope that you are successful."

Arnaud nodded curtly and swept out of the tent before saying anything rash.

He stomped through the line of grey tents blending easily into the mountain. Most of them were empty, their owners lying beneath the rock and dirt. Grey clouds cast ominous shadows on them: the final shelters of the dead.

I'll go alone, Arnaud thought fiercely. The beast can't have gone far. King Eochan punctured a wing with his blow. The small wound that had cost him his life and the ruby sword. He halted suddenly and pawed through his tunic. The ruby necklace lay still beside the emerald.

Queen Brighde. He hadn't seen her since the battle a day ago. King Eochan had told him to give it to her immediately. His last request.

Arnaud redirected his steps to the tents of the wounded. There were twelve injured men and one faun spread out among three large tents. Lucas darted in and out between them, apparently in charge, and another young farmer followed with bandages and burn salve. They were too distracted to notice Arnaud or the coming rain.

"How are they doing?" Arnaud asked solemnly as he entered one of the tents.

Lucas quickly checked under the blood-soaked cloth pressed on the stomach of a hunter. Arnaud knew the man's name was Bernard. He groaned in severe pain and Lucas began changing the soaked bandage for a new one. He looked at Arnaud and back at Bernard.

"Here, finish this, Marius." The young farmer set his load down and picked up Lucas's work. A stranger's blood was caked on his face where he'd stopped to wipe sweat from his brow.

"They're dying," Lucas told Arnaud in a low voice as they left the tent. "That man's bleeding to death, and I don't know enough about healing to save him, or . . . several of the others." He sounded worn and frustrated.

Arnaud wished they had some sort of doctor with them, that they could have even brought Grainne along. But then he might have her death on him as well and Arnaud couldn't take that.

"Well, just keep trying," Arnaud said as encouragingly as he could manage. The moans of dying men could be heard from where they stood. "Maybe the fauns have someone; perhaps you could ask."

Lucas nodded. Raindrops began to fall with increasing rapidity. They ignored them.

"Which tent is Queen Brighde in?"

"Queen Brighde?" Lucas sounded confused.

"Isn't she here?" Could all that blood have been King Eochan's?

Lucas shook his head. "I haven't seen her."

Arnaud felt a sudden panic. King Eochan had obviously sensed or dreamed his own death. Had he seen something concerning Queen Brighde as well? He'd been adamant about Arnaud finding her directly after the battle.

"Everything alright?" Lucas stared at him.

"I've got to go." Arnaud clapped him on the arm distractedly. "Don't give up."

He ran past the tents with no idea where to look but in her own. It was empty. The rain fell harder, dampening his clothes and plastering hair to his forehead. Where would she be? Arnaud passed by a few uninjured men looking pale and lost, shuffling to their shelters.

Queen Brighde had just lost her husband, perhaps she had gone to his grave? He turned back toward the makeshift cemetery where he'd spent the night digging resting places for corpses. The rain dropped rapidly on two men digging for the twenty-fourth. The swaddled body lay still and ready beside them.

"The queen! Have you seen her?" Arnaud called.

They shook their heads and continued digging.

Where? And then a thought struck him. He knew where she was. Arnaud began to run.

"Queen Brighde!"

She was standing on a ledge overlooking the dragon's narrow valley; where the battle had taken place. Where King Eochan had died. She was very close to the edge, her toes almost sticking out over the steep plummet, staring down at the spot where he'd last lived.

"Queen Brighde," Arnaud repeated more softly.

He moved forward slowly until he stood beside her. "Look at me." He took her arm and gently turned her to face him, away from the death-stained valley. She was ghostly pale with thick black circles rimming her bloodshot eyes. Her dark hair was limp and wet and stuck to her face. She looked profoundly lost.

"What are you doing?" Arnaud asked.

"He . . . I shouldn't have asked him to come," she said so quietly it was almost a whisper. Her eyes were still watching the valley.

"He would've come whether you asked him or not," Arnaud told her, still gripping her arm.

Queen Brighde shook her head softly. She looked anything but stately now. She looked broken. "What's to become of me? I'm alone. I can't go back to Ardgal. They hated us."

She seemed to be speaking more to herself than to Arnaud. "He . . . he didn't . . ."

Arnaud reached up with one hand and pulled the ruby necklace over his head.

"He told me to give this to you." He took her hand and closed it over the ruby.

Queen Brighde stared at it weakly. She began to sob. For several long minutes her tears mixed with the rain and Arnaud waited patiently. She suddenly turned angry, but it was weak anger and she continued to cry.

"He thought I didn't know!" She wept through clenched teeth. "He's left me alone with the people who hated him, who will hate me when they find out."

Her tears suddenly stopped. She stared down at the necklace hanging from her limp hand, looking entirely exhausted. She glanced back down into the valley. Arnaud studied her weary face. He could see how desperate she was, where that feeling might lead her.

"It's a boy," he said.

Queen Brighde turned to him suddenly with wide, sad eyes.

"Our sons play together in the castle gardens." Arnaud recalled his dream. He didn't know how he knew it, but the brown-haired boy was King Eochan and Queen Brighde's son.

She pressed the necklace to her belly and stared wearily down at the rocks.

"You won't be alone, Queen Brighde," Arnaud said. "I promise you'll be well taken care of. Both of you."

It took her a long moment to lift her gaze from the ground, but she did, and she stepped away from the ledge.

***

They made their slow way back to the camp through the now steadily falling rain. Queen Brighde clung to the necklace, holding it against her stomach with one hand and gripping Arnaud's arm with the other to support herself on the crooked ground. She didn't seem to be aware of him or their surroundings.

Eventually the tops of tents popped into view over a rocky precipice looking like a flat stone table on a barren land. He led her directly to Lucas's tents, feeling a little guilty for adding to the man's already overwhelmed state. But he wouldn't dare leave Queen Brighde alone now. He would lend Lucas a hand and keep an eye on her as he did so.

"Arnaud, what ha—"

Arnaud gently removed Queen Brighde's hand and gave it to Andre who stood in one of Lucas's tents weighed down with blood soaked cloths. Andre dropped them and took it as Arnaud swept over and seized a thin blanket. He draped it over Queen Brighde's shoulders.

"Is there somewhere she can—?" He glanced around the wide tent. Two of the four men laid out on the ground were obviously dead.

"Probably the fourth tent," Andre said.

"But there were only three."

"There's four now."

They tried to move her quickly through the rain this time, but her steps were awkward and she stumbled.

"What happened to her?" Andre asked when they'd sat Queen Brighde down in a dry corner.

"King Eochan," Arnaud whispered, afraid of what the sound of his name might do to her.

"Oh." Andre stared at her. She sat extremely still, her hand still pressed protectively over her belly and her eyes closed tight.

"How are the men?" Arnaud peered around this tent, calmer than the others: less blood, less moaning.

"Five more dead," Andre said gravely. "Lucas tries not to show it, but he's going crazy. There's nothing he can do for them. Not even lessen the pain."

Arnaud clenched his jaw. There were maybe eight injured here. Minor cuts and burns compared to the gaping wounds of others. "Where is he? What can I do to help?"

"Likely the second tent," Andre told him, moving to leave. "Last I saw him he was attempting to stitch up a man whose side had been torn up by the dragon's talons."

Arnaud knew exactly what that felt like. He glanced at Queen Brighde, still lost in her deep grief. "I'll come with you."

"Arnaud?" Their way was suddenly blocked by Marc whose head stuck through the tent flap. "I was told he came in here."

Arnaud was extremely relieved to see the man alive and well. Perhaps his dream had only been that. A dream.

"I need to speak with you," Marc said, finally catching sight of him. He glanced at André who passed through the flap without a word.

"What is it?" Arnaud stepped out after him. The rain had decreased to a heavy sprinkle.

Marc looked extremely nervous. He bit his lip. "Gaspar."

Arnaud waited for him to continue.

"He's . . . it's the . . . the burned bodies. They . . . bring up memories." Marc grimaced as if in sudden pain. "I'm worried about him. He hasn't said a word in almost two days. Just stares."

Arnaud sucked his teeth and nodded. "What can I do for him?"

"If you could . . . find a reason to send him away. Make sure he doesn't continue after the dragon with us; without him knowing why you're doing it." Marc looked apologetic. "I know it's a lot to ask, but—"

"No, I understand," Arnaud said thinking quickly. "I was hoping to find someone to go to Calais for me, to bring my family here. I know Gaspar would keep them safe."

He looked wearily at Marc and saw the man as he had in his dream, charred and writhing in pain, at the brink of death. "Are you sure you won't go with him?" he asked.

Marc shook his head decidedly. "You'll need all the help you can get here. If the dragon lives, all of this will have been for nothing."

Arnaud nodded sadly. "I agree."

***

Andre, Lucas, Marc, Nicolas, Damien, Gregoire, Philippe, and Morey. These were the men who volunteered themselves for the good of the people; who would more likely than not die in pursuit of freedom from the dragon's bloody reign. Arnaud began to understand what Andre had said. He would much have preferred the lives of strangers sacrificed than the lives of his friends.

It was a dark, brooding day. Clouds hung low over their heads, and heavy fog crept around every corner. It was maddeningly dismal being unable to see their surroundings, never knowing for sure whether or not their foe lurked behind the mist.

Not a word was uttered as they climbed up and over the mountain. Silence pressed down like the clouds, threatening to crush them and their already shaky spirits. Even with Damien's guidance, they were forced to backtrack many times, always scanning the grey for an easier path.

Arnaud thought it would never end. Never. That
they would just keep on walking into nothing and never
find the castle, and never face the dragon. It was a
painful journey. Climbing in tense quietude with only
thoughts to keep him occupied. Bleak thoughts that this
might be their last day on earth, that the sun may never
shine on them again, that their final careless farewells to
friends, family, even strangers would be their last.

Arnaud stumbled on loose rock and was forced to
reach out and grab a boulder to prevent himself from
sliding down a steep incline into the valley below.

What's wrong with me? Why is my footing so
unsure? He was slightly dizzy and out of focus. Must
be the fact that I hadn't really slept in three days. When
we make camp I'll recuperate.

Andre stopped and watched him set himself right,
but he didn't say anything. Arnaud wished someone
would speak, would shatter the solemnity. But they
simply walked on with heads bowed mutely, following
the trackers, Damien and Nicolas.

But after that moment Arnaud had something new
to occupy his mind. A pain in his upper right arm that
had begun a few days past was very suddenly increasing
with intense rapidity. It was only a small cut, Arnaud
knew that he'd received during the first battle. A little
red, a little swollen; he'd ignored the soreness assuming
it would heal on its own. Jarring his arm against the
rock seemed to have somehow awakened its existence.

As the day dragged on the pain increased until
Arnaud's arm was stiff and he had to grind his teeth to
keep from crying out in pain.

"Arnaud?"

He looked up. They were no longer walking on
mountains and loose rock. There was no longer any mist
or even much light. He stood on a grassy stretch. The
sky was clear and dark. When had that happened?

"Arnaud," Damien said as if he'd been repeating himself over and over. Arnaud looked at him. "Caen is only a few miles away. It's a deserted city. Do you with to make camp there?"

"Yes. That sounds fine," Arnaud said quickly. Damien nodded once and redirected them with purpose.

What's wrong with me? Arnaud thought, attempting to shake confusion from his eyes. These men were depending on him to lead. They'd trusted him. He concentrated his will on cleaning his head and it seemed to help. If I could just get a good night's sleep.

A cool breeze blew around them right over the flat plain. It whipped the waist-high grass against them, slapping their skin like a thousand tiny whips. Arnaud stumbled even on the steady ground. He was incredibly weak, exhausted to the point where it was an effort to even lift his legs. The sporadic gusts of near-freezing air served to momentarily awaken him, but it was fleeting and a second later he was back staring blearily at the ground.

"Arnaud," Andre grabbed his arm and pulled him to the right. Arnaud sucked his breath through his teeth. It felt like his arm was on fire. "You were headed right for that animal," Andre said releasing his arm quickly.

Arnaud stared weakly at a large cow, calmly chewing cud, its black hide shining blue in the starlight. Andre studied him with an expression of extreme concern. He stood very close the rest of the journey.

They saw the city long before they were upon it. Hundreds of houses looking like shadows spread out across the empty plain, giving the illusion of a sleepy, peaceful village. The wind whistled as it blew through the stale homes. Arnaud took one step on the overgrown dirt road and knew there was not a living soul within its borders. But there had been. As one, they immediately stopped and stared. Marc took a step back.

Bodies, picked clean by insects and the elements until only piles of white bones glittered in the moonlight. Ragged bits of charred cloth clung to a few. The chill of shock hung heavy in the air around them. Survivors had not remained to bury their dead. Arnaud closed his eyes. So many dead.

"Is there another part of the city?" Arnaud turned to Nicolas.

"The . . . northern section was least affected," he said, keeping his countenance carefully blank.

Arnaud took the lead. The shock of seeing so many bodies in the streets, lying still where they had died, snapped him a bit from his painful reverie.

They skirted around the outskirts, careful not to enter again into the tainted streets. Still, Arnaud felt a morbid fascination drawing him to look, and several times he thought he could see the light glinting on skulls and piles of bones.

Relief was temporary, and the severe, stabbing pains and the fogginess of mind returned.

"Yes, these should be empty," Nicolas said stepping forward.

Arnaud suddenly stumbled over his own feet. His pack felt so heavy. Andre discretely pulled him upright, steadying him.

"Can we build a fire?" Gregoire asked rubbing his arms and chattering as they walked past empty houses. They looked like tombs, their gaping windows and doors welcoming death.

"I wouldn't suggest it," Damien said to Arnaud. "We don't know where the dragon is, or how it might react."

Arnaud nodded as strongly as he could. "We'll have to do without a fire. Just stay together in the houses. Get some rest." Oh, how he needed rest.

"We'll take this one," Andre announced, grabbing Lucas's arm and barely touching Arnaud's shoulder.

Arnaud let Andre lead him into one of the small buildings. The smell of musty cloth and stale wood hit him as he shuffled over the dusty floors.

"Wha—" Lucas shut his mouth and stared at Arnaud. He quickly pulled up a rotting chair and had him sit on it. Moonlight poured through the windows as Lucas carefully ripped open the right sleeve of Arnaud's shirt.

He swore. "Arnaud, when did you get this?"

Arnaud looked over at his arm. The inch-long cut he'd gotten in the battle had swollen to half the size of his fist. Even in this light he could see green infection under the skin surrounded by a thick ring of black.

"During the first battle," Arnaud breathed. His head was now pounding with the same biting pain as his arm. "It was just a little red yesterday."

Lucas leaned in and examined it. He bit the inside of his cheek. "It's healed over the infection. Probably the work of that sword. I'm going to have to reopen it."

That was the last thing Arnaud wanted him to do right now, but he nodded.

"Do you have any of that salve?" Lucas turned to Andre who was peering suspiciously out the window.

"No, but I can get some."

Andre left and Lucas pulled out a small knife. "Let's get more into the light."

Arnaud let Lucas carry two chairs to the window. He collapsed back into one.

"Ready?" Lucas asked.

"Just do it."

Lucas posed the blade over the pus-filled wound, then drew it away. He leaned over and pulled several long cloths from his bag. He rolled one up and shoved it into Arnaud's mouth. "Bite on that."

It was by far the most pain Arnaud had ever felt. It took all of his will-power to hold still and not push Lucas away. He gripped the chair until his hands splintered and bit down on the cloth until his teeth ached. He moaned involuntarily, but the gag thankfully muffled the sound.

Arnaud didn't want the others knowing his vulnerability. There were too many independently-spirited men here who would try and take over if they found out he was wounded. And Arnaud needed to keep control. For reasons he couldn't explain he knew it was vitally important.

"Here, I—" Andre entered the house. He crinkled his nose and looked away when he saw Arnaud's oozing arm.

"How did you get that?" Arnaud mumbled weakly through the cloth in his mouth.

Andre smiled. "I'm glad you've forgotten."

Lucas took the salve and set it aside. "Go hold him down. I have to get all the infection out. Arnaud, are you ready?"

Andre walked around and put a hand against Arnaud's left shoulder. Arnaud braced himself and nodded. This was, if possibly, even worse. But with Andre holding him back, Arnaud could concentrate on not screaming. He squeezed his eyes shut over tears of pain.

"Are dragons poisonous?" Lucas asked after an endless span of time. Andre shrugged.

"I don't know how this infection could've spread so fast. And it's not . . . normal." He peered at the small cut. "But I think I've got it all now."

Arnaud exhaled, just now realizing he'd been holding his breath.

"I'm not sure how much you'll be able to use your arm, though." Lucas cleaned the wound with water from his skein and smeared thick yellow salve over it. He took one of the bandages and began to wrap it tightly. Arnaud was reminded of the day a few months ago when the man had accidentally stabbed him. Always in the right arm.

"Here." Andre handed him another skein of water. "Drink this."

Arnaud took it. He was beginning to feel better. His headache was gone and his vision was clearing. Had the dragon nicked him in the shoulder without him realizing it? It was such a small cut.

"You'll have to hide it somehow," Andre said gravely. "I don't think some of these guys could take you falling weak right now."

Arnaud nodded. "I know."

Lucas stood up. "Good thing you learned swordplay from a left-hander then."

"Good thing you stabbed me so I had to learn that way."

Andre slapped Arnaud on the arm.

"Ow!"

"Coincidences!" he said holding his arms out as if this proved everything.

***

Chapter Seventeen

He stood on a wide platform in a room he had never seen. A crowd of five hundred people filled it from wall to wall, watching him, listening to him say something he could not hear. He felt his lips move but the words were unknown. He hoped he was saying something inspiring. The people's expressions seemed favorable and they were nodding in agreement.

Arnaud gazed over the crowd. His sisters were there at the front. He was incredibly relieved to see this; that Gaspar had gotten them here safely.

There was Gaspar looking comical without even saying anything, and Anais was beside him, holding his hand.

Arnaud stared. Gaspar and Anais? That was unexpected.

Clarice stood with a smile on her face between Andre and Lucas. But where was Mother? Arnaud wanted to continue looking around for her, but the speech was over and he was stepping down from the pedestal.

Genevieve walked over to him and Arnaud put his arms around her. She smiled as she spoke and he replied. Her eyes were velvety blue. Somehow he'd never noticed that in any of his other dreams.

She climbed up on her tiptoes and kissed him.

***

For two days they trekked along the base of the mountain hoping to stumble upon another lair of the beast. Damien suspected it might have a den within sight of the glittering castle, near the place of its first desecration. So they looked to the stronghold which lay several miles out of Caen, built up into the rock.

The entire situation was so surreal Arnaud had a difficult time taking it seriously. As, on the third day, they crept alongside the rock to stay clear of a sudden downpour, he found himself in a type of daydream. A small butterfly had inexplicably appeared in their area. It floated along ahead of him, staying free of a wetting as they did, gracefully dipping and swaying in the heavy wind, struggling to stay aloft. Its hue was a rich blue that sparkled in the heavy lighting. Arnaud had never seen a blue butterfly before.

"What's that?" Philippe suddenly said from behind.

Arnaud heard the man but was too caught up in the delicate blue wings, in his strangely dream-like state, to listen. The butterfly had slowed, was closer now. He was dimly aware of some commotion around him, but paid no heed. Infinitesimal black-blue veins stood out on the paper-thin aqua. It reminded him of translucent leaves.

A thick crimson drop suddenly pelted the fragile creature. It struggled desperately for a moment and then sank to the earth, damaged and disabled, leaving him with an intensely macabre feeling. Painfully torn from his reverie, Arnaud leaned back and peered above for the cause of this destruction. A wide stone precipice hung out high over them.

He shut his eyes quickly as fresh blood splattered down upon his face. A low moan shook the rocks and he could hear the crunching down on thick bones. The beast was above on the rocks, feeding on some poor animal, shaking its carcass wildly.

He looked around at the men. Their eyes brimmed with poorly disguised terror, their mouths gaped open. Arnaud ran through the situation, thinking swiftly on his feet. The dragon was yet unaware of them. If they could surround it somehow and attack as one, they might have a chance. He gestured for the men to spread out on either side of the rocks and climb. They were on the low ground, but he felt the element of surprise more important in this situation.

Arnaud laid his own hands softly on the rock, and realized it was wet. Rain was still falling steadily down upon them. He hadn't noticed it. Thank God, he thought. Perhaps the rain would help disguise any vibrations of their movement.

He seized a corner of stone and pulled himself up with his left hand, steadying against the rock with his right. It was awkward and difficult but he managed to situate himself and reach for another wide crack, and another. Thick rain drops slid down his face as he looked over at the others. Andre and Marc, and Philippe were parallel to him. They'd found another smaller precipice, apparently within shooting range of where the dragon feasted, yet unaware. Philippe's hands shook as he fitted an arrow to his bow.

"No." Arnaud mouthed. They didn't see. "Wait!" he whispered hoarsely. They weren't all in position. If Philippe shot now he would only irritate the beast and draw its attention to their presence.

But Philippe was too caught up in nerves to think of the others. His bow gave a muffled buzzing twang as he let it loose.

Time seemed to slow down as Arnaud watched the arrow fly up and out of sight, onto the precipice. True to its target.

A curdling screech shook the air. It grated through Arnaud's ears into his head and rattled his teeth. His heart stopped in sheer horror as he watched the beast lean over the edge, cock its neck, and spit fire down on the three men. Its wings beat unevenly as it did so, and Arnaud could vaguely see the ragged hole King Eochan had cut in his last moment.

The beast's aim was deathly accurate. Philippe received the brunt of the blow. His body exploded into flames. His last screams echoed from the rocks as he fell. Marc's entire left side met with the fire as well. He stumbled back in shock, almost over the edge but Andre, who had managed to dodge the fire completely, seized him by the sleeve and pulled him back. He quickly pounded out the fire with his own sleeves.

All of this happened within the span of a few seconds, and Arnaud looked on in shock.

Marc. He was burned just as in the dream.

"Back!" Arnaud whispered to them loudly, gesturing downward with his stiff right arm. "Back."

Lucas already waited beneath the smaller ridge to help Andre lower Marc down to solid ground. No one looked to Philippe; not now. He was obviously dead.

"There was a cave back—" Damien gestured the way they'd come.

Nicolas hurried up to Marc whose eyes fluttered in pain.

The men all stood around staring at Arnaud or up at the dragon's precipice.

"Move!"

They shuffled after him along the mountain breathing heavily. Philippe must've managed to wound the dragon or frighten it. It didn't immediately come down after them. Arnaud thanked God with every step for it. They could do nothing if the beast pursued now. They would be nothing more than embers burned upon the rock.

The cave was slanted down. It was more a hole in the ground than the elaborate faun's caves. The rain that had been pouring steadily, soaking them through, gathered at the back leaving several inches of water to slosh up against their feet.

"Over here," Lucas told Andre as they dragged groaning Marc to the very back of the cave where it slanted up above the water.

Arnaud stared down at his boots. He looked out toward the cave opening. The sun was poking through the clouds, blinding in the grey and the dark cave.

"Arnaud." Andre grabbed his arm. Arnaud stared at him: his exhausted eyes, sweaty forehead, and the blistering burn running down his face. "Do you have any cloth? A handkerchief or anything?"

Arnaud dug into his pocket and retrieved a large handkerchief, feeling the incredible eeriness of intense déjà vu.

Andre nodded curtly as he took it and strode quickly back to Lucas's side.

He followed Andre knowing exactly what he would see, what he would face, but he had to. He had to know exactly how Marc was doing. Whether he would actually die.

Nicolas crouched beside his adoptive son, gently brushing burnt hair off of his ghostly pale face. His eyes were dry but very red.

Arnaud wanted to ask Lucas how Marc was doing, whether he thought the man would live, but the words wouldn't come. He only stared at the withered skin in amazement.

A heavy hand turned Arnaud away from the horrific sight.

"We must act now," Damien said in a low voice, "before the dragon has a chance to move on."

Nicolas stood slowly to his feet, still staring at Marc's mutilated form.

Arnaud nodded. Damien was right. They couldn't afford to waste any time. "It would be suicide to try and climb back up there."

"A watch," Nicolas said blankly. "It was a watch tower. Difficult to ambush."

Arnaud nodded at him, his mind running. Gregoire and Morey had taken Philippe's unrecognizable corpse out from the open. They walked over and stood beside him. "We'll have to draw it out." He looked warily around at them.

"How?" Morey asked.

"Bait." Damien spoke the word without apology.

Silence struck like a hammer. All were utterly still except Lucas and Andre who frantically worked to save Marc. Arnaud was reminded of Phynnaeus suggesting the same thing at the High Council. He had absolutely refused then, but he could see no other way. They were out of time and out of strength.

"I'll go," he said finally. The sword might help, and either way the cause was greater. If Arnaud could save thousands of lives with his own life, he would do it.

"No. We will need you to break the enchantment," Damien said. "And you must remain to rebuild this country."

Arnaud was surprised by his words. Damien had seemed to him too selfish to consider the good of the country.

"I'll go," Nicolas announced quietly but with determination.

"N—" Arnaud began to speak but the old hunter stopped him.

"I have nothing left here. The dragon has taken everything from me."

"Marc and Gaspar—"

"Will live their lives," Nicolas said gravely. "Mine will soon be ending as it is. I'm an old man. I'm going, Arnaud."

They stared at each other for a long moment. The man's lined, caring face was set with purpose. Finally Arnaud dropped his gaze and nodded, feeling like he signed a death warrant by doing so.

He turned to the others. "We four will spread out hidden among the rocks. Do not fire until the dragon is within sight upon the ground. Understood?" Arnaud looked sternly at each of them. They nodded solemnly. "Aim for the eyes, and if possible the open mouth. Don't waste arrows on scales." He glanced at Nicolas, who stared at a now unconscious Marc. "Let's go."

The rain had stopped temporarily. Clouds parted to make way for a blinding sun. It beat down on their wet clothes and wet hair, making them feel sticky and heavy. The air was humid and difficult to inhale.

Arnaud crouched behind a wide boulder with his sword posed ready in his unsteady left hand.

Lucas had said in a sword lesson that it helps to focus on breathing. It aids in a clear mind and quicker reflexes. Relax. Relax. Tight muscles mean restricted movements. Your actions should be fluid, second nature. Try again . . .

That lesson felt like the far distant past, but he focused on breathing slowly and deeply and filling his mind with peaceful thoughts of white gowns and blue flowers in long brown hair. He could feel his heart rate steadily slow.

Then Nicolas stepped boldly out into the open. He shouted deeply and rattled his bow against the rocks. He let loose an arrow into the dark hole above and made sudden deliberate movements. The rest watched quietly from their places. Waiting for the beast to appear and swoop down and engulf the poor man in flame.

Deep breaths. Focus on deep breaths.

343

Nicolas hollered and stomped and shot another arrow. This one had deflected uselessly off thick scales. He stopped moving.

The dragon reminded Arnaud more of a scorpion than a lizard. It scuttled somehow when it moved and its armor reflected like hundreds of black mirrors. It screeched and hissed angrily at the one visible man below.

The hunter shot another arrow. It plinked off the beast's head. The dragon twitched angrily and roared as it sprayed a stream of fire down into the valley, but Nicolas was too far to reach. He backed up and shot another arrow.

The point bounced off right between the beast's eyes. The dragon moaned in anger and moved to the very edge shooting fire as it went. Nicolas stepped farther back and fit another arrow.

The dragon suddenly swooped down at him, but clumsily. Apparently flying was difficult, even impossible with that wounded wing. It spit fire angrily at him in quick succession. The hunter managed to dodge the first two, but the third lit his pant leg on fire. He stopped to pat it out and the beast leaned its long neck forward.

"Now!" Arnaud shouted.

They all stepped out from behind their rocks. The three other men immediately loosed their arrows. Two tore through the thin membrane of wing and the third soared past. The beast shrieked its wrath. Arnaud leapt forward. He couldn't fire a bow with one arm. His only weapon at this point was his sword.

But he wasn't quick enough. Nicolas was distracted by the fires burning into the flesh of his leg. He never moved out of the way, and he never saw the jaws coming. Arnaud heard the crunch of bone and of

flesh as the monster snapped. He felt a noble soul fly
from the arena.

"Left!" Arnaud shouted to Damien across the
space. His voice echoed loudly from the rocks, and the
beast turned to the sound heaving fire as it went. The
blaze swept over Damien. The man stumbled back and
then lay still upon the ground.

Arnaud didn't have a moment to spare for the
man. He sprang forward and buried his sword into the
nearest piece of flesh visible through spread scales. It
was just above the creature's back leg, but the blade
went deep and the dragon bellowed in pain.

Arnaud could feel the beast's extreme body heat.
He could smell its putrid earthy scent. He was near
enough to touch its scales. For one moment he was
mesmerized by its beauty. Up close the scales were not
black, they were not any color, or they were all colors.
They were wrong and beautiful, and in spite of himself
he began to lose himself in their luster.

Searing pain suddenly ripped into the daze. The
beast had whipped its tail around, and a great spike had
planted into Arnaud's side. It flung back, throwing him
up and away and down hard into the sloping rocks.
Arnaud didn't notice the excruciating pain, or
acknowledge his luck at surviving such a blow. He
focused only on keeping his left grip on his sword and
crawled weakly over to the meager shield of a boulder.
His eyes stung and watered as he peered through the
cloud of smoke now covering where the beast had been.
It had hidden itself in the swirling black and grey.

Arnaud panted and squinted down at his beaten
body. The tear in his torso was severely soaked in
blood. He closed his eyes tight and pressed his right
arm into it feeling the hot gush upon his skin. He had to
fight off hacking and coughing that pulled at his ripped
side as he caught his breath. It seemed useless, facing

an opponent who held all advantages, but he must try something. If the beast would not show itself, Arnaud would have to draw it out again. Hopefully Gregoire and Morey would be able to strike the beast down while it went for him. It was a slim chance, but he was out of options. And time.

But even though Arnaud knew it was necessary, knew it was their only chance, he found himself paralyzed. The muscles in his legs and chest tightened so that he was physically unsure if he could move. In the corner of his eyes he could see Damien's and Nicolas's lifeless bodies lying limp upon the rocks. His mind was suddenly bombarded with visions of the charred corpses of his companions, his ears filled with the memories of their shrieks. He was afraid. And he was ashamed of his fear.

He stood alone seething with inactive adrenaline, torn between primal self-preservation and what he knew to be right. He glanced wearily down at the bloodied sword.

What he knew to be right.

It seemed Arnaud turned to God only when he had exhausted all other options. "Lord, help me. Give me strength," he whispered.

He took deep breaths and focused on these words, repeating them over and over in his mind. And he found his thoughts clearing once again; his muscles and nerves calming. Hot courage flowed into him. He took a last deep breath and prepared to step into the open. A loose stone clattered down the slope next to him and out over the plateaued clearing of rock. Angry flames leapt out from smoky fog and pounded the rock until it became red and molten.

Arnaud almost laughed in realization and relief. The dragon could not discern between the sound of his movements and those of a rock. He transferred the sword to his right hand still clutching his side, bent over, and gathered up some large pebbles. He tossed them and they skipped and popped over the flat clearing. Hasty fire leapt out at them and the dragon moaned angrily. Arnaud bent to gather more, but rocks already came clattering from the other side of the mist. Flames jumped out again. The dragon was confused and overzealous. It was coming closer, hasty to be rid of its pestilence.

Arnaud braced himself, feeling the numb strength spread through his limbs. He stepped silently out from behind the boulder, staring at the foggy source of fire so intently his eyes hurt.

The rocks clattered out again, as Arnaud knew they would, but further back this time, forcing the dragon to step forward into view. Arnaud pressed his body against the rock wall preparing himself to aim the blade, when the beast was suddenly upon him; its head near enough to reach out and touch; its blood-stained jaw wide and snapping. Arnaud spun quickly to the side.

Time seemed to slow again as he caught sight of the beast's furious yellow eye. He pulled his left arm back and with all his remaining strength he drove it into the eye all the way down to the hilt, deep into the dragon's brain.

The beast quivered violently and then fell without a sound, dead before it landed in a rumbling thunder of noise and movement.

***

Chapter Eighteen

Even though he knew in his heart that he would not fail, relief overwhelmed Arnaud. He stumbled over to lean against the rock, not wanting to crumble before his men. His face was wet, but whether from the smoke; the sudden sprinkle of rain; or from tears of pain, exhaustion and relief; he did not know.

"Arnaud." Andre was suddenly standing next to him. "Arnaud, are you alright?"

"I thought you were helping Lucas." Was all Arnaud could think to say.

"I figured you needed it more," Andre said taking his arm to steady him.

Arnaud nodded distractedly. He turned and looked out over the clearing in a strange confusion.

There were two bodies unmoving on the ground. Arnaud braced his side and stumbled over as quickly as he could. Andre followed.

Nicolas's body was barely recognizable. Arnaud looked quickly away both to keep from vomiting and being overcome with grief. The man had died nobly, honorably. But he deserved better.

Rain dripped steadily again on him, sliding over and into his eyes. Arnaud blinked them out and rubbed his face with his hand.

"Nicolas was a good man," Andre said quietly.

Arnaud looked across to where Damien lay. Perhaps he wasn't dead. Perhaps he could be saved. He began hobbling over to the man's side.

"Arnaud. Arnaud, don't! You're bleeding badly."

Arnaud ignored him and hurried along. Andre shuffled quickly alongside and then fell. Andre simply and suddenly collapsed down on the ground near Damien's still body.

348

"Andre!" Arnaud crumbled down to his knees beside his friend. "What is it?" Had he been injured? Arnaud hadn't seen, had only assumed the boy was in rights. He reached forward to examine him for any unseen ailments, but before he could touch him, Andre abruptly opened his eyes and sat up looking baffled, but well.

"What happened?" he asked, shaking his head quickly to clear it.

Arnaud stared. "I have no idea."

His eyes shot down to the emerald pendant glowing brilliantly on his chest and then over to Damien lying still, but whole. He crawled the few feet over on his hands and knees.

"Blood, Arnaud! You're bleeding!" Arnaud reached up and pressed his fist into his side. He crawled on three. "Arnaud, you've got to—"

Arnaud reached out, and before he could touch him, Damien began to stir. He looked around blinking heavily and laid a hand on his head. "What—" He stared at Arnaud. "The dragon?"

"Gone." Arnaud glanced back at the hide of the beast. A thick smoky fog curled around it glinting off the reflective scales.

Damien glared at the half-concealed corpse as well and then back at Arnaud. "You're bleeding badly."

"I know I'm bleeding." He was beginning to feel light-headed and wanted to just sit back. Curl up on the ground. But Andre had already seized him under the left shoulder and pulled him up. Damien stood to help.

"Wait!"

He saw something through the low clouds and the rain, shining in the dim light. He peered hard through the thick drops. Was he mistaken? Was he hallucinating?

Andre began to pull him gently away.

There! It was metal. Black iron rusted with neglect and time. A winding fence leading out from the rock and on into obscurity. A fence. Were they really that close? Had the dragon really been that close to her? Arnaud was filled with sudden anger and fear. The beast had lived so close. Who knew what damage it might've wreaked? What it might've done.

"Wait." Damien laid a hand on Arnaud's arm. He'd been preparing to move toward the gate without realizing. "You'll have to wait. In your state you wouldn't make it to the front door."

Arnaud looked at the man and sensed Damien knew exactly what he was saying. If she is still there, she will remain a few minutes longer. It didn't matter. He wanted to go now, to find her, but Andre was already pulling him back and Arnaud was too weak to protest.

Lucas said nothing as he gently moved Arnaud's hand and examined the wound. He grimaced and swallowed hard and began rapidly tearing long strips from a cloak. Arnaud looked away. It hurt more when he looked.

"How's Marc?"

Lucas paused his work for a moment and then continued ripping the strips and tying them around Arnaud's waist. "It's up to him now; how much he wants to live. And God."

Arnaud sucked in a sharp breath and swayed as Lucas pulled one of the knots tight.

"I've done all I can."

Arnaud's eyes flitted involuntarily over to Marc's body through the cave's dark light. He didn't know Nicolas was dead; that the man he considered his father had sacrificed his life so they could live.

He winced as Lucas pulled the final strip unbearably tight. "Hopefully that'll stop the bleeding;

for now. You need to see a physician. Someone who really knows what they're doing. This is . . . nasty."

Arnaud nodded, but he wasn't really listening. The rain had increased and was slowly dissipating the smoky fog. The corpse of the beast now lay before them in full view. Arnaud had known the dragon was large, roughly the size of a large building, but from this view and angle it appeared positively gargantuan. And its form; claws curled and twisted unnaturally, tail draped over near boulders, head thrown back and limp, was disturbing and weird. The hilt of Arnaud's sword still shone deep in its eye socket. And the dissipating mist swirled around in an evil, otherworldly way. Arnaud could not take his eyes from it.

"Will you be taking a trophy?" Damien asked following Arnaud's gaze.

"It is not to be touched," Arnaud replied, his voice loud and stern. He felt like he needed to warn Damien, to make sure this hunter wouldn't disturb the corpse of an amazing kill. "We've sacrificed too much to welcome the same evils. Especially for a relic." He stared hard at the hunter until he nodded and broke the gaze.

"Did the rain follow us?" Andre said in amazement.

Arnaud looked down at his boots and found them, even at the cave's high-leveled opening, deep in water. The rain couldn't have done that; it was little more than a sprinkling now.

"What's that sound?" Morey asked suddenly, sounding frightened.

Arnaud could barely register what resembled applause or thunder before a great wave rose up and over the mountain's low peak, and crashed recklessly down into the valley directly on the dragon's corpse. It was the single most awe-inspiring, thing Arnaud had ever seen in his life; literally snatching the breath from his lungs. Spray rose up and hit them, mixing with the rain, and they instinctively braced themselves for a tide of water.

It never came. The earth seemed to simply soak up the water, and when they opened their eyes, the shell of the horrifying tyrant of a beast was gone. Disappeared. Only Arnaud's sword marked where it had been, planted neatly in the soft rock and mud and small inches of water lapping up against their mountain wall. They just stood and stared, listening to the thunder and watching the steady rain form ripples in thick puddles.

The fog slowly dispersed and a blue sky began to peek out in sparse patches through the clouds. Arnaud's sword shone amazingly clear in this light, like a beacon, but he looked past that to the iron fence perhaps fifty yards beyond. So close. His heart skipped. He began to walk toward it feeling acutely his slashed side and his bruised and aching body, but ignoring them all. Determination numbed him.

"Arnaud," Damien said following him. "Arnaud, this can wait."

"Going for a physician is more important." Lucas followed as well.

"There is a small village perhaps fifteen miles away. We should look there," Damien offered.

Arnaud's sword made a schinking sound as he pulled it from the ground with his left hand and gracelessly slipped it into its sheath. "You're right. Go for the physician. I won't wait any longer." He didn't turn to see their reaction. He didn't care. He began to limp toward the fence.

"I'm coming with you."

Arnaud turned to see Andre striding boldly beside him.

"Andre, I'd rather do this along."

"I don't care what you'd rather," Andre replied evenly. "I'm not going to let you die on me now."

Arnaud stared at him. Why the stubborn little . . .

"Stay behind me."

Andre nodded and stepped back to let him break the enchantment before him.

They walked slowly along the winding fence as if in funeral procession, anticipating a sight never before seen and never to be seen again. But whether it would be disturbing or awe-inspiring was unknown. The dragon had ruled in these parts and seemed generally unaffected by enchantment. The castle could now be in ruins, helpless bodies desecrated.

Arnaud pushed sickening thoughts from him as they neared the double-door gate. It was ten feet tall and cast of the same heavy black iron. The metal had been formed and twisted into winding intricate shapes and a great black rose graced the meeting of the doors.

They stood silent for several minutes, staring past the gate into a courtyard. A sudden heavy fog tried and failed to conceal hundreds and hundreds of rose bushes, dead, leaving only evil twisted thorns. The sight was foreboding, more chilling than the cold rain.

Arnaud took a deep, steadying breath and reached for the gate. It was worn and rusted like the fence and wouldn't budge until both he and Andre used their remaining strength and body weight to push it inwards into the thorn patch.

Then there were the thorns, one hundred yards of them and no visible away around. Arnaud drew his sword and hacked and chopped with his left arm while his right continued to push down against his side. On top of the deep gash, several of his ribs had been broken and each movement was more acutely torturous than the last.

His breathing quickly grew laborious and shallow. Each inhale stretching his deep wound, each exhale pushing down on his battered ribs. His muscles screamed and burned in agony from exhaustion and overuse. But he ignored all of it. His one thought and one goal was getting to her, waking her; freeing her and all the people inside from an enchantment too long in place.

It took them several hours to cross the thorns. And when they finally made it through Arnaud had to lean against the stone wall to try and steady his breathing. His side was bleeding afresh and his sword hung limply at his side. He could no longer lift it.

He stood for a long while staring out at the thorns, letting the rain slide over his face. It reminded him horribly of that night he'd broken down soon after his brother's death. It seemed so very long ago. The pain he'd felt had lessened or perhaps only the anticipation he felt now dulled all other emotions. Andre waited patiently and silently while he recovered, and did not offer to help, perhaps realizing how solemn and important this was.

Arnaud recovered then used both hands to sheath his sword.

They walked along the stone wall in search of an entrance, their boots sloshing in mud and mulch soaked by rain, until they came upon it. The back entrance; a wooden door deeply set in the stone, and around it slept five armor-hung guards, propped up against the wall or curled up on the ground. As Arnaud passed them he felt the enchantment lift, and as he walked under the stone arch before the door he heard one of them grunt something about fresh cod.

He pushed on the door expecting the hinges to have rusted as the gate's had, or the great lock upon it to be effective, but it swung easily open at his touch.

There was no light inside. They carried no torch or candle nor anything to light them with, so they stepped blindly into the darkness. Arnaud stood still trying hard not to remember their time under the mountain. His eyes adjusted very gradually to the light. Windows were set high above in the tall room. They lined a wide staircase up until it wound out of view, and were set above dulled and musty tapestries along the walls. The clouded light was weak and the glass was glazed and dusty. But it was enough for them to see the mosaic floors, the red velvet curtains and the two women asleep upon the stairs. They were dressed in outdated servant's garb and two large piles of linens sat next to them.

Arnaud felt the breath of the enchantment huff out as he stepped carefully over them and up the dust-caked stairway. He wondered if he should stay and help these people understand what had happened to them.

"Andre . . ."

"I'll be here," Andre answered from the bottom of the steps.

Arnaud nodded and turned up the steps. His only thought was of finding her, making sure she was safe in a tower where the dragon may've frequented.

He climbed and climbed. The stars were endless and steep just as they'd been in his dreams. Every step was excruciating, the next always seeming impossible, yet he ascended without pause or hesitation.

Each landing was filled with doors and often a sleeping servant or guard, a century ago in the middle of some task. Arnaud seemed to know exactly where he was going, which doors to pass through, which halls to walk down to find the next staircase. Though he could not recall dreaming it, he was filled with a feeling of familiarity. But he passed over these thoughts as he

355

passed over the rooms and waking people he barely saw. They were not important right now.

He kept climbing up endless steps, praying for the strength to make it all the way. Feeling heavier and weaker with each movement, but pushing past it all, never slowing; relying upon adrenaline and God to get him to her.

And then they ended.

Arnaud stood at the top step and wavered on his feet. He reached out and steadied himself against a wall. His hand left a crimson stain. He tenderly touched his side and found his fingertips wet with hot blood. He already needed fresh bandages.

Her door stood before him. He looked at it and fresh energy shot through his body. Bandages could wait. He limped forward, hesitated a moment, and then laid a blood-tipped hand upon her door, pushing it gently open.

There was no moon. And the wind was not blue, but he could feel it as he stepped inside. It whipped his damp hair and tunic about for a moment and then was gone as if a lid had been snapped over its source, entirely snuffing it out.

And through an overgrowth of still-green vines and the thickness of dust and residue magic, Arnaud saw her. Lying on a heavily canopied bed near a window where grey peered in and rain clattered on the pane. But she was different from the dreams; fresher, lovelier, more real and more alive. He had not realized until that moment how fiercely he loved her.

But they were only dreams.

He wondered vaguely if the pain was finally getting to him. If he should perhaps go find Andre to tend his wounds before he lost too much blood. But he kept walking until he slumped down upon the foot of her bed.

"I might die." He almost laughed. "I finally found you and I might die."

Arnaud looked over at her, between dreams and waking, and knew it had all been worth it anyway. He reached out and took her pale little hand, deliriously wishing his were not covered in dried blood and grime. He closed his eyes weakly.

"You're – you're hurt! I—"A voice, sweet and high like bells, one he'd memorized by heart, was the last thing Arnaud heard before the world went dark.

***

"Friends."

Arnaud looked around him at the crowded hall. As many people as they could fit into the castle to celebrate his official coronation and the death of the dragon. He was struck with remembrance. He'd had this dream.

"Many of you have fought alongside me. Have paved the way for this victory. I . . . applaud your strength and determination to resist defeat. To never accept surrender , to never give into despair and death. You are the bravest, most honorable men I have met, and I am proud to have you by my side."

He thought of Marc still under Collette's and Grainne's watchful care, recovering from his burns. He looked at Andre and Lucas even now both vying for Clarice's attention.

"Most of you have lost much due to internal terrors and foreign enemies. I feel your loss. Its pain is deep and lasting."

He remembered the loss of his own father and brother. His mother had also died of grief before Gaspar could reach her.

"And yet I cannot promise that there will be fewer deaths, for lasting peace carries a price. I cannot promise life will be easier; there may be difficulties as we rebuild. But I can promise action. No longer will we stand by and wait for evil to take over. We will act to defend ourselves. We will fight back. And no matter how difficult it is, how long it takes, we will win."

Applause ensued that Arnaud wasn't really listening to. He stepped quickly down from the platform and pulled Genevieve close.

"I feel like I know you well already," she said smiling.

"What do you mean?"

"It's like . . . like we knew each other before, in another life."

"Or in a dream," Arnaud replied distractedly. He'd not mentioned his dreams to her.

"Yes, a dream." She nodded and stood on her toes to kiss him. "I remember this."

***

Juliet Peterson is the author of two books: <u>Through the Wise and the Wicked</u> and <u>The Enchantment</u>. <u>The Enchantment</u> was written when she was seventeen. Juliet resides in Oregon and can be contacted at jalynp@gmail.com.

Made in the USA
Las Vegas, NV
04 April 2025

20471635R00203